THE LAST MASTERPIECE

JOHN STANDARD
BOOK FIVE

TOM TOWSLEE

To Herb and Carol

CHAPTER 1

THE MID-AFTERNOON SUN HUNG OVER ZIHUATANEJO BAY like a heat lamp. It sent the temperature into the low nineties and drowsy tourists into the boozy comfort of bars and restaurants or the welcome shade of beach umbrellas and thatch-roofed cabanas. Sailboats and catamarans anchored in the bay baked under the unrelenting sun while bobbing on the gentle swells lazily working their way in from the ocean.

Jet skis and banana boats cut white wakes through the bay's blue water. Parasails towed by speed boats floated overhead, fearless tourists hanging from harnesses like smoked hams.

Comandante Alejandro Vega of the *Policía Judicial del Estado Guerrero* watched it all from the deck of the private pool of a new luxury hotel built high on a hill with a view toward the Pacific Ocean. White-washed apartments, homes, and condos on the west side of the bay stood out like chalk against the dull-gray hills. To his right were the beaches of la Madera and El Centro. Below was the hotel district and *Playa la Ropa*. On the south side of the bay was *Playa las Gatas* with its palapa restaurants and white sands.

Vega looked at it through tired eyes that had seen it all before. It was early December, and another tourist season with its beer, tequila, and limes was just starting to get its buzz on. In the next four or five months, he would see a rotating cast of visitors here for a couple of weeks to escape the ice, rain, snow, and winter temperatures of the States and Canada. They would mingle with the more familiar ex-pats who came and went as they pleased, most arriving before Thanksgiving and staying until April.

Vega used his fingers to crush out the last of his cigarette and put the butt in his pants pocket. He swept the ashes off the front of his uniform and hiked up pants weighted down with a gun that he had never drawn in anger but felt naked without. He sighed, wiped his face with a handkerchief, and went back to the reason he was there: the body of a man floating face down in the water.

The man's legs were together, and his arms stretched out as if frozen in a swan dive gone bad. The smell of chlorine mixed with the iron-laced odor of blood, enough of which had oozed out of the three bullet holes in the naked man's back to turn the water in the long, narrow pool a cotton-candy pink. A gentle breeze off the bay made the dead man's long hair wave back and forth like kelp in a tide pool.

"Who found him?" Vega asked, turning to one of his sergeants. He was slender with a thin mustache stuck on a face too serious for someone that young.

"*Novia*," the sergeant pointed to the far end of the pool where pastel curtains waved in the breeze and a wide set of stairs led up from the pool. "She's in the bedroom."

"Witnesses?"

"None so far."

"*¿Nombre?*"

"Not all of it. I believe the girl is hired help. *Prostituta.* She doesn't seem to know much other than his name. She called him Raj. The manager is on his way. He has the registration information. He can also open the room safe. That should tell us more."

Vega walked back to the far end of the pool to look out at the bay again. He had seen the same scene every day for twenty years, but from a slightly different angle. His own house was a quarter mile to the south and further up the hill. When he and his wife built the place, most of the slopes on the east side of the bay were nothing but scrub trees, dirt, and vermin. Now, it was rapidly filling up with condos and private homes like his. Lately, three high-end hotels had opened. So far, this was the only one with a dead body in a private pool.

As the local comandante, he had made it his life's work to keep the violence and mayhem that plagued most of the State of Guerrero away from the *comercio turístico* on which Zihuatanejo relied. He didn't fight crime. He sparred with it. A few left jabs, but no knockouts. He was happy to keep the scum in the pond by convincing the drug lords that the beaches, restaurants, and bars frequented by visitors were no place for drug dealers. The message was simple, even for them: Tourists aren't going to buy your drugs and the locals can't if they don't have jobs.

It had worked, for the most part, but it remained a fragile although personally lucrative alliance that could shatter at any moment.

Now, the body in the pool gave him an uneasy feeling that everything he'd worked so hard to avoid was about to crumble along with his hopes of quietly spending his last days on the job. The man's death was not the result of some domestic dispute or suicide. This was Mexico. A drug deal gone bad was always an option. It just didn't feel that way.

Whatever it was it meant more work than he wanted to deal with.

Vega wiped his face again with a handkerchief. "Three months, sergeant, and I'll be done with this *mierda*. No more bodies, drug dealers, narcos, or drunks. Just a nice, comfortable, quiet retirement. *Sol, cerveza, viaje.*"

"*Sí, comandante. Lo siento.*"

Vega took one more look at the floating body, then sighed. "Alright, get everyone in here and pull him out of the pool. The coroner can take care of the rest. Now, let's talk to the girlfriend."

Vega moved slowly along the pool, up the stairs, and through the curtains into the bedroom. The girl sitting on the bed looked to be in her early twenties with short black hair and a welcoming face that was more Spanish than Mexican. Red circles surrounded brown, doe eyes filled with fear and uncertainty about what would happen next. Streaks of dried mascara lined her cheeks. Store-bought tits out of proportion to her slim body spilled over the top of a bikini so small it made Vega wonder why she even bothered with it. He went into the bathroom behind the king-sized bed, took a terry cloth robe off the hook on the back of the door, walked back, and handed it to her. She slipped it on, pulling the front around her as if she were cold.

"*¿Cómo te llamas?*" Vega asked.

"Chantelle."

"*Jesús, sálvame,*" Vega muttered, then pulled a chair over from a small table at the end of the bed and sat down in front of her, elbows on his knees. "Let me tell you how this works. If you lie to me, you'll spend two or three weeks in a dirty jail cell as either a material witness or in protective custody. Longer if I decide you had something to do with this. You don't want that.

Bad things can happen there to a beautiful woman like your-self. *¿Entender?*"

She nodded and wiped tears off her cheek. "*Sí.*"

"On the other hand, if you tell me the truth and it checks out, then you'll spend a couple of days in a hotel in Ixtapa. After that, you're free to go. *¿Entender?*"

The girl thought for a few moments, then nodded her head again.

"Good. Now, let's try this one more time. "*¿Cómo te llamas?*"

"Blanca Mendes."

Vega knew most of the hookers in Zihuatanejo. They were mostly independent, working the town's three show bars, which were a combination of strip club and *burdel*, instead of walking the streets. They earned a few hundred pesos a night either pole dancing, doing lap dances, or giving the occasional blow job. None of them looked anything like Blanca Mendes.

"Acapulco?" Vega asked.

"*Sí,*" she said, then explained that she was hired five days earlier through her service. Everything was paid in advance. She got some money upfront then drove her own car to Zihu-atanejo. It was parked in the hotel lot. She was supposed to stay for another four days. She found the man who hired her dead in the pool when she returned from shopping in Ixtapa.

"I bought this bikini," she said, opening the front of the robe. "I thought he might like it."

Vega guessed she'd spent two thousand pesos for something with a hundred pesos worth of fabric and string.

"*Muy bonita,*" he said. "And then?"

"I put it on and walked out to the pool. That was when I found him. I screamed and ran outside. A maid came. She went inside, then came back out and called the police."

"Your ... client's ... name was Raj. He have a last name?"

She shook her head. "I just called him Raj."

"What did he do while you were here?" When she gave him a confused look, he added, "I mean did he do business? Use a computer? Talk on the phone? Have visitors?"

"He talked on the phone a lot. I didn't understand it. It was a language I didn't know."

"Did either of you do drugs while you were here? Cocaine? Heroin? Marijuana?"

She shook her head. "Only champagne and wine, but he never had much. I think he was very religious." She paused for a moment. "Most of the time anyway." She gave Vega a sly smile then pointed toward a small rolled up rug in the corner of the room. "He would pray several times a day. He used that rug over there. He always bowed that way." She pointed toward the east.

Vega slumped back in his chair. Blanca Mendes was only a few years older than his two daughters. Soon they would be off to college in Mexico City or Guadalajara. They would have a future. Blanca would probably never get that chance. Sadly, like most Mexicans, she was too busy worrying about today to think about tomorrow. She made her money with beauty and luck without thinking about what would happen when both ran out. Whatever it was, he was too tired and jaded to judge her or anyone else. Just looking at her told him almost all he wanted to know. It also told him she had nothing to do with the body in the pool.

Blanca Mendes may be a lot of things, but she was no killer, at least not with a gun.

"Okay, Blanca. Get dressed. Pack up all your things. One of my men will drive you to Ixtapa," Vega turned to the sergeant. "Find her a room at the Radisson. Tell the manager she's a guest of the state. If he gives you any trouble, have him call me."

"I'll have one of the female officers drive her," the sergeant said.

Vega smiled and pointed to his head. *"Bueno idea,"* he said. That he didn't think of that himself only reinforced his belief that it was time to retire.

He walked out of the bedroom, across the hallway leading to the front door, and up a few steps to a raised kitchen. It overlooked a large front room with a U-shaped couch covered in tropical-colored fabric and large pillows. In front of the couch was a coffee table four feet square and topped with inlaid tile. Colorful paintings with scenes of local beaches and hanging fruit covered the walls. On one side of the room was a full bar lined with expensive bottles of tequila, scotch, and vodka. Fresh limes and oranges filled a hand-painted bowl. A half dozen bottles were visible through the glass door of the wine cooler. A tall vase on a glass-topped end table contained fresh flowers. A wide terrace with lounge chairs and natural wood railing offered an uninhibited view of the bay with the Pacific Ocean in the distance. The pool was off to the right where one of his men was using a long pole to pull the dead man's body closer to the edge.

Vega knew the hotel had the reputation for being the most expensive and exclusive in the city, a sign that each year Zihuatanejo was becoming more of a tourist destination for upscale travelers seeking luxury and anonymity. It was a place for the rich. It was not for those on a seven-day package trip from Manitoba.

"Comandante," the sergeant said, standing at the door. "The manager is here. He opened the safe. We found a few thousand US dollars, his wallet, and a passport. His name is Rasheed al-Amir. He's from the United Arab Emirates. His business card says he's deputy director of acquisitions for..." the sergeant looked at the card, "...the Louvre Abu Dhabi."

"The Louvre? Isn't that in Paris?"

The sergeant shrugged. "I guess there's two."

Vega took the passport and thumbed through the well-used pages with stamps from a dozen different countries. The most recent were the United States and Mexico. The photo showed a handsome man with dark eyes, a neatly trimmed beard, and longish black hair. He was thirty-seven years old.

"How many rooms in this hotel?" Vega asked.

"Twenty-four."

"Other guests?"

The sergeant thumbed through his notebook. "Two couples, according to the manager. Both Americans. They were gone all day. They just got back. They don't look happy."

"Where's the ambulance and the forensics people?"

"They should be here by now."

"Check on them. I want that body out of here as soon as possible. Understand?"

"Si, comandante. I will call them again."

"Okay and do this as quietly and discreetly as possible. No sirens, flashing lights, or hazmat suits. The fewer people and vehicles the better. No sense getting the tourists riled up until we know more about what happened."

Vega handed the passport back to the sergeant, then looked at the business card and muttered to himself, "Arab Emirates? The Louvre? What the hell is he doing in Zihuatanejo?"

CHAPTER 2

It was a busier-than-usual Thursday night when Itchy Donlan arrived at Mango's a little after eight. He sat down on a vacant stool next to John Standard and ordered a Corona. The bartender looked at Standard, who nodded. The beer would go on Standard's tab. That was Itchy's price of admission.

Standard couldn't remember the first time he met Itchy Donlan, but it was probably in a bar. It could have been The Lusty Crab, aka *El Congrejo Lustroso*, where American retirees stretch their pension dollars drinking cheap beer served in ice-filled buckets under the watchful eyes of velvet paintings featuring Elvis, bullfighters, and dogs playing pool. It might have been Footloose, a hole-in-the-wall with a beer-stained plywood bar top, six wooden stools, and twelve different brands of tequila. A sign out front read "Cold Friggin' Beer." It hung next to a second sign that read "We Speak Canadian."

Most likely, though, it was Mango's, the upscale restaurant and bar that was the epicenter of Zihuatanejo's expatriate crowd that showed up sober and pale in October and left hungover and tan in April. Standard thought of the place as Zihuatanejo's answer to Rick's Café from the movie *Casablanca,* but without the Nazis, or at least none in uniform.

The parade of expats was a mixture of retirees and trust fund babies from the States and Canada. It didn't matter where they stayed if it was never more than a cheap taxi ride to the nearest bar, restaurant, or liquor store. Zihuatanejo didn't always attract the rich. Just the frugal.

After watching them for a couple of nights each week for two years, Standard was starting to have a hard time telling them apart. Best he could tell, they all just traded clothes.

"So many bars. So little time. Maybe we need to find a new place to hang," Standard said. "Everyone here is starting to look like Norma Desmond and her butler."

"Who?"

"Google it."

Itchy Donlan was never a part of the tight-knit group of regulars. He was more like an adjunct hanger-on scorned for always being poorly dressed, broke, and looking for anyone to buy him a beer. Their money and Itchy's needs made for a fraught and precarious relationship. Most shook their heads or turned their backs on him. Occasionally, a newcomer would wander in, usually a lonely, well-tanned widow or divorcee well past her sell-by date who would buy him a drink, fall for his bullshit, and let him stay with her for a few days where he drank all their liquor and treated room service like it was Door-Dash. Those that didn't were generous enough to keep him afloat for a few days until they eagerly flew back to the States, wiser for the experience. In other words, Itchy was the male version of Blanche DuBois in *Streetcar Named Desire,* always living off the "kindness of strangers."

While others scorned Itchy, Standard liked him. Maybe it was his blarney-filled Irish charm. It could have been his entertaining stories about living hand-to-mouth in an obscure Mexican beach town. Maybe the lurid tales of seducing the easily seduced. Mostly, though, it was knowing that by befriending Itchy he earned the further disdain of Mango's regulars. Fine with him. Standard had something they had all wanted at one time or another. Most still did.

Itchy was a short man with a long story. He was all of five-foot-five with a doughy body, thin hair, and pudgy fingers. He was probably in his mid-forties, but five years of a hardscrabble life in Zihuatanejo made him look a little older and shopworn. A Celtic fire hydrant with fashions by Goodwill: straw porkpie hat, threadbare aloha shirt, seersucker shorts, and Topsiders. While most visitors wore their hard-earned tans with pride, Itchy's face and legs were a permanent blotchy red. While he did his best to stay out of the sun and protect his Irish skin, it was hard to do in the tropics, especially in Itchy's sketchy line of work.

Best Standard could tell, Itchy had two sources of income: Kickbacks for steering tourists toward SCUBA trips or tequila-fueled sunset cruises on a catamaran or doing some cruising of his own for widows and divorcees staying at luxury hotels in Ixtapa. The pop-up resort area five miles north of Zihuatanejo catered to families on air/hotel package trips or people afraid of coming in close contact with anything that resembled the real Mexico.

How Itchy ended up in Zihuatanejo was part rumor, part legend, and part who cares. The most credible story was that he arrived five years earlier on a vacation with his wife and two pre-teen sons. They left him behind and flew home when Itchy, after an all-night bender, was arrested and jailed for allegedly propositioning a young girl on her way to church. After he was released without being charged but with a stern warning, his wife and kids were gone, a sign that he was no longer welcome back home. He not only lost his family, but any means of financial support once his wife got back to Topeka and closed their bank account.

So, he stayed.

Standard had always planned on asking Itchy for the real story, but never got around to it. It was Itchy's business, not his. Instead, he asked him how he got the name Itchy. Turns out his real first name is Richard. Growing up everyone called him Richie, except for his little brother with a speech impediment. Richie became Itchy, and the rest is history.

"Where's Emma?" Itchy asked, more for the sake of conversation than any real interest in Standard's girlfriend. For good reason.

Emma Parrish didn't think much of Itchy and while she never said anything, it was easy to tell that she felt Standard needed a better class of friends. In their nearly two years together, she had introduced him to her small circle of artists, writers, rich clients from Mexico City, and the mayor. Everything went fine until someone asked him what he did for a living. He told them "Just visiting" when the real answer was "Nothing."

"Having dinner with some clients from Mexico City," Standard told Itchy.

"She should be here soon."

Itchy used a bar napkin to wipe his face then stared wistfully at the well-heeled patrons on the other side of the bar slurping Margaritas, gin and tonics, and frosty bottles of Corona. He scanned the crowd for a fresh face that might be interested in his services as a "Tourist Consultant." Apparently not seeing anyone worth pursuing, he went back to drinking his beer.

"Tough day?" Standard asked.

"They're all tough these days, John boy. More and more

tourists every day, but they aren't falling for the usual bullshit. Maybe COVID made them smarter, or they've grown afraid of anything involving human contact. Not only that, so far this season's crop of old gals in Ixtapa has been a bit sparse. I'm down to my last few pesos."

"What's your plan?"

"The news is good and bad. The good is that my business back in Topeka sold and my divorce is final. That means I should have the money from both by the end of the month, assuming anything is left after the lawyers and my ex-wife are finished."

"And the bad?"

"The end of the month is a month away. Not sure I can last that long. It's a mess, John. A fucking mess."

Standard knew what was coming next, but this time he was ready with something more than a handout.

"I may have something for you. It may not be much, but it might help."

Itchy's eyes lit up. "You're on another case, right? You want to get the band back together. Do the ol' Spade and Archer thing again like the last time with that guy we kidnapped."

Helping Itchy always came with a certain amount of risk. Two years before, the little man had gotten into his head that he and Standard were a team, even though all the trouble Standard had gotten into since coming to Mexico was pretty much self-inflicted. Any part that Itchy played in getting out of trouble was minor at best. Even though Standard's "adventures," as Emma liked to call them, had been lucrative, people ended up dead.

"There were no cases," Standard said. "We were not partners, and the guy we snatched out of that condo ended up shot in the head by a gang of cartel soldiers. So, drop it."

"What is it then?"

"I don't know yet. I'm meeting a guy tomorrow to hear what the deal is. Something about a package arriving at the airport in a few days. Depending on what it is, I can cut you in."

"Is there money in it?"

"If not, we won't do it."

"Where's this meeting?"

"The VistaPacifica in Ixtapa. Ten o'clock. Can you make it?"

Itchy did some damage to his beer. "I've got a date tonight with a gal staying at the same hotel. In fact, she should be here soon." He looked toward the front door. "She's from the east coast. Boston maybe. Could be New York or Philly. Anyway, she's down here looking to buy a condo. I'm showing her around." He nudged Standard with his elbow. "If I get lucky, I'll still be there in the morning."

CHAPTER 3

A VISIT TO MANGO'S BY EMMA PARRISH ALWAYS CAUSED something of a stir, which was exactly the way Emma liked it. Having been the girlfriend of the guy who owned the place before dying several years earlier in a SCUBA diving accident gave her legendary status among the regulars, at least those still able to remember back that far. Emma did her best to take full advantage of it.

When word got out two years earlier that Standard had moved in with her, it earned him the undying disdain of Mango's regulars—men and women—who would give anything to change places with him. Standard took it in stride. Being Emma Parrish's boyfriend far exceeded any advantages that came with being part of the tequila-and-cellulite crowd across the bar. He knew who the winner was. So did they.

When Emma finally walked in, Standard couldn't take his eyes off her. She was so perfect she made everything and everybody around her look broken. A ballerina gracefully working the room like she owned it. She eased her way along the bar, greeting those she knew with hugs and air kisses, sometimes stopping to talk, smile, and laugh. As for those she didn't know, she'd pirouette quickly by and on to someone familiar. Somewhere along the way, a margarita magically appeared in her hand, delivered by a knowledgeable, eager-to-please bartender.

Emma may know how to work a room, but she knew more about how to dress for the job. She wore a silver necklace and a simple dress—sleeveless and a bright white that showed off her deep tan. Sun-bleached, shoulder-length hair carefully tucked behind ears with diamond studs. Her mouth a bit downturned; her cat-like eyes an emerald green. When she spotted Standard on the other side of the bar, she flashed a smile that made him feel like he was the only person in the room.

It was a look that never failed to take his breath away.

When she moved around the bar to greet him with a kiss on the cheek, he ran his hand over her ass.

"I beg your pardon," she said, feigning offense.

"Just checking to see if you're still going full commando."

"Just for you," she said, then turned to give Itchy Donlan a look that made him wither a bit then quickly get up and offer her his stool.

"Nice to see you, Emma," he said.

Emma gave him a polite thank you then drained her drink and motioned to the bartender for another.

"How was dinner?" Standard asked.

"Excruciating. Those clients think I'm the maid rather than the leasing agent. They kept rambling on about dirty baseboards and dryer lint. Anyway, we agreed to raise the rent on the two places I handle for them and hire another maid. They make more money, we get an extra thousand pesos a month during tourist season, and a maid gets a job."

"Guess you're buying tonight."

Emma downed her shot then motioned for another. "I see

you're still on the outs with the in-crowd," she said, discreetly nodding toward the glaring regulars on the other side of the bar.

"They don't know what you see in me."

"Neither do I," she said, then whispered in his ear. "Why don't you take me home and remind me."

They each ordered another drink then Standard called Arturo, a taxi driver who was ready to take Emma and Standard anywhere they wanted to go, even if it meant forsaking longer trips with higher fees. Standard and Emma accommodated him as best they could. He was bilingual, friendly, and always available. If he wanted to pretend he was some kind of chauffeur, that was fine with them.

Itchy Donlan drained the last of his beer, slid the bottle across the bar, and pointed toward the entrance. "I need to go. My date is here."

Emma and Standard looked across the bar at a woman standing at the front door. She had the lost look of someone unsure where she was or why she was there. Other than that, Standard thought, she looked a lot like Itchy's other "dates," although a bit younger, no gray hair, overdressed, and underweight.

"Good to see you, Emma." Itchy said. "John, tomorrow, ten a.m., VistaPacifica. That right?"

Standard nodded.

"I don't know what you see in him," Emma said after Itchy left.

"Comfort the afflicted and afflict the comfortable. It's an old newspaper adage."

"I can see Itchy is afflicted, but where's the comfortable?"

"They'll show up. They always do."

"So, what's this about tomorrow?" She gave Standard a look of concern he'd seen before. Some of his "adventures," as she liked to call them, had left Emma continuously on edge. With good reason. She'd been kidnapped, threatened with a knife, chased by *soldados* from a drug cartel, and seen a house full of dead bodies. She was never shy about reminding him that none of that would have happened without him.

"I may have found some work. Itchy's having a hard time. Thought I'd cut him in on it."

"What work?" Concern had turned to outright suspicion.

"Not sure. I'll find out more tomorrow."

Emma grabbed his arm. "John, you promised me. No more of your little adventures. I know what happens. Something starts out looking simple and easy and then the next thing you know you're in so deep you can't or won't want to get out. It's that whole 'I need to know the truth' thing. Something left over from your days as a reporter. In case you've forgotten I can run through the list for you. It started with ..."

"I know. I know. This is nothing like that. If it is, I'll walk away and let Itchy take care of it."

"Promise?"

"Promise. Now, let's get out of here."

CHAPTER 4

ARTURO WAS WAITING WHEN STANDARD AND EMMA walked out of Mango's. They climbed in back, sitting shoulder to shoulder in the small white taxi while he expertly weaved his way through the narrow streets, then along the canal before turning south on the road to *Playa la Ropa*. They passed the hotel district then down the hill to a straight stretch.

More than once, Emma had told him about what this area was like when she moved here. There were little more than a few shacks, cheap hotels, and a pop-up restaurant or two. She'd heard stories of the days when there was no road to *Playa la Ropa*. Everything had to be carried down the beach.

The way it looked now was fine with Standard. He never tired of the drive despite doing it at least five or six times a week. The smell of bougainvillea and gardenia mixed with the intriguing and ever-present aroma of sea air, wood smoke, and rotting garbage. It all reminded him of why he came here in the first place and why he stayed. After two years in Mexico, he had learned to relax and surrender to the glacial pace. He enjoyed the cool mornings, reveled in the hot, humid days, and marveled at each night's sunset. He had even endured a rainy season, something he promised himself that he would never do again.

Not to take anything away from Emma. She had changed his life in ways that he still had trouble understanding. Her spirit and passion saved his life and kept him in one piece. No way could Zihuatanejo look or feel the same without her. She was as much a part of the city as the culture, food, and scenery.

Even after two years, he still wasted days wandering around the city, ducking into dark bars, finding the best Caesar salad or pozole, and carefully buying meat, fish, vegetables at the bustling *Central Mercado*. He traded his clumsy Spanish with the broken English of the Avocado Lady. *"Uno para hoy,"* she'd say, handing him a ripe avocado. *"Uno para mañana,"* she'd say, handing him another that was not quite ready to eat. The fish and shrimp were always fresh and kept on ice. The rest was a different story. He preferred his meat refrigerated and his chickens with their heads removed.

Over time he'd met dozens of waiters, waitresses, bartenders, taxi drivers, and beach vendors. They all added up to a network of people who loved to talk, gossip, and ask for advice. If Standard ever needed to find something or someone, he knew the people who could make it happen. To the locals, John Standard became either *Juan Estandar* or "that gringo who lives with Señora Emma." He was happy to answer to both. He counted among his friends a charter boat captain, the local chief of the state police, a DEA agent, and, of course, Itchy Donlan. It was a motley crew, but one he could trust. Well, maybe not Itchy so much.

The taxi stopped at the end of the road at a beach access. Small seafood restaurants and a tienda specializing in beer, candy, chips, and ten different types of cupcakes lined the street and the beachfront. It was early evening, the beach vacant except for a few stragglers on their way to or from dinner. The waves made perfect scalloped marks on the hard sand along the water line. Lights from the sailboats moored in the bay reflected off the mirror-like waters. To the north, lights from the city stretched along the waterfront and up the hillsides. The diamond-like lamps that worked their way up the slopes highlighted the prosperity of the bayfront while masking the poverty that grew up behind it. In most places, only the wealthy lived on the hilltops. Here it was the opposite.

"The first time I met you all you could talk about was how beautiful everything was," Emma said. "You've never stopped feeling that way, have you?"

"No. This is one of those places you want to freeze in time. To keep it as something that never changes. That's not going to happen, so I'll enjoy it while I can."

Before getting out of the taxi, Standard handed Arturo the fare. "Can you pick me up here tomorrow morning at nine-thirty?"

"Of course. Anything for Señora Emma."

"It's just me, Arturo." The taxi driver looked disappointed. "Sorry, pal."

Standard and Emma followed the now familiar path along the beach, then up a long, crude cement stairway to the palapa house they shared. It was roomy, open air, and welcoming, thanks in part to a view of the bay through a stand of towering mimosa trees and coconut palms. When Emma went to change clothes, Standard plopped down in the living room, his feet on the wooden railing that encased the house. Soft guitar music drifted up from one of the beachfront restaurants, mixing with the low rumble of waves hitting the sand.

Emma showed up wearing a short robe. She had a shot of tequila in one hand and a joint in the other. She handed Standard the glass while taking a long drag.

"So, tell me about this guy you're meeting tomorrow."

"Not much to tell. I got a text from him asking me if I was interested in picking up an important package at the airport and delivering it to his hotel in Ixtapa. That's all I know."

"How did he find you?"

"Vega. He contacted the police, but they wanted nothing to do with it. Vega's a few months from retirement and I hear he has a murder on his hands."

"Murder?"

"I talked to him earlier today. The dead guy was staying at that new high-end place on the ridge above the hotel district. That's about as much as he would say. I think he wants to hide under the bed and hope the whole thing goes away until he retires."

"What kind of package?" Emma asked.

"I don't know."

"John, this is Mexico. I've already had my cartel moment. I'm not going through that again. You know as well as I do that a package here doesn't mean the same as in the states. These people aren't ordering from Amazon or Chewy."

"I know. If it smells bad, I'm out of there. By bad, I mean drugs."

"This guy have a name?"

"Simon Nazareth."

"Biblical. What does he do?"

"Don't know. I'll find out tomorrow."

Emma put her joint in an ashtray, disappeared into the bedroom, and came back with her laptop.

"Let's see what we can find," she said, sitting down at the kitchen table and typing. Standard got more tequila. "Here he is. Simon Nazareth. Art dealer. Galleries in New York City and London. Specializes in emerging artists." She scrolled through more websites, then stopped. "This is interesting. He was sued ten years ago for selling a fake Chagall to some Wall Street investor. Looks like he settled out of court, but it doesn't say for how much or with whom."

When she looked at Standard, he shrugged. "That should make tomorrow's meeting all that more interesting. Is there a picture?"

Emma clicked on the Nazareth Gallery website, then on a picture of Simon Nazareth. He looked to be in his sixties with a shock of gray hair, glasses with dark frames, a bulbous nose, and a thin beard that matched his hair. He was broad-shouldered and plump-cheeked with three chins and a good start on a fourth.

"He looks harmless enough," Emma said.

"Unless you're a piece of pie," Standard said. "I wonder what this package is and why it's coming here."

Emma searched the website some more, finding a picture of Nazareth's wife. Her name was Mai. She was at least thirty years younger, a classic Chinese beauty with dark almond eyes and a face framed in silky black hair. She had the title "Director of Acquisitions."

"Is Mrs. Nazareth going to be there tomorrow?" Emma asked.

"Hmm. Let's hope so."

"Asshole." She closed the laptop. "This all smells bad to me. Art dealers. Forgeries. Mysterious package at the airport. Vega investigating a murder."

"You may be right, but like I said, let me at least check it out."

CHAPTER 5

A<small>LL</small> C<small>OMANDANTE</small> A<small>LEJANDRO</small> V<small>EGA</small> <small>COULD</small> <small>DO</small> <small>WAS</small> shake his head, wipe the sweat from his face, and ask himself for the thousandth time what he'd done to deserve this. Another man lying face down. The second in the last twenty-four hours and killed in the same way. Three bullets in the back. Oozing blood creating a halo around his body. The only thing different was that this guy was on a tile floor instead of in a swimming pool and there was no bikini-clad, top-drawer hooker in the bedroom.

"*Madre de Dios*," Vega muttered, then turned to his sergeant, looking for answers. "What do we know?"

"His name is Bernardo Braceros. Fifty years old. He's been here three days. Came in on a Spanish passport that lists his hometown as Bilbao. He had a business card from the Prado Museum that says he has something to do with acquisitions."

"Prado? Art museum, right?"

The sergeant nodded. "*Sí, comandante.*"

Vega sighed and took another lap around his face with the handkerchief. First the Louvre and now Prado. Try as he might, even someone in denial and with a short-timer attitude couldn't miss the coincidence.

The hotel was a modestly priced five-story affair in the La Madera section of Zihuatanejo. It was painted adobe red, had a small swimming pool, and offered guests a free breakfast, Wi-Fi, and HBO. The dead man's room was spartan, even by Mexican standards, with little more than a king-sized bed, tiled floors, a wall-mounted, flat-screen television, small bathroom, and a balcony with a view of the bay.

"What did the staff say?"

The sergeant flipped through his notebook. "According to the manager, he showed up without a reservation. Demanded a room with a view of the bay and would pay extra if needed." He flipped another page. "He told the manager he'd be here a week, maybe longer. Paid in advance."

"Witnesses?"

"The woman at reception said Braceros came back at around five p.m. today. He walked through the lobby then up the stairs toward his room. A few minutes later a tall, slender man with blond hair came in. She thinks he was muscular, maybe a body-builder type, dressed in a T-shirt and tight jeans. She noticed him because guests always wear shorts and colorful shirts. She'd never seen him before and doubted he was staying here. She remembers he went up the same set of stairs as Braceros."

"Anybody hear anything? Arguing? Shots?"

"*Nada todavía,* but we're still talking to guests and staff. The hotel was close to empty at that hour."

"Who found the body?"

"The maid. She came in to turn down the bed and bring fresh towels."

Outside, the sun was in the mouth of the bay, five degrees away from sinking into the ocean. Gradually, almost like a wave, the lights of the city came on, covering up the bad and illuminating the good. Vega ran his hand over his face again, then rubbed his eyes. "Two guys from art museums. One from the Middle East. The other from Spain. How many more art museums are there?"

The sergeant shrugged.

There were probably as many art museums in the world as there were hotels in Zihuatanejo and Ixtapa combined. No way could Vega find out if there were more representatives from other art museums in town. Even if he knew, it didn't explain why they were here or why they might be in danger.

Zihuatanejo and Ixtapa had their share of artists and a few galleries, including the *Museo Arqueológico de la Costa Grande*. None of which made it the epicenter of the art world. Now, two people who might have been able to tell him why they were here were dead. He had no idea who killed them. There was the blond bodybuilder in a T-shirt and tight jeans, but that didn't tell him much.

"Okay," Vega said. "You know the drill. Cordon everything off. Get the technicians in here, then call the coroner. Get the body to the morgue as quickly and quietly as possible. They will want to do an autopsy. Fine, but all I want to know is if the two men were killed with the same gun. For the time being, tell everyone to be on the lookout for some bulked-up slender man with blond hair wearing jeans and a T-shirt, for all the good it will do. I'll take care of the rest."

Vega dreaded the thought of calling the secretary of foreign affairs to let her know that two foreign nationals had been murdered in a town that lives and dies on tourism. He needed to choose his words carefully. If the drug cartels, eager to kill each other for no apparent reason, wasn't bad enough, now he had two international incidents on his hands.

Not only did the victims have targets on their backs, now so did he.

At least it would be the secretary's problem to inform the governments of the UAE and Spain. He knew his job: Find the killer. He may be a short timer, but this was still his town. Vega had his own way of doing things and he didn't need a bunch of ham-handed federales and foreign diplomats mucking things up. They hadn't cared about Zihuatanejo before. It just needed to stay that way.

Tough talk, he knew, but he'd survived worse, and he would survive this. Something told him, though, that he was going to need some luck. He may have doubts about what had happened and where things might be going, but he had a fine-tuned sense for trouble. More than two decades of salary, kick-backs, and bribes had made Vega know when things weren't right. Still, it was a race against the clock: Find the killer, then hang on for another three months and get that significant bump in his retirement. That didn't keep him from having a feeling that some malevolent force in nature was giving him one last challenge before crossing the finish line.

CHAPTER 6

VISTAPACIFICA WAS PURE IXTAPA ARTIFICIAL GLITZ. Stucco walls painted a baby-shit yellow. Marble-floored lobby that echoed with the sound of flip-flops and whining children. Three swimming pools surrounded by palm trees and lounges covered in colorful cushions. Swim-up bars. Five restaurants, each one more expensive than the other, all with ocean views. Beachfront cabanas for those seeking to escape the smell of chlorine and Coppertone. Miniature golf. Water slides. Iguanas basking in the sun on a tree-filled island in the middle of the largest pool. Fiesta night on Wednesday with fake cock-fights and buffets lined with steam trays filled with dishes featuring corn, pork, vegetables, and even a few things vaguely resembling authentic Mexican cuisine.

During his time in Zihuatanejo, Standard had developed a love-hate relationship with Ixtapa. He knew most of it: Marina in the north with its extravagant yachts, the high-rise hotels at the south end of the beach, and the exclusive condominium complexes in between. He accepted it for what it was—a vacation mecca that supported thousands of jobs for locals and millions in revenue for hotel chains, bars, restaurants, and shop-keepers. Huddled across the street from the hotels and condos was a playground of upscale shops, more restaurants, bars—and, of course, the prerequisite Carlos 'n Charlies and Señor Frog's. If that wasn't enough, there was a 24-hour casino.

None of this held any appeal for Standard. It just wasn't his idea of a good time. He felt that every hour spent in Ixtapa was an hour off his life. On the other hand, he'd made a lot of money during his infrequent trips. If this was another chance to make more, then he could suck it up for a couple of hours.

When Standard arrived at the VistaPacifica, waiters in starched white uniforms were already bustling poolside, deliv-ering Bloody Marys, Mai Tais, and Margaritas to those up early enough to grab the coveted lounge chairs closest to the bar. The only restaurant open at that hour featured a sixty-foot buffet covered in steam trays offering *huevos rancheros, chilaquiles, huevos divorciados, tamales,* a mountain of different pastries, and bowls of salsa, sour cream, guacamole, and pitchers of fresh-squeezed juice. A young chef in a tall, white toque stood at attention, ready and eager to make an omelet on demand. He wasn't getting many takers. This time of year, the hotel's guests were more the pancake-scrambled-egg-and-bacon crowd. Maybe with a Molson chaser.

Standard spotted Itchy Donlan sitting at a booth with the woman he'd met the previous night at Mango's. Getting a closer look, Standard could see that she was attractive, in her early sixties with gray-free hair cut short, fashionable glasses, and only a touch of makeup. She wore a printed dress and had a good start on a Mexican tan. A toothy smile with a hint of lipstick lit up a round, friendly face. Next to her on the table was a floppy straw hat with a wide brim and a purse that doubled as an upscale beach bag.

From the way they looked at each other, Standard could

tell that Itchy had charmed his way into a few comfortable days and nights of companionship with another Miss Lonely Hearts. While she was a cut above Itchy's usual conquests, Standard stuck to his determination not to judge. There was a reason that Itchy always hummed the tune of "Stayin' Alive. Stayin' Alive."

"John! Sit down," Itchy said, jumping out of his seat. "This is my friend, Marie Mitchell. Marie, this is John Standard. We're sort of partners."

Standard scowled at Donlan, then reached across the table to shake Marie's hand. "Nice to meet you."

"Marie wants to check out some of the local condos for sale," Itchy said. "I'm going to show her around later today. There are some nice ones further down the beach, but I think she would like those new ones that just went up on *Playa la Ropa*. What do you think?"

"Sounds great, Itchy, but we need to go," Standard nodded to Marie. "It's nice to meet you. Zihuatanejo is a great place, and nobody is better to show you around than Itchy. Whatever you're looking for, he'll help you find it, but for now, we need to go."

While Itchy promised Marie to see her that afternoon, Standard scanned the restaurant looking for anyone who matched the picture of Simon Nazareth he'd seen on the Nazareth Gallery website: overweight, gray hair, bulbous nose. He spotted him sitting in the far corner, filling up one side of a table for four. He was wearing a rumpled linen suit right out of a World War II spy movie. On the table in front of him was a plate of *chilaquiles*. He had a knife in one hand, a fork in the other, a napkin tucked into his shirt collar, and a look on his face that said he was unsure about what was on the plate or how to eat it.

"Mr. Nazareth? I'm John Standard."

Nazareth looked surprised for a second, then put down his knife and fork.

"Mr. Standard! Of course! Sit down, sit down," he gestured to his plate. "Forgive me, but I was just trying to figure out what this is."

"Think of it as a kicked-up enchilada," Standard motioned to Itchy. They both sat down. "This is my ... friend ... Mr. Donlan."

"Call me Itchy."

"Of course. Thank you both for coming."

Everybody shook hands and made small talk about Mexico, the weather, and the food. Nazareth seemed a bit skeptical of all three. The fact that he was wearing a suit confirmed he had no idea where he was or what to wear. What he had on was appropriate for a café in Casablanca, but not a resort hotel in Ixtapa.

"Interesting name," Standard said.

"Yes, I get that a lot. It was one of those Ellis Island things. When they asked my great-grandfather his name, he thought they were asking where he came from. The rest is history."

"My people came from Limerick," Itchy said. "Guess I got off lucky." He smiled at his own joke.

"I understand from Comandante Vega that you need help with a package," Standard said. "Care to fill us in?"

"Yes, of course. Down to business. I appreciate that. Thank you. I was hoping the local police could help me, but this comandante or whatever you call him, didn't seem interested, or I didn't make myself clear. He looked distracted and said something about being short-staffed and not having the time or manpower. I was going to offer to pay him, but I wasn't sure what the protocol was. I haven't had to bribe anybody since I was in Russia two years ago. I didn't want to embarrass him or get myself thrown in jail. When he gave me your name and contact information, it seemed like an easy way out."

"And the package?"

"I have a very valuable item arriving here in two days by private plane. The item needs to be picked up, transported to this hotel, and brought up to my room," he looked at Standard then at Donlan. "I can pay you two thousand dollars each for what I believe will be only a couple of hours' work. Plus expenses, of course. I have no idea what you need down here or how you get it."

"This package," Standard said. "If it's anything illegal, we can end this right now."

"No. No. Nothing like that," Nazareth acted both offended and surprised by the suggestion. "It's valuable, but not in a way that you would associate with... Mexico."

Nazareth had an easy way about him, the kind of person who talked and acted like they knew what they were doing as well as being clear and upfront about it. Confident. Self-assured. All traits that made Standard suspicious. There was something about him and his story that didn't sit right.

"So, why not pick it up yourself?"

"Mr. Standard, I'm an art dealer. I spend most of my time in Europe or the US. My knowledge of Mexico begins and ends with Frida Kahlo, Diego Rivera, and Taco Bell. I'm not a fan of any of them. This is my first time in this country, and I need someone who knows the language and the territory. I can't be driving around a place I've never been, and certainly not with something of value. I explained all this to the comandante, but he didn't seem to care."

"This item. What is it?"

Nazareth leaned back in his chair and eyed the two men sitting across from him.

"I'll tell you, but if you decide not to take the job you must promise me that you won't repeat it." He looked at Standard then Itchy.

When Itchy shrugged, Standard said, "Sure, let's hear it."

"There are actually two items," he said. "One is my wife, Mai. You'll like her. Very smart and no nonsense."

"And the second item?" Standard asked.

Nazareth gave the two of them a look like he was about to share a deep secret. "Let me tell you a story."

CHAPTER 7

FIVE YEARS EARLIER. THE SOUTH OF
FRANCE.

Tiffany Bergen looked up at her husband standing
on the steps of the abandoned nunnery in front of massive oak
double doors with rusty hinges, rivets, and wormholes. Over
and around the doors was a granite arch engraved with images
of angels in diapers, saints with halos, and the Virgin Mary
with a child.

"This is it," Fred Bergen said, turning around to look at his
skeptical wife. She stood on the weed-filled gravel driveway
next to their rental car, arms crossed, face blank. "I can feel it."

"Are you sure?" she said, glancing at the abandoned garden,
dead olive trees, and rye grass burned brown by a summer sun.
The dark mold covering the stucco sides of the L-shaped
building looked like something from a leaky car engine. Every
other window was broken, shards of glass hanging in the frames
like frozen tears. Fern-filled rain gutters tilted at odd angles.
Broken slate tiles on the roof made her think of missing teeth. If
this was her husband's dream, then her first reaction was that
he needed to wake up before making a huge and expensive
blunder.

"I'm positive," her husband gushed. "Look over there. That's the perfect place for the swimming pool and an outdoor kitchen and dining area." He pointed toward the deserted vegetable garden. There were rusty tomato cages and a lattice work, presumably for string beans or peas, surrounded by a row of depressed looking sunflowers, their heads bent sadly toward the ground.

Tiffany was having a hard time being impressed. She wasn't even sure where they were or how Fred found the place. They'd met with a realtor in the nearest town, but the best she could tell, even he didn't know exactly where the nunnery was. With vague directions, they drove an hour from their hotel then another two hours going around in circles on roads barely wide enough for the car. She had no idea how long it would take to get back or if it was even possible. They could be lost for hours if not days.

She originally liked the idea of an upscale hotel and restaurant, but now all she could think about was who in the world would drive all the way out here? It was too far for dinner and too close to spend the night. After all the driving around they did, the best she could tell was that the closest village was five miles away, and there wasn't much there, certainly nothing that she wanted other than flowers and baguettes.

Why couldn't her husband have decided to make movies rather than cook food? He could have been a producer. They should be hanging out with A-list actors on Oscar night rather than wandering around an abandoned nunnery in the middle of nowhere. That's the problem with men with too much money. They see nothing wrong with pissing it away on unrealistic dreams. Lose a few million here. Make a few million there. No harm. No foul. It was all a zero-sum game to them.

Fred Bergen rattled the chain on the huge rings that served as door handles, then pulled a key out of his pocket and slipped it into the rusty padlock. After jiggling it a few times, it popped open, the chains clattering onto the rock porch.

"Shouldn't we wait for the realtor?" Tiffany said.

"He said he'd be late. Besides, he gave us the key. He probably can't find the place anyway. Come on. Let's go inside."

When Fred pulled open the doors, Tiffany could feel a blast of stale air and the odor of mold, rotten food, and animal droppings. Reluctantly, she walked up the stairs and carefully followed Fred inside, fully expecting Vincent Price to pop out at any moment to welcome them in.

Sunlight streaming in sent rats and squirrels scurrying across the floor into cracks in the foundation. Inside was a large room littered with broken tables and chairs. A breeze from the open door sent dried leaves slow rolling across the uneven floor inlaid with tile in the shape of a cross. Stone pillars held up a vaulted ceiling. Peeling frescoes covered chipped plaster walls. Faded depictions of the fourteen stations of the cross looked down from crumbling cornices. Broken windows with shards of stained glass sent multi-colored shafts of light that lit up the room and the dust motes floating in the heavy air.

"This must have been the dining room or a meeting room," Fred said. "Maybe they had their religious services here." When he turned around, his wife stood in the doorway looking like she wanted to either run away or throw up.

"Come on. Let's look around. Don't worry. It's safe."

At the far end of the room was a massive, ash-filled fireplace, the brass andirons charred a deep, sooty black. The huge grate, maybe three feet across, was covered in more soot and the blackened remains of a log the size of a railroad tie.

Tiffany watched her step as she moved further inside, following Fred to the far side of the room. An open doorway across from the fireplace led to a small chapel with four pews in various stages of disrepair and covered in dust, shredded pages from a hymnal, and rat droppings. On the far wall was the dim outline of a cross, six-feet high and four-feet across. In front of it sat a wooden table covered with what looked to her like decades of melted candle wax. More creatures disappeared into holes. Something flew by her head and out the door.

"This could be the wine cellar," Fred said. "Just imagine this room temperature-controlled and covered in racks holding some of the best wines in France."

Tiffany nodded, then started to say she could use one of those bottles right now but stayed quiet. Fred was having too much fun enjoying the chance to spend a small fraction of his wealth to make his dreams come true in what she thought was the least likely place. She hoped his dream didn't become her nightmare.

"Now, let's check out the kitchen," Fred said, heading out the chapel door with her two steps behind him.

In the kitchen was another ash-filled fireplace, stained wooden tables, rusted country sinks, and a well-used wood-burning stove. Rusty pots and pans hung from hooks on the wall. Broken dishes littered the floor. The few plates, cups, and saucers still in one piece sat in glass-front cupboards above the sinks. When they looked in the large pantry, they found broken shelves and a handful of dusty jars of what looked like canned fruit and vegetables. Dried herbs hung from hooks next to something that Tiffany thought at one point might have been a sausage.

"Honey, close your eyes and imagine this with all the best kitchen equipment in the world. Stainless steel refrigerators, two hand-made French stoves with six or eight gas burners each. Meat, fish, and poultry cooking on a grill burning only local wood. A world-class chef creating authentic French food and giving orders to a small army of sous-chefs. Food from the farms here in this valley. Local vegetables, farm-raised ducks and chickens, grass-and-acorn-fed cattle and pigs. A classically trained pastry chef. A sommelier. Waiters and waitresses carrying gourmet dishes going out the door to guests. It'll be incredible!"

Tiffany could only manage a weak smile. Owning and operating an upscale hotel and restaurant in the south of France had been all Fred talked about since they were married five years earlier. She had an art history degree from Vassar, but since graduation, her major occupation had been finding and marrying someone like Fred Bergen. He had made billions as a Wall Street hedge fund manager. At age 58, he'd made all the money he needed and was eager to move on and realize his dream. If people wanted to think of her as a trophy wife, it was fine with her. At age 31, she was more than happy to indulge his fantasy and soldier on. Not that there was anything she could do about it. Their prenuptial agreement made sure of that.

She would need to warm up to the idea of living in the south of France and become the supportive spouse. She just never thought about owning a restaurant and cringed at the thought that Fred would screw up the courage to ask her to work there. The best she could hope for was being the hostess, taking reservations, seating guests, and handing out menus. No way was she going to schlep plates from the kitchen.

Telling Ophelia, "Get thee to a nunnery," was fine coming from Hamlet. It didn't carry the same weight coming from Fred Bergen.

After walking through the kitchen, they took a left into what had apparently been the nun's living quarters. It was two stories with a large, three-story turret on the far end. They moved slowly down the gritty hallway, sticking their heads in the doors of cell-like rooms with sagging bedframes, rotting mattresses, broken wash basins, and cracked mirrors. Tiffany had images of nuns with their habits, wimples, and rosaries getting ready to run off to some obscure religious service. Not that she knew that much about nuns or their activities.

"I can't wait to see what the architects will do to turn these rooms into luxury suites," Fred said, showing the first signs that restoring the nunnery may be a bigger challenge than he thought.

Tiffany tried to imagine what it must have been like for the nuns who had lived here and who they even were. As an Episcopalian, her knowledge of nuns was limited to what she picked up watching an old Whoopi Goldberg movie. The realtor said they belonged to some obscure religious order that he couldn't remember other than it had a loose affiliation with the Catholic Church. All he could learn from the locals was that nuns had occupied the place for a few hundred years, surviving on donations from the overly devout farmers and shopkeepers. When that money dried up, they scratched out a meager living selling fresh fruit, vegetables, and bread at local open-air markets in the nearby villages. They even tried their hand at macramé and tie-dye. She imagined them working in the garden and taking fresh produce and baked goods to market in the old pickup that now sat abandoned in a nearby grove of trees covered in ivy, a young tree growing out of the broken windshield.

The realtor didn't know when the nuns left, just that for twenty years the local, cash-strapped diocese had been trying to sell it, but with little luck.

Tiffany thought that for some of the nuns, this may have been the only place they'd ever known. They came young, grew old, and left. She tried to imagine what it must have been like for them to leave, putting their faith in God that He would take care of them. Tiffany hoped they were right.

While Fred inspected more rooms, Tiffany walked to the

end of a hallway littered with more of the detritus left behind by those who had taken the veil and then moved on. The turret was at the far end. When she opened a small, arch-shaped door, she jumped back as a rat ran out, stopping long enough to give her the stink eye, then scurrying out a broken window. Inside the door was a winding stone staircase with rusted iron handrails anchored in rough-hewn rock walls. She carefully navigated the steps made of the same rock, not sure if around the next corner she was going to run into another resentful and inconvenienced rodent. She suddenly felt like one of those characters in a horror movie who wanders off alone to be hacked to pieces by someone in coveralls and a hockey mask.

The landing at the top of the stairs led to a doorless room filled with the same dirt, dust, and broken furniture as downstairs, only more of it. It was also larger and felt different, as if it belonged to someone more important, maybe some stern, sanctimonious abbess who ran the place with a harsh, demanding hand.

Pushed up against one wall was a single bed with a mattress chewed to tatters by rats or other vermin. Two small arch-shaped windows, the glass in each broken, offered a view across the valley to the west. A bird landed on the sill, took one look at her, and flew away. If this was where the abbess, mother superior, or whatever they called her lived, it must have been a stark existence. At least it gave whoever she was the ability to look out and thank the Lord for all the things they didn't have.

Stopping at the window, she had to admit the view was breathtaking. Rolling hills covered in green fields broken up by stands of trees, rock walls, and narrow roads. Cattle and sheep grazed in the distance. The church spire in the nearest village pierced a bright blue sky.

She moved slowly around the room until reaching a small writing desk pushed up against a wall. A spindle-backed chair with a broken leg leaned to one side. What caught her eye, though, was a painting in a heavy ornate frame hanging on the wall, the image barely visible behind a thick layer of dust and spider webs. She pulled a handkerchief out of her pocket, carefully wiped away as much of the dirt as possible, then moved back to take a closer look. After two steps all she could do was gasp.

"Fred," she yelled. "You need to see this. Now!"

CHAPTER 8

STANDARD AND DONLAN LOOKED AT EACH OTHER, THEN AT Nazareth. "What was it?" Itchy said, "What was the painting?"

Nazareth leaned forward, put his elbows on the table, and looked around as if afraid someone was listening. "Have the two of you ever heard of Raphael?"

Donlan gave a confused look toward Standard and then at Nazareth. "You mean the waiter at El Pelicano?"

"I think he's talking about the painter, Itchy," Standard said.

Itchy looked embarrassed for a moment. "Oh, yeah. Right. Sorry. Who?"

"Keep going, Mr. Nazareth," Standard said.

"Raphael was a 16th Century Italian painter. His real name was Raffaello Sanzio de Urbino. He died in 1520 at the age of 37. He, along with Leonardo da Vinci and Michelangelo, formed what art authorities like to call the traditional trinity of great masters of that period, the architects of the Italian High Renaissance. His style built on the works of the other great painters of the era. He was also very prolific. A master of the

42

fresco style with works such as *The Expulsion of Heliodorus*, *The Miracle of Bolsena*, and *The Liberation of St. Peter*. Most of them are either stored or on display at The Vatican. His most famous work was *Portrait of a Young Man*, which many art historians believe was a self-portrait. The painting is of a man dressed in a tunic, velvet hat, and cape draped over his shoulder. It's considered the world's most famous missing painting."

"Missing?" Standard said.

"To say the least. Let me explain. Over the centuries the portrait had several owners and was stored at various times in London, Paris, and around Poland. When the Nazis entered Poland in September 1939, the painting, along with another by da Vinci, was hidden away in a house in a small Polish town. Unfortunately, the Nazis discovered the hiding place. Eventually, the portrait became part of Hitler's private collection that was supposed to go to his *Führermuseum*, which was never built. When the war ended, the Germans destroyed much of the art they had stolen, including, many believe, *Portrait of a Young Man*. There are some who believe the painting survived the war and is stored in a bank vault somewhere in Poland. Extremely unlikely. I believe it was destroyed. It sounds like something the Nazis would do. But the story doesn't end there.

"Legend has it that Raphael painted a companion piece called *Portrait of a Young Woman*. The woman in the painting could have been Raphael's sister or his lover. There are two schools of thought about what happened to it: Either it is lost forever, or it never existed."

"Until now, I take it," Standard said.

Nazareth nodded. "The best anyone could tell, the painting had been hanging in that nunnery for at least a hundred years and maybe longer. Who knows where it was or who had it before then? The nunnery was built in the mid-1700s. It's hard to believe it was there that long, but none of the experts we hired could rule it out. My guess is that one of the nuns picked it up at some archaic version of a flea market and took it back to the nunnery, not knowing what it was. It's happened before."

"And the Bergens?"

"They're clients of mine. I helped them buy millions of dollars of contemporary art by Murakami, Koons, Rothko, and others for their Manhattan penthouse. They even have a Warhol or two, although I'm not a fan. Soup cans and Marilyn Monroe. I never quite got it. Anyway, after they discovered the painting in France, they purchased the nunnery. Of course, never telling the realtor or the owners about the painting. Bergen is no fool. He eagerly laid out a few million dollars for the place knowing full well that inside was a painting that could be worth hundreds of millions. That's how the rich get richer."

"How did they know the painting was the real thing?" Standard asked.

"Educated guess that hit the jackpot. Tiffany is what you might call a trophy wife. She is beautiful and half his age. Smart, in a street sense sort of way. And, as luck would have it, had a minor degree in art history from Vassar. It wasn't much, but enough for her to recognize that the painting she found wasn't just some run-of-the-mill portrait. When I asked her about it, all she could say was 'It just had that look.'"

Nazareth explained that the Bergens took the painting back to their apartment in Paris and for the next five years spent hundreds of thousands of dollars getting it restored and establishing its provenance.

"Provenance?" Itchy asked.

"Provenance tells the story of the painting. Who did it? Where it's from? Where has it been? Why is it here now? We had to prove it was real. Without the provenance, the painting was worthless. I helped the Bergens find and bring in experts from all over the world to do the work and create the necessary paperwork.

I even found Raphael scholars from Oxford and the University of Milan. We made them sign non-disclosure agreements to keep the discovery a secret. As it turned out it didn't do much good.

"Establishing its authenticity was not easy. Some of the experts were convinced it had to be a fake because they had always believed the original never existed. Others felt the same way for other reasons. But the longer they looked at it, did the tests on the paint and the wood, examined the brush strokes, and compared it to other works by Raphael, they gradually concluded it was real."

"You didn't bring in experts from The Vatican?" Standard said. "You said it has a collection of Raphaels."

"No. The Vatican believes anything painted by an Italian belongs to the church. I didn't want to deal with it and neither did the Bergens. Besides, there's no shortage of experts in 16th Century masters. So, when everything was in order, Fred Bergen decided to try quietly selling the painting without a lot of publicity.

"Why sell it?" Itchy asked. "They had other masterpieces. Why not one more?"

"Fred Bergen is a money man. Making money is what he does best. Buy low. Sell high. That kind of stuff. This looked simple to him. Buy a nunnery for a few million. Sell a painting for a few hundred million. Besides, he's more of an investor than a collector. There isn't a painting he owns that he wouldn't sell for more than he paid for it. This was the perfect investment since he basically got it for free. In other words, he was determined to sell the painting for as much as he could get. Since they'd worked with me up to that point, they asked if I'd help with the sale. They made it clear upfront that they didn't want a public auction or a high-profile donation to an art museum. No nightly news, Associated Press, or some gossip-riddled art-centric websites. A discreet private sale would suit their purposes, particularly when it came to the IRS."

"And you agreed," Standard said.

"Reluctantly. I believe the painting belonged where the public could view it, but if I didn't sell it for them, they'd find someone else who would. Then there was my fee, which in this case is substantial and life changing. No way I would walk away from that."

"Why all the secrecy?" Standard asked. "Seems to me the more people who knew about it the more people would want to buy it."

"None of us wanted a repeat of what happened with *Salvator Mundi,* a painting that was thought to be a da Vinci but is still wrapped in chaos and controversy. What was believed to be something by the 'hand of the master' had a murky provenance. It may not be a da Vinci but da Vinci-ish. Maybe the work of one of his students. In the end it was all about the ego and dreams of academics and the power of those rich enough to own it and create their own provenance.

Fred Bergen wanted nothing to do with anything like that. All he wanted was to quietly increase his wealth by thirty percent and avoid paying taxes by keeping the money in a series of offshore accounts. Or something like that. Anyway, he had it all thought out. Discretion was the key factor. Unfortunately, word got out. Now, the sharks are circling. Beautiful art is an ugly business."

"What's this got to do with Zihuatanejo?" Itchy asked.

"When people in the art world got wind of the painting's possible existence, the Bergens started getting messages from The Vatican, the Louvre, Prado, the Metropolitan Museum of

Art in New York City. The list goes on, and don't get me started with the auction houses. The weirdest offer was from this Russian oligarch. A guy named Drago Dragovich. I looked him up. Bad dude, at least on paper. He sent my wife, Mai, a few emails threatening her if we didn't sell him the painting. We both blew him off as so much bluster. Besides, I hate Russia. The whole country is a criminal enterprise.

"Anyway, as their agent, I handled all the inquiries. The figures being thrown around were staggering. I took down all the offers and told each one that I would get back to them. After that came calls from the auction houses: Sotheby's, Christie's, a few others."

Nazareth took a couple of more stabs at the *chilaquiles* before giving up and motioning to a waiter for more coffee.

"It was about this time that I was contacted by a private collector, a man named Carlos Strasser. You can look him up, but you won't find much. He's totally off the grid. No Facebook, Twitter, Instagram, or any of that stuff. Best I could learn is that he's the heir to a South American meat packing fortune. He lives on a 300-foot ship, spends almost all his time at sea, and runs the business from there."

"Sounds like Captain Nemo," Itchy said.

Nazareth laughed and nodded. "That's what I thought. Then he made an offer that was something out of *The Godfather*. You know, the kind you can't refuse. It was well above what anyone else was offering. When I told the Bergens, they jumped at it. If they wanted to keep everything as quiet as possible, selling the painting to a recluse like Strasser was just the ticket. Don't ask me why, but it was Strasser's idea to meet here, hand over the painting, and collect the money via wire transfer. He's on his way here now. His ship is a few days away."

"A South American named Strasser," Itchy said. "Is there something I'm missing?"

"I know," Nazareth said, shaking his head. "Draw your own conclusions. All I know is that he's not one of those billionaires spending his money recreating something Alan Shepard did sixty years ago. Best I can tell, he has one of the largest private art collections in the world, and that's just not my opinion. Ask anyone who's familiar with the art world. All I know is that he's willing to spare no expense making it larger."

"How did word get out?"

"The art world is full of critics, collectors, dealers, and hangers-on who thrive on gossip and rumor. Sometimes I think there are more people writing about art than producing it. Being an art critic does not require a lot of time or energy, just a self-made reputation as a so-called expert. So, they talk, they guess, they speculate. Occasionally, they are right. This is one of those times. The painting was real, and an enormously rich collector was going to buy it. It was all going down right here."

"What's this painting worth?" Itchy asked.

"A lot. The most expensive painting ever sold at auction was da Vinci's *Salvator Mundi* at just less than half a billion dollars. The next is Picasso's *Les Femme d'Alger* at nearly two hundred million. I can't divulge what Strasser is paying for *Portrait of a Young Woman*, but it falls somewhere in between."

"How does this wire transfer work?" Standard asked.

"Pretty simple really. Strasser brings his laptop. We bring ours. He sends the money to an account already set up in The Caymans. When the money shows up in the account, we hand over the painting. Strasser and the painting sail away in his yacht and the Bergens are hundreds of millions of dollars richer than they already are. Welcome to the world of high finance in the 21st Century. Art lovers should turn away and try not to watch."

"And Strasser and the painting are coming here to Zihu-atanejo," Standard said, thinking again that something didn't sound right. He kept getting the feeling that he was about to be dragged into one of those "adventures" that Emma keeps warning him about.

"I know, but it's not my doing," Nazareth said, then stood up. "Let's find a place that serves food I'm more familiar with and I'll tell you the rest."

CHAPTER 9

After leaving the VistaPacifica, they crossed the street to the array of strip malls that featured upscale clothing stores that had yet to open and a collection of small restaurants, each claiming to have the best tacos in Ixtapa, which, to Standard, was a pretty low bar. Sunburned tourists in cargo shorts, baseball caps, and tank tops roamed the narrow walkways in search of a cheap breakfast and a michelada.

Nazareth lumbered along a few steps behind Standard and Itchy until they settled on a place with a menu out front that included *tocino y huevos*. When Standard explained that it meant bacon and eggs, Nazareth eagerly nodded. They went inside and sat down at a table where he quickly ordered scrambled eggs, bacon, toast, and a side of pancakes. When he tacked on a Bloody Mary, Itchy quickly did the same. Standard stuck with coffee.

"So," said Standard after Nazareth finished explaining to the waitress the meaning of crispy bacon, "when does this painting arrive?"

"The day after tomorrow, probably in the afternoon. I'll

know later today. My wife is bringing it. It's coming in on a private jet from New York City via Miami. It's in a specially designed metal case to protect it from the humidity." He looked back and forth between Itchy and Standard, then brought back the conspiratorial whisper. "What I need you to do is pick up her and the painting and bring them to the hotel. I'm staying in the penthouse. Deliver her and it to me. I'll keep it safe until Strasser arrives. Each of you get two grand, after that, you're done."

Standard's antenna was up. He believed the story about Raphael and the long-lost painting. What he didn't understand was why Nazareth would trust them with it and his wife.

"That's a valuable cargo and you just met us," Standard said. "What's the catch?"

"No catch. Vega, the police chief or whatever he is, said I can trust you. Why would he steer me wrong? He knows the both of you and probably where you live. Besides, my wife will be with you. She and the painting are a package. She won't let anything happen to it."

None of that eased Standard's suspicions that something wasn't right. He was ready to pull the plug and walk away when Itchy came to the rescue ... as only he could.

"Let me see if I understand this, Mr. Nazareth," Itchy said. "You want John and me to play FedEx for your wife and a priceless painting by some guy I never heard of. Fair enough, but back in the States I was an accountant with some clients who liked to invest in art. You know? Nothing serious like this. More like buy something for a million, hang on to it for a year or two, then sell it for two million.

"I didn't need to know anything about art. My only job was to find a way for them to avoid paying taxes on the difference. Now, I figure this painting of yours is worth, let's say, three hundred mill for the sake of argument. As the agent for the owners, your bite is twenty percent, minimum. That's sixty million dollars." Itchy sat back in his chair and smiled at Nazareth. "And you want to pay us two grand each?"

Nazareth quickly flashed the look of someone who'd just been busted. When his breakfast conveniently arrived, he dove into it like there was a time limit, washing it all down with long pulls on his Bloody Mary. "I assume you have a number in mind."

Itchy smiled. "Twenty thousand each once the deal is done and this guy Strasser has his painting, and you have your money. I figure you're sitting here right now with five thousand dollars—the two thousand each you wanted to pay us and one thousand for expenses. We can take that money now to cover the cost of playing errand boys. All in the name of art. Agreed?"

Standard smiled to himself. It was a side of Itchy he'd never seen. Gone was the sketchy low life, living hand to mouth, and mooching overnights with widows and divorcees. In its place was a savvy ex-accountant who knew how to negotiate. Standard watched while Itchy, never flinching, eyeballed Nazareth and waited for an answer.

"Clearly, I've found the right two men for the job. It's a deal." Nazareth said it with a smile, raising his drink in the way of a toast. He reached into the inside pocket of his jacket and pulled out an envelope. "Here's the five thousand. You'll get the full amount when the painting is safely in the hands of Mr. Strasser."

They shook hands and exchanged phone numbers.

"One more thing," Standard said before Nazareth left. "If one of us needs to wait for Strasser then we're going to need a room on the same floor as yours."

"Fair enough. I'll take care of it and leave the key at the front desk."

"Nice work on the money end, Itchy," Standard said after

Nazareth left to walk back to his hotel. "I was about to walk away until you called him out. Twenty K is nothing to sneeze at."

"Two thousand each sounded like a scam to me. Upping the ante ten-fold tells me there may be something to this."

"It still smells bad. A priceless painting. Zihuatanejo. Some mysterious South American meat-packing mogul. Pickup and delivery. Not the kind of thing we see a lot of around here."

"I know, but given my current finances, I don't have a lot of options." Itchy gave Standard a worried look. "Don't bail on me. I need this and I can't do it alone."

For Standard, it wasn't so much about the money as it was helping Itchy. Twenty thousand was more than Donlan had seen since showing up in Mexico. Given the way he lives, it would keep his head above water for a year or more. That made it hard to say no.

"Okay, but we're going to need a few things," Standard said. "That means talking to Fat Tony."

"Good idea, but can you handle that end?" Itchy said. "I'm supposed to meet Marie for lunch. You know? That gal I introduced you to at breakfast. I promised to show her some condos for sale."

"Would you rather have lunch with someone twice your age than go to a titty bar where I have an open tab?"

Itchy thought for about two seconds. "I'll get a taxi."

CHAPTER 10

STANDARD SHOWED UP IN MEXICO FEELING LIKE
Raphael's painting must have looked: lost, faded, and in need of
restoration. He had a few drops of color, a little black and
white, and a whole lot of gray. His role in the traffic deaths of
two young girls turned his routine life upside down and made
him a pariah in his own city. He went from a married man with
a good job to living in a two-room apartment in a squalid
building on Portland, Oregon's Park Blocks and scratching out
a meager living as a freelancer writing grants for school
districts, op-eds for a couple of food banks, and newsletters for
homeless advocates.

Then things changed. He thought it was for the better. It
just didn't stay that way.

He stumbled into a short-term and dangerous side hustle
helping rich people find other rich people. It refilled his bank
account, gave him back some of his self-respect, and forced him
to learn how to handle a gun. It didn't last long. A face-to-face
encounter with a knife-wielding, cross-dressing serial killer put

him in the hospital for a month. He came away with a nagging and disturbing sense of his own mortality, a scar across his chest, and a fear of knives. Along the way, he picked up an inexplicable willingness to risk his own life for the sake of others, something that fate seemed determined to never let him escape.

Heading for Mexico and a badly needed change of scenery came in the form of a gin-induced epiphany that Portland, Oregon, was tired of him, and he felt the same. With crime, homelessness, high taxes, and seasons that alternated between blue and gray, it wasn't a hard decision.

Three days out of the hospital, drunk, and caught in a rainstorm, he hid in the doorway of a travel agency in the heart of downtown. In the window was the right poster at the right time. White sand beach. Bikini-clad model. Palm trees. Blue water. At the bottom, the words: "Zihuatanejo—A World of Its Own." He'd never heard of the place but took it as both omen and invitation. After a few hours on the Internet learning as much as he could, he packed a bag; and left behind friends and lovers; to escape crime, homelessness, and dank winters for the sun, tacos, and tequila of Zihuatanejo.

The place never quite lived up to the idyllic scene on the poster, but it didn't matter. He fell in love as soon as he stepped off the plane. He escaped the airport's stink of jet fuel to suck in air that was both humid and invigorating. He ducked back inside to an airport bathroom, changed into a pair of shorts, and left his slacks in a trash can. He was even more convinced that this was where he needed to be when he found a house to rent at the far end of *Playa la Ropa* and met the woman who owned it: Emma Parrish.

Looking back, the accident that changed his life triggered a series of cascading events that eventually landed him in

Mexico. While the deaths were never far from his thoughts, it was impossible to escape the fact that had it not happened, he never would have come here and never found Emma. Sort of a twist on the adage "No good deed goes unpunished." As far as he was concerned, "No bad deed goes unrewarded."

He never planned to stay, but once he found Emma there was no way he could leave, certainly not without her. Not after what she'd done for him. With patience, persistence, and stern words, she knitted him back together. He healed with her love, a warm sun, gentle breezes, and the sound of waves hitting the beach.

Unfortunately, he unwittingly paid her back with a series of events that quickly threw her idyllic life into intermittent periods of turmoil and self-doubt. The dangers he'd encountered in Portland had followed him south. First was the death of an American woman that cost Emma a few days as the hostage of a Mexican pimp trading in underage girls. Something she still won't talk about. When he helped the DEA bring down a cartel money manager responsible for the death of Emma's best friend, she got a first-hand view of a house full of mutilated corpses. Despite the trail of dead bodies, none of them had been his fault unless you count the cartel soldiers who burned to death in a van on the highway to the airport.

The way Standard saw it, he couldn't help himself. He kept getting sucked into things that started out small, then quickly exploded into something much more dangerous. Little did he know that all that mayhem inflicted on him and on Emma would lead to becoming a major investor in a show bar, which he quickly learned was part strip club, part whorehouse, and all money.

Standard met Fat Tony two years earlier when Tony was managing a sports bar near the Catholic Church in El Centro not far from the bayfront. For a few pesos upfront, Tony guar-

anteed Standard and Emma the best tables for the college foot-
ball playoffs and the Super Bowl. Over time, as they became
friends, Standard learned that Tony's job as a bar manager was
more of a sideline. His real job was as a local fixer, capable of
getting anything from a few bags of cement for a patio or girls
for a weekend sleepover.

After moving on to two other bars, he popped up as the
owner of a show bar called Sticky Fingers. It was housed in a
garish purple building on a street running parallel to Ruta 200
at the north end of town. It was not exactly a street anyone
would confuse with San Francisco's Tenderloin District. It was
huddled between a welding shop and a hardware store. The
only other source of nearby entertainment was an open-air
theater showing pirated versions of first-run movies. When a
trio of *sicarios*, Mexican hitmen, looking for Standard shot up
Sticky Fingers one night, three people died and more were
injured. Tony ended up with a destroyed knee and facing a lifetime in a walker.

Feeling partially responsible, Standard loaned Tony some
of the money he'd been paid by the DEA to help rebuild the
place. Six months later, Sticky Fingers II opened for business
again at the same location. Tony recovered enough to supervise
the remodel and host an open house with music, free lap
dances, and a no-host bar. He also promised to repay the money
Standard had loaned him and throw in a lifetime open tab that
included everything from a cold beer to a hot stripper. Standard
stuck to the beer but stopped in every couple of weeks to check
on his investment, which was earning him a thousand dollars
US each month. The money came in an envelope ready for him
whenever he showed up.

He hadn't told Emma any of it and since they kept their
money separate, she didn't notice that he had a little extra
income to help pay the bills, buy groceries, and take her to

dinner three times a week. Eventually, she would figure it out.

That's when Standard would have some explaining to do.

Tony was well over six feet tall and tipped the scales at something short of two-fifty, which was sixty pounds lighter than before being shot up and spending weeks on hospital food and painkillers. He wore loose-fitting white pants, a black T-shirt that looked too big even for his bulk, and a Panama hat. Since Standard last saw him, Tony had improved enough to trade in his walker for a cane. Despite the pain of being shot and the hard work getting Sticky Fingers rebuilt and open, the smile never left the big man's face. He lit up even more seeing Standard, his grin so wide it turned his eyes into tiny slits.

"Señor Juan!" Tony said when Standard walked in with Itchy Donlan. "It has been too long."

Even at mid-day, the place was doing a good job. Men nursing beers filled half of the twelve tables surrounding a raised platform with a brass pole. Topless waitresses carrying trays moved between the tables taking orders, delivering bottles of beer, and giving suggestive smiles. The girl on stage was slowly slipping out of a gold G-string and bra as she swung clumsily around the pole to the smoky beat of the piped-in music of Tito and the Tarantulas. A machine pumped out just enough fog to give the dim neon lights a frosty glow. Neon signs advertising Corona, Pacifico, and Dos Equis added to the dark ambiance. The bar with two bartenders did a brisk business in one corner. In the other, a steel-cage booth where a woman took in money through a slot in a Plexiglass window and handed out change.

"So, what's up *jefe*? Just checking in?" Tony said, leading them to a booth off the dance floor. Standard and Tony talked business for a few minutes while Itchy stayed glued to the dancer as she said goodbye to the last of her costume.

"You own this place?" Itchy said to Standard without taking his eyes off the stage.

"It's a long story, but if you need anything, Tony's got your back."

"I'll remember that," Itchy said.

Tony ordered three Coronas from a topless waitress who gave Itchy a smile suggestive enough to pull his attention away from the stage.

"I've been meaning to ask you," Standard said. "Did you ever find that boa constrictor that disappeared the night the place was shot up?"

"You mean the one that dancer was using?" Tony said with a shiver. "No, and it was a Burmese python. Thing gave me the creeps. It was eight feet long, at least. I have a feeling it may still be around somewhere. Seems like there are a lot fewer *ratas y ratones* around here than I remember."

Tony leaned against the back of the booth and gave Standard the kind of look that said he knew they were there for a reason. "So, let's hear it."

"We need some help, Tony," Standard said.

"I figured that."

"And we need it pretty fast."

"Name it."

"An SUV, preferably a Tahoe or something like it. A handgun, a Glock if you can do it. Two men in another car for backup. They need to be armed as well. I think a shotgun would work."

Tony whistled. "You planning to rob a bank?"

"No. It's a simple job of picking up two important packages at the airport and taking them to the Vista Pacifica. Couple of hours. Three at the most."

"Why all the iron?"

"Better safe than sorry. The packages are ... vital, if you know what I mean."

"This package. Is it ...?"

"No. No. I had the same concern. It's nothing more sinister than an old painting and a beautiful woman. I'm just preparing for the worst and hoping for the best."

"Must be either quite a painting or quite a woman."

"Both."

Tony sipped his beer and watched as one dancer replaced another. "Given our history, Señor Juan, I think you better tell me more."

Standard gave him the short version of what he'd learned from Simon Nazareth. Tony didn't recognize the name Raphael, but looked surprised at hearing what one of his long-lost paintings would sell for. That was enough to explain why the Louvre, Prado, and other museums would want it.

"¿Cuándo?" Tony asked.

"Day after tomorrow. It's two grand. Cash. Can you do it?"

When Tony shrugged like he wasn't sure, Standard nodded to Itchy, who counted out two thousand of Nazareth's five thousand dollars and slid it across the table. Tony eyed the money, then smiled. A gold tooth glinted in the light from the disco ball. Standard nodded to Itchy, who peeled off another thousand.

"I'll arrange it and call you," Tony said, taking the money and slipping it into his pants pocket. "I'll drive backup and get my cousin Emilio to ride shotgun ... with a shotgun."

"I'll figure out the details and fill you in when the time comes," Standard said. They shook hands followed by one of Tony's bear hugs.

"You saved my business," Tony said. "I would give my life for you."

"Let's hope it doesn't come to that."

When Standard got up to leave, Itchy didn't move. "You're part owner, right?"

Standard nodded. "Sort of, but that stays between the two of us."

"Open tab, right?"

Standard gave Itchy a pat on the back then nodded at Tony. "Just tell Tony what you need."

CHAPTER 11

AFTER STANDARD LEFT FOR IXTAPA TO MEET WITH SIMON Nazareth, Emma Parrish got up, showered, and dressed. Having the house to herself felt good, reminding her of all those years she lived alone before John arrived. She made coffee, heated up some day-old pastries, and savored both as she sat down in the living room gazing out at the bay.

She decided that this was the day she would tell him. She had lain in bed for an extra hour that morning making up her mind. She knew what to tell him, just not how.

Needing time to figure it out, she packed her beach bag with a bottle of water, some lotion, and a copy of *Jane Eyre* that she'd been struggling with for the past two months. The walk down the hill to The Tortuga was familiar and comfortable. She'd made the trip thousands of times, but not so much lately. There just wasn't enough time. The longer she stayed in Zihuatanejo the more work she got from rental owners wanting her to handle their property. Six clients and guests coming and going every two weeks during tourist season made her busier than she wanted. It was time to stop taking on more work. The money was welcome, but Zihuatanejo was not a place to work hard. It was too warm, welcoming, and beautiful.

The Tortuga was little more than a thatch-covered cement pad large enough for a cramped kitchen, a few plastic tables with chairs, and a dance floor. Outside on the beach were wooden lounges, more chairs with Corona logos on the back, and thatched-roofed cabanas, all situated a few yards above the bay's anemic waves.

She got a cabana as far away as possible from the noisy kitchen and the other guests. To her surprise, Pablo showed up in record time. After ordering a Bloody Mary, chips, and salsa, she stripped down to her bikini and pulled a lounge chair into the sun.

She didn't understand why she was having so much trouble finding a way to tell John something she had been thinking about for a long time. In their two years together, she had learned that it was change that brought him to Mexico, but it was inertia that kept him here. Although she liked to think that she had something to do with it. He may move from bar to bar and restaurant to restaurant to trade gossip with bartenders and waiters, but that was because there wasn't much else to do here. That seemed fine with him, most of the time.

John's "adventures," as she liked to call them, had made her question her love for him more than once. While she missed the calm, quiet days before he showed up, she would miss him more. Since he moved in, things had happened to her that she still can't talk about, and she'd seen things she'd just as soon forget.

The upside—and what she valued the most—was that he never took her for granted. When they made love, he made it more about her than him. Still, despite the intimacy and passion, there was always a part of him he kept hidden. Not just from her, but from everyone. Maybe it was that mystery that made her love him more than any man she'd ever known.

She thought of him as a tattered and torn Peter Pan living in Always Always Land, meaning that trouble was always coiled in the shadows ready to strike.

What she valued least was how he kept getting into the kind of trouble that made her not just scared, but questioning why she stayed in Mexico, and why she stayed with him. That explained why she laid down her own marker, stating her independence by leaving him alone the first summer they were together so he could learn for himself what it was like to live through a monsoon season with its three months of near-constant rain. If her leaving for a few months in the States made him believe she needed to get away from him and all the trouble he'd caused, then so much the better.

"You could have just told me," a bored Standard had said when she got back.

"Yeah. I could have."

In her fifteen years in Zihuatanejo, she had one boyfriend who died in a SCUBA diving accident. He left her two things: a 1960s-era fully restored, low-mileage Plymouth Fury and a feeling of relief. She had never loved him or even liked him that much. Mostly because he didn't need her, and she needed to be needed.

Enter John Standard.

She remembered what he was like the day two years ago when he showed up at her door looking to rent the small palapa house on her property. Sad, broken, and lost. She took him in in more ways than one. Over time she could see him regain some feeling of self-worth that came with knowing that she tolerated him as much as she loved him. He promised her long ago that he would do everything in his power to protect her. He'd failed a few times when things happened that made it hard for her to outlive. That she eventually did was a testament to her own strength. Still, loving him came with a price. Sometimes she grew tired of paying it.

Knowing him and what she needed to tell him, the best thing to do was just come right out with it and see what happens.

By two in the afternoon, the sun was high in the western sky, the temperature in the mid-eighties, and the smell of wood smoke and cooked meat drifting out from the restaurant's kitchen. Tourists wearing tank tops and Bermuda shorts paraded barefoot on the hard sand above the waves. Some had dogs that tottered along behind them happily holding sand-encrusted tennis balls in their mouths. Children splashed in the warm water under the watchful eyes of parents or nannies. Four cabanas away, the usual collection of retirees sitting at a table playing backgammon traded lies about the last time they got laid. They had real names, but Emma only knew them as Ranger Bob, Señora Lenora, Tan Man, and Fall Down Phil.

They all had a backstory. Bob, a retired Texas Ranger living in Mexico to stretch his pension and smoke the same dope he once arrested people for. Lenora, a librarian from central California so desperate for a husband she once swam out to a yacht owned by a bachelor. Tan Man, a furniture salesman from New Jersey who spent hours in the sun determined to achieve the perfect shade of deep brown. Phil, an epileptic electrician prone to occasionally passing out and falling into the bushes, prompting hectic searches by the other three.

"A little late in the day for you," Standard said when he showed up, sitting down in one of the plastic chairs across from her. He looked around to see if Pablo was slogging through the soft sand to take his order. He didn't see him but knew he would show up eventually. Being regulars didn't get them much. Being big tippers did.

"I slept in then came down for a late lunch and decided to stay." She drained the last of her drink and, like Standard, looked around for Pablo. "I sat here thinking about all the time I used to spend at this place. I rented one of those little casitas behind the restaurant while the house was being built. Over the last fifteen years the place has had at least five different owners who gave it five different names. I only remember the first one: *El Crocodilo*. That's still the name I think of whenever I'm here."

When Pablo finally showed up, Standard ordered each of them a beer and a shot of tequila.

"How was your meeting?" Emma asked.

"Pretty interesting. Simon Nazareth is going to pay us to pick up his wife and an expensive painting at the airport and deliver it to his hotel in Ixtapa."

"Us? So, you did cut Itchy in." When Standard nodded, she shook her head. "You have more heart than brains. So, tell me about this painting."

As soon as Standard said Raphael, Emma put down her book and sat up.

"What? Raphael? You mean *The* Raphael? One of the great masters?" She shook her head. "Jesus, John! What's a painting like that worth and what's it doing here?"

"A lot, and this is where the seller and the buyer agreed to meet. Don't ask me why. These art people seem a little... unconventional."

"I hope you know what you're doing and that you're getting paid for it."

"How does an extra twenty thousand sound? Helps pay our bills and keeps Itchy's head above water for a few weeks, probably longer."

"You promised me, John. If this is another one of your..."

"I know. I've done everything I can to make sure it isn't."

"That's not a reassuring answer."

Emma was still shaking her head when Pablo showed up with a tray full of beer and tequila in small ceramic cups.

"Next time bring the bottle," Emma said, then looked at Standard. "When does this painting arrive?"

"Day after tomorrow."

Emma gave him one more suspicious look then went back to her book. Standard stared out at the bay and the sailboats moored just offshore. An hour later, after another beer, they walked up the hill to their house, showered, and dressed. A little after six, they walked back down the hill and up the beach to a rooftop restaurant overlooking the bay. Emma waved at a table of four people she knew, but Standard didn't. He did know the waitress, and she knew them, which meant that when they sat down, she showed up with a bottle of their favorite white wine and an ice bucket. They ordered grilled lobster, drank wine, and watched the sun go down in the mouth of the bay.

"When's the last time you had a steak or anything that requires a knife?" Emma said it while leaning on the table, her chin on her hand.

Standard reached for his wine glass. "It's been a while."

"Two years by my count. Don't you think it's time to get over it."

"You weren't there; besides, I like things that are soft and edible, if you hadn't noticed."

"Cute," she said, took a sip of wine, then reached across the table to hold his hands, a gesture that usually preceded bad news. "I have something we need to talk about. I can't think of the best way to tell you, so I'm going to come right out with it." Standard braced for the worst. "I think we should move."

"What? Where did that come from?"

Emma had owned the house they lived in for fifteen years,

designing it herself, navigating Mexico's byzantine ownership laws for non-citizens, and supervising the construction. She paid for everything, scratching, saving, and draining the inheritance she got from a late uncle to make sure she had enough to make the place exactly the way she wanted. The result was a comfortable combination of simplicity and elegance that reflected who she was and how she lived her life. She appreciated that Standard was happy to chip in all he could. Why wouldn't he? Beautiful house. Beautiful woman. Beautiful place. She knew that he woke up every day feeling like the luckiest man in the world. At least that's what she told him.

"I've been thinking about it for a while. I could sell the place I have here for enough money that we could buy or build a palace on the beach in Troncones. You've been there. You know what it's like. Quiet and cute. Not many year-round residents."

"I thought you loved it here."

"I do, but Zihuatanejo is not the place I came to. It's getting bigger and busier. Troncones is more the Mexico I remember. Like here used to be. It's far enough away to escape the crowds, but not so far that we'd be isolated. It's only thirty minutes north."

It didn't take Standard long to see that this had nothing to do with Emma wanting to recapture the old Mexico. They had been to Troncones once on a day trip. Standard remembered it as a dusty stretch of road lined with modest beachfront homes, vacant lots with million-dollar ocean views, a few palapa restaurants, and stalls selling fresh fruit and vegetables. Stray dogs slept on the shoulders of the road. Chickens dodged cars while scratching in the dust for crumbs, bugs, and seeds. Not exactly Emma's kind of place.

"This isn't about a nice house in a serene setting, is it? This is more about getting away from any future possibility that I'm going to get you involved in more of my self-inflicted trouble. No more living on the edge, waiting for another murder, kidnapping, or car chase. Do I have that right?"

He could see it was right and the look on her face said she resented him for it.

"Troncones might be more than a new place to live," she said. "It might mean a new start, one out of harm's way. That's not a bad thing. What's happened in the past has been as hard on you as it has been on me. Moving to Troncones would reduce the chances of those things ever happening again. You know all the things that happened and the effect they've had on me. Can you blame me?"

They drank in silence before the waitress took their plates away, and he ordered two snifters of Amaretto. When they showed up, he held up his in a toast.

"Maybe we should drive up there and look around," he said. "See what's available."

"Really?"

"Why not? It's been a while since we've taken a road trip. It's probably time to get *El Furioso* out of the garage and blow off the dust."

El Furioso was her old boyfriend's Plymouth Fury. He'd driven it once, and only once. When he almost wrecked it during an encounter with a trio of cartel *sicarios*, she let him know that there wouldn't be a second time.

"You know, John, if you could squeeze another thousand dollars a month out of your share in Sticky Fingers, we could make just about anything work."

It was Standard's turn to shake his head. "How long have you known?"

"Does it matter? You'd think by now you would have learned not to underestimate me. I've been here longer than you have."

He gave her the shy smile of someone who'd just been busted. "Okay, let me finish this little delivery job. Then maybe we can even find a little place in Troncones to spend the night then take a day to look around."

Emma leaned across the table to give him a long, wet kiss. "You've made my day. Now, pay up, take me home, and I'll make your night."

CHAPTER 12

FATHER STEPHEN O'MARA GROANED AS HE STOOD UP, stretched his back, and rubbed his temples. It seemed like he'd spent half of his fifty years as a Catholic priest on his knees. Every year it became as hard to get down as it was to get up. Lately, his legs ached, his feet hurt, and thanks to the rampant humidity of Mexico he'd developed an annoying heat rash.

Once on his feet, he crossed himself while looking up at the crude life-sized crucifix above the small church's simple wooden altar. The tallow candles on each side flickered from the breeze coming in through the open doors and windows. On an easel next to one of the candles sat a crude painting of Madonna with child. On the other side was an equally crude rendition of a serene-looking Jesus sitting under an olive tree. Behind him in one of the front pews, a woman wearing a mantilla sat with her head down, her lips moving, a small child fidgeting on the seat next to her. Further back, an older man in a work shirt and dusty pants prayed over a handful of lottery tickets. Yellow-eyed mynah birds watched it all from the sills of the open windows.

The scene was a far cry from the opulence of The Vatican, the Sistine Chapel, and St. Peter's Basilica, but something about its simplicity made it seem much more holy and blessed. Much more Christ-like. More reverent rather than ornate. Jesus was, after all, a simple man. O'Mara sighed. If only the church were this simple.

He often wondered what Jesus must think of all the pomp and ceremony surrounding his birth, life, and death. Does he approve or look down with disdain at all the glorification and celebration? How does he view those who mix politics and religion or wage war in God's name, as if God would approve? Under the current Pope, the church was gradually moving away from hide-bound orthodoxy. O'Mara welcomed it, but would the next Pope be forced to conform, see things differently, and roll back the clock?

All good questions best left for another day.

Three days in Zihuatanejo, a place he had never heard of until a week ago, and he still hadn't recovered from the long flight from Rome. Despite its wealth, the church steadfastly refused to pay for business class, not even on international flights for missions ordered by the Pope. To make things worse, he'd made no progress on why he was sent there in the first place. Rumors—and they were just that—that a long-lost masterpiece by Raphael had been found and restored were enough to send the curators of the Vatican museums into high alert, particularly those at the Villa Farnesina Linceian Center for Research on Cultural Heritage. They already possessed Raphael's *Madonna of Foligno*, *Oddi Altarpiece*, and the *Transfiguration*. The chance to add *Portrait of a Young Woman*, a painting most people thought didn't exist until a few months ago, was irresistible.

But was it true? That's what he was there to find out and to obtain the painting if he could.

Raphael was, after all, Italian, and the Raphael Rooms, with their vast collection of his works, were a major tourist attraction. The Holy See believed, and he agreed, that any art by an Italian master belonged in the Vatican. He also knew from experience that the church strongly believed that art by any master anywhere in the world also belonged to the Pope. It didn't matter that only a fraction of the Vatican's vast art collection was on display at any one time. The rest was stored away out of sight. That's why some countries wanted their art back. Fortunately for Father O'Mara, that was someone else's problem. His job was to acquire art, not give it back. His orders, sent down by none other than the Pope, were clear: Get the long-lost Raphael.

As a Vatican lawyer, he had negotiated the purchase of hundreds of pieces of art for popes going back to John Paul I. Fortunately for him, but unfortunately for the church, the days of the Vatican buying art to hide away in its vast collection were over. The world was now full of people with too much money who were willing to spend on art, even if they knew little about it and in many cases weren't even sure what they were buying. The church was no longer as rich as it once was. Now, all Father Stephen could do was try his best to get those who could afford to acquire a great work of art to lend it to the Holy See.

If rumors of the previously undiscovered Raphael were true, he needed to find the buyer and attempt to convince him or her that the masterpiece belonged with the Vatican's other Raphael paintings. His most successful selling point was convincing the owners that they were punching their union cards to heaven. Sacrifice in this life for rewards in the second. It was a plausible argument when negotiating with Catholics. A much harder sell when it came to everyone else. He could also try buying the painting but doubted that what the church could offer would come anywhere close to what the rumored buyer was willing to pay. The church had other obligations, including feeding the poor and settling myriad lawsuits against dissolute priests filed by choir boys.

Like most people in the art world, Father Stephen was familiar with Carlos Strasser, but only by reputation. He was one of the world's avid collectors wealthy enough to pay any price for the long-lost Raphael. The church was in no position to compete.

So, each day Father Stephen would walk down to the waterfront with a cup of coffee and a bag of churros, find a bench, and stare out at the bay waiting for Carlos Strasser's mysterious ship to arrive.

His research found that while most of those in the art world had heard of Strasser, few knew him, and those who did had nothing good to say. Coming from Argentina increased the chances that he was Catholic, which might be an opening. That he was at least part German, however, created other, less godly hurdles to cross. Lutherans were never easy to comprehend.

Learning that the reclusive Strasser had arranged to purchase *Portrait of a Young Woman* and where the deal would take place was a testament to the Vatican's ability to gather information from distant and often suspect sources, especially when it came to priceless pieces of art by Italian masters. In this case, the source was a little more mundane—an auction house jilted for being denied the opportunity to sell the historic piece of art that would garner worldwide attention and a sizeable fee. How the auction house found out was something Father Stephen didn't want to think about.

Not that any of that mattered to him. All he needed to do was get to Strasser, make his pitch, and see what happens. To do that, he needed Strasser. That meant waiting, for lack of a better term, for his ship to come in.

Father Stephen bowed his head in one more silent prayer, then walked out the church's side door into another warm and humid night that would reignite his heat rash. Dim streetlights on the other side of a concrete wall gave off a faint glow. It mixed with music and laughter from a nearby cantina and the annoying honking of taxis circling the streets of El Centro looking for fares. If he closed his eyes, he could imagine being back in the hustle and bustle of Rome, which reminded him of the often-irritating intrigue of the Vatican bureaucracy, and the crowds of worshippers outside St. Peter's. He often thought about what it would be like to escape the rarefied air of Rome for the simple life of a parish priest. Maybe in England, Scotland, or, better yet, his native Ireland. Reading the Gospel, delivering sermons, and offering communion to the faithful. Presiding over funerals or the occasional exorcism. It all seemed a lot closer to doing God's work than chasing paintings and other works of art around the world.

He left the church by a side door for the short and increasingly familiar walk along a tree-lined path to the rectory and his sparse room with its double bed, desk, mirror, and small closet where he kept his three cassocks and an extra pair of shoes. He would pray again, spend another restless night, then get up in the morning to walk down to the bay to see if Strasser's yacht had arrived during the night. It had to show up sooner or later. The researchers at the Vatican had reassured him that he was close. Maybe tomorrow would be the day.

He didn't recognize the tall, slender man with white hair who stepped out from behind one of the trees. He was dressed in a T-shirt and jeans. His first thought was that he was one of the parishioners coming for a late-night confession. He could also be lost, homeless, and eager for a meal and a place to sleep.

Only he looked different—more fit, less tan, and definitely not a local.

"Can I help you, son?"

"Forgive me, Father," the man said, then grabbed the priest by the shoulder, turned him around, and shot him three times in the back.

CHAPTER 13

THE NEXT MORNING, STANDARD HIT THE TORTUGA FOR breakfast and a chance to read a well-used, two-day-old Los Angeles Times he bought from a beach vendor. He was halfway through his *huevos revueltos* and an article about ten feet of snow in the Sierra Nevadas when Aurelio showed up. He had his bucket of homemade cheese and the three street urchins that followed him everywhere he went. Standard had named the kids the La Madera Irregulars. Their knowledge of the city and all its nooks and crannies had come in handy more than once.

As for Aurelio, he roamed the beaches of *la Ropa* and *la Madera*, trying to convince wary tourists to buy a few feet of his string cheese. Standard knew from experience that the cheese was good—salty, fresh, and the consistency of mozzarella. He also knew that Aurelio didn't get many takers but was generous enough to cut off three-inch pieces and give them to those who had politely declined.

The street urchins came in three sizes: small, smaller, smallest. They wore dirty T-shirts, baggy shorts, and worn-out flip-flops or taped-up sandals. They followed Aurelio around, hoping that those who didn't want his cheese might be interested in their array of cheap bobble-head toys or a package of Chiclets. At night, they hit the bars and restaurants trying to interest many of the same tourists in the same plastic frogs, turtles, armadillos, and gum. In Mexico, a child's work is never done.

If there was anyone in town who needed to be found, the Irregulars were the ones to ask. And they worked cheap. Once, Standard gave them a hundred-peso note for some earlier work. All they could do was stare at it and babble in Spanish.

The note was worth about five dollars US.

"Have you heard the news, Señor Juan?" Aurelio was always eager to fill Standard in on local gossip. "Last night a priest was killed at Our Lady of Guadalupe. They say he was murdered. *Asesinado!* I walked by there this morning on my way to the beach. There were police everywhere and people standing in the street. A woman told me he was shot. Another woman was crying. The nun who found him had to cross herself five times before running to tell the other priests. I was told that he was not a local priest, but that he was visiting from the Vatican."

When Aurelio crossed himself, the Irregulars did the same, although Standard wasn't sure they knew what it meant. "Murdering priests is not a good thing, Señor Juan. *Muy mal.*"

Standard passed on the cheese but distributed a handful of coins to the four of them, then left to get a taxi into town. His antennas were up. The Vatican meant art, and art was becoming the city's newest common denominator.

The taxi dropped him in front of the Artisan Market. He walked a block up the street to the church, but all was quiet. The crowd and police were gone, the church doors open as if nothing had happened. While Aurelio was usually a reliable source, Standard knew a better one.

He found Comandante Vega at his favorite barbacoa place on *Avenida Morelos* across from Scotia Bank, a short walk from the church. He was staring into a plate of *tacos al pastor*, his hand wrapped around a frosty bottle of Pacifico. The floor was tile. The tables were Formica. The woman behind the counter wore a hair net and used a cleaver to chop whatever meat you wanted. Pork, beef, chicken, goat, and some pieces Standard didn't recognize.

Standard's relationship with Vega was complicated, going back to not long after he came to town. They first bonded over a shared interest in a high-end pimp whose body was found after someone blew holes in his yacht. They both knew who it was but never talked about it. Standard saw Vega as a lazy, over-the-hill cop living off bribes, kickbacks, and payoffs from business owners, contractors, and the occasional drug lord looking for someone to turn a blind eye to a torture killing or two. Vega viewed Standard as a meddlesome *norteamericano* who made his life more difficult with his knack for attracting trouble, but resourceful enough to come away unscathed.

After Standard saved Vega's marriage and Vega saved Standard's life, they forged a fragile friendship based on mutual respect and distrust.

"It's only noon, Alejandro. Things can't be that bad already."

Vega pushed the plate of tacos to one side then drained half his beer. "I have three murders on my hands. An Arab, a Spaniard, and a Catholic priest from the Vatican. The Vatican, John! Do you know how many Catholics there are in Zihuatanejo? Thousands, including me and my family. This is not going to go over well."

"Three? I heard about the priest."

"One from the Louvre and one from Prado. They all had something to do with acquiring art for famous museums. All shot in the back. Looks like the same killer, but we're not sure yet. It's only a matter of time before I have sheiks, bullfighters, and the Pope crawling up my ass. Three months from retirement and I get hit with this. *Tres meses* and I can put all this behind me. *Increíble.*"

Standard was enough of a friend to sympathize. No one looked toward retirement more than Vega. He had used his ill-gotten gains to build a huge house in the hills overlooking the bay. Standard had been there a few times. It came with a full-time housekeeper, a swimming pool, and a fountain in the courtyard with peeing cherubs. Vega and his wife designed it and had been living there for the last two years. After retirement, the two of them dreamed of enjoying winters in Zihuatanejo and the summers traveling to the US and Europe. During their infrequent lunches, Vega had talked about seeing the Eiffel Tower, the Coliseum, the Pyramids of Giza, and the Washington Monument.

"You know, John, things like this never happened around here until you showed up. The list of dead people is long for someone who's only been here for two years. It has been two years, right? It seems like five. Whatever it's been, I don't need to count the bodies. You know the number as well as I do."

"So, this is all my fault? Really?" When Vega shook his head and offered a weak apology, Standard changed the subject. "Tell me about these murders."

Vega gave a quick rundown of each one along with descriptions of the victims. He had no suspects other than a slender man with white hair wearing a T-shirt and tight jeans. It was little or no help. When Vega described the phone call he made to the secretary of foreign affairs about the dead men, their nationalities, and that one of them was a Vatican priest, Standard thought he was going to start crying.

"Bad for you. Worse for the dead guys," Standard said. "Any theories?"

Vega shook his head. "I can't figure out why they were here. The Louvre in Abu Dhabi, Prado in Spain, and now some lawyer from the Vatican. What are they doing here and why would anyone want to kill them?" Vega was in full whine. He ordered another beer for himself and one for Standard. "I'm hoping the people in foreign affairs can reach out to the museums these guys worked for and get me some answers. All I know is that if I don't find this killer, I'm going to have investigators from the federales here. Those guys are a pain in the ass."

"Look at the bright side, Comandante. This is your big moment. Solve this and you can go out on a high note, a fitting end to an illustrious career. Dinners. Plaques. A gold watch. A phone call from *El Presidente.* Not only that, but you no longer need to do favors for drug lords in exchange for keeping their *soldados* out of the tourist areas. Think about how many visitors you've saved by confining the bloodletting to your own people living in the hills above town and away from places like Carlos 'n' Charlies. It really is quite a career."

"Don't be a *sabelotodo*, a smart ass. I'm not in the mood." Vega pulled the plate back in front of him and picked up a taco. "That guy I sent to you. The one who wanted something picked up at the airport. Did he get in touch?"

"He did."

"And the package?"

Knowing what he did about Vega and his bumbling police force ruled out telling him about Simon Nazareth and a priceless painting. Besides, one more mention of art and Vega would put a gun to his head. The Comandante had his own business to take care of. Standard had his. If one bled over into the other, he would take care of it then. Now was not the time.

Then there was twenty-thousand dollars at stake—forty counting Itchy Donlan's end—all of which would be at risk by telling Vega more than he needed to know. Best he could do now was roll the dice. Pick up the painting, deliver it to Nazareth, collect the money, and pretend it never happened. He needed to be careful.

"The package is his wife." It wasn't a total lie. "That's why I stopped by. I wanted to say I appreciate the referral. We connected and it will all be taken care of by tomorrow. And I earn a little money."

Vega seemed too worried about three murders and who the victims were to take much interest in what Standard was up to. "Is there anything going on that I should know about?"

"I told the guy that if it was something other than his wife, anything out of bounds, he can forget it. He promised it wasn't. If it turns out he's lying, I'll let you know."

"You believe him?"

"Enough for a nice payday. Maybe enough to kick in a few hundred for your retirement fund."

"Thanks, but a few hundred pesos isn't going to make much difference in my retirement."

"I was thinking dollars."

Vega smiled and they drank a toast to Standard's growing knowledge of how things work in a third-world country.

"When do the federal investigators show up?" Standard asked.

"*Depende*. They move at their own pace. Sometimes fast, sometimes slow. The more progress I can make finding the killer or killers, the less likely they are to want to solve it themselves. I probably have a few days, no more than that." Vega sighed then reached for his plate of tacos only to push it away again. "And it's not just my government. I've received messages from the Arab and Spanish embassies in Mexico City asking what happened. It doesn't end there. The Archbishop of Mexico called me directly. Now even the Pope knows what happened. Jesus!"

Standard thanked Vega again, then left after deciding that once he and Itchy had been paid, he would tell Vega about the painting and all the people who wanted to get their hands on it, probably including the dead ones. Why else would they be here? First, though, he needed to clear up a few things with Simon Nazareth.

CHAPTER 14

STANDARD FOUND SIMON NAZARETH SITTING AT A
poolside table with a laptop, a cell phone, and a Piña Colada.
Cheaters clung to the end of his nose as he peered at the
screen. A dozen older guests were doing water aerobics at one
end of the pool.

At the other, children wearing inflated rings around their
arms laughed and splashed under the watchful eye of parents
coated in zinc oxide and drinking Margaritas. The air smelled
of chlorine and food from the lunch buffet. Nazareth barely
noticed when Standard sat down across from him. When a
waiter in a starched-white coat and Bermuda shorts showed up,
Standard waved him off.

"Mr. Standard, how convenient," Nazareth looked up just
in time to order another drink before the waiter got too far
away. "The drinks they make here are quite delightful, especially something called a Piña Colada. Fruity, I would say.

They tell me there's booze in it, but you could fool me.
Anyway, I'm glad you're here. I was just going to call you with
an update on our packages, as you like to call them."

"And?"

"The plane carrying the Raphael and my wife has just left New York City headed to Miami. It will refuel there and leave early tomorrow morning. It's about an eight-hour flight, so they should arrive here mid-afternoon. You can meet them at the south end of the airport. Customs has already been taken care of,"

He gave Standard a sly wink. "Don't ask. The plan arrives at 2 p.m. Once you take delivery of the painting and my wife, of course, bring them both here. There will be two private security men on the plane, but they only come as far as the gate. They do air, not ground. That's your job. After that, the responsibility for everything is on you and your friend until you get here. I trust everything else is in order."

Standard had talked to Fat Tony earlier in the day. The Tahoe he requested was ready along with a back-up car and two people. Same with the guns. Standard and Donlan needed to be at Sticky Fingers whenever they were ready to go to the airport. He needed to call Tony again with what time to meet.

"We're good, but something else has come up," Standard leaned across the table, the look on his face serious enough that Nazareth closed his laptop and drained the last of his drink. "Did you know there were people in town from Prado, the Louvre, and The Vatican?"

Nazareth waited until his new drink showed up before answering. "No, I knew the museums were interested in the painting, but I had no idea they sent representatives here. Why would they? This is a done deal. They were outbid. End of story. Their argument was that anything as valuable as a long-lost Raphael belonged in a museum where people could view it rather than hanging on a wall in someone's mansion or yacht. I told them I agree, but the ultimate decision rested with the owners. I told them to submit their offers in writing and as their agent, I was obligated to pass on their bids. I never heard back from them, not that it mattered. There was no way they would come close to what Strasser is ready to pay."

"Not even The Vatican?"

"These are hard times in Rome. The Vatican expressed interest in buying the painting but first wanted a chance to convince Strasser to donate it. I passed that on to Strasser and got a quick no. Same thing with the other museums. I guess they decided to keep trying."

"Did you know all three of them are dead?"

"What? That's impossible! How do you know that?"

"Trust me."

"There must be some mistake."

"There's no mistake. From what I've been told, all three were killed the same way. Three shots in the back. I've talked to the local police. They have no suspects and no motive. The comandante who referred you to me thinks the valuable package I'm picking up at the airport is your wife. He knows nothing about the painting. If he did, even the police in this place could make a connection. Now, level with me. Did anyone else besides those three contact you about the painting?"

"There were several, but the only one that appeared serious was this Russian, Drago Dragovich. I told you about him. Oligarch. Gangster. Sort of the same thing. He sent emails saying he represented a private party interested in acquiring the *Portrait of a Young Woman*. My guess is that the private party was him. Not that it mattered. I told him the same thing I told the others: Send me an offer. When it came in, it was so low that I almost didn't bother the owners with it. When I did, their reaction was the same as mine. Thanks, but no thanks. Just as well. I don't like dealing with Russians, especially now. They're all crooks. Wait! You don't think..."

"Representatives of the three most famous museums in the world are murdered just before a lost masterpiece arrives in an obscure Mexican beach town. I went to public school, and even I can connect those dots."

"Jesus," Nazareth rocked back in his seat, then gave Standard a scared look. "You're still okay with picking up the painting, right?"

It would have been easy to say no. Walk away and let Nazareth deal with his own damn painting. The promises Standard made to Emma about not getting involved in another "adventure" made the idea of ditching the whole thing sound better and better. But twenty K couldn't be ignored, especially if Emma was serious about moving to Troncones. That kind of money goes a long way in small Mexican beach towns. Then there was Itchy. While Standard could get by without a payday, Itchy was a different story.

"Mr. Standard, believe me. If all this was up to me, I'd be right now sitting around the conference table in my lawyer's office in New York City taking care of everything. You and your friend would never be involved; might not even know the sale took place. Coming down here," he waved his arm around. "Wherever here is, was all Strasser's idea. The guy is paranoid at the least. Batshit crazy at the most. Maybe somewhere in between. The one thing he does have is money, and he's eager to part with it to get that painting. Fine. The kind of money he wants to toss around is too big to ignore. So, we do everything his way. All I can say is stick with me, and in a couple of days, you and your friend will be forty thousand dollars richer."

The old Standard, the one before Emma, would have said yes without much thought. It would have been one of those "fuck it" moments because he had no choice or because any risk involved acted like a drug. He didn't have a death wish, but that doesn't mean death didn't wish him dead. The one after Emma wanted to take a step back, think before acting, weigh the pros and cons. Not that any of that mattered. Trouble was knocking at the door again. Might as well say hello and hope for the best.

"There's one other thing, Mr. Standard. My wife got another threatening email from Dragovich earlier today. I'm not taking it seriously. His offer is far too low, and he knows it. Besides, this deal will be done before he has a chance to do anything about it. I just thought you should know."

"We made a deal," Standard said. "We'll keep our end and hope nothing goes sideways between the airport and here. You keep your end. When the painting and your wife show up safe and sound tomorrow, have the money ready. We get paid, and we are out of there. After that, if someone is running around Zihuatanejo killing anyone involved with that painting, it's on you. Am I clear?"

"That's not exactly right," Nazareth said. "You don't get paid until Strasser has the painting. That's what you agreed to. Not that it matters that much. He'll be here soon, probably not long after the painting arrives. You won't have to wait long. And I did get a room for you down the hall from mine. The key is at the front desk."

The vise grip of doubt squeezed Standard's throat until all he could say was, "Fine."

"And your friend, Mr. ... Itchy."

"I'll take care of him."

It took Nazareth a few seconds to take it all in. "I appreciate your honesty and your loyalty. My wife is more important than the painting, but I hope that you can take care of both."

"I'll see you tomorrow afternoon. I'll need to give some money to Itchy to keep him happy. I'll let him keep what's left of the five thousand you gave us."

Standard got up, walked around the pool, and into the

lobby. On the way, he called Fat Tony to meet the next day at Sticky Fingers. He'd explain his plan then.

"You have the guns, right?"

"*Asegurado y cargado,*" Tony said. Locked and loaded.

In the lobby, he went to the desk to pick up his room key. He was almost out the door when he ran into Itchy Donlan and his girlfriend.

"John!" Itchy said. "What a surprise. You remember Marie."

"Of course. Nice to see you again," Standard nodded toward Marie. She was dressed for a day poolside: one-piece bathing suit, a sarong around her waist, floppy straw hat, beach bag. "Pardon us for a moment, Marie. Itchy and I need to do a little business. It won't take long."

Standard pulled Itchy into a corner near the bank of elevators. "We're on. Meet me tomorrow afternoon at one in the parking lot next to Sticky Fingers. I've talked to Fat Tony. Everything is ready to go. If things turn out right, you'll be twenty thousand richer before you know it."

Itchy gave an unconvincing nod. "Is this dangerous? I'm not really a bang, bang, shoot 'em up kind of guy. You know, other than what you might think."

No sense telling Itchy anything that would cause him to get cold feet. He needed him for his plan to work. "There are no guarantees, Itchy. My advice is that tomorrow you do everything I tell you. Enjoy your date, or whatever you call it, with Marie and I'll see you then. We good?"

"Yeah. Yeah, of course."

Standard looked toward Marie who was still standing in the middle of the lobby staring intently out at the pool.

CHAPTER 15

THE SLEEK BELL 206 HELICOPTER HOVERED OVER THE *El Obra Maestro* before gently settling down on the front deck of the slowly rocking superyacht. The copter's engines still whining and the rotors still spinning when Carlos Strasser stepped out, instinctively ducked down, and walked sixty feet toward the ship's massive superstructure. His pants and shirt flapped in the last of the prop wash.

Strasser was in his late sixties but looked ten years younger thanks to a rigid regimen of exercise. No carbs. Three miles a day on the treadmill in the ship's gym. His paleo diet heavy on beef raised on his own ranches. A stiff, almost militaristic bearing made him look taller than his medium height. He had a pale complexion. A full head of blond hair combed back over a high forehead was held down by a cap with the same blue and white colors as the Argentinian flag. An aquiline nose sat above a mouth with thin lips and narrow chin. As always, he was dressed in a black turtleneck, sport coat, and pants. In his left hand was a well-worn leather briefcase that he carried more for effect. Most of his business was done on his cell phone.

Lorenzo de Leon, the captain of the *El Obra Maestro,* waited, dressed in white, hands behind his back, a peaked military cap on his head. If he was nervous that the yacht's owner had arrived, he didn't show it. Sailing the world together, de Leon and Strasser had learned to like and trust one another. "Welcome back, sir. I hope your trip went well."

After the long flight from Sweden to Oaxaca then a two-hour helicopter flight, Strasser's legs felt weak, and his head throbbed. Jet lag would set in soon, which left him little time to get things done.

"Thank you, captain. Stockholm is a beautiful city but if I ever see another pickled herring, it will be too soon." They shared a laugh and shook hands. "Fortunately, it was also very profitable, so worth the time and trouble. Now, I'm eager to hear where we are, and your plans for the coming days. We also need to discuss the logistics of what we do when we reach our destination. Give me an hour then let's meet on the bridge. I want to know where everything stands."

Strasser crossed the deck, then down the port side of the ship and through a hatchway. Inside, he walked up two flights of stairs to his cabin. His luggage was already there, sitting on a stand at the end of the king-sized bed. He undressed and went into the bathroom to stand under the shower for ten minutes trying to wash away all that was behind him and get ready to close the greatest deal he would ever make, that anyone in the art world would ever make.

He'd done all the work. Did all the research. Read all the books. He knew more about Raphael than any man alive. He didn't own one of his paintings, but it didn't matter. Nothing could compare to *Portrait of a Young Woman.* Owning it would be more than enough. Every expert he'd ever consulted believed the painting was either destroyed or never existed in the first place. His father had told him that he was sure the painting hung in the dining room at Hitler's Bavarian retreat of Berghof, but that it had been destroyed along with other price-less pieces of art at the end of the war.

He had always believed they were wrong. He just couldn't prove it. He was positive the painting had probably existed in somebody's house or cellar, someone who had no idea what it was. He was sure his father was wrong—the painting never hung on Hitler's mountain. Instead, it had miraculously survived the war when so many valuable pieces of art didn't. Now he had been vindicated, his long-held belief validated. As a solitary man it did little good to gloat. Still, he enjoyed a few private moments of satisfaction thinking about his competitors and detractors.

There would be no more scoffing about Crazy Carlos and his wild goose chase.

For what may have been hundreds of years, the painting hung unappreciated and collecting dust in the turret room of an obscure nunnery in the south of France.

Probably one of the sisters bought it for a few francs at what passed for a yard sale.

He had to laugh. Those crazy nuns sold carrots, potatoes, and parsnips to make ends meet when all the time they were sitting on a gold mine. Strasser's shallow Catholic roots made him want to cut the nuns a little slack, but he had a hard time understanding how they could fail to see that they possessed a priceless piece of art.

It had always been Strasser's dream to one day find the painting himself.

What better way to prove he'd been right all along. Most of the self-proclaimed experts he talked to had never heard of the painting. Those that did had no idea where it might be. The best guess by those few who believed in its existence was that it was somewhere in Eastern Europe. That led to years of on-again, off-again visits to castles, art museums, and private homes in every country east of Germany. Nothing. He kicked himself for not putting the south of France on the list, but why would he? Monet, Matisse, and Van Gogh lived in Provence, but that was four hundred years after Raphael.

That a wealthy hedge fund manager from New York had stumbled across it was deflating but may turn out to be little more than a very expensive inconvenience. Strasser would have to pay millions to get what he couldn't find on his own. Not that any of that mattered now. What did was that his instincts had been right.

Refreshed and fighting off creeping jet lag, Strasser dressed then walked up another flight of stairs to the bridge. De Leon was waiting.

"What's our position?" he asked.

"Twenty miles off the coast of Mexico and two hundred miles south of Acapulco. The passage through the canal went smoother than I thought so we are a little ahead of schedule."

"Your plan?"

"Top speed to Acapulco. Refuel. After that it's a short trip up the coast to Zihuatanejo."

Strasser looked out the curved bank of windows, then at the array of computer screens that made the yacht one of the most advanced in the world. Just under a hundred-seventy meters in length with a top speed of thirty-five knots, *La Obra Maestro*, The Masterpiece, had taken him around the world in search of priceless art. None of those journeys were anywhere near as important as this one.

He needed to make sure everything was perfect.

"Make whatever adjustments you need, but I want to arrive in Zihuatanejo at night to attract as little attention as possible. Also, put any non-essential crew ashore in Acapulco. I want as few people on board as possible. You can either send them home or pick them up on the way back. Once I have the painting, I'll take the helicopter to the airport in Zihuatanejo. I've arranged for my plane to remain in Oaxaca then meet me there. By that afternoon I'll be in Montevideo, and you'll be on your way before noon. We'll decide where later on. Let me know if anything changes. I'll be in the salon or my office."

The salon that covered three quarters of the main deck was lined with some of Strasser's favorite paintings. Not the most expensive, but the ones he enjoyed the most. There was a Vermeer and a Manet, just not their best. The others were lesser-known 19th Century artists. The star of the show was an enormous J.M.W. Turner depicting a large sailing ship partially hidden by a shadowy mist. With the push of a button, the painting disappeared into the ceiling to reveal an 85-inch QLED television used mostly to watch replays of Argentina's three FIFA World Cup championships.

Strasser knew that his reputation in the art world was one of an eclectic collector, a dilettante with a lot of money, but with no particular specialty when it came to expensive art. One critic referred to him as a vacuum cleaner rather than an art connoisseur, sucking up valuable paintings, carvings, and jewelry like dust bunnies.

Strasser bristled at the criticism. He considered himself an expert, a shrewd authority with a deep appreciation for all types of art. His expertise was finding rare pieces, using his personal fortune to buy them, and enjoying watching the disappointment on the faces of those who lost out. Over the years he'd collected thousands of pieces of art ranging from ten-foot marble statues of Greek gods to delicate hand-carved cameos. What wasn't on the yacht was either in his house or one of the warehouses on his estate in Uruguay.

Strasser poured a drink then sat in one of the captain's chairs in front of the wrap-around windows with a 180-degree view. Outside, the ocean offered little more than gentle swells. Further out to sea, a cruise ship silhouetted against the light-blue sky moved south. On the foredeck, the helicopter he came in on had been securely lashed down. Soon it would be refueled and ready when he needed it.

Now came the hard part. The waiting. He was not a patient man by nature but now he had no choice.

He picked up the satellite phone on the table next to his chair, then swung around to look out at the ocean on the port side just as the ship's powerful engines picked up speed. He dialed. The man answered after three rings.

"Where do things stand?" Strasser asked.

"Three of your four competitors are no longer in the game."

"Good," Strasser said, avoiding asking about the details. "Am I right in assuming that it's the Russians still standing?"

"For now," Heinz Richter said.

Strasser smiled to himself. What Heinz meant was that it was only a matter of time before all threats to possessing the painting were eliminated. Once again, he would have outsmarted them all. He'd even outmaneuvered a Russian oligarch.

Fortunately, that's not a hard thing to do.

If a little blood was shed along the way, that was the price for playing in the big leagues. The dilettantes and bedwetters from museums would come up short again. Thinking about the look on their faces when he sailed away with what could very well be the last masterpiece made him smile.

"And the painting?"

"I believe it will arrive before you do. That means tomorrow at the earliest. The only way it can get here safely is by plane. The seller will need to get it from the airport to his hotel. I will watch the airport for the next two days. When it arrives, I will let you know."

"And the seller's agent has checked into the appropriate hotel, I assume, and taken a room on the top floor."

"Yes sir. The penthouse near the roof access."

"Very good. I'll let you know when we are close to arriving. After that I'll contact Mr. Nazareth to complete the transaction. You can meet me at the hotel. It shouldn't take long. You've done good work, my friend. We are almost there. When it's over, we shall meet at my ranch and toast our new acquisition."

"It would be an honor. I look forward to it."

Strasser hung up, poured another drink, then walked down a short flight of stairs to his office. He logged on to his laptop and started searching for any news about missing representatives of Prado, the Louvre, and The Vatican. He found nothing but knew that wouldn't last. He was surprised that the local authorities had managed to avoid any bad publicity. Murder and a legendary masterpiece were too juicy for the press to ignore. Eventually word would get out. Reporters and cameras would start showing up. So, the sooner he left with the painting the better.

CHAPTER 16

Standard got up late, made coffee, and found some news on the internet that was more current than the old LA Times he'd just read. He needed to know about Strasser, and there was only one place to go. He killed a little time making more coffee, warming up a day-old pastry, and going back to the internet for more news about what was happening in the US. The more he read, the more he appreciated being in Mexico.

At eleven o'clock, he called Benny Orlando. Portland, Oregon, was two hours behind Zihuatanejo, and Benny liked to sleep late. It was always best to catch him in the morning.

"Benny. It's Standard."

There was a long pause followed by a muffled groan. "What time is it?"

"Nine o'clock your time."

"Morning or night?"

"Morning," Standard said. "I need your help. Get dressed, make some coffee. I'll call you back in half an hour."

Benny had been Standard's landlord since losing his newspaper job and, in fact, still was since Standard continued to pay rent on an apartment in a building Benny managed if you call collecting rent and ignoring complaints managing. Benny was a little person who spent most of his adult life as a clown named "Baby Benny" in the Ringling Bros. Barnum & Bailey Circus. He retired and moved to Portland after his aunt died and left him everything she had, including a rundown apartment building on the city's South Park Blocks. After living there for several years, he sold it to an investment company with the agreement that he could stay on as manager and live there for free until it was destroyed and replaced with a modern high-rise. Something that had yet to happen.

Negotiating a job and free rent was the least of Benny's talents. His true calling was as a top-shelf hacker with a special ability to find out pretty much anything about anybody. And if he couldn't, he had a worldwide network of hackers, nerds, passive-aggressives, and snitches who could. From what Benny had told him, they were the prototypical collection of disgruntled cops or socially awkward, overweight geniuses living on Red Bull, ramen, and DoorDash pizza. Like most of them, Benny did all his work from a darkened room in his apartment filled with the latest in high-tech whizbangs and gizmos.

Benny's idea of amusement was destroying the lives of those who had made fun of his stature. He'd hack into their bank accounts, send the money to PETA, destroying their credit ratings, send obscene resignation letters to their employers that included multiple uses of the phrase "you fucking douchebag."

In his previous life as a struggling freelancer, Standard would sometimes sit in Benny's office watching the little man's fingers fly across a keyboard while his eyes darted between more screens than a multiplex. The sound of a window-mounted air conditioner mixed with the blare of calliope music coming out of a stereo system too big for the room. The muted movie *Trapeze*, starring Gina Lollobrigida, played on a continuous loop on a flat-screen TV in the corner. Looming over it all was a large poster from another movie, *The Greatest Show on Earth*.

Benny was also Standard's best friend. After becoming something of a pariah in his own hometown, Benny rented to him when no one else would. He even let him slide on the rent for a few months until he found work. Standard once asked him why he rented to him.

"I needed to send that month's rent receipts to the investment company," Benny had told him, then winked. "I was a little short."

Along the way, Benny used his finely tuned skills to help Standard find people who didn't want to be found and got paid handsomely for it. He was more than willing to help if it meant Standard could cover his overdue rent. Benny was the last person he talked to before leaving for Mexico. He didn't have to explain anything. Benny just knew. They'd kept in touch ever since.

After calling Benny, Standard left the house and walked down the hill to The Tortuga. He ordered *huevos revueltos* with *tocino, pan*, and *jugo de naranja*. Scrambled eggs with bacon, toast, and orange juice. He was still waiting for the sloth-like Pablo to show up with his food when it came time to call Benny again.

"You awake?"

"Barely," Benny said. "Whatever you want better be good. I'm underwater here on a bunch of projects. The only one I can tell you about is a website for a pueblo casino in New Mexico. So, what's up?"

"I need you to find out as much as you can about a man named Carlos Strasser. All I know about him is that he's rich, collects art, and his family is part of some South American cattle business. If it's beef, then he's Argentinean or Brazilian. That's just a guess. Also, he travels the world in a yacht."

"When do you need this?"

"Sooner the better."

"You and everybody else," Benny said. "Okay, but one of these days I'm going to start charging you for this kind of work."

"You're collecting double rent on my apartment by listing it on VRBO. That should cover it."

"I need to rent to dumber people," Benny grumbled. "So, give me the guy's name again." Standard listened to the sound of Benny rummaging around for something to write on, then repeated Strasser's name. "I'll need a few hours," Benny said, then hung up.

When Pablo came to clear away the breakfast dishes, Standard ordered a Corona then called Fat Tony to make sure everything was still good for the next day. "The woman and the painting will ride with us in the Tahoe. Itchy will drive. I need you and your cousin to stay as close on our tail as you can until we get to the hotel."

After reassurances from Tony that all was good, he called Itchy to check in.

When he didn't answer, Standard figured he was still playing slap and tickle with his new friend Marie. There was always the chance that Itchy would bail on the whole plan, but with twenty-thousand dollars on the line, the odds were slim. Then he called Emma.

"Where are you?"

"Ixtapa, waiting for guests to show up at one of those condos I handle. Have I ever told you how much I hate this place?"

"Many times. Just don't hate the money you make. It's what Ixtapa is all about. When you get back, I'll take you to dinner. There's that new place in La Madera. Italian, I think."

After she promised to be home by five, Standard pulled a lounge chair out into the sun and ordered another beer. It was one of those lazy days that made him love Mexico. The sun was warm. The parade of tourists was a never-ending movie. The calmness of the bay was broken up by jet skis and banana boats. The "click click" of the usuals playing backgammon two cabanas away provided familiar background music.

Two hours later, he packed up his things and climbed the hill back to the house. Emma wouldn't be back for another three hours at best. Plenty of time for a shower and a nap. Then the phone rang.

"This guy Strasser is a pretty interesting character," Benny Orlando said. "How much do you need to know?"

"Everything you have."

"His father was Ludwig Bauman, a mid-level accountant for the SS during World War Two. It's believed he siphoned off millions from the bank accounts of Jews and Gypsies sent to concentration camps. In the last days of the war, he packed up his money, left his wife and son in bombed-out Berlin, and boarded a freighter from Odessa to Rio. He disappeared for three years, then popped up in Argentina where he bought up thousands of acres of land and went into the cattle business. Along the way, he picked up a new wife, started a new family, and changed his name to Strasser. He has two daughters and a son. The girls married well. One to a French doctor and moved to Paris. The other to a banker in Buenos Aires. The son, Carlos, never married. He took over the cattle business forty years ago when his father died. He used his degree from the London School of Economics to turn it into an empire that includes feedlots, slaughterhouses, meatpacking plants, distribution, and a string of beef-centric restaurants. It even branched into sidelines like cutlery, kitchen appliances, and recipe books. Before they died back in the eighties, Carlos's parents were the king and queen of the South American meat-packing glitterati. Regulars at royal weddings, New York City galas, and Hollywood premiers."

"And Carlos?"

"He's known in the industry as The Baron of Beef. Not exactly a cut off the old prime rib, if you know what I mean. Elusive, reclusive, and exclusive. He avoids the limelight, preferring to run his various businesses from his yacht while collecting priceless paintings and other pieces of art, most of which he keeps on an estate near Montevideo. His business conglomerate has offices all over the world, but for some reason, the headquarters are in Johannesburg, South Africa. Probably a tax dodge of some kind. If he has any philosophical ties to his father's days with the Third Reich, there's no mention of it. He stays totally off the grid. No social media and very little mention in the press. Today, that makes him something of a ghost. A man of mystery in a world where there are fewer and fewer mysteries. Several art magazines have done profiles of him, but most of it was hearsay and rumors. He never talked to any of them."

"Where did you find all this?"

"The Israelis mostly. I have a couple of contacts there. The Mossad keeps an eye on the heirs of Nazi Germany, thinking that fortunes built with stolen money are ripe for reparations."

"What about his yacht?"

"*La Obra Maestra.* Means The Masterpiece. Not the largest or most expensive in the world, but impressive. Almost three hundred feet. Like I said, he spends nearly all his time there. Global trackers have the yacht in Southeast Asia, India, and Portugal. And that's just in the last year. Right now, it shows it off the west coast of Mexico near Acapulco. Isn't that where you are?"

"Close. What about his art collection?"

"Believed to be the largest private one in the world. Name an artist, dead or alive, and he probably owns one of their paintings. He also seems to own a few marble statues from Italy, jade necklaces from China, and a diamond ring that once belonged to the queen of Romania ... supposedly. One of his profiles claimed his life-long obsession is finding some long-lost painting by Raphael. Now, care to tell me what this is all about? Fine art seems a heavy lift. I always saw you as more of an anime guy."

Standard gave Benny the short version about why Strasser was coming to Zihuatanejo, talking in vague terms about an expensive piece of art, and leaving out any mention of Raphael or murdered representatives of art museums.

"In other words," Benny said, "trouble has found you ... again."

"Life without risk is not worth living."

"Evel Knievel?"

"Good guess. Charles Lindbergh."

"Be careful. I'm loving the double rent on your apartment. There's a refugee family from Kabul staying there now. They think it's a suite. The feds are paying for everything. So, just don't come back anytime soon. I may have a problem getting them to leave."

"Thanks for the help. I'll let you know how things turn out."

Standard hung up, sat down, and rubbed his eyes. Russians like Drago Dragovitch. Nazis like Strasser's father. Zihuatanejo was starting to feel more like Leningrad 1942. But as ominous as it sounded, he couldn't back out and walk away from twenty thousand dollars.

CHAPTER 17

Heinz Richter gave five hundred pesos to the waiter he'd convinced the night before to come back to the hotel with him, then hustled him toward the door with a smile and a pat on the back. Richter didn't remember the kid's name, if he ever knew it. Whatever it was, he wasn't the best he'd had. Certainly nothing like what he'd found in places like Hong Kong and Bangkok, but good enough for a one-night stand and a few hours of diversion.

Richter smiled when the kid tried to kiss him goodbye, then gently let him leave, promising to see him again while knowing he never would. Strasser never approved of his occasional dalliances. Like the others, he would keep this one to himself as well.

Richter stripped back down to his underwear and did his daily exercises: fifty push-ups, two hundred sit-ups, and twenty-five squats while holding the room's ottoman. It was a regimen he started during his days in the military. It kept him fit, his muscles well-toned, his body fat at under ten percent. Finished, he showered, dressed, grabbed some food from the tienda across the street from his hotel, and got in his rental car. Not sure when the plane carrying the painting would land, he took a calculated guess that it would be sometime in the afternoon.

He just didn't know if it was this day or the next. He would need some luck.

Richter wound his way through Zihuatanejo's confusing streets before finally finding Ruta 200 more by mistake than intention, then heading south toward the airport. Thirty minutes later, he was sitting in the parking lot munching on chips, choking on a tasteless taco plate, and washing it all down with a tepid orange Fanta. It was the kind of food he'd come to expect in Mexico, which made him want to get this over with and back to civilization as soon as possible. After traveling the world with Strasser, he had found the one place he never wanted to come back to.

For the next six hours, and with occasional trips into the terminal for bathroom breaks, he watched the area of the tarmac reserved for private planes. Not knowing what kind of jet, its number, or when it would arrive made him anxious. He didn't like uncertainty and definitely not in this case. There was too much at stake. Hard as it was, he had no choice but to sit, wait, and try not to eat too much bad food, which to him meant not eating at all.

In the years he'd worked for Carlos Strasser, Heinz had learned about the importance of patience, of watching, waiting for the right moment. He just hadn't learned it from the chronically edgy and unpredictable Strasser. Instead, he wondered if it was a trait he'd inherited from his father, who worked for the Stasi in the former East Germany. His career consisted of spending hours watching and waiting for those trying to escape into the West. When the wall came down and the country collapsed in 1990, he became a mercenary for a company made up of other discarded agents of the old spy service. Heinz was eight when his father was killed in some obscure, bullet-ridden East African country fighting in a war that pitted one corrupt tribal chief against another. He would later learn from his own experience that when it came to Africa there was no other kind of war or chief.

Heinz still remembered the tall, stern man with the buzz cut who showed up at their door on a rainy February morning in Potsdam where he lived with his mother in a third-floor, three-room apartment. The man handed his mother a small box filled with money and a letter saying that her husband was dead. It was unsigned. The man said *"Es tut mir leid"* then left. She sat down on their threadbare couch and stared at the money. She didn't cry. His parents were never close.

Ten years later, Heinz joined the German army, eventually becoming a member of an elite military force, serving two tours in Iraq and Afghanistan under NATO leadership. During his first night patrol, he wondered what he would feel the first time he killed someone. It didn't take him long to find out. He came up behind a Taliban sniper, put his pistol to his head, and pulled the trigger. He felt nothing that night nor the next five times.

He left the army when he turned twenty-five and went to work for a private security company where he spent most of his time protecting rich executives, crime bosses from Russia, and soccer players. One of the company's clients was an Argentinian meat-packing conglomerate run by a reclusive billionaire. That was where he met Carlos Strasser, who eventually hired him as the company's chief of security for twice the salary. Over time, the job became less and less about corporate security and more about doing Strasser's personal bidding. That was when he learned about Strasser's passion for art and the lengths he would go to get what he wanted.

As a result, this wasn't the first parked car he'd sat in. He'd done the same thing in cities all over the world. Sometimes it might be a bar, restaurant, coffee shop, or hotel lobby but it was all for the same reason. If there was some piece of art out there —painting, mural, statue, whatever—that Strasser wanted, it was Heinz's job to make sure he got it. Sometimes it involved a candid face-to-face, innuendo-laden conversation. After all, he was dealing with smart, rich people. They don't understand anything that's too direct or to the point. Sometimes what he wanted required something more ... aggressive. Only a few died under strange circumstances. Others were badly injured. Sometimes all it took was finding the family dog hanging from a tree in the backyard.

Whatever he had to do, things always seemed to work out in Strasser's favor. He had the magic touch when it came to finding what he wanted and getting his hands on it. Sometimes he paid for it. When he didn't, well, that's where Heinz came in. Over time they had worked out an arrangement in which Strasser talked about what he wanted, who had it, and where it was. It didn't take long for Heinz to know when to take the hint. The code gave Strasser deniability and Heinz a Swiss bank account full of Euros. Not enough to retire, but he was only in his forties. Plenty of time to earn more.

This thing with the painting, however, felt different. Something worth nine figures was not the same as talking some dot-com bozo in Hong Kong out of his desire to own a jade dragon or a pimply-faced thirty-something entrepreneur out of an obscure Degas. *Portrait of a Young Woman* was Strasser's Holy Grail. A validation of his decades-long belief that the painting existed somewhere. But just being right wasn't enough. Possessing it was. During long voyages on his yacht, Strasser would spend hours talking about Raphael, his paintings, and his life. He would endlessly speculate about where *Portrait of a*

Young Woman might be and why no one had found it. He was convinced that one day it would be his and the world would know about it.

In addition to being impatient, Strasser was also paranoid, erratic, and capricious. Always thinking outside the box. Always staying one step ahead of the competition, and not just the dead ones. But wanting to do the deal of a lifetime in a place like Zihuatanejo, made Richter shake his head. He always took Strasser as more the Monte Carlo, Majorca, Santorini type. This place was totally off his usual grid, but then again, that was Strasser. Always in search of the new and unusual.

Strasser had made it clear in his uniquely obtuse way that it was Heinz's job to make sure he got what he wanted. "Do whatever it takes," he'd told him. "Use your best judgment." Richter knew the code words. No one had to lay it out for him. That's why three of Strasser's competitors were dead. Unfortunate for them, but Heinz had his orders and obligations.

Three bodies didn't mean the field was clear. Museums and churches were not the only ones interested in great art. There was still one more player left on the field. A wild card. In his experience, very wild. Heinz hadn't found him yet, but he knew he was around. He could feel it. Taste it. Either he or his men were out there looking for their chance to steal the painting. When they showed themselves, Heinz would be ready.

CHAPTER 18

Heinz was on his second bottle of Fanta and ready for another bathroom break when just before two p.m., a black SUV pulled into the lot, circled the parking area twice, then stopped in front of a metal gate at the south end of the terminal. It idled for a few minutes before a battered white van with a sliding door on the side pulled in next to it.

As if on cue, a Bombardier Learjet landed on the airport's single runway. It went out of sight behind the terminal before reappearing and taxiing as close to the gate as possible. The whine of its engines slowed as it pivoted and came to a stop. Two minutes later, a door on the plane's right side dropped down.

Heinz picked up the cheap binoculars he had bought at a stall in the Central Mercado, peered through them, and held his breath. The next few minutes would tell him if he had guessed right about when and where the painting would arrive. If he was right, then the waiting was over. All he had to do now was make sure it would get safely to where it needed to go.

He watched as a short, pudgy man in a straw hat and flowered shirt got out on the driver's side of the SUV. He pulled up his baggy Bermuda shorts and looked around as if expecting something or someone else. One look at him, and Heinz had a hard time believing that this was the guy Simon Nazareth had hired to pick up and transport a priceless painting. The man's head was on a swivel, looking all around as if expecting someone to start shooting.

Heinz's concern eased when another man, younger, better looking, with dark hair and a deep tan got out on the passenger side. He wore shorts, sandals, and a Polo shirt. One look at him, and Heinz knew that he'd seen men like him before. Not in sleepy Mexican beach towns but in jungles and mountains. The kind that was easy to overlook until things went bad, and they saved your life. Whoever he was, everything about him said he was the leader, the guy in charge.

They both walked around the SUV to the driver's side of the white van.

Heinz couldn't see the driver, only a flabby arm resting on the open window. After talking for a few seconds, the van backed up across a driveway into an empty parking spot. The two from the SUV walked over to the gate that opened onto the tarmac and waited, watching the private jet.

Heinz stiffened when two federales in full military camo with helmets and combat glasses came out of the south end of the terminal. They had AK-47s across their chests and pistols on their belts. In unison, they took ten steps toward the jet, then stopped. This was not what he expected. He never thought that armed soldiers would be a part of things, let alone show up at the same time as the jet. Customs had always been Heinz's biggest concern. After talking about it, he and Strasser agreed that getting the painting into the country might be the most complicated part of the operation. But there was nothing they could do about it. Neither of them had any idea what arrangements Nazareth had made, if any. Now, all Heinz could do was hold his breath and see what happens.

After another few minutes, a woman dressed in a bright white business suit and a pair of blood-red heels carefully came down the stairs from the plane, carrying a leather briefcase. She was tall, statuesque, and Asian. Her jet-black hair was pulled into a tight ponytail. Heinz guessed Hong Kong or Shanghai, but with her large sunglasses, it was hard to tell. It didn't matter. He knew the type: smart, arrogant, beautiful. She looked as much in charge as the man who got out of the SUV.

He watched as she walked across the tarmac to stand three feet in front of the nearest federale. After speaking for a few seconds, she reached into the briefcase, pulled out her passport, and handed it to him. The soldier took it, looked at it, then handed it back. Next, she reached into the briefcase again and pulled out a sheet of paper and an envelope. She handed both to the soldier. He unfolded the paper, seemed to read it, then gave it back as well. He slipped the envelope behind his flak jacket and took ten steps back. He nodded to his partner, who did the same.

"Slick," Heinz thought as he watched the entire prearranged dance through the cheap binoculars. "Everything in order, including the bribe. God, I love corruption."

The woman had to be Nazareth's wife, Heinz thought. She would be the only person he would trust to take care of details such as dodging customs, paying off federales, and getting the painting this far.

With the soldiers paid off, the woman walked back to the plane, up the stairs, and disappeared inside. Heinz put down the binoculars and leaned forward, arms on the steering wheel. He knew what was coming next, the money shot. After several minutes, she emerged followed by a man carrying two expensive-looking leather suitcases. He wore black pants, a white shirt with epaulets, and aviator glasses. A few seconds later, a second man dressed the same way came out carrying a large silver metal oversized briefcase, about three feet by four feet. The way Strasser described it, *Portrait of a Young Woman* was small—just seventeen inches by twenty-four, but with a heavy ornate frame. With protective packing, it would fit comfortably in the bag.

Heinz excitedly banged his fist on the dashboard. "Yes. Yes. Yes."

The painting and the seller were together or soon would be. Strasser was a day and a half away. There was every reason to relax a little, but Heinz forced himself to stay alert. This deal wasn't over yet until Strasser sailed away with the Raphael. Also, the wild card was still out there.

The passenger from the SUV, the one in charge, opened the gate, took the oversized briefcase, and walked toward the back of the car. The other man took the luggage and followed him. When the SUV's back gate opened, the briefcase went inside and under a blanket. The luggage went in the back behind the front passenger seat. The woman hung back long enough to shake hands with the two men from the plane, then walked out the gate to the SUV. The short fat guy held the door for her as she got in the seat behind the driver.

With everybody in the SUV, Heinz started his car, put it in gear, and waited. His plan was to follow them as closely as possible without getting noticed until they got to the hotel and the painting was safely inside. That was the key to everything. After that, it was nothing more than a routine transaction, only one involving hundreds of millions of dollars.

When the SUV pulled out of the lot, the white van was on its back bumper. Heinz waited a few seconds, then followed, staying back far enough to keep the two vehicles within sight. For the first three miles toward town, the van was never more than three feet behind the SUV. In tandem and at a steady pace, the two cars stayed in the left-hand lane, meaning anyone trying to pass had to do it on the right.

"Smart," Heinz thought as he shadowed the two cars from a hundred yards back. If trouble was coming, it would need to sneak up on the right. Drivers don't shoot well. Passengers do. Sliding side doors are easily pushed open. It was a savvy move that made him think that he was right in not underestimating the men hired to pick up the painting, particularly the one in charge.

Another mile toward the city, and Heinz was beginning to think that it was going to be a cakewalk. He hoped so. The tension had made his neck hurt and the meager lunch was not sitting well. He kept a close watch on every taxi, truck, and passenger car that sped by him, changed lanes, and raced past the van and the SUV. The more that went harmlessly on their way, the more he relaxed. That didn't last long.

The car that came up behind him seemed to come out of nowhere. When, at the last second, it darted into the other lane and started passing him on the left, Heinz glanced over at it. It was a late model bronze Mercedes sedan. The driver had a nest of unkempt brown hair, a large forehead, and pale skin. He was wearing a sweat-stained tank top and sucking on an inhaler. The passenger could have been his brother but with a cigarette hanging in the corner of his mouth that bobbed up and down as he talked on a cell phone and pointed ahead at the van and SUV. Once it was past him, the Mercedes veered back into the right lane and sped up even more.

These were the people Heinz had been waiting for. The last obstacles standing between Strasser and the Raphael. Drago Dragovitch's thugs. He was sure of it. His muscles tightened. Breaths short and shallow. While he knew something would happen, he didn't know what. Time to think fast.

Getting rid of them was going to be more complicated. The three museum representatives never knew what was coming. These guys don't dance.

Only one thing to do.

He stomped down on the gas to squeeze every mile per hour out of the underpowered rental car. He started gaining precious ground. The Mercedes pulled up next to the white van. It slowed slightly to keep pace. Heinz inched closer. A man popped out of the Mercedes's moonroof. It had to be the passenger. The one who had been on the cell phone. His upper body cleared the car's roof. Slowly he pulled up what looked to be an assault rifle of some kind. Heinz checked his speedometer. All four cars were doing just over sixty miles per hour. The man struggled to raise the gun toward his right shoulder. Buffeted by the wind, he wasn't making it easy.

If this was their plan to get the painting, it was typical Russian: Steal what you can't buy. Kill who you can't negotiate with. The problem was that shooting up the van and the SUV put everybody and everything at risk, including the Raphael. Some plan, Heinz thought.

Heinz stomped the gas again. Banged on the steering wheel in a useless effort to get another mile per hour out of the car. Maybe this wasn't going to be as much fun as he thought. One shot from the rifle might send the van off the road, leaving the SUV with the painting on its own and unprotected. He watched as the Russian bent over the top of the car. Braced himself then tried to take aim at the van's passenger side door. Just as it looked like he was about to fire, the sliding door on the right side of the white van flew open. Out came the barrel of a shotgun followed by a flash that blew out the Mercedes' windshield.

Heinz was close enough to ram the left third of the Mercedes's bumper. Then the driver slammed on the brakes. A tap that would send the Mercedes careening off the road quickly turned into a collision. The right fender on Heinz's car crumpled. Pieces of glass and chrome flew into the air joined by shards of glass from the Mercedes's shattered windshield. The shooter's upper body jerked backward. The rifle flew up in the air. It sailed over the top of Heinz's car to join the rest of the debris.

The Mercedes immediately swerved hard right. Slid left as the driver tried to correct, then right again. Tires on the left-hand side buckled. The smell of burnt rubber. Skid marks on the asphalt. Totally out of control, it slid across the shoulder of the highway, bounced off a bridge abutment, and disappeared down a brush-filled culvert.

Heinz had to choose between staying with the SUV and the painting or taking care of the Russians. It was not a hard decision. He hated Russians.

Heinz hit the brakes, pulled over, and stopped the car on the right-hand shoulder. He got out and, gun in hand, ran back down the road to where the Mercedes had disappeared. He followed the car tracks through the mowed-down brush, through a culvert, and into a stand of coconut palms, the trees perfectly aligned like aisles in a grocery store. When he saw the car, he pulled up twenty feet short and waited. The Russians no longer had an assault rifle, but that didn't mean they were unarmed.

After clearing the culvert, the Mercedes had smashed through a makeshift wire fence and T-boned into one of the coconut palms. Steam with a rubberized smell poured out of the crushed hood. A half-dozen coconuts had already banged down on the car's trunk and hood. Two more crashed down as Heinz watched to see what came next. The man who had the rifle was draped across the roof. He raised up and turned left then right. The dazed look on his face said he was trying to figure out what just happened. As soon as he straightened up and turned around, Heinz shot him in the forehead.

Heinz waited and watched, not sure if the second man, the driver, was dead or alive. Finally, the car door opened with the screech of metal against metal. Slowly, the driver half fell, half climbed out of the car, his face covered in blood from gashes on his forehead and nose. His pant legs were torn. More blood came from a deep cut in his left thigh and right arm. He tried to stand up but fell once then again, each time while trying to hold up both hands and begging in Russian and then bad English.

"Drago," he yelled. "We from Drago. No shoot. Drago."

"Turn around," Heinz yelled. "Hands in the air."

When the driver did as he was told, Heinz shot him three times in the back. "Stupid Russians," Heinz muttered, then followed the car tracks back to the highway and his car.

CHAPTER 19

While Itchy Donlan drove, Standard sat in the passenger seat, the Glock in his right hand held tight against his thigh. He kept one eye on the road ahead and the other on the right-side mirror. If he had a third, it would be on Itchy, who probably hadn't driven a car in five years.

Standard stiffened each time a car came up on the right, then relaxed when it passed. If all he saw from the airport to the hotel were taxis, vans, and passenger cars, so much the better.

That didn't last long.

When they were four miles north of the airport, he looked in the mirror and saw the bronze Mercedes. Something about it made him suspicious. Maybe it was because he hadn't seen a Mercedes since he arrived in Mexico, and certainly not a bronze one. A rental, he thought. From Acapulco.

"Speed up a little, Itchy," Standard said.

"Why? What's wrong?" Itchy looked back and forth between his mirrors and the road ahead. He was nervous before they reached the airport. One word from Standard about speeding up, and he was flat-out scared. "Are we in trouble? Is it bad?"

"Just do what I tell you, Itchy. Don't worry about anything but the road ahead."

Standard called Fat Tony. "I don't like the car coming up on the right. We're going to speed up a little. See what happens. Stick with us." He hung up and checked on Itchy again. "You still with me?"

"Yeah. Yeah. Fine." The sound of Itchy's voice told Standard just the opposite. He just needed the little guy to hang in there for a while longer.

Standard turned in his seat to look at Mai Nazareth. "Just a precaution. You don't see a lot of late-model Mercedes around here."

"Russians," she said, barely looking up from her open laptop.

"Russians! What makes you think that?"

"A Russian named Drago Dragovich has been after the painting ever since word got out that it had been found. I get three emails a day, demanding that we sell it to him."

"Yeah, your husband told me about him," Standard said. "Called him a bad dude."

"Whoever those men are, they're probably trying to steal it." She looked up from her laptop and took off her sunglasses. Her dark eyes were all business. "This is where you earn your money, Mr. Standard."

"Did she say Russians? What kind of Russians?" Itchy said. "John, you told me..."

"I said do what I tell you. Now, keep driving and stay in this lane. Same speed."

Standard turned back around, rolled down the window, and raised the Glock. He looked in the mirror again. The Mercedes was easing over to the left to get close to the van. A head came out of the moonroof, followed by a man's upper body. Then a rifle. He called Fat Tony.

"Trouble on the right. Tell Emilio to get ready."

Standard turned around in the seat and leaned out the window. He didn't see the side door of the van slide open, but he couldn't miss the shotgun barrel pointing at the Mercedes. A muzzle flash. The car's front window shattered. It swerved violently as the driver slammed on the brakes. The Mercedes jerked forward as if hit from behind, veered to the right, and disappeared.

Standard called Tony again. "The Mercedes? Where did it go? What happened?" He heard Tony say "¿Qué sucedió?"

Tony answered after a few seconds. "Emilio says it went off the road. He thinks there was another car behind it, maybe. It got rear-ended after Emilio shot at it. Is that a problem?"

Standard took a deep breath. "Not anymore." He leaned back in the seat and looked over to check on Itchy.

"Were those really Russians?" Itchy's face was pale, his hands gripping the steering wheel as if he were afraid it would fly away. "They're gone, right? The Russians? What happened?"

"I'll tell you later. Keep going. Let's get this over with."

Twenty minutes later, Itchy pulled the SUV into the driveway of the VistaPacifica, turned off the engine, and took a deep breath. "I'm glad that's over," he said. "Whatever the hell it was."

"We're not home yet," Standard said, getting out of the car and looking around at the parking lot and the street. He wasn't sure what he was looking for, unless it was another car with gun-wielding Russians. "Let's get her and the painting up to Nazareth's room as fast as we can. Go find a luggage cart."

Tony's van pulled in behind them. "Wait here," Standard said to Mai Nazareth, then got out to talk to Tony.

"Thanks." He handed Tony the Glock.

"You sure you don't want to keep it?" Tony asked.

"Probably a good idea." Standard put the pistol in the small of his back under his shirt.

"That Mercedes?" Tony asked. "Who was it?"

Standard pointed at the SUV. "She thinks it was Russians trying to steal the painting. If it was, be careful. I don't know what happened to them, but they can be unpredictable. You might want to hide the van away for a few days. Do the same with the Tahoe when Itchy brings it back. I'll let you know when this gets settled."

Standard watched Tony drive away, then walked back to the SUV to open the door for Mai Nazareth and help her out. By the time he got her and her luggage out of the car, Itchy had shown up with the cart. He loaded her baggage on it, then opened the back of the SUV. He gently pulled out the case holding the painting and put it on the cart with the luggage. The three of them maneuvered their way through the crowd of guests waiting to check in and around a corner toward a bank of elevators.

On the ride up, Itchy checked off each floor as if it were a countdown to a big payoff. Standard couldn't stop thinking about Russians, her warning, and what happened to the mysterious Mercedes. He tried to relax. No sense worrying about something that didn't happen. Whatever uneasiness he felt was tempered by the fact that he was just a few floors away from handing his wife and painting over to Simon Nazareth. After that, all he had to do was wait for Strasser to show up, collect his money, and put the whole thing behind him.

"Itchy," Standard said when the elevator doors opened on the top floor. "I've got this from here. Go back downstairs and take the car to Sticky Fingers. Tony will know what to do with it. I'll meet you there later. Have a few drinks on me, and anything else you need. You've earned it."

"What about the money?" Itchy said, rubbing his fingers together and whispering in a voice low enough that Mai Nazareth couldn't hear. Itchy looked disappointed and a little anxious. The money was his only reason to get involved in the first place. Leaving without it wouldn't sit well.

"Don't worry. I'll take care of it. Enjoy yourself until I get there."

When Itchy got back in the elevator, Standard pushed the luggage cart down the hall towards the double doors marked "Penthouse." Mai Nazareth stayed a few steps behind, but close enough to run into him when he stopped in the middle of the hall.

"Did you tell your husband we were here?" Standard asked.

"No," she said. "I called him when we left the airport to tell him we were on our way. I tried to reach him after what happened, but he didn't pick up. Why?"

Standard pointed up the hallway. "If he doesn't know we're here yet, then why's the door to his room open?"

"Probably just the maid," she said, squeezing by him, walking quickly up the hall, and pushing the door all the way open. Standard shrugged and followed, feeling more and more like a bellhop. She held the door while he steered the cart down a short hallway to the living room.

The first thing that hit Standard was the smell—a mixture of iron and chlorine—then the sound of bubbling water and finally the persistent humidity oozing in from the open patio doors. The second thing was Simon Nazareth. He was in the hot tub on the balcony, his back to the room, and facing the ocean with haystack-shaped rocks offshore.

CHAPTER 20

⁓

Standard's fear of knives was like a malevolent merit badge earned through blood and a near-death experience. Memories of the night in Mason Gage's basement, the fillet knife, the blood, the ambulance, and a long hospital stay lay coiled somewhere in the back of his head. He'd emerged from the hospital a month later with a scar from armpit to armpit and what his psychologist called aichmophobia, a fear of sharp objects. He'd dealt with it by downing pills, drinking anything that boasted 80-proof, and losing endless nights of sleep. None of it worked until he started avoiding knives altogether. Slowly, things came back into focus. Moderation trumped excess. He still made waiters take knives off his table.

He moved the ones in Emma's kitchen to a separate drawer. He avoided foods that needed to be cut up and stubbornly resisted Emma's taunting offers to do it for him.

Phobias are, after all, phobias.

Now, seeing the knife in Simon Nazareth's chest brought back a renewed level of the once-vanished darkness.

He'd seen his share of bodies. Some he knew. Others were

strangers. Some deserved to die. Others not so much. A couple were his fault. The rest their own. As luck would have it, only one involved a knife, which was one too many. Too bad his luck just ran out.

Nazareth's arms were draped along the side of the tub, his head slumped forward and to one side. Blood still seeped out of the wound. Foam the color of cotton candy filled the hot tub. The ice in the drink next to him was still cold.

"Jesus," he said, then remembered Mai Nazareth. He rushed back into the living room and grabbed her by the arm. "Come with me," he said, then steered her into the master bedroom and into a chair.

"What is it?" she said, looking both confused and scared. "What's wrong? Where's Simon?"

"Stay right here. Don't move. I'll be right back and explain everything. Okay?"

She nodded, then put her hand over her mouth. The look on her face said she knew something was wrong. He just needed time to tell her what it was.

His reactions were all instinct. It wasn't like he had made plans on what to do when finding a dead man in a hot tub. The two thoughts that came to mind were Mai Nazareth and the painting. Mai first. She had feelings. The painting second. It had value. Simon Nazareth was the fourth murder in two days. Standard was learning firsthand about art's dark side.

After closing the bedroom door, Standard went back to the living room, grabbed the case with the painting, then sprinted down the hall to the adjacent room Nazareth had reserved for him. The key card was in his wallet. He opened the door, went inside, and slipped the case behind a luggage stand in a closet with a mirror-covered sliding door. The painting was as safe as he could make it given the circumstances.

The "Do Not Disturb" sign was on the inside handle of the

door to the hallway. He took it off, hung it on the outside, and sprinted back to the penthouse. The door to the bedroom was still closed. Mai Nazareth had stayed put.

The hotel phone was on the wet bar. He dialed the front desk while pouring a shot of tequila. His hand shook. As much liquor went on the bar top as in the glass.

"I need security up here right away," Standard said when the receptionist answered. "And I mean right away."

Standard took a deep breath then went into the bedroom to tell Mai Nazareth her husband was dead, and that *Portrait of a Young Woman* was safe.

"Dead? How? Why?" Sorrow joined the fear and confusion on her face.

"All good questions, but first you need to listen to me," Standard said, kneeling in front of her as she sat on the edge of the chair. "Do you have any idea who would do this? Who would want your husband dead?"

For a few seconds, all she could do was open and close her mouth. Finally, she whispered the name "Drago."

That didn't make sense. He didn't know what happened to the men in the Mercedes, but there was no way they could have gotten to the hotel before them.

Whatever it was, now was not the time to deal with it.

"Security will be here soon. After that, it will be the police," Standard said. "Don't mention Drago and don't tell them about the painting. We'll both tell them the same thing: We got here from the airport and found him. Just say you were here on vacation. Plenty of time for the truth later. Have you got that?"

She nodded dumbly then broke into tears.

CHAPTER 21

For the time being, the truth about PORTRAIT OF A *Young Woman* and why the Nazareths were in Zihuatanejo was between him and Mai Nazareth. It needed to stay that way. There was plenty of time to tell the police the whole story, but not until he had time to figure out what was going on. Vega would look for the path of least resistance. Round up a few suspects. Comb the jails. Find someone who might have done it and, no matter how thin the evidence, charge them. Standard didn't see it that way. It wasn't that Mexico or Zihuatanejo didn't have murders, not by a long shot, but this was off the leash. He needed to find out on his own.

Then there was the painting. He was the only one in the world who knew where it was. That made him both a target and indispensable. If Strasser or anyone else wanted it, they would have to come through him.

The four hotel security guards who showed up looked unsure of what they were walking into. It didn't take them long to figure it out. One look at Simon Nazareth and half of them wanted to throw up while the other half wanted to put Standard in handcuffs. He explained that he had picked up Nazareth's wife at the airport and brought her to the hotel. They found him dead when they walked into the room. He stuck to that story for the next hour then repeated it when Comandante Alejandro Vega showed up.

"I should have known you would be involved sooner or later," Vega said, looking down at Nazareth's body still in the hot tub. "Maybe I should let those security guards lock you up while I figure out what the hell is going on."

"Wrong place, wrong time, Alejandro. Simple as that. He hired me to do a job and I did it."

"For money."

"Only if the widow comes through on her husband's promise. If not, all of this is on the house."

Vega gave Standard a suspicious look when a team of technicians showed up and started going over the room and dealing with Nazareth's body, now pale and wrinkled from too long in the hot tub. Two men in white scrubs showed up with a gurney and waited to take the body away. Vega and Standard had seen enough. They went outside to stand in the hallway.

"So, you and Señora Nazareth show up and find the door to the room open. You walk in, find the body, hustle her into the bedroom, and call security," Vega said. "That about it?"

"Pretty much."

"So, all Nazareth wanted was someone to pick up his wife at the airport, and he chose you."

"You sent him to me."

Vega glanced in the open door to the penthouse, watching the technicians scurrying around with their cotton swabs, fingerprint kits, and cameras. "That's four murders in two days. That's more than I've had in the last fifteen years if you don't count the drug dealers, addicts, and prostitutes shooting each other."

"You told me the other three were shot. Nazareth was stabbed. That makes this a little different."

"Dead is dead," Vega said. "What do you know about Nazareth and why they are here?"

Tricky questions, Standard thought. "They own some kind of gallery in some city on the East Coast. She told me they were here on vacation. Her husband came down early. She followed."

"Wouldn't be an art gallery by any chance?"

"Could be." Standard had gotten adept at playing innocent around Vega. "Why?"

"If it's art, then all four are connected."

Standard fought the urge to tell Vega about the painting and where it was, but decided this was not the time. For now, all he could do was hope that Mai Nazareth understood what he said and not tell Vega or anyone else the real reason they were in Mexico.

"We'll have to question the widow," Vega said.

"I know but give her some time. She's pretty shook up, as you can imagine. I was the one who told her about her husband. Delivering bad news face-to-face is not easy. It may not have come across as well as it should have."

"Okay, I'll leave that to the hotel security people. I've got other things to deal with and Ixtapa has its own way of doing business. Their first loyalty is to their own reputation. Their motto is don't scare the guests. The widow and victim are a distant second. The less they see of me or anyone else with a gun and a badge, the happier they'll be. If they find who did it, they'll call me, and we'll come and get whoever it is."

"Can I go now?" Standard asked.

Vega nodded, but with the warning that he would need to sign a statement and that they might need to talk again depending on what more he learned about Nazareth's death.

Standard wasn't in the mood for Sticky Fingers or explaining to Itchy why he wasn't getting his money, at least not yet. Riding in a taxi in the late afternoon traffic toward Zihuatanejo, through town, and on to the road to *Playa la Ropa*, he thought about what to tell Emma. There only one answer: Full disclosure.

Before that, he needed to know more about Drago Dragovich. Only one place to go for that. He dialed. "Can you meet me at Footloose?" He waited for an answer, said thanks, and hung up.

CHAPTER 22

Before leaving the two dead Russians behind, Heinz sent a text to Strasser.

"The playing field is now clear."

Back on the highway, he figured he was ten or fifteen minutes behind the SUV, the van, and the painting. He hit the gas and got the expected anemic response from the rental car. He was never going to catch them. That was okay. He knew where they were going.

He drove north, patiently navigating the heavy traffic and endless stoplights through Zihuatanejo. Twenty minutes later, he was parked across the street from the VistaPacifica with a clear view of the black SUV sitting in the driveway in front of the open-air lobby. He looked around for the white van, not seeing it, he guessed that it had already left.

He watched as the little guy with the straw hat and baggy shorts showed up with a luggage cart. He pulled the suitcases out of the back seat as the woman in the sunglasses stood on the lobby stairs watching. The younger man, the one in charge, opened the back gate of the SUV, and pulled out the canvas bag with what Heinz assumed was the painting. With everything loaded on the luggage cart, they headed toward what he figured were the elevators. Ten minutes later, the little man in the straw hat came out, got in the SUV, and drove away.

Heinz's best guess was that Simon Nazareth's wife, and the Raphael were now in one of the hotel's penthouse rooms. So far, things were going according to plan. Still, he decided to stick around to see if the guy in charge came out. That would mean the Nazareths were alone with the painting.

Heinz was still in his car a half hour later when the police cars and an ambulance showed up in front of the hotel. He traded in waiting in the car for sitting on a bench in front of the hotel and closer to the action. He ran through the options of what could be going on. The only good one was that the ambulance was there for some other reason that didn't involve Nazareth or the painting. All the other options were bad.

After an hour, the man he assumed was in charge came out, got in a taxi, and left. Two men pushing a sheet-draped gurney showed up an hour later. They loaded it into the ambulance and drove away. Things were not looking good. He forced himself to wait another hour, tolerating the annoying parade of buses, taxis, and sun-burned tourists in cargo shorts and sundresses, some with children in tow. Something was seriously wrong, and until he found out, everything else was going to be irritating.

The confidence he'd felt a few hours earlier was all but gone. Ambulances and police cars have a way of doing that. If his guess was right about what was happening, getting the painting just got more difficult. Telling Strasser was going to be even harder. The multi-billionaire didn't take well to bad news, and if the body on the gurney was who he thought it was, this could be as bad as it gets. He just had to be sure that the bad feelings he was getting were justified.

Finally, relatively sure that the hotel had returned to some semblance of normal, Heinz walked up the driveway and into the lobby. The long wait had given him time to come up with a sketchy plan to confirm what he already suspected. It was time to act. Strasser's yacht was somewhere north of Acapulco and due to arrive sometime after dark the next day. He would want answers. Heinz was determined to have them.

The young woman at the reception desk had dark hair, red lipstick, and a toothy grin. She wore a brown uniform with epaulets and a name tag that read: Bianca.

"Excuse me ... Bianca," Heinz said, trying to look and act as friendly as possible. "I have an appointment with one of your guests, but I'm afraid I've lost his room number. Could you call him and let him know I'm here?"

"Of course," she said in heavily accented English. "What is the guest's name?"

"Simon Nazareth."

She started typing on her computer, then stopped and looked around as if for help. "Excuse me a moment," she said, then disappeared into a door marked "Supervisor." A few minutes later a tall man in a starched white shirt and matching pants came out and walked around to the front of the desk.

"My name is Julio Hernandez," he said. "I'm the daytime supervisor."

"Gunther Schmidt. I'm here to see a friend of mine, Simon Nazareth. Is there a problem?"

"I'm afraid there is," Hernandez said. "Please come with me."

He led Heinz to a group of couches arranged in a quiet corner of the lobby. When they sat down across from each other, Hernandez leaned forward, elbows on his knees. "I'm afraid there's been a tragedy, Señor Schmidt. Your friend passed away earlier this afternoon, just a few hours ago in fact. I'm sorry to have to tell you this."

Heinz didn't have to fake a stunned look. While he knew something was wrong, this was more than he expected. He fell against the back of the couch. "But how? I talked to him just a few hours ago. He sounded fine."

"It is not my place to say. I think you should talk to the police. I can arrange to have you taken to the station."

"Police? What do they have to do with Simon's death?"

"That's a question best put to the authorities. *Lo siento.*"

"What about his wife, Mai? Is she okay?"

"Señora Nazareth remains a guest of the hotel. She has asked for privacy, but I would be happy to pass on any messages."

Heinz thought for a moment, then nodded. "Yes, if you wouldn't mind."

"Of course." Hernandez left and came back with a pad of hotel stationery, a matching envelope, and a pen.

Heinz thanked him, then wrote: "My condolences, but nothing has changed. The buyer will be here soon. Have the painting ready." He added his phone number, then folded the note, put it in the envelope, and handed it to Hernandez.

"Thank you. You've been very professional."

Heinz left the hotel, took up his spot on the bench out front, and waited. His phone rang an hour later.

"I don't have the painting," Mai Nazareth said.

Heinz let that sink in for a few seconds, then asked, "Who does?"

"I believe it is with one of the men who brought it from the airport. His name is John Standard."

CHAPTER 23

Adam Bovary Jones wasn't your typical DEA agent. He loved the Grateful Dead, quoted Shakespeare, and once gave Standard a government-issue Glock that he used to kill a drug cartel *sicario*. He also liked to drink beer at corner bars and gleefully trade gossip about who killed whom in Mexico's rampant and violent drug wars. At over six feet tall with a barrel chest and a cue-ball head, he was easy to spot in Mexico, harder if he was undercover in a biker gang. His "uniform" included aloha shirts, cargo shorts, and sandals. It probably wasn't what he wore to work, but there was no way to be sure.

The Footloose was a corner bar with six stools, two tables, and a bar menu that started and ended with roasted *cacahuetes*, peanuts in the shell. It specialized in margaritas and bottles of Pacifico that came in ice-filled buckets. At five in the afternoon, locals and a few tourists cruised by on their way home from work or looking for an early dinner. Taxis navigated the narrow streets. The sun sinking behind the mountains to the west helped cool off what had been a hot and humid day.

"You need to find a better place to hang out," Standard said, grabbing a seat next to Jones and ordering a beer. The only other customers were a sunburned couple wearing T-shirts and Minnesota Twins caps.

"I've tried, but I keep coming back here. I think it's the barmaid." He nodded toward a heavily made-up twenty-something with a pushup bra, hot pants, and fuck-me pumps. "And the beer's cheap. Government stipends being what they are. Besides, I consider her bra a miracle of engineering."

The two met the previous spring. Jones was looking for information about a beautiful accountant whose father was the leader of one of Mexico's largest drug cartels. She lived in a secluded compound on the west side of the bay. Standard obliged and between the two of them, the accountant ended up dead, temporarily throwing a wrench into her father's operations. That adventure earned Standard sixty thousand dollars in purloined drug money, some of which went into helping Fat Tony remodel Sticky Fingers. He did return the Glock.

"How goes the drug wars?" Standard said.

"The same. Cocaine and heroin always in demand. Marijuana not so much anymore. Fentanyl a growing scourge. I don't get it. Selling a drug that kills the user. It's like Ford killing everybody who drives. But it must make money, or the cartels wouldn't be doing it."

"I need a favor," Standard said.

"Talk slow. Remember, I'm an employee of the federal government."

Standard ran through everything that happened, starting with meeting Simon Nazareth, a short rundown on Carlos Strasser, and ending with the art dealer's death.

"Can't say I've heard anything quite like that," Jones said, shaking his head. "You're a piece of work. You know that, right?"

"So, I've heard."

"What's the favor?"

"I keep running across the name Drago Dragovich. Simon Nazareth mentioned him, and so did his wife. She thinks this Dragovich killed her husband. She also thinks it was his men who chased us from the airport. He's Russian. Probably an oligarch of some kind."

"Dragovich is after the painting, so he kills the person who has it without knowing where it is," Jones said, shaking his head. "That's stupid even by Russian standards. It doesn't add up. What am I missing?"

"There's a lot about this that doesn't add up. This Dragovich. Ever heard of him?"

Jones laughed and threw up his hands. "Jesus Christ, Standard. First, this Strasser sounds like some ex-Nazis, and now you want to know about Russians. What is it with you? You're lucky that drug lord didn't kill you over what happened to his daughter and now this."

"So, you've heard of him?"

"Yeah, and when it comes to Dragovich, DEA stands for Don't Even Ask."

"That bad, huh?"

"Worse."

Standard sipped his beer while Jones gave him chapter and verse about Dragovich. "He started out as a mid-level apparatchik in the Finance Ministry of the old Soviet Union facing life buried in a nameless, faceless, soulless Russian bureaucracy. Then the USSR broke up. Dragovich, being a finance guy, saw his chance and snapped up several oil and gas leases in eastern Russia along with a couple of refineries and a pipeline. Became a millionaire overnight. Tens of millions became hundreds of millions and soon he started to branch out and, like all Russian oligarchs, not into philanthropy. The only thing he liked more than being rich was getting richer. Charity was not the way to go. Arms dealing, drug dealing, and sex trafficking were more appealing and profitable. So was laundering money for his gangster buddies. It was the drug dealing that got us interested in him. Opium from Afghanistan mostly, but we haven't ruled out fentanyl from China and Mexico. The more we found out the more his name was linked to rivals who either decided to take their business elsewhere or ended up dead. Then Russia invaded Ukraine. Being a Putin guy, Dragovich got hit with sanctions."

Jones ordered two more bottles of beer, calling the barmaid "Honey," and giving her a generous tip.

"A few years ago, he spent thirty million dollars for a house in the ritzy Moscow suburb of Rublyovka and another five million on furnishings and some remodeling. It was intended to be a palace for him, his wife, and their kids, but thanks to Putin's war and sanctions by the west it seems to have turned into more of a prison. Now he's having cash flow problems. His yacht has been impounded. His flat in the French Quarter of Paris and a house on Grosvenor Square in London have been seized. The mistresses who lived in them are out on the street. He has another house in Davos, but with no mistress in residence he has little reason to go there. Embargoes and price caps are cutting into his gas and oil revenue. The war in Ukraine is sucking up every available weapons system, which seems to have an adverse impact on his arms sales, but don't ask me how that works. He still makes money selling drugs. The sex trafficking was always more about fun than profit. We've heard stories that are right out of Caligula."

"In other words, tough times," Standard said.

"Don't sell him short. His transition from pasty-faced bureaucrat to brutal oligarch was nothing short of miraculous. He's become wily, ruthless, and probably feeling a little cornered and desperate. We've been chasing him for years, along with every other civilized country. He's been hard to track down. Harder still now that travel is difficult with all the sanctions." Jones gave Standard a sideways glance. "You're not suggesting that Dragovich is going to show up here."

"The painting is here. The buyer is here. So is the seller. Whatever his reasons for wanting that painting, Dragovich needs to be here as well."

"Anything to do with Dragovich you need to tell me. If he shows up, I'm going to need reinforcements. This guy doesn't dance, and he doesn't work alone."

"Any chance you can tell me where he is now?"

"I could if I knew. Like I said, he's hard to track down. If I were him, I'd hole up in my dacha in Russia and wait for the war to end and the sanctions lifted so he could get back to getting richer than he already is." Jones drained the last of his beer. "I have some contacts at the CIA. Let me check with them. See if they know where he is. Shouldn't be a problem. Thanks to the war, Russia is full of wanna-be spies willing to do anything to fuck Putin and his cronies if it gets them out of the country."

Jones threw some money on the bar then blew a kiss to the barmaid. "So, what does your girlfriend think of all this?" he asked. "As I remember she wasn't too happy the last time you ran into trouble."

"Not much, and probably even less when I tell her what happened today."

CHAPTER 24

EMMA PARRISH LEANED AGAINST THE KITCHEN COUNTER, arms across her chest, and glared at Standard.

"Only you could drive from the airport to a hotel in Ixtapa, see some guy pop out of the top of a car with a rifle, and end up with another dead body." If she made any effort to keep the irony out of her voice, it wasn't working. "You told me once that you were a magnet for trouble. I keep trying not to believe it, despite everything that's happened. I wrote it off to a series of coincidences, a run of bad luck. Now, I believe it. I'm all in. I've tried to think of some character in fiction to compare you to. All I can come up with is that guy trapped on a lifeboat with a live tiger."

Standard sat at the kitchen table, knowing that the more he tried to explain, the faster he would lose the argument. He had promised Emma no more trouble. She had every right to be angry.

"So, what now, John? The guy who owes you and Itchy forty thousand dollars is dead, you've stashed away a long-lost piece of art, and the dead guy's wife thinks he was killed by a

Russian gangster. You know, John, it's impossible to make this stuff up."

"If it's any consolation, the piece of art is a masterpiece worth hundreds of millions of dollars."

"Care to tell me where it is?"

"It's better you don't know."

"And this Argentinian mega-billionaire, this Howard Hughes of hamburger or whatever he is, who wants to buy it is supposed to show up in his yacht, sail into the bay, drop anchor, pick up this masterpiece, and leave. Is that what you just told me?"

"Yes."

"Let me guess. You're not going to tell anyone where the painting is until you find out who killed this Nazareth guy. You're going to do what you always do: put yourself out there to find the truth and right the wrong. If that's not true, then you're not the John Standard I know and love."

"It's what I do best," he said. "And don't forget the three dead guys from the Louvre, Prado, and The Vatican. They could be all connected."

"And the painting?"

"Collateral. The painting for the truth."

"Does this Strasser have the truth?"

"Only one way to find out."

Emma came over to the table, pulled a chair around to sit in front of him, and put her hands on his knees. "After two years I know that nothing I can say or do is going to stop you from doing what you think is best, no matter how much I disagree. You've been lucky in the past, but this feels different. We're not talking about brain-dead narcos, thieving accountants, high-end pimps, or crazed, bi-polar assassins. We're talking about a painting with a price tag that would make a drug lord blush. Just imagine what kind of people something like that brings out of the woodwork. The world may have changed, but three hundred million dollars or more is still a lot of money. Now, tell me. Who knows you have the painting?"

"No one, really. Mai Nazareth could probably figure it out. If she did, there's no one to tell ... except."

"Strasser," Emma said, shaking her head. "That's just great, John. Russians with rifles and the son of a Nazi. Any other deviant criminals out there with a few hundred million dollars to spend on an obscure painting? The Mafia maybe? How about the Yakuza? Maybe some drug cartels are interested, but lucky for you they like hippos and submarines more than art. You put a target on your back and mine as well, I suppose. It wouldn't be the first time."

Her voice was louder, her face redder. He'd seen her steamed a few times before, but nothing like this. It was part anger, part fear. She dodged a few bullets, but always feared that her luck would run out. He needed to find a way to calm her down.

"I know what I'm doing. This is different than those other times because I've told you all of it. No surprises. You know everything I know except where the painting is. Maybe you could help me figure this out."

"How about give the painting back and be done with the whole thing? Is that an option?"

"No. At least not yet."

"I didn't think so. Hanging on to the one thing that probably got four people killed, and you want to keep it. Incredible."

"I know that. You got any other suggestions?"

She thought for a few seconds while going to the kitchen counter to pour herself a shot of tequila. She downed it and poured another.

"Just one," she said. "Don Pedro Serrano."

CHAPTER 25

PLAYA LAS GATAS IS TWO HUNDRED YARDS OF WHITE SAND beach in the southwest corner of Zihuatanejo Bay. Standard and Emma would go there on days when they just wanted to get away from town without taking a long, hot road trip. They'd find a table with chairs and lounges at one of the beachfront palapa restaurants that catered to locals on their days off and tourists looking for something out of the ordinary. A reef built offshore centuries ago by some long-lost culture created a protective cove that kept the water warm and the waves little more than ripples.

They'd dine on shrimp, fish, beer, and tequila while enjoying the sun and watching little kids play in the shallow water. A few of the restaurants also rented beach toys or sold swimwear, flip-flops, and T-shirts. Waiters dressed in white and carrying menus offered passersby "the best food on the beach," and free shots of tequila with every meal order. Wind off the bay sent smoke from wood grills behind the restaurants into the hills to the south.

Standard climbed out of the boat that brought him across

the bay from the City Pier, negotiated a rickety dock, and then down onto the beach. While it was not yet ten in the morning, the over-eager waiters were out in full force. He waved them off with a smile and polite "*más tardes.*" He stuck to the hard sand along the shoreline as he walked west.

At the end of the beach, he took a hard right through a stand of palm trees toward the mouth of the bay. Coconuts lay on the ground like severed heads. Dried palm fronds covering the dry sand felt and sounded like a crunchy carpet.

Going to see Don Pedro Serrano made sense once Emma explained who he was, where he lived, and how he might help. She reminded him that he'd met Serrano at a party the previous spring. Standard remembered a small, shy man who looked to be in his fifties with a wiry build, leathery skin, thin hair, and graying goatee. He seemed to spend most of his time in a corner sipping a margarita and chatting amiably with anyone who approached him. Standard didn't remember seeing him leave, only that he was gone, apparently slipping out the door without anyone noticing.

He was surprised when Emma described him as one of Mexico's most successful artists. Not as well-known as Frida Kahlo or Diego Rivera, but his paintings of local scenes still sold for low six figures, mostly from his galleries in Taos and Beverly Hills. She believed that if anyone in Zihuatanejo would know what to do with *Portrait of a Young Woman,* it would be Serrano. She was confident that he knew art and the art world, two things that Standard was only beginning to appreciate, and not in a good way. He just hoped she was right.

Sharing things about the painting came with certain risks for himself and anyone else who knew what and where it was. Then again, who better to tell than an artist.

On the other side of the stand of palm trees sat two plat-forms thirty feet by thirty feet raised a foot off the ground.

They had wooden railings with slim tree trunks holding up thatched roofs, creating open-air houses much like the one where Standard and Emma lived. One house was furnished with chairs, couches, and tables. Toward the back he saw a kitchen and bedroom behind a bamboo screen. The other looked to be a studio with easels, crude wooden benches and shelves, and a floor covered in paint drippings. He looked in both the houses before seeing Serrano sitting in an Adirondack chair with a pencil and a sketchbook.

He was dressed in a white T-shirt, white pants, and paint-splattered sandals. His thin black hair stuck out from under a battered straw hat. His goatee was closely trimmed and seemed grayer than what Standard remembered. His forehead a jumble of wrinkles as he stared at the bay, deep in thought. His fingers long, thin, and permanently stained by paint and pencil. On his pad was the beginning of a sketch depicting Zihuatanejo as seen from across the bay.

"Excuse me, Señor Serrano," Standard said. Serrano looked up, a little startled, then put his sketchbook on the ground and stood up. "My name is John Standard. We met last spring at a party. I'm a friend of Emma Parrish."

Serrano looked confused for a moment then brightened. "Of course. Of course. I try to forget parties as soon as I leave them, so forgive me. The best artists are the loneliest. Not that it matters." They shook hands. "Any friend of Señora Parrish is always welcome. Please, join me." He motioned to a second Adirondack chair. "Can I get you something to drink? I have fresh orange juice or a cold beer if you'd like."

"A beer would be great," Standard said.

As if on cue, a young boy, barefoot and wearing only a pair of white shorts, appeared on the steps leading to the house with the kitchen.

"*Dos cervezas, Esteban,*" Serrano said, then turned to Standard. "Sit down. I don't get many visitors, certainly none with your ... *reputación.*"

"Reputation?"

"You're exploits during your short time in Zihuatanejo are well known and spoken of with great awe. I have heard of them all. Both good and bad. I think the truth lies somewhere in the middle. Still, they are impressive feats." They sat down. Serrano crossed his legs, letting one sandal dangle from his foot. "None, however, as great as winning the hand of the stunning Emma Parrish. She is the most beautiful woman in the State of Guerrero and maybe all of Mexico. Trust me. I have met most of them and none compare to her. Over the years, she and I have shared many dinners together and talked long into the evening. She is as smart as she is lovely. You are a very lucky man."

Standard was searching for a way to answer when Esteban showed up with two bottles of Corona topped with lime wedges. "To Emma Parrish," Standard said. They clinked bottles. "Beautiful place you have."

The triangular-shaped piece of property sat on the south side of the entrance to the bay. A half mile away to the right was the white sand beach and hotels of *Playa la Ropa.* Directly across the water was the City of Zihuatanejo just coming to life for another day of catering to tourists and locals. Small white pangas ran back and forth between the City Pier and *Playa las Gatas.* More pangas carrying tourists on deep-sea fishing trips were either heading out to sea or on the way back.

"I have lived here for twenty years. Ten of those I have spent arguing with the government over who owns this land. I have offered many times to buy it, but each time they refused. So, the matter stays unresolved. Occasionally, out of spite I suppose, the government turns off my electricity. Then I must go into town to see Comandante Vega. He has two of my paintings. Not my best, but good enough to get the power turned on again."

They shared a smile at the expense of Vega and his dogged determination to accumulate as much wealth as he could with as little effort as possible.

"I know Comandante Vega well," Standard said. "He tolerates my getting involved in things that seem to make his life harder. I regret it, but some things can't be helped. Occasionally he keeps me out of trouble and in the good graces of the local bad guys."

Serrano gave him a sly smile. "I'm sure you're right." He squeezed the lime into his beer. "So, Señor Standard, should I assume that you are here for a reason?"

"Call me John, please, and yes, I am. I need your advice."

"That I have plenty of."

"What if I told you that I have a priceless painting by one of the great masters sitting in the closet of a hotel room in Ixtapa?"

"Are you talking about Raphael's *Portrait of a Young Woman*?"

"What makes you think that?" Standard tried not to look surprised.

"In the art world, rumor and gossip are the appetizers. Money is the main course." Serrano poked the lime wedge down into the bottle, then took a sip. "I think you had better start from the beginning."

CHAPTER 26

Don Pedro Serrano nursed his beer and stayed silent as Standard walked him through the entire story from meeting Simon Nazareth to finding him stabbed to death. For good measure, he added the murders of the men from the Louvre, Prado, and The Vatican. Serrano's ears perked up when he mentioned Carlos Strasser and Drago Dragovich.

When he was done, Serrano stood up, went into the house, and came back with a bottle of Don Julio Añejo tequila and two glasses. "You forgot to mention the two dead Russians found in a coconut plantation south of the city."

That was the first Standard had heard of what happened. He wasn't surprised to learn the men were dead, he just didn't expect to hear it from a reclusive artist. "You're pretty plugged in for a guy who lives like a hermit in paradise."

Serrano laughed. "I've lived here a long time, John. I have many friends. Some know things. Some don't. I listen anyway."

"I take it you know Strasser."

"Personally? No. I have never met him, but he is well

known in the small world of people rich enough to own master-pieces such as the one you have."

Serrano poured two healthy shots. "From what I hear, he is not a man to be trusted. Ruthless, obsessed, and single-minded when it comes to getting what he wants."

"And Dragovich?"

"Never heard of him, but if he is a Russian oligarch well known to the DEA, then I would be very careful."

"What about Nazareth?"

Serrano thought for a moment. "I have heard the name but know very little about him or his galleries. The New York City art scene is a nest of vipers I prefer to avoid. If they want my paintings, check my website, or visit one of my galleries."

"Strasser? Do you think he is obsessive enough to pay hundreds of millions of dollars for a painting that most people thought was lost forever or is something else going on here?"

"Perhaps," Serrano said.

"Meaning?"

"How much do you know about art forgery?"

"You think ...?"

"I am always suspicious on those rare occasions when a painting from one of the great masters comes on the market. And with good reason. I have seen reports that two hundred billion dollars a year is spent on art. Six billion of that involves forgery or other illegal activity. That is a lot of money, but it's complicated and not always what it appears. It is not unusual for some billionaires to spend ten million dollars for a painting, then spend five thousand on a forgery to hang in his house while the original is placed somewhere safe. Then there's the guy who buys a fake Renoir, then tells his friends it's authentic while the real one hangs in the Louvre. Then, of course, there are those who are simply duped into buying a forgery thinking it's an original. There was a forger living in Switzerland who would use the same materials and techniques as a great artist to create works he would sell as never-before-seen originals. He made millions."

"Sounds sort of harmless."

"To some extent it is. Foolish people spending millions on things they know little about. Buyer beware, and all that. On the other hand, art forgery is fraud. That's why it's a crime, especially if the seller knows the painting is fake. Even the FBI has an art crime team. The definition of fraud is finding a weakness in a system then exploiting it. The exploitation in this case involves uneducated buyers with too much money."

"Who does these forgeries?"

"Talented artists who should know better. Art students looking to pay tuition. To be honest with you, John, I dabbled in it a bit myself as a way of paying for art school in Paris."

"Is this a new thing?"

"Hardly, art forgery has been going on for centuries. The list of scandals is endless. Never, however, on the scale it is today."

"Nazareth mentioned the *Salvator Mundi*."

"Possibly. Its provenance is a bit murky," Serrano said. "Not as egregious, however, as most forgeries. There are more artists now producing fakes. At the same time, there is better technology capable of identifying them, but it can't outpace the increase in the number of naïve millionaires and billionaires who know about business but not art. Many of them are young. They only see art as a short-term investment. That kind of ignorance is ripe for the forger. Sadly, it is art as collateral, as a commodity. It exists as an asset rather than something to be enjoyed and appreciated. If you are a purist like me, it is all very sad."

"Nazareth told me the painting had been restored and inspected by experts. He had what he called a provenance."

"Provenance proves that the painting is authentic. It can be forged the same as the painting itself. That's what makes it more complicated."

"So, it's possible that Strasser is about to pay hundreds of millions for a fake Raphael. Unless of course it's real. Can you tell the difference?"

Serrano poured each of them another shot of tequila. "Without a doubt."

"Sounds to me like *Portrait of a Young Woman* is better off with you than in a hotel room."

"I agree. We should bring it here, but we're going to need some help. I know just the person."

They looked at each other, nodded in unison, and shared a long laugh.

CHAPTER 27

Special Ed picked up the phone only after debating whether to answer it at all. It was time for a nap, and since he already had a charter for the next day, there was no one he wanted to talk to. Then again, maybe it was someone wanting to book a trip for another day. He sighed and ran his hand through his hair. If he wasn't careful, his deep-sea charter fishing service might turn into a real business.

"Ed? It's Standard."

"Yeah. Glad you called. I need a deck hand for tomorrow."

"I need your help."

"Music to my ears."

Calls for help from John Standard always gave Ed equal amounts of joy and unease. In the two years of their friendship, they had skated well past what is borderline illegal, even in Mexico, onto the thin ice of outright criminal activity. As a multi-millionaire who bailed out of the dot.com boom before it crashed, paid his taxes, and moved to Mexico, Ed felt he had enough money to buy his way out of any jam. He just didn't want to find out.

At the time he sold his high-tech business, he put his net worth as somewhere in the low nine figures. It was probably still in the same neighborhood, not that he paid much attention anymore. He had a will that left a couple of million to each of his two ex-wives and the rest to the World Wildlife Fund and public broadcasting. He amended his will a few months earlier, leaving Standard his charter boat. He just hadn't told Standard. He wanted it to be a surprise.

The charter boat was the *Tuna Warrior* he bought five years earlier, more for fun than profit. It was forty feet long and tricked out with all the high-tech equipment that made him rich in the first place. His charter prices were twice what the local panga captains charged, but he only got half as many customers. Being a businessman, that made sense to Ed: Same money for half the work. More time to kick back and enjoy his success.

Standard had crewed on several of Ed's charters. Once he cured him of his seasickness, Ed felt that Standard did it more for the experience than the meager wages he paid, which usually came in the form of sailfish or Dorado fillets.

"Can you meet me at the City Pier in an hour?" Standard asked.

"What kind of trouble are you in now?"

"I'll explain when I see you, but it involves something irreplaceable."

"You mean Emma?"

Standard laughed. "No, nothing like that. I'll have a friend of yours with me. Don Pedro Serrano. He tells me you do some work for him."

"I help him get some of his paintings from his house and out to the airport. It's more a labor of love. He doesn't pay squat, so I don't ask, but he's an easy guy to like."

"One more thing. We're going to need your car."

Ed was waiting on the City Pier when Standard and Serrano got off the panga from *Playa las Gatas*. He'd left the *Tuna Warrior* tied up at the dock below the pier ready for the next day's charter.

"So, what's this thing that's so irreplaceable?" Ed asked as they walked up the pier toward the bayfront.

"It's a painting," Standard said, then gave him a quick explanation.

"Sounds boring compared to what you've gotten me into in the past."

"We're not done yet."

Ed's 1995 Pontiac Bonneville was parked in a gravel lot a block from the pier. The car looked too big to fit through the city's narrow streets and too rusted to hold together on the cobblestones. It had a tattered rag top, a dented hood, and bald tires.

"You'd think someone as rich as you would have a better ride," Standard said, getting in the back and letting Serrano ride shotgun.

"Why bother. Anything better and someone would just steal it or strip it. Besides, I only drive it from my condo to the marina and back. If it goes missing, no great loss."

The car coughed and sputtered when Ed started it up. It dropped into gear with an ominous thud. They bounced and rattled through the cobblestoned city streets out to Ruta 200 then north toward Ixtapa. Twenty minutes later they pulled into the driveway in front of the VistaPacifica. It was dusk, darkness still a half hour away.

CHAPTER 28

STANDARD WAS IN NO HURRY TO GO INSIDE. HE WANTED TO bring the painting out as discreetly as possible. A little less daylight might help.

"I don't think you want to come out through the lobby," Serrano said, looking out at the people milling around the reception desk. "The loading dock is around the corner on the right. We can figure out a way to get there. Come out that way. We'll be waiting."

Standard agreed but insisted on staying in the car for another few minutes until it was darker. "Okay," he said, finally. "Let's do this."

Hoping to avoid being recognized by either the staff or what passed for hotel security, he put on a battered baseball cap he found on the back seat. He got out of the car and walked toward the open-air lobby, pulling the cap down, and giving the reception desk a wide berth. He ducked around a corner to the bank of elevators, stepped in the first door that opened, and pressed the button marked "Penthouse." He took it as a good omen that the elevator turned out to be an express, rather than a local that stopped at each floor. When he stepped out, he saw the police tape in front of the double doors leading to what had been Simon Nazareth's room. He took the absence of guards as another good sign that he might pull this off without being seen.

Halfway down the hallway on the left was the room where he'd stashed the painting. The "Do Not Disturb" sign was still on the door handle. Another good sign. He used the card key and stepped inside. As far as he could tell, the room had been untouched. In the bedroom, he slid back the door on the closet. The painting was where he left it.

He wondered what the hotel had done with Mai Nazareth. He assumed they were putting her up somewhere, probably in the penthouse at the other end of the hall. That would seem like the right thing to do. Since the VistaPacifica catered to package trips that included air and hotel, the penthouses probably didn't get a lot of use. Not wanting to run into her or anyone else, he carefully opened the door wide enough to look outside. The hallway was still empty. He grabbed the painting and headed back to the elevators.

Instead of going down to the lobby, Standard stopped the elevator at the third floor. He got off, looked around, and spotted a door marked "Stairs." He went down a flight of metal steps, nodding to a group of confused-looking housekeepers on their way up carrying towels and sheets. They were dressed in black with white aprons and sensible shoes.

He wondered what the maids would think if they knew he was carrying a piece of art worth more than the hotel they worked in.

The door at the bottom of the stairs opened onto a storage area with a cement floor. Shelves filled with canned goods and cleaning supplies lined the far wall. The handful of hotel workers at the other end either didn't see him or didn't care as he walked out one of the two huge metal garage doors and onto a long, wide loading dock. Outside, Standard spotted Serrano still in the front seat of the Pontiac and Ed behind the wheel. Just as he was heading for the car, a security guard came out of the storage area.

"*Alto ahí,*" he yelled.

Standard froze. He was twenty feet away from the car. No way he could reach it and get away. As the guard got closer, he reached for his gun. Standard started thinking this could get ugly, when Serrano got out of the car and walked up the short set of stairs to the dock.

"*Fácil, amigo,*" Serrano said to the guard, then introduced himself.

The guard looked confused, glanced back and forth between Standard and Serrano, then put his gun away. The two men talked in Spanish for several minutes, while Standard stood still, waiting. Finally, the guard nodded and shook Serrano's hand. He left after giving Standard a look of disgust.

"I told him you are returning one of my paintings because you didn't like it," Serrano said. "He knows my work. He thinks you are *estúpido.*"

"He's probably right."

Standard put the briefcase with the painting in the back seat, then got in next to it. Twenty minutes later they were back at the City Pier. Special Ed fired up the *Tuna Warrior,* opened a beer, and lit a joint.

"Compared to our other adventures, that was pretty tame," Ed said, letting the boat idle for a few minutes while he blew smoke into the night air.

"I'll try to do better next time," Standard said.

"So, there is a next time?"

"Isn't there always?"

They crossed the bay in the dark. When they reached *Playa las Gatas*, Ed feathered the boat's powerful engines, cranked the wheel to the right, and eased up against the rickety dock.

"As far as I go, boys," Ed shouted down from the bridge. "I'd love to join you and find out what the hell this is all about, but I got business in the morning. But don't worry, I'll catch up with you. If you need me, you know the drill."

After Ed and the *Tuna Warrior* were headed back across the bay, Standard and Serrano carried the briefcase up the beach and set it on an easel in the artist's studio.

"As curious as I am, I think I'll wait until morning to take a look at it," Serrano said.

They were back in the Adirondack chairs doing more damage to the Don Julio and staring at the lights of the city. The night was warm with just a slight breeze coming off the ocean. The scent of wood smoke mixed with the salt air and odor of fried fish. Inside, Esteban was cooking what smelled like chili rellenos. Neither one said anything for a while. The painting was safe and in the hands of someone Standard trusted. The only thing left to do was wait.

He didn't have to wait long.

Standard was about to leave and catch the last panga back to the city when a huge yacht seemed to appear out of nowhere and enter the bay. It cruised by so close that Standard felt as if he could reach out and touch it. The black boat was dark except for running lights and the dim glow of computer screens on the bridge. Spotlights pointed down at the foredeck where a helicopter looked like a spider caught in its own web. A hundred yards into the bay, the yacht dropped anchor, pivoted until the bow was pointed back out to sea, and dropped a stern anchor.

"It looks like your buyer has arrived," Serrano said.

Standard nodded. "Now I know why Nazareth chose the VistaPacifica. It's the only hotel in Ixtapa with a heliport on the roof."

CHAPTER 29

Standard said goodbye to Serrano, then joined two waiters from one of the palapa restaurants as the only passengers on the last panga back to the city. The boat needed to take a wide arc around the yacht sitting in the middle of the bay. As they passed the stern, Standard saw the brass plate:

El Obra Maestro
Rio de Janeiro

The Masterpiece seemed like an appropriate name for why the yacht was there and for the vessel itself. Sleek, black, even a little mysterious given that there were no signs of life. He assumed Strasser was onboard, anticipating getting the Raphael and quickly leaving. If that was the plan, he was in for a big surprise.

When the panga reached the dock below the City Pier, Standard jumped off, climbed the stairs to the top, and called Adam Jones.

"That Mercedes I told you about," Standard said. "There were two Russians in it. They're both dead."

"I know, and that's not the worst of it. We think one of the dead guys is Dragovich's brother. The other is his nephew. That's not going to sit well with him."

"Meaning what?"

"You tell me. If I have this right, those Russians were shot while they were chasing you and the painting that you said Dragovitch wanted."

"They were shot! I didn't shoot anybody."

"I didn't say you did, but somebody shot them. Whoever it was, it's not what's important right now. I checked with my guy at the CIA. It seems Dragovitch is missing. No one knows where he is. They had eyes on his dacha then realized he'd slipped out somehow. He's not in his apartment in Moscow or any of his four other homes. He keeps his private jet at Sheremetyevo airport. It's not there. Looks like he's on the loose. All I can tell you is to be careful and, like I said, let me know if he shows up. I'll need help if he does."

"Thanks a lot, I guess," Standard said. "For what it's worth, I think that yacht that just anchored in the bay belongs to Strasser. He's here for the painting."

"You going to give it to him?"

Standard had been asking himself that same question. "I'm not sure yet."

"Think about this," Jones said. "Maybe the painting is a way to lure Dragovitch to Mexico. We might be able to bust him."

"Good for you. Bad for me. Let's see what happens."

Standard hung up and called Itchy Donlan. By now Itchy would have heard about Simon Nazareth and probably freaked out that he was never going to see the twenty-thousand dollars he'd been promised. Best talk him off the ledge and keep him from doing something stupid. Although it had happened before.

"Meet me at Mango's," Standard said when Itchy answered.

"I'm already here." Itchy hung up.

It took less than ten minutes to walk from the City Pier to Mango's. Standard knew from Itchy's voice that the little man was not happy. Standard had a solution, but it would require Itchy to be patient, not something he could afford to do given his money situation.

Standard spotted Itchy on the other side of the bar. What he wasn't expecting was that Marie would be with him. Although "with" was a relative word.

She had the glazed and confused look of someone who didn't know where they were but still amazed by being there.

"What's with Marie?" Standard asked after sitting down next to Itchy.

"Not sure." Itchy looked over his shoulder at her. "Someone died back in New York. Could be a friend or her cat. Could be both. Whatever it was she seems determined to toast the deceased as often as possible."

"Itchy, listen. About the twenty thousand. We're still in the game, but it's going to take a little more time."

"How are we still in the game? The man with the money is dead."

"But his wife isn't. She has the check book now. I'm just not sure that she knows what her husband agreed to pay us. I need to talk to her, but now is not a good time. Try to understand. The good news is that we have a bargaining chip."

Itchy's eyes got large. He looked around, leaned closer to Standard, and went into full conspiratorial mode. "You have that Ralphy thing. John, it's worth millions!"

"Hundreds of millions, actually."

"Well, fuck the twenty thousand. We're talking real money here. What are you going to do?"

Standard was back to asking himself questions. The painting wasn't his. It still belonged to the couple who found it in France. Mai and Simon Nazareth were a team, which meant she was still their agent. If Strasser wanted the painting, he had to go through her. Their dilemma made him smile. Only two people knew where the painting was. One more than he wanted but that didn't change his plans to hang on to it until he knew more about the six murders.

"I'm going to be patient and see what happens. I suggest you do the same thing. I can give you a little boost to get by for a while. Do you need it?"

Itchy shook his head. "No thanks. I've got Marie to keep me going. If that changes, I'll let you know. Thanks for the offer, though."

Standard was in the back seat of a taxi on his way home when his phone rang. It was a call he'd been expecting. When he answered, he was quick to pull the phone away from his ear.

"Where's my painting?" Mai Nazareth wasn't quite screaming, but close. "Strasser just called me. He's here. He told me his boat is in the bay and that he's going to be here tomorrow morning at ten. I need that painting."

"I'm sorry, but Strasser needs to wait. I have questions. Six people are dead, including your husband."

"Six?"

Standard told her about the dead representatives from the museums and the two Russians in the coconut plantation. "I think Strasser may have some answers. When I get them, I'll consider returning the painting. Until then, the ball is in Strasser's court."

"You can't do that. That painting isn't yours."

"I know that, but it's not yours either, and it's not Strasser's.

Tell him we need to talk. He can reach me at this number. By the way, your husband promised my friend and me twenty thousand each for delivering the painting. You're on the hook for that. Pay up when this is over."

"And when is that?"

"When I say it is."

"If that's your idea of a plan, I'd be careful. I have no idea what Strasser will do when he learns your name and that I believe you have the painting." She hung up.

Standard leaned back in the seat, stared out the window at a line of palm trees, and wondered if he was about to have a little fun with the mega-rich or get into the kind of trouble that always found him. He hoped for the former but feared the latter.

CHAPTER 30

While Emma got up early, Standard stayed in bed, listening to her get dressed, then rummage through the refrigerator and her closet. He knew her well enough to sense that something was up. He pulled on a pair of shorts and a T-shirt, then went into the kitchen. It didn't take him long to find out what she was up to.

Emma never did anything without a reason.

"We're going to Troncones. I'm packing some stuff to take with us. You need to do the same. We might spend the night." She walked away, then turned around. "And we're taking *El Furioso*."

Standard had little choice but to agree. He'd already promised her a trip to Troncones to check the place out as a future home. He left it to her to decide when. That she was already eager to go told him all he needed to know about how serious she was about moving.

He asked her for an hour to go to The Tortuga for breakfast. She agreed but insisted that they leave right after he got back.

Standard walked down the hill to the beach that was just beginning to fill up with tourists, most of them couples walking on the hard sand above the waterline.

He ordered coffee, toast, and scrambled eggs. *El Obra Maestro* sat a hundred yards off the beach, its bow still pointed out to sea as if eager to escape Zihuatanejo's meager and mundane surroundings. A limo at a bowling alley.

Standard figured Strasser's plan would be pretty simple: Take the helicopter to the VistaPacifica, land on the roof, go down to the penthouse, pay for the painting, and leave. The plan would get him and his yacht underway before noon. Too bad it wasn't going to work out that way.

Standard looked at his watch. It was a few minutes before ten. As if on cue, *El Obra Maestro's* helicopter lifted off the bow, hovered for a second, then did a ninety-degree pivot and headed north toward Ixtapa. He watched as it cleared the cell phone and radio towers on top of the hill and disappeared.

It wasn't hard to imagine how the conversation would go once Strasser reached the hotel. It would start with Mai Nazareth telling him what happened to her husband and who she thought killed him. When he asked where the painting was, she would say she didn't know but she knew who did. After that, she would give him Standard's name and phone number. That's when things would start getting interesting.

Standard finished his breakfast and went home to pack for Troncones. On the way, he called Arturo for a ride to Ixtapa where Emma kept *El Furioso*. He knew it was at one of the rentals she managed, but she would never tell him or anyone else exactly where.

Turned out it was in a well-maintained condo complex of about twenty units near the marina and overlooking a golf course. After Arturo dropped them off, Emma used a remote to open the garage, then went inside and pulled the cover off the

Fury. Standard never got tired of looking at it. Eye-popping red. Fins. Hardtop. White leather interior. Four hundred-plus horsepower V-8. Since he wasn't allowed to drive it a second time, he didn't complain when Emma announced, "I'm driving," and got behind the wheel. She fired it up and let the powerful engine idle for a few minutes. The rumble of the tailpipes was like hearing a favorite song.

After throwing their bags in the trunk, she backed the car out and headed south out of Ixtapa to catch Ruta 200 that would take them north to Troncones. On the way, Standard leaned out the window far enough to see the top floor of the VistaPacifica. He wondered how the conversation was going between Mai Nazareth and Strasser. Not that it mattered. He was going to hear all about it sooner or later. Probably sooner.

He put his phone on the dashboard, then sat back to enjoy the thirty-minute drive up the coast, made longer by slow-moving buses full of school children and gear-grinding trucks loaded with vegetables and livestock. The trip gave Emma time to describe in vague terms more of why she thought they should move to Troncones. Twice the house for half the price and a return to the Mexico she remembered. She stopped each time his phone rang. After the fifth call, she asked if he was ever going to answer it.

"Not yet." He turned the phone off. "This Troncones thing is more important."

"So, I hope you're not totally opposed to moving there. I know it's a big decision, but I think it makes sense. Troncones is getting more popular but will never be anything like Zihuatanejo. It would be an investment."

"You may be right," Standard said, quietly trying to convince himself how living in Troncones would significantly reduce the chances of getting into the kind of trouble he was already in, and that Emma detested. "Let's see what we find."

It turned out Emma was right. Even though they had been there before, on closer inspection Troncones is what Mexican beach towns used to be. There were a few small hotels, B&Bs, and a slew of private homes, and some rentals stretched along a wide sandy beach lined with bougainvillea, hibiscus, and palm trees. There was a surf shop, a yoga retreat, and several beach-front palapa restaurants. Nothing to brag about, but at least it didn't have a Carlos 'n Charlies, Señor Frogs, or faux cock fights on fiesta night at an over-elaborate resort hotel. It was not Ixtapa. The waiters in front of the restaurants were less aggressive, the arts and crafts more rustic, the people less edgy. The few *norteamericanos* roaming the streets looked like they were actually interested in what the real Mexico had to offer.

Emma pulled the car into the dirt parking lot of one of the first thatch-roofed palapa restaurants she saw. They joined a handful of adventuresome tourists sitting at small tables drinking Margaritas, eating chips and salsa, and staring out at the waves. They ordered grilled shrimp and cold beer. She waited until the food came before asking him about the painting.

"It's safe."

"Safe where?"

"It's better you don't know. Pretend it's *El Furioso* and all those times that you wouldn't tell me where you kept it."

"This is different," she said. "We're not talking about a car. We're talking about a priceless painting. You won't tell me because you don't trust me."

"I trust you to know that too many people who know about that painting are already dead. Six at last count. The painting is collateral until I find out who killed Simon Nazareth and the others and why."

"Are you feeling that target on your back yet?"

To a certain degree, Emma was right. He may have overplayed his hand a bit but had no intention of folding. Having the one thing everybody wanted gave him a certain amount of protection to go with the amusement of toying with the spoiled and privileged. His only concern was whether it protected the people around him.

Emma pushed her plate away, the shrimp and rice half-eaten. Instead, she drained her beer and held the empty in the air, hoping for another. "John, you always do this. You're not the police. What makes you think that you're not the next one to die because of that damn painting?"

"As long as I have it, I'll always have options."

"Didn't Sam Spade say the same thing in *The Maltese Falcon?*"

"Not exactly, but close."

"That painting and all those dead people says everything you need to know about why I think we should move here," she said, confirming what Standard had felt ever since she brought up the idea. "It may be the only way to keep you out of trouble. I should say keep *us* out of trouble. Remember, I have had my own experiences with your little adventures."

"Things you've never told me about."

"And never will. Now, let's get out of here."

After leaving the restaurant, they drove along the beach road looking at vacant properties or houses that could be fixed up. Emma took pictures of realty signs on places she liked. They parked in a turnout and walked along the beach to view the same properties and houses from the ocean side. Standard had to admit that the houses and vacant lots may be cheap, but the views were worth millions.

At mid-afternoon, they checked into a beachfront hotel with only four rooms and a swimming pool. They stocked up on fruit, beer, and tequila at a store down the street. Walking back to the hotel, Standard got the feeling that they were the

only people in town. There was quiet. Then there was Troncones. This could take some getting used to, he thought.

Emma sliced up and plated the pineapple, papaya, and
bananas then squeezed a lime over it. They picked at it while
sitting by the pool overlooking the beach. They sipped tequila
and chased it with cold beer. A cool breeze came off the ocean.
Rollers hitting the beach put off an insistent but soothing roar,
unlike the anemic waves of Zihuatanejo Bay. The sun sat ten
degrees above the horizon and sinking fast.

"All those calls today? They were about the painting,
right?" Emma asked.

"It was Strasser. I'll call him after he stews a while."

"And?"

"Maybe he'll be impatient enough or want the painting so
badly that he'll tell me what he knows about the murders."

"Those people who were killed? The ones from the museums? What if he doesn't know anything."

"Then I'll figure something else out," Standard said. "But
he has to be involved somehow. It's the only thing that makes
sense. Eliminate the competition. Make sure he's the only one
to get the painting. From what I can tell, he's obsessed with it.
Maybe by getting other bidders out of the way he would be
sure to get what he wants."

"What about Nazareth?"

"Killing him makes no sense. All Strasser had to do was
give Nazareth the money, then sail away with his painting.
Nazareth's death only makes things more complicated. There's
something else going on. I just don't know what. I'll hang on to
the painting until I do."

CHAPTER 31

CARLOS STRASSER FLEW BACK TO *EL OBRA MAESTRO* FROM VistaPacifica with the name John Standard, a telephone number, and a gut-wrenching panic that things were moving beyond his control.

Simon Nazareth was dead. His wife thought this Standard guy had the painting but didn't know where it was. To make things worse, she thinks Drago Dragovich killed her husband.

"Drago! What's he got to do with it?" he'd asked her.

"I think two of his men were trying to steal the painting when we were bringing it here," she'd explained. "I don't know what happened to them." Strasser looked at Heinz, who nodded and shrugged.

"Drago's men are dead," Strasser said.

"Doesn't he have other men?"

Strasser and Drago were no strangers. In the exclusive world of the megarich, they had been competitors, but not friends. He considered Drago a cynical brute who only knew the price of art, never the true value of it. If there was ever anything of value that the two of them wanted, Strasser always came out ahead. The only expensive pieces of art Drago owned were ones Strasser didn't want and let him have. While he had never considered Drago stupid, maybe it was time to change his mind. He was not surprised that Drago wanted the Raphael, but killing the man who had it before finding out where it was seemed to him like vintage Russian bungling.

Strasser knew that Drago had fallen on hard times since the war in Ukraine. Since there was no way he had the money to match Strasser's offer, he apparently decided to steal the Raphael then sell it for a badly needed cash infusion to his floundering empire. Drago had no idea what it takes to sell a priceless piece of art on the open market. A corrupt Russian oligarch selling only a painting worth hundreds of millions would create nothing but suspicion. The first thing any smart person would think is that if a Russian is selling it, it's got to be a fake. Not an unreasonable assumption.

Strasser could only shake his head. "Fucking Russians," he muttered.

Whatever Drago was trying to do it clearly hadn't worked out, at least not yet. Drago's two men were dead, but Mai Nazareth might have been right. He does have other men. Strasser needed to get his hands on the painting as soon as possible and leave. Drago was unpredictable. Best not to be around if he shows up.

But where was he?

As the helicopter circled the bay before setting down on *La Obra Maestro,* Strasser looked down at the city that was a mixture of storefronts, streets, and shanties. The hotels along the beach looked pleasant enough, but he had a hard time imagining himself—or anyone he knew—staying in any of them. And only one hotel with a heliport? That makes no sense.

When the copter landed, Strasser jumped out, crossed the deck, and up the stairs to his office. He sat at his desk and dialed John Standard's number yet again. He'd already called him a half dozen times, left voice messages, and texted another ten times. Nothing.

This was not what he was used to.

He sat atop a worldwide conglomerate that included cattle ranches, livestock transportation, meat processing and distribution, a few high-end restaurants in Paris, London, and Rio, and a successful online cutlery business. He had all the power he could ever want and if he needed more money, he could drive up the price of beef by cutting back production. It worked for OPEC with oil. It worked for him with hamburger, prime rib, and filet mignon. All of it built up over three generations with money his father stole from Jews and gypsies, something he tried not to think about.

It made him rich enough to travel the world in a mega-yacht, running his dynasty from a laptop and cell phone, and indulging in his love of expensive art. He hired competent people to run his businesses day to day, paid them well, and earned their loyalty. As he got richer, so did they.

Now, the only thing standing between him and what could be the last masterpiece, the one thing he coveted above all else, was someone who sounded like they were little more than a beach bum.

Who was John Standard and what did he want? The way Mai Nazareth described it he was someone willing to play errand boy to make a few bucks. If that was the case, then getting the painting shouldn't be that hard. Everybody has a price. What's his? A six-pack of beer? Some marijuana? A few bottles of tequila? Maybe a night in a Mexican brothel. Whatever it was, fine if it got him the painting. Not only that, Strasser knew he had other options. Chief among them: Heinz Richter.

Mai Nazareth had also mentioned a second man whose

name was either Izzy or Icky or Ozzie. She wasn't sure but made it clear that Standard was in charge and if anyone has the painting he does. She described them as friends, rather than boss and employee.

After she described what happened when she and Standard walked in and found Simon's body, she had to be right. Standard had the painting.

He was also sure that she didn't know where it was. If she did, why lie about it? What would be the point? He was there to buy the painting. She was there to sell it to him, her dead husband notwithstanding.

Yet here he was. Anchored in a tiny bay surrounded by worm-riddled sailboats with a view of shabby shacks and even shabbier hotels. Coming here seemed like a good idea. A perfect out-of-the-way place to do a nice, quiet transaction. Easy for *El Obra Maestro* to get in and out. A hotel with a heliport right over the penthouse. Sail in. Fly over and back. Sail out. Besides, it's what the Bergens wanted. Something quick, quiet, and efficient. No publicity. No auctions. No reporters or art critics. How hard could that be?

Pretty hard, thanks to whoever killed Simon Nazareth.

But solving murders was not why Strasser was there. If Drago killed him, then fine, let the police or whatever they have down here deal with it. Strasser was here for the painting.

He picked up his phone again and called Heinz. "I have two names for you. John Standard and some guy named Izzy or Ozzie or something like that. They're the ones who brought the painting from the airport to the hotel and I believe still have it."

"I saw them when the plane arrived. I know what they look like."

"Good. I'm going to see what I can find out about John Standard. I want you to track down this Izzy or whatever his name is. I'd suggest starting at the bars in town because the best I can tell all anyone does around here is drink."

After hanging up, Strasser called his corporation's data center in Johannesburg, South Africa. The phone rang on the desk of Blessing Sbuso, the head of research.

"Ms. Sbuso, this is Carlos Strasser. It's nice to see you still at work."

"Mr. Strasser! What a pleasure!" she said.

Strasser could tell from the sound of her voice that she was doing her best not to sound suspicious about why the chairman of the board was calling her from halfway around the world.

"I have a couple of projects for you, and I'm afraid they are rather urgent. First, I need you and your team to find out everything you can about a man named John Standard. All I have is a telephone number and that he lives somewhere in Zihuatanejo, Mexico. He looks to be in his late thirties. Can you take care of that for me, Ms. Sbuso?

He knew it was not the kind of research Blessing Sbuso and her team usually did. Their expertise was marketing, economics, and geopolitics. Missing persons was not a core competency. The good news was they had resources. He should know. He paid for it.

"Of course, Mr. Strasser. We'll get right on it and send you everything we find as soon as possible. You mentioned a second project."

"I need to know the whereabouts of Drago Dragovich. Russian oligarch. Oil and gas mostly. Guns, drugs, sex trafficking as sidelines. Maybe money laundering for his friends in the Russian mafia. Half-assed art collector. Homes all over Europe. Same as the other request. The sooner the better, Ms. Sbuso."

He gave her Standard's phone number along with spelling

the name of the city, then hung up, and muttered to himself, "Mr. Standard may have my painting, but I have people."

Strasser made it a practice never to drink before five p.m., but he was willing to make an exception given what had happened. Easy had become hard. Hard required thinking. Thinking required alcohol.

He poured a glass of scotch, drank it, poured another then began running through the short list of people with a reason to kill Simon Nazareth. It wasn't Heinz. He knew better. It couldn't have been the people from the Louvre, Prado, or The Vatican. They weren't killers and, besides, thanks to Heinz they were already dead. That left Drago. Mai Nazareth might be right. So, what would Drago do next? Not much, Strasser thought, unless he knows that John Standard has the painting. That would be a stretch. Best Strasser could tell only he and Mai Nazareth knew that Standard had it.

Strasser had one more drink, then called the steward to order lunch. After eating, he laid on the bed to think but fell asleep. Two hours later he woke up to the sound of an email alert on his computer. He opened the message from Blessing Sbuso. He started reading, then decided to print out her report with its attachments.

He poured another scotch while waiting for the printer to spit out the documents, then found a comfortable spot on the couch.

To: Carlos Strasser, Chairman of the Board
From: Blessing Sbuso, Director of Research
Re: Request for information regarding John Standard.

John Kennedy Standard is a 39-year-old American citizen, born in Wheaton, Illinois, USA. Both his parents and his older brother are deceased. He graduated from Northwestern

University with a degree in journalism. After jobs at two Midwestern newspapers, he was hired as a reporter by the largest daily newspaper in Portland, Oregon. He eventually became a columnist. A review of his columns indicates a recurring theme that appears to chip away at the city's liberal reputation, particularly when it comes to race relations and dealing with the rampant homelessness, crime, and protests, all of which are a significant part of daily life in Portland.

Following a hit-and-run accident in which two young girls were killed, he was charged with vehicular homicide and leaving the scene of an accident. A jury found him innocent, but that didn't prevent his employer from firing him, after which he became something of a local pariah. The incident also seems to be the reason behind the divorce from his wife of five years, leaving him in debt, without a place to live, and more or less unemployable.

He spent several years as a freelance writer. (As an aside, freelancer is a term from Sir Walter Scott's novel Ivanhoe, referring to a mercenary soldier—a free-lance.) Articles with his byline appear on several tabloid-like websites. His main source of income at the time seemed to be the city's alterna-tive weekly, Inside Oregon. He is believed to be responsible for an article on the late industrialist Proctor Scofield and his involvement in the apparent suicide of Scofield's stepdaugh-ter. (See Attachment #1) While working on another article (See Attachment #2) about the disappearance of several young women, Standard was nearly stabbed to death by a deranged killer named Mason Gage. According to the police report (See Attachment #3), police killed Gage before he could kill Standard. Standard spent a month in the hospital before dropping out of sight.

Activity on his passport (See Attachment #4 w/ photo) shows that he left Portland for Ixtapa/Zihuatanejo in January *nearly two years ago. Since then, he has made two trips back to Portland, each time returning to Mexico after only a few days. He has no known address other than an apartment in Portland. His only asset appears to be a Vanguard account containing $242,000. The money was deposited four years ago shortly after Standard's return from a round trip to the Cook Islands in the South Pacific. The account (See Attachment #5) shows little activity other than a $10,000 withdrawal around the time that he left for Mexico and the required tax filings. The account appears to do little other than accrue interest. Statements are sent to Benjamin Orlando at the same Portland address as Standard. It is an apartment building in the mid-town area. Orlando is the manager and former owner. He is also an accomplished website designer, hacker, and researcher. Formidable and numerous firewalls have prevented us from accessing Orlando's computer. We will continue trying.*

Standard holds no current debit or credit cards, which is an indication that he deals mostly (if not entirely) in cash. Based on the cost of living in Mexico for the last two years, we estimate that the $10,000 he took with him nearly two years ago has likely run out. We are unaware at this time of any other sources of income or if he is living rent-free somewhere in the city.

A search of government databases turned up a reference to Standard in a DEA report on cartel activity in the State of Guerrero, which is where Zihuatanejo is located. (See Attachment #6) The report mentions, in vague, bureaucratic terms, Standard's apparent involvement in the traffic deaths of three cartel soldiers and a massacre at an estate in which several people were killed, including an accountant for one of Mexico's most powerful cartels. She was also the daughter of a local drug lord.

During his month-long hospital stay after being stabbed, Standard underwent a psychiatric evaluation (See Attachment #7) in which he was diagnosed with post-traumatic stress syndrome, depression, and self-destructive tendencies. All those maladies were the result of the traffic accident that killed the two girls and his own later injuries at the hands of Mason Gage. Those incidents led to a period of alcohol abuse and self-medication. The evaluation describes Standard as "engaging, humorous, and insightful" but prone to becoming distracted and distant. The evaluation cites two lingering effects of the attack on him: a fear of knives and a near-total disregard for his own wellbeing.

Our assessment of the information we have obtained so far suggests that Standard is resourceful and not overly concerned with self-preservation. A reading of the psychiatric evaluation appears to indicate that he is more concerned about the wellbeing of those around him than for himself. We are unaware at this time who those people might be. Given the string of deaths that have followed him since the hit-and-run incident, he is no stranger to death. We suggest that Standard be approached with caution. While we do not believe he is dangerous, danger appears to follow him around, jeopardizing those with whom he becomes involved.

Please consider this a preliminary report provided to meet your request for a quick response. We will continue our research and provide you with updates as they become available.

Strasser read the report a second time then thumbed through the attachments, lingering over a copy of Standard's psychiatric evaluation by one of the hospital's staff doctors. He kept coming back to one sentence: "I believe that the only thing that would return Mr. Standard to his previous mental and emotional state is an event that adds value to his life and allows him to, in some way, address his empathy for others in a real and tangible way."

Reading a few of his columns gave Strasser the impression that Standard enjoyed needling the city's elite without using the term "limousine liberals." He just came close a few times. Several columns chronicled the reaction to an arson fire that destroyed a historic black church, the city's inept responses to a homeless crisis and rising murder rate, and a plague of riots that turned the center of the city into a ghost town. None of what he read gave any indication that Standard was an art lover. It seemed to Strasser that Standard was more interested in dead bodies than dead artists.

When he'd finished reading, Strasser had a hard time believing Standard was anything other than the beer-soaked-and-pot-steeped beach bum that Mai Nazareth made him out to be. Someone continuing to live a life that made him what he is and where he is. If he was more than that, as Sbuso's report suggested, then what was he doing here? What would someone with all that baggage be doing in a dreary beach town on the west coast of Mexico other than getting drunk and hiding out? While the information from Sbuso made it sound like someone much more complicated, unpredictable, and, at least to some degree, threatening, Strasser wasn't buying it. Even if experience had taught him that lack of concern for self-preservation can make for a dangerous enemy, Standard didn't fit the bill. So, what was he, and what did he want?

There was only one way to find out. He needed to meet with Standard, or at least talk to him. If this was about money, then it should be easy enough to resolve. If his refusal to return phone calls and text messages were any indication, nothing about John Standard was going to be easy.

Strasser opened a second email with a document titled "Dragovitch" attached:

To: Carlos Strasser, Chairman of the Board
From: Blessing Sbuso, Director of Research
Re: Drago Dragovitch

Drago Dragovitch's private jet left Sheremetyevo airport at 11:38 p.m Moscow time yesterday. According to the flight plan, the plane was headed to Tripoli, Libya. We believe he chose Libya because sanctions and other limitations resulting from the war in Ukraine have restricted his travel. His passport is more welcome in countries allied with Russia.

The plane is currently on the ground in Tripoli. A flight plan has been filed for Havana, Cuba. We believe the plane is already in the air. We will track it and provide you with necessary updates.

The report on Dragovitch created more questions than answers. Was Drago even on the plane? If he was, is he going to Havana to drink rum and fuck whores? If he's coming to Zihuatanejo, there was no way of knowing when he would arrive or what he would do when he got here.

Strasser assumed the worst and that Drago was on his way. He could do nothing about it except find the painting and leave before Drago arrived. He picked up his phone to leave yet another voicemail and then a text message for Standard.

CHAPTER 32

Emma and Standard left Troncones the next morning after breakfast at a palapa restaurant and checking out two more beachfront properties. One was a large vacant lot with two hundred feet of beachfront. The other was a house that was little more than a cement foundation sprouting rusted rebar that the builder apparently thought would sprout a fully finished house.

Emma drove while Standard scrolled through the text messages from Carlos Strasser then listened to his voicemails. They all started out polite, morphed into subservient, then ended in outright anger. The tone of Strasser's last message twelve hours earlier was that he was done asking. That took the ball out of Strasser's court and put it in Standard's.

"Are you going to call him?" Emma asked.

They were ten miles north of Zihuatanejo stuck behind a flat-bed truck loaded with live chickens with nowhere to pass. Feathers flew by like pieces of torn tissue. A half dozen of the caged birds stared back at them as if aware of their fate and begging for help.

"I'm not sure. I know what he wants. He just doesn't know what I want. Sooner or later, I'll have to tell him. Probably later."

"When we were dealing with rich pimps and cartel *soldados* I at least had some idea what to expect. They were bad people. Bad things were going to happen, and they did. Mostly to them, but that's beside the point. This feels different. Strasser is not a criminal. He's just some guy with too much money who wants to buy an overpriced painting that's been lost since the 15th Century. Why not just give it to him?"

"There is the matter of a few hundred million dollars," Standard said.

"That's between him and this Nazareth woman. If you won't give the painting to him, then give it to her, and let them do whatever deal they have. That gets you out of the middle."

Standard knew she was right ... up to a point. That six people either directly or indirectly associated with *Portrait of a Young Woman* were dead kept ringing in his head. While Emma may think Strasser is no criminal, he wasn't so sure. He felt like a poker player holding good cards but wanting to see one more.

"I'm sorry, Emma, but people are dead. You know me. That's not something I can just walk away from."

She sighed and went back to staring out the windshield at the chickens and swatting away feathers.

Standard and Emma had this same conversation more times than either of them could count. It always came out the same. While he would figure things out in a way that kept her safe and him alive, she would wonder what made him do it. She knew enough of his history to get some level of understanding, but she would never know all of it. He was a mystery she would never stop trying to unravel.

Two miles north of Zihuatanejo and with the chicken truck

and feathers in the rearview mirror, Standard called Mai Nazareth.

"Tell me about your meeting with Strasser?" he asked before she had a chance to say hello.

"Just what you'd expect. He asked to see the painting. When I told him I didn't have it he acted stunned for a few seconds. He seemed speechless, sort of dazed. Then he wanted to know where it was. I told him the last time I saw it you had it. I gave him your telephone number like you told me."

"What else?"

"He wanted to know about the trip from the airport to the hotel. I told him what I saw and everything you told me. He asked me who I thought killed Simon. I told him Drago Dragovitch."

"How did he take that?"

"Not well. I got the impression the two of them have a history."

"Did you tell him about Itchy Donlan, the man who was with us in the car?"

"Yes, but I couldn't remember his name. I said it was Izzy or Icky or something like that."

"Where did you leave it with Strasser?"

"He just stared at me, then left. Has he contacted you?"

"He's left a few messages."

"Mr. Standard, I hope you understand the gravity of the situation. That painting belongs to my clients. They expected Simon, now me, to sell it to Strasser and put the money in their account, minus our fee. They are waiting for word that the sale has gone through. What would you like me to tell them?"

"I really don't care. This is between Strasser and me now. Tell your clients whatever you want while I figure things out."

"There's one other thing. Strasser didn't show up alone. He had a man with him that could have been his twin. The man didn't say or do anything. He just stood in the background. Strasser introduced him as his accountant, there to make the transfer happen. I've seen a lot of accountants in my life. He doesn't look like any of them. I got the feeling he was something else, someone that would do anything Strasser asked. And I mean anything, Mr. Standard."

"Name?"

"He called him Heinz."

CHAPTER 33

It took stops at three different sketchy bars scattered around the center of Zihuatanejo before Heinz Richter learned that "Izzy" was actually "Itchy" and that his last name was Donlan.

Finding him proved to be more difficult.

None of the bartenders or waitresses in places with names like The Lusty Crab, *El Gordo Camaron*, and *Cocodrilo* knew his name. His questions about where Donlan lived were met with blank stares and laughs that said, why would anyone want to know that? What he did pick up were bits and pieces that left him thinking that Donlan spent most of his time moving from bar to bar looking for someone to buy him drinks or hanging out in the hotel restaurants, night clubs, and discos of Ixtapa preying on widows and divorcees.

That was a lot of territory to cover. If he didn't get lucky, it could take days to find Donlan. He didn't have days.

After a day working the streets of Zihuatanejo, he took a taxi to Ixtapa. The bartenders, bellhops, waiters, and waitresses had no idea who he was talking about. That included the Vista-Pacifica, which is the last place Heinz saw him. Donlan may have been some kind of tattered celebrity in Zihuatanejo, but he was a murky presence in garish Ixtapa.

Heinz ended up finding a quiet bar across the street from the resort hotels, ordered a beer, and marveled at how someone as despicable and nondescript as Donlan could be involved with a priceless work of art. From what he could tell, the art world had its share of low-lifes. He just didn't expect to find one on the west coast of Mexico. All he could do was keep looking. If he found Donlan then he might find Standard. He could tell from the sound of Strasser's voice that Standard was the prize. Donlan was nothing more than bait. He could work with that.

He headed back to Zihuatanejo to hit four more bars and chat up eight more bartenders and ten more waitresses before wandering into what looked like the city's only upscale restaurant.

Mango's was a couple of blocks off the bay front in the middle of an intersection of three streets. While exploring El Centro, he had walked by it several times, each time thinking that it was too upscale for Zihuatanejo. He felt the same way about Itchy Donlan, but it was worth a try.

From outside, its wooden doors and whitewashed walls reminded Heinz of a Spanish hacienda. Inside the elegant dining room was decorated with stunted palm trees, blossoming bougainvillea, and moon lights. A small mariachi band roamed through the tables serenading a handful of diners.

He sat down at the end of the bar that was filling up with older Americans that looked and acted like regulars. He watched them order drinks, shake hands, and give man hugs and air kisses. He ordered a beer and asked the woman sitting next to him if she knew Itchy Donlan. She was a porky, sixty-something blonde with too much lipstick, and wearing shorts and a tank top that showed too much well-tanned cleavage.

"Jose," she said to the bartender, "he wants to know if Itchy Donlan ever comes in here." They both started laughing.

"Yeah," the bartender said. "He's been in a few times."

The five people sitting at the bar overheard him and started laughing as well.

"I take it he's a regular," Heinz said, joining in the laughter. "Does he come in at any particular time?"

"What do you want with Itchy?" a man sitting two stools to Heinz's left said. He was old and bald. His skin burned a blotchy red from too much sun. He wore baggy shorts and a frayed aloha shirt. He had a Margarita in his hand and looked ready for another.

"I'm a friend from the States. I heard he was living down here. Thought I'd look him up. I'm having a hard time finding him."

"Here's an idea," the old man said. "Buy a round of drinks for the bar. Word will get out and Itchy will show up like a shark smelling blood."

Heinz smiled and tried to be a good sport. "Any of you know where he lives?"

That produced another round of laughs. "Anyone care?" the woman said.

That earned more yuks.

"Somewhere on the other side of the marina," a woman four seats away said. She looked younger than her bar mates. Her deep tan said she might be a permanent resident.

Heinz looked at the others. They just shrugged. Someone muttered "Could be."

He politely bought a round for the bar, then left and

walked back toward the bay. On Paseo del Pescador, he waved off waiters clutching menus and ignored the stalls selling T-shirts and bathing suits. He walked past the naval base, the foot of the City Pier, and groups of tourists headed to dinner or back to their hotels. It was early evening, not yet dark. Lights glittered on the homes, hotels, and condos on the west side of the bay. The smell of salt and fish past its prime filled the air. *El Obra Maestro* sat a hundred yards off the end of the pier, a dark shadow against the mountains.

He thought about calling Strasser to give him an update on his search for Itchy Donlan but decided against it. The multi-billionaire was in a sour mood after what happened at the VistaPacifica. Hopefully Strasser's search for John Standard was keeping him busy but that was only for the short term. He would never be happy until he gets his hands on *Portrait of a Young Woman.* Things had gone off the rails. The question was how far and where it would end.

Heinz first learned of the painting right after he was hired. It was during a long sea journey from Johannesburg to Kuala Lumpur that Strasser shared his theories about where it might be, who had been secretly hoarding it, and what he would do to get his hands on it. Knowing next to nothing about art and even less about Raphael, Heinz had a hard time understanding his employer's obsession or his frantic searches around eastern Europe. Over the years, he would come to know more about the painting, Raphael, and his employer. That was why it came as no surprise that the closer Strasser came to realizing his dream, the more erratic he became.

Heinz knew that his job was to find Donlan and see where things went from there. During his time in Zihuatanejo and his exploration of its streets and neighborhoods, he'd learned that there were only two ways to reach the hillside shanties above the marina where Donlan supposedly lived. One way was on the main street that snaked through town then out toward the bay. That was the best way by car. The other was a bridge over the marina entrance, easiest for anyone on foot. Deciding that fifty-fifty were the best odds of any, he took his chances and found a bench near the entrance to the bridge and waited.

CHAPTER 34

Itchy Donlan eased out of bed and started to get dressed. He looked for his socks, then realized he hadn't worn any. His shirt was on the back of the chair next to his shorts. His hat was on a hook next to the door. On the way out, he grabbed five hundred pesos out of Marie Mitchell's purse. He left her passed out on the bed after she downed several more Margaritas in what he took as a further effort to mourn who or what had died back in New York City. He intended to spend the night, but by ten p.m., he decided that even the hard bed in the hovel he called home was better than sleeping with a comatose widow.

Too bad, he thought. In many ways she was so much better than the other old gals he'd picked up in Ixtapa. She was a bit younger, a lot smarter, more sophisticated, and, more important, very enthusiastic. At least until lately. Maybe it was time to cut his losses and find fresher fields to plow. The tourist season was picking up and COVID was over, all of which meant that more and more widows, divorcees, and spinsters arrived every day.

When it came to women, Itchy had one rule: Never get involved with one who has more problems than he does. In his case, that was no easy task. Sadly, Marie fit the bill. Too bad. She would be hard to replace.

As he shoved the money into his pocket, he thought about how different his life is now from what it was six years ago. Then, he had a thriving accounting practice, a wife, two sons, and a twenty-something mistress he visited every Tuesday afternoon. He never imagined coming to Mexico on vacation and having that fall apart because of one night of drinking and propositioning the wrong girl at the wrong time. He still can't believe that in a place like Mexico, they can come down so hard on drinking. After all, that's what everybody does. It's like a national sport, right behind soccer. Cut some slack. He can't be the first American to say or do something stupid.

After a week in jail, Itchy got out only to learn that his wife and sons had gone back to Topeka without him. That explained why they didn't come to see him or try to bail him out. If that was the way they wanted it, then fine, he would just stay. Knowing his wife, he felt safer staying in a place where he knew no one rather than going home to her.

The whole purpose of coming to Mexico in the first place was to give him time to think over a job offer from a large accounting firm located outside Washington, D.C. It was a big decision that meant selling his practice to take a job that would require a major change in lifestyle and location. Turns out he got both, just not the way he thought it would be.

As hard as things were over the next six years, he had come to enjoy the simple uncomplicated life of living hand to mouth. He honed his skills at seducing vulnerable women, which, while less financially rewarding than being an accountant, was more fun than helping rich guys find ways to fuck the IRS.

He used some of Marie's money to take a taxi into Zihuatanejo. He got out at the Central Mercado to get something to eat at a late-night taco stand. While munching on tacos al pastor, he tried to figure out what to tell his live-in girlfriend Yolanda about where he'd been for the last two days. In the year they had been together, she had never once questioned him about where he went or how long he was gone if he came back with enough money to help pay the rent and buy a few groceries. Still, he felt he needed to tell her something.

Two days was a long time, and Yolanda tended to worry when she couldn't find him. She was young, sweet, and devoted to him. He hated deceiving her about where he'd disappear to, but telling her the truth wouldn't go over well, no matter how trusting she was. Between what he swindled out of old babes in Ixtapa and the meager sums Yolanda pulled in selling hand-made baby clothes at the Artisan Market, they could just afford the three-room, cement block house on the hillside above the marina. Itchy hated the place but appreciated having his own roof over his head and what she had done to make it livable.

On the other hand, things were looking up. In a few weeks, he'd have the money from his divorce and sale of the accounting business. Then there was the twenty thousand he was owed for his short stint as a delivery boy for Simon Nazareth. He thought he'd have the money right after he and Standard pulled up in front of VistaPacifica with the painting and Nazareth's wife. Just his luck that Nazareth turned up dead. Now, all he could do was hang on, be patient, and wait for Standard to take care of business.

Standard. At least he had that going for him. Standard seemed to have a magic touch. He'd barely been in town a month before moving in with Emma Parrish. Donlan sighed. If only he could be that lucky. There were more times than he could count when he wanted to be more like Standard. Tall, handsome, confident, a dogged determination to learn the truth, and a bedrock belief that no matter what he did, things would turn out alright for him and those around him. Standard cutting him in on a shot at a twenty-thousand-dollar payday was evidence of that. Although, that was looking a little iffy. Then there was the painting. No way of telling how that might go.

Finished eating, Itchy walked south through downtown toward the bayfront.

Most of the restaurants were closed at that hour, but a few bars were still open. Music and laughter spilled out onto the street mixed with the rattle of beer bottles and ice cubes and the whir of blenders. Still unsure what to tell Yolanda, he decided that maybe a drink at Mango's would help. If Standard was there, he might get a status report on their payday and find out more about what was going on with the painting.

Donlan was positive Standard stashed it somewhere after finding Nazareth's body, but where? If he did have it, then why was he hanging on to it? It seemed anyone even loosely connected with it were either already dead or risking their lives. Knowing Standard, he had his reasons, and he wouldn't let his own safety get in the way. No need to worry, he thought. Standard always figured things out.

No way he would leave him out of the money.

The usual crowd of sunburned expats was crowded around the bar, including Nigel, a former submarine captain who owned a restaurant in Porto Mio on the west side of the bay. He was an aging horn dog who liked to chat up the old babes that were Mango's regulars, most of whom he'd hit on before but forgot. He may have even been successful at one time but was too lost in the fog of booze, humidity, and creeping dementia to remember.

"There was some guy in here asking about you," Nigel said. "Said he knew you from the States and wanted to say hello."

Itchy was immediately suspicious. He didn't have that

many friends in Topeka, and those he did have didn't know where he was and wouldn't just drop in even if they did. "Did he give you a name?"

"No. He was a blond guy in jeans and a T-shirt. Had an accent of some kind. German, I think, but don't hold me to it. He looked to be about your age, but more fit. Kind of muscular, but in a thin, wiry way. Sound familiar?"

Itchy could count on one hand the number of times anyone wanted to find him. Usually, it was one of his Ixtapa conquests wanting to either say goodbye or get back the money she'd loaned him. But they were all women and none of them had German accents. He thanked Nigel, drained his beer, and left.

He stopped at a tienda to spend some more of Marie's money on a cheap bottle of wine that might serve as a peace offering to Yolanda, even though having been raised by nuns she didn't drink. He headed down the street that led to the arched, cement bridge over the entrance to the marina. He was still trying to come up with an explanation for his absence when he reached the steps going up. He looked up long enough to notice the man sitting on the bench, gave him a polite "Hola," then kept walking. The man had blond hair, a T-shirt, and jeans, but Itchy didn't put two and two together until he reached the top of the bridge. When he stopped and turned around, the man was gone.

Itchy shook it off and kept walking. Bodybuilders were a new demographic for Zihuatanejo, but it could be a trend.

On the other side of the bridge, he headed two blocks north then up a dirt path between two open-air restaurants, one of which was still doing business. Plates rattled, customers laughed, smoke from the kitchen mixed with the aroma of carne asada, chili rellenos, and fresh, handmade tortillas. Beyond the restaurant, he passed a half-dozen sheet-metal-and-plywood shanties, their doors open, dim lights and music oozing out onto makeshift patios with oil drums turned into barbecue grills.

The house he shared with Yolanda had a living room, bedroom, and small kitchen. It smelled of packed dirt and masa. On the shelves above the small sink were a few canned goods from the local food bank and salt and pepper shakers stolen from restaurants. There was no closet. Just a few clothes hanging on a rope stretched over a double bed held up by cement blocks. The bathroom was a shack outside they shared with six other hovels. The front door was wood. Same with the back door out of the kitchen. Threadbare carpets and burlap sacks covered the hard-dirt floors. The tin roof was painted white to reflect the sun but didn't do much to keep the rain out during monsoon season.

Yolanda wasn't home yet, which was fine. Maybe when she got there, she'd be too tired to ask him where he'd been.

Itchy had just screwed the top off the wine when a man busted through the front door. He recognized him immediately as the guy who had been sitting on the bench by the bridge. He kicked himself for not paying closer attention.

"What the hell! Who are you?" Itchy said as the man stood in the doorway looking around then marched toward him. "If you're here to rob me, you picked the wrong guy and the wrong house."

"You're a hard man to find, Mr. Donlan," he said.

"Not hard enough it seems."

"You need to come with me. I know someone who would like to talk to you."

CHAPTER 35

STANDARD WOKE UP THE NEXT MORNING THINKING ABOUT
how stressed Itchy Donlan must be over not getting the twenty
K and how he was going to get by for the next three weeks. He
tried calling him a few times. After getting no answer, he
walked down to The Tortuga for breakfast, then took a taxi to
the Artisan Market.

He wandered through the narrow, stuffy aisles lined with
stalls selling clothes, shoes, hand-painted plates, mugs, and
hammocks. He found Yolanda sitting in a folding chair sewing
what looked like a baby's christening dress. She was young, a
little overweight, and had a scar across her upper lip. Standard
met her once by accident at the Central Mercado where she
and Itchy were shopping. She struck him as very shy, polite,
and totally devoted to Itchy.

"Señor Juan." Her smile quickly turned to a look of
concern. "Itchy? He is okay, *si*?"

"I've been trying to find him. I was hoping you had seen
him."

"Not for *dos dias*, but that is Itchy. He *viene y va*, but I love him anyway."

He reassured Yolanda that Itchy was fine and to have him call when he showed up.

Itchy wasn't much of a morning guy, so looking for him in his usual haunts early in the day would be a waste of time. Besides most of them weren't open or serving liquor yet. Not that it mattered. Itchy was broke, unless he'd cajoled a few pesos from Marie. He dialed Itchy's number again. Still no answer. Ixtapa was the only other place he could be. Standard had no stomach for another visit to the VistaPacifica. Finding Itchy would have to wait.

Since he was in town, he went to the Central Mercado for fruit and pastries to take home. He picked up a bottle of tequila and some limes at a liquor store. Stuffing everything into his backpack, he stopped for lunch at a noisy taco place in El Centro. He found a table overlooking the street, ordered a plate of *tacos carnitas* and hoped Itchy would just walk by.

After an hour, he took a taxi back to *Playa la Ropa*, dropped the fruit, pastries, and tequila at the house, then walked back down to The Tortuga. He tried Itchy's phone two more times along the way. Nothing. More and more concerned, he called the VistaPacifica and asked for Marie Mitchell's room. She answered with a slurred hello.

"Have you seen Itchy?" Standard asked.

It took her a few seconds to answer. "He was here last night, I think. I guess he left."

"Do you know where he went?"

"I don't even remember his leaving."

Standard hung up. He was getting worried, and his options limited. Itchy never left town because he had no money and no place to go. Besides, he would never walk away from the twenty thousand he was owed. He could call Vega and report Itchy missing, then see how long it would take the comandante to stop laughing.

He had one last idea. Paying his bill and picking up his backpack, he headed up the beach. Not seeing what he was looking for, he walked over the hill, past several cliffside restaurants mingled in among the high-end and moderately priced hotels to *Playa la Madera*. He found Aurelio explaining the finer points of bathtub cheese to a pair of skeptical-looking tourists wearing Green Bay Packers caps. The three members of the La Madera Irregulars stood in his wake waiting to step in to sell a few bobble-head toys if they passed on some cheese.

After nodding to Aurelio and motioning down the beach, Standard stopped at a palapa restaurant, ordered a beer, and waited. Aurelio and his posse showed up ten minutes later.

"You come to buy some cheese, Señor Juan," Aurelio said. "I'm sure Señora Emma would be most grateful."

"Not right now." Standard pointed to the three boys. "I need to find Itchy Donlan. Can I get you to send your search party out to look for him?"

"Señor Itchy is missing? That is not good." Aurelio started talking to the Irregulars in rapid Spanish. When he said "Itchy," all three nodded. After Standard gave each of them a ten-peso coin, they ran off in different directions.

"If they learn anything, I'll be at The Tortuga," Standard said. He bought three feet of Aurelio's cheese then caught a taxi back to *Playa la Ropa*. He had plenty of time. It would take hours for the Irregulars to comb the city for any sign of Itchy then report back to Aurelio. And only then if they found him.

At five o'clock, he was still at The Tortuga drinking beer and waiting. An hour later he spotted Aurelio and the Irregulars headed up the beach in his direction. When they arrived, the three kids plopped down in the sand, looking exhausted. Aurelio took a chair on the other side of the table.

"Any luck?" Standard asked.

Aurelio nodded toward the oldest of the three boys. "*Dile al Señor Juan,*" he said.

Instead of answering, the boy pointed out at the bay and *El Obra Maestro.*

CHAPTER 36

❦

Standard looked at the boys then turned to Aurelio for an explanation.

"They told me that a cook at a restaurant near Señor Itchy's house saw him leave with another man, a man with blond hair," Aurelio said. "Señor Itchy did not look happy. They walked off toward the City Pier. A panga captain leaving for the night to go fishing told one of them he saw Señor Itchy in a ... *bota de goma.*"

"A rubber boat. A Zodiac."

"*Si.* The bota was headed toward the *yate.*" Aurelio pointed at the *El Obra Maestro.*

Standard didn't like where this was going. Strasser had Itchy and Itchy's phone. That explained a lot about why Standard wasn't getting any call backs. Turnabout was fair play. Strasser would now use Itchy as leverage to get the Raphael.

Standard handed Aurelio a handful of fifty-peso bills. "This is for all of you. Divide it up any way you want, just take care of them." He nodded toward the trio of kids hanging in

Aurelio's wake while eyeing the money. "Gracias," he said to all of them, then left to walk home.

After explaining it all to Emma, they agreed that calling Itchy's phone wasn't going to work. The only option was to wait.

"He wouldn't hurt or kill Itchy, would he?" Emma said, showing more concern for Donlan than at any time in the past.

"Hurt? Could be. Kill? Doubtful. He wants to trade Itchy for the painting. Kill him and he has nothing to trade."

By ten o'clock, Standard had paced around the house a few hundred times waiting for the call from Strasser that he knew would come sooner or later. At almost midnight, he and Emma were still up, resisting the urge to drink and going back to trying to figure out what mysterious something was creeping through the dry leaves along the fence line. After thinking it could be anything from a rat to a boa constrictor, they decided they really didn't want to know. They turned instead to impatiently watching the always-entertaining gecko races inside the lamp shades and fantasizing about what a house in Troncones would look like.

Emma tried to take Standard's mind off Strasser and Itchy by speculating what she could make selling their current house in the hopes it would be more than enough money to buy a vacant lot and build pretty much whatever they wanted, within certain limits. Even though it could be a while before they had a house that was as good as what they already had, she was convinced they could make it happen. Standard favored buying an existing house and remodeling it but didn't make an issue of it. The house they were in now had been hers long before he showed up. She could sell it and do whatever she wanted, but he appreciated at least being consulted.

They were still talking amenities, décor, and the logistics of living thirty minutes away from the city when his phone rang. Caller ID announced that it was Itchy Donlan.

"It's Strasser, isn't it?" Emma said.

He was sure she was right. He let it ring a few times. He'd already decided to play along and see what Strasser had in mind.

"Itchy?" Standard said when he finally answered. "What's up?"

"This is Carlos Strasser, Mr. Standard. Since you refused to return my calls or texts, I'm afraid I had to take more drastic steps."

"Define drastic."

"Drastic with a small D. At least for now. I'll get to the point. I have your friend Mr. Donlan. I propose a trade. Him in exchange for my painting."

Standard saw that coming. He was ready. "The painting isn't yours."

"Yes, it is! I'm the only person who believed *Portrait of a Young Woman* was real. Everyone else said it was either destroyed or never existed. I deserve it. I made a deal with Nazareth. I know you have it. Give it to me and I'll let your little friend go unharmed."

"And if I don't?"

"Then he will die an ugly death."

"And you'll never see the painting again."

"You have other friends I assume."

"You plan on paying for this painting?"

"That is between me and Mrs. Nazareth," Strasser said. "It has nothing to do with you. From where I sit, you stole it. Give it back."

"Let me talk to Itchy."

Standard heard mumbling in the background and then some scratching noises.

"John?" Itchy sounded stressed, with good reason. As much as he liked to think of himself as a partner in their so-called adventures, Standard knew Itchy shied away from anything that smacked of danger, no matter how small. He'd come in handy in the past, but only up to a point. Being held captive was about as far outside his comfort zone as he could get.

"Are you alright?"

"I'm fine if you call getting slapped and punched a few times fine. Nothing broken, at least nothing I can tell." Itchy's voice was strained, his speech a little slurred. "Get me out of here. These guys are nuts. Some goon named Heinz dragged me out of my house and out to that yacht in the middle of the bay. It's nice, other than the occasional beating. The yacht is sort of creepy. Lots of art on the walls. I feel like an extra in *Boys from Brazil*. I don't think this is going to end well. I need you to do something."

"Okay. Hang in there and I'll work this out. Give the phone to Strasser." Standard waited until Strasser came back on. "You win, but I need time to get the painting and figure out how to give it you in a way that no one gets hurt. I'll call you back in twenty minutes."

"Don't disappoint me, Mr. Standard."

Standard hung up then explained everything to Emma.

"That solves it," she said. "Give him the painting, save Itchy, and you're out of the middle of the whole thing."

"That's one option," he said.

"Any others? By others I mean ones that don't get you or Itchy killed."

"If things get dicey, I'll pull the plug, give Strasser the painting, and be done with it. Deal?"

Her nod of agreement came with a skeptical look.

Standard made a quick phone call, talked for ten minutes then listened. He hung up and called Strasser.

"Meet me at the end of the City Pier in one hour. Bring Itchy with you."

He hung up before Strasser could answer.

CHAPTER 37

AT ONE-THIRTY IN THE MORNING, THE CLOSED-UP bayfront restaurants and bars looked tired and spent after a day of catering to picky tourists new to town and demanding expats complaining about the lack of anchovies in the Caesar salad. The streets were empty, the stalls that sold hats and T-shirts shuttered. The day's heat had gradually cooled the cement walkway, but he could still feel the warmth in his sandals and into his feet. Despite the hour, the air clung to his body like a night out on a bad date: clingy, needy. The persistent odor of fish and wood smoke mixed with the smell of diesel fuel lingered persistently in the night air that had shed the daytime humidity and turned cool and comfortable.

A dozen pangas were pulled up on the beach in front of the open-air fish market that would open in a few hours. Another dozen would still be out at sea catching the fish and shellfish that would at dawn be sold to restaurant owners and seafood markets. The only sounds were the gentle waves coming in from the bay and the faint music from one of the nightclubs blocks away in the center of town that was still open.

A handful of pelicans slept standing up on an abandoned panga twenty yards off the beach. Lights from the condos, hotels, and restaurants ringed the bay like a diamond necklace. Two stray dogs ran by, one carrying a large bone, the other trying to steal it. Standard, watching as the dogs disappeared around a corner, thought they could either be a metaphor or an omen for what was about to happen.

At the end of the sidewalk along the bayfront was a statue of Mexican patriot José Azueta standing behind a machine gun, his arm raised in triumph. Fittingly, the machine gun was aimed down the hundred-yard length of the City Pier—an odd way to greet visitors but appropriate for this particular night.

Standard stood in the statue's shadow. The lamps lining both sides of the pier stretched out in front of him, casting halos of dim yellow light on the concrete deck. Beyond were the bobbing lights of anchored sailboats and the dark shadow of Strasser's yacht.

The plan he'd sketched out over the phone would play out in the next few minutes, hopefully with the same ending he had in mind. He gave it a fifty-fifty chance at best. Not great odds, but worth it if it got Itchy out of a jam that Standard had put him in. The role of the Raphael would be more complicated.

He'd been there for ten minutes staring through Azueta's legs and waiting to see if Strasser showed up and who was with him. He hoped it would be just the billionaire and Itchy, but he doubted it.

Standard held his breath when he heard an outboard motor approach the rickety dock beneath the pier. He couldn't see it, but at that hour it could only be one thing: the Zodiac from the yacht. He didn't move, waiting for the motor to shut off and watching the stairs to the top of the pier about two-thirds down on the left.

The silence lasted a couple of minutes before the unmistable figure of Itchy Donlan appeared first. He had a cloth bag over his head, hands tied behind his back, a blond man pushing him from behind. If Itchy groaned or protested in any way, Standard was too far away to hear it. The good news was that Itchy was at least upright and walking on his own. The third man up the stairs was older and taller with the same blond hair as the man pushing Itchy. He was dressed in black—pants, shirt, lightweight jacket with *La Obra Maestro* embroidered on the front—and stood ramrod straight. He moved past Itchy to stand in the middle of the pier, acting like he owned it, which he probably could if it was for sale. Light from a three-quarter moon mixed with the soft glow of the pier's lamps, creating a black-and-gray kaleidoscope of competing shadows.

Standard waited another minute before coming out from behind the statue.

He made sure Strasser and the other man saw him before walking toward them. After ten steps he started feeling like he was in a scene out of *Gunsmoke*. He figured the older man for Strasser. The one with Itchy must be the man Mai Nazareth described as Strasser's "accountant." She was right. He didn't look like any accountant Standard had ever met, then again neither did Itchy Donlan. His hopes that it would be just Strasser and Itchy were out the window, but that wasn't going to change anything.

"Mr. Standard, I presume. I'm Carlos Strasser. This is my associate Heinz Richter. You know Mr. Donlan, of course. Now, where's my painting?"

"It's safe," Standard stopped ten feet away, Strasser in front of him, Richter and Itchy five paces off to the right.

"You said you would bring it."

"Not really. I need to know a few things first."

When Strasser looked toward Richter and nodded, Richter

pulled a pistol from the waistband of his pants and put the muzzle to Itchy's head. Even with a bag over his head, Itchy seemed to know immediately what it was. His screams were muffled, loud enough for Standard to hear but not understand. Not that he needed to.

When Itchy's screams began to sound more like begging, Standard's guilt for getting the little man involved grew even larger. All he wanted to do was put a little money in Itchy's pocket to help him get by for a few weeks. Now Itchy had a gun to his head and was pleading for his life.

"What is more important to you?" Strasser said. He had the smug look of someone who thinks he's holding all the cards. "My painting or your friend's life?"

If Standard wasn't pissed off before, he was now thanks to Strasser's arrogance. He'd just met the guy, and he already hated him. Some people just do that.

"Do you really plan on paying for that painting?" Standard said.

"Of course, I do. Why would you say that? Give me the painting and Mrs. Nazareth will get her money."

"Six people are dead and your lackey over there is holding a gun to my friend's head. Doesn't exactly inspire confidence in your honesty."

"Six?" Strasser's surprised look was weak and unconvincing. "I know of only one, Simon Nazareth, and I had nothing to do with that. Why would I? If he were still alive, we wouldn't be standing here. If you believe Mrs. Nazareth then it was Dragovitch responsible for her husband's death, not me. Besides, Dragovitch isn't here. He's in Havana, but maybe headed this way."

"Fine. That leaves five others. My guess is that your lackey over there killed them on your orders. They wanted the painting. So did you. Now they're dead and here we are. Am I right?"

"I don't need to explain anything to you. Give me the painting or your friend dies."

"If you want the painting, then tell me the truth."

"Let's say that sometimes the art world can be ugly and leave it at that," Strasser said. "Now, the painting?"

"Fine. So, here's what we're going to do. Let Itchy go, and I won't tell the police that you probably had a hand in the deaths of five people. I could make a pretty good case that they were competitors trying to outbid you for the Raphael. I'm fairly familiar with the police here. They may not believe me, but I think I can convince them that you and your boy make plausible suspects. Since they don't have any, they'll take just about whoever they can get their hands on to clear the books. At the least, they'll bring you in. Question you. Throw you and your man in jail for a few days. Let you sit in a dark cell with rats and roaches while they impound your yacht. After that word gets out that the baron of beef and his side dish are in jail on suspicion of murder. That won't be a pretty picture."

Standard looked at Strasser for some kind of reaction. All he got was an icy stare.

"They'll probably put a couple of men on board your yacht just to be safe. Can you imagine what two underpaid cops would do aboard a luxury yacht like yours? My guess is that your boat has a wine cellar, a few paintings, and a bunch of laptops. Probably a freezer full of steaks. You can kiss all that goodbye. By the time you get out of jail your little boat will be stripped and covered in pelican shit. Another ugly picture."

"Sounds to me like you've chosen the painting over your friend," Strasser said. "Regrettable. I've sort of enjoyed our short time together. He has told me a lot about you, your partnership, and the adventures you've had together. He made this boring shithole town sound like it might be more exciting than it looks."

"This isn't getting us any closer to what I need," Standard said. "Your boy Heinz turns himself in, admits to the killings, and you get the painting. Simple as that."

Strasser didn't say anything for a few seconds, then turned toward Richter. "This is a waste of time. Shoot him, Heinz, and then let's get out of here." He looked back at Standard. "I'll deal with you later, Mr. Standard. I don't lose."

Just as Itchy gave out another muffled scream, Standard pointed over Strasser's shoulder. "You might want to rethink that."

Special Ed stood at the end of the pier, the flying bridge of the *Tuna Warrior* rising behind him. He looked every bit like a washed-up pirate: baggy shorts, a sweat-stained shirt, do-rag around his head, and a black patch over his left eye. The shotgun against his shoulder was pointed at Strasser.

"If anybody is doing any shooting around here, it's me," Ed said.

Ed swung the gun around to point at Richter. "Let him go," he said. Richter pressed his gun harder against Itchy's head. "I wouldn't do that, blondie. I've known Itchy Donlan for five years. Believe me, he is not worth dying over. Now, do what I told you. Let him go."

Richter looked at Strasser, who waited a few seconds then nodded. When Richter pulled the gun away, Itchy stumbled forward and collapsed on the cement deck and did his best to crawl away.

"Now, lose the gun and kick it over here."

When Richter got another nod from Strasser. He dropped the gun and used his foot to slide it toward Ed.

Strasser glared at Ed then turned to face Standard again. "I was warned that you are a resourceful and clever man and that

I should treat you with caution, Mr. Standard. I didn't take that warning seriously enough."

"It's happened before."

"It won't happen again, at least not by me. That painting is mine. You have no right to it."

"You know my terms. Richter for the Raphael."

"I'm afraid that's impossible. What is possible is that you name a price, I pay it, and you give me the painting."

"Fuck your money."

"Don't you want to know what I'm willing to pay you?"

"No. It's Richter or nothing."

"You can't prove any of this. You're bluffing."

"I don't need proof if Richter turns himself in and confesses."

Standard waited for Strasser's answer. Not getting one, he nodded to Ed.

"Okay, party over," Ed said, bending down to pick up Richter's pistol and putting it in his waistband. "Now it's time to go, and I would hurry." He held up his cell phone, the timer visible on the screen. "While you were here chatting, I cruised by your yacht and put a bomb on the fan tail. As soon as I press start, you have fifteen minutes to get back there and disarm it. I think throwing it in the bay is the best bet. If you don't make it, well, sorry." He pressed the timer's start button. "Tick tock. Véncelo. Off with both of you."

Strasser and Richter looked at each other, then ran toward the stairway leading down to the dock. Standard and Ed moved to the edge of the pier to watch the Zodiac roar away, zigzagging at high speed through anchored sailboats toward the *El Obra Maestro.*

"Thanks for coming," Standard said.

"You had me at Germans. Not a fan. Bad food. Warm beer. Ugly history. Besides, this is the kind of party I had in mind."

"Did you really put a bomb on the yacht?" Standard asked.

"Fuck no! I filled an old backpack with wires, a handful of dead batteries, a broken cell phone, and some toilet paper rolls. One look inside, and if they heard me, they'll throw it over the side."

Standard shook his head and smiled. "You know you just pissed off one of the ten richest men in the world."

"Whoever said the rich don't suffer. Besides, I used to be on that list. It's no big deal. It's not about the money. It's more about keeping score."

"So, you were really that rich?"

"Yeah, but don't tell anyone. It ruins the image."

They both laughed then walked across the pier to untie Itchy and pull the bag off his head. He coughed, sputtered, and complained about why it took them so long. The left side of his face was covered in bruises and blood seeped from a cut lip. "I couldn't tell if those Nazis were going to fuck me or each other." He rubbed his wrists, ran his hand through his hair, and gently probed his damaged face. "This is getting out of hand, John. Did someone call the police? Kidnapping is a crime, even in Mexico. I think."

They propped Itchy up on a bench. Ed handed him a flask that Itchy eagerly grabbed and took a long swig.

"What did Strasser want?" Standard asked.

"You. Who else?" Itchy said, taking a second drink. "You heard him. He wants that damn painting, and he knows you have it. He asked me where you live. I told him I didn't know, which is the truth. It's not like you've ever had me over for dinner. What really pisses me off is that if Strasser killed Nazareth then he's the reason we're out twenty grand each. I'm not going to forget that. The fucker."

"You heard him. He said he had nothing to do with Nazareth's death."

"You believe him?"

"It makes sense."

"After spending twenty-four hours with that bastard, I wouldn't believe anything he said."

Ed and Standard talked about what to do with Itchy, deciding that sending him home might not be the best idea. Strasser already knew where Itchy lived and might take him again out of spite for what just happened. Finally, Ed agreed to let Itchy stay on the *Tuna Warrior* for the night and send him home in the morning.

"I'll track down his girlfriend in Ixtapa," Standard said. "Maybe he can stay with her until this gets settled."

"This painting," Ed said. "Must be pretty important. What's it worth?"

"Not sure exactly. Probably three hundred million for starters."

Ed whistled. "So, now what?"

"Good question."

"You sure Strasser and that other guy had something to do with those murders?"

"Who else? They all had something to do with buying or selling art, and the Raphael is the only thing in town they would be interested in."

"But no proof?"

"Not yet."

Ed pulled Richter's pistol out of his waistband and handed it to Standard, holding it by the trigger guard. "Maybe this might help. Just be careful. Richter's fingerprints might come in handy."

CHAPTER 38

The next morning, Emma left early to meet with a realtor who specialized in properties in Troncones. The night before, he'd told her what had happened at the City Pier. All she did was shake her head and go to bed, mumbling something about Standard and a death wish. She didn't bring it up when they got out of bed the next morning. Neither did he.

When she was gone, Standard stood in the front room, drinking coffee and staring out at the bay at *El Obra Maestro*. Pangas swerved around it. Kids on jet skis circled it like hungry sharks. He imagined Carlos Strasser sitting in luxury, looking at his paintings and brooding over his previous night's humiliation and plotting revenge.

Threatening to sic the police on Strasser was a calculated bluff that worked when it needed to. It wouldn't hold up for long, and not at all if Vega wouldn't be willing to haul Strasser and Richter in for questioning. Standard wasn't ruling it out, but the chances were slim. Vega going face to face with a multi-billionaire. Standard could pretty much figure out how that would end up: another contribution to Vega's retirement account.

Then there was the pistol Ed took off Richter. It could be the murder weapon, but that would require matching bullets from the gun with ones found in the victims. Not sure what a Mexican ballistics test looked like, he decided to hang on to it for the time being.

Standard got dressed, walked down the hill, and got a taxi into town. On the way, he called Special Ed to see how Itchy was doing.

"Still asleep," Ed said. "He drank everything except the bilge water and passed out. Can't blame him. He's pretty beat up. I think he was afraid things were going to get worse. And not just threats in exchange for information about you and where you are. At one point, he thought Strasser and his buddy were going to pull out the thumb screws. He figured he was a dead man. Pretty grateful for being rescued, though. I haven't been thanked that much since my days handing out six-figure employee bonuses."

When they agreed to keep Itchy on the *Tuna Warrior* until he feels up to leaving, Standard hung up and sat back in the seat. Maybe Emma was right: Give Strasser the painting, let him and Mai Nazareth work out the payment, and he could get out of the middle of it.

Then again, maybe not. That would mean leaving everything in Vega's hands. Since he doesn't know about the Raphael, there was no way the comandante could figure things out on his own. He could tell Vega about the painting, but that could lead to telling him where it was. That wouldn't work. At least not yet.

He had the taxi drop him off at the Central Mercado where he had breakfast at a food stall called Fonda Irma. While eating *huevos rancheros* and drinking coffee, he called Adam Jones.

"You still interested in Drago Dragovitch?" Standard asked.

"Always," Jones said.

Standard could hear the sound of scraping in the background, which meant Jones was in a *pulqueria* somewhere getting his head shaved. "He's in Havana but might be headed here."

"How do you know that?"

"I had a meeting with Carlos Strasser last night. He let it slip."

"Thanks. I'll pass it on. Strasser? How did that go?"

"Jury is still out. I'll let you know."

Standard hung up, finished his breakfast, then headed through town toward the bay front. Along the way, he stopped at a liquor store for a bottle of high-end, boutique tequila that came in a hand-blown and numbered crystal bottle. Six blocks later he was back at the City Pier. He walked down the same stairs Strasser and company had used the previous night. He boarded a waiting panga and paid the ten-peso price for a trip across the bay to *Playa Las Gatas*.

It looked as if Don Pedro Serrano hadn't moved since the last time Standard was there. He sat in his Adirondack chair, sketchbook on his lap, gazing out at the bay. He stood up to greet Standard and offered him a chair.

"I brought you this as a way of saying thank you for your help with the painting," Standard said, handing Serrano the tequila.

"Wow," Serrano said, looking at the label and smiling. "I've heard of this brand. Very ... boutique-ish. Shall we try it?"

"A little early for me."

"You're right. Some other time. Coffee would be more in order. I'll be right back."

While Serrano was gone, Standard looked at the *El Obra Maestro* moored less than two hundred yards away. What would Strasser think if he knew the painting he so passionately coveted was so close?

"Here to check on the Raphael?" Serrano asked, handing Standard a cup of coffee. His houseboy, Esteban, stood behind him holding a plate of pastries.

"Only to find out if it's real." Standard took the coffee and a chocolate croissant then sat down.

Serrano sipped his coffee, seeming to choose his words carefully. "I believe it is. Hand-ground pigments in a solution of oil. You can still detect tiny notes of linseed. And the species of wood panel does appear to be poplar. The soft, luminescent style also mirrors that of Raphael. Unfortunately, I can't be positive without seeing the provenance. I assume Ms. Nazareth has it."

"I need to bring you up to date," Standard said, then told Serrano what had happened the previous night on the City Pier. "Strasser only asked for the painting. Not the proof it's real."

"Mr. Strasser is a true believer. Proof is for everybody else."

"Mai Nazareth and I are not on great terms these days. Getting the provenance from her is probably not in the cards."

"It's not imperative, but if you want to be sure."

Standard nodded. "Let me figure something out. I have other business with her."

"Do you have any plans for the Raphael?" Serrano asked after Esteban came out to pour more coffee. "I don't mind keeping it here. In fact, it is something of a privilege. But based on what you have told me and what has happened in the past, keeping it here comes with a certain amount of risk."

"Plans? Sort of. There's the easy way and there's the hard way."

Serrano smiled. "Something tells me you're going to take the hard way."

CHAPTER 39

MAI NAZARETH COULD DO LITTLE MORE THAN PACE BACK
and forth across the living room of the penthouse at VistaPacifica. Trying not to start drinking until at least midafternoon was
taxing her rapidly eroding self-discipline. Nothing had worked
out as planned and she had no idea how to set things right
again.

A priceless painting was missing. The buyer was threatening everything from a lawsuit to torture. The painting's
owners were livid. And worst of all, her husband had been
killed in the penthouse next to hers.

She shared a wall with a crime scene.

The deal that would net her somewhere around sixty-
million dollars was teetering on the brink of collapse. Her and
Simon's dream of spending the rest of their days in a seaside
villa in Majorca was in shatters. Now, everything was in the
hands of John Standard, a man she barely knew but who
seemed to know what he was doing, not that he shared it with
anybody. She only knew that he had no intention of returning
the painting until he got answers from Strasser.

"Good luck with that," she muttered.

Her one meeting with Strasser told her that he was not the negotiating type, particularly when it came to *Portrait of a Young Woman*. The emails and text messages she'd received from him over the last few months focused on one thing: The Raphael. Everything else was at times incoherent and incomprehensible. She wrote it off as a fanatic with a lot of money.

The look on his face when he learned that her husband was dead, and the painting was missing still scared the hell out of her.

"What a shit show," she said, then headed for the bar at the far end of the room. Since it was early, maybe a Bloody Mary would make a good compromise. It really wasn't a drink. More of a breakfast condiment with a peperoncino. Throw in some celery and a couple of olives and it qualified as a salad. Not that it mattered. Drinking wasn't going to bring Simon back to life or make the painting magically appear.

She had been around the art world all her life. Her mother was a successful artist, painting delicate watercolors of koi ponds and lotus flowers in the garden of their Hong Kong home. They were mostly gifts for her friends, but she sold enough to small collectors to earn a decent income. Her father owned an art gallery in Hong Kong, specializing in jade carvings, Chinese vases, and intricate landscapes. She went to art school in Paris, lived in the French Quarter, and toyed with becoming an actress or a model. In the end, she decided to stay with what she knew best and loved the most, eventually moving to New York and opening a small gallery in Soho.

She met Simon when he came to one of her showings of paintings by new, young artists. He was charming, smart, and knew the art world better than she did. Her friends thought it was an odd match. He was twenty years older than her and a little eccentric and a lot overweight. She married him after deciding that prospects trumped appearance. They joined forces and within two years the business exploded, and they added another gallery in London.

Nowhere on that ten-year journey did the word murder ever come up. Now, if that fat police chief is to be believed, six people with some connection to the art world were dead. At least he didn't know about *Portrait of a Young Woman.* She had Standard to thank for that.

Standard had told her not to talk about the painting. Agreeing meant putting all her trust in him that it was safe. Only she was beginning to have her doubts. There was too much at stake, including millions of dollars and a few reputations, including hers. With Simon dead, it was now all on her.

Every time she thought about the painting it brought back memories of Simon and their time together. He satisfied her in ways other men couldn't. Loving. Trusting. Smart. While she knew art, Simon knew how to make money selling it. Their shared love of art and money far outweighed the difference in their ages, education, and background. If he knew about her brief and forgettable affairs, he never mentioned it and never let them get in the way of his expressions of love and devotion.

She remembered how excited Simon was when the Bergens called to tell him about the painting and ask for his help proving it was real. It was one of those moments when preparation meets opportunity. Simon may have been forgetful and absent-minded at times, but he would never miss a chance to succeed on an international level. He threw all his energy into it—finding experts to restore and inspect the painting, gathering the provenance, urging the Bergens to be patient. He had taken care of everything, then, on the verge of the biggest payday either one of them could ever imagine, he was killed. For his sake, and for hers, she had to complete the deal. Their dream of Majorca could still be within reach, just not with poor Simon.

In her mind, a twenty percent fee for selling a painting worth hundreds of millions made grief an inconvenient emotion.

She shook thoughts of Simon out of her head. She would mourn him later in her own way. For now, she was in charge. Pick up the pieces and take care of business. First and foremost being the Raphael.

Her only regret is that they didn't find someone other than Strasser to sell the painting to. She wished she knew then what she knows about him now.

There were other offers, but Strasser's was not something they or the Bergens could say no to. Her brief meeting with the multi-billionaire confirmed everything she had learned about him. The threats he made after learning the Raphael was missing scared her to death. And if Strasser wasn't horrifying enough, there was the man he called his "accountant," Heinz something. He looked bloodless, pale but not albino, menacing.

To make matters worse, she'd received two more emails from Drago Dragovich. The Russian oligarch turned gangster insisted that he could outbid anyone for the Raphael. She knew that wasn't true but continuing to ignore him was risky. His emails were becoming more and more threatening, and they weren't going to stop if he thought she had the Raphael.

Which she didn't.

If she could get it back, she could give it to Strasser, collect the money, and get out of town. Once that was done, if Dragovich still wanted it he could deal with Strasser, and she would be rid of both of them. The only thing standing in the way of making all that happen was John Standard.

Standard fascinated her. He was an easy man to like but a hard one to figure out. He inspired both confidence and confusion. Why would he put himself in the middle of all this? Sure, people were dead, but what did that have to do with him? Maybe he had a warped sense of justice that was missing in most people. Maybe he liked playing cat and mouse with the super-rich, risking his own life in exchange for a little amusement. Whatever it was, it made no sense to her.

Then there was that funny, little friend of his. Ozzie. Ollie. Something like that. What an odd couple. On the drive in from the airport, all she could figure out was that Ozzie did whatever Standard told him, and Standard did everything he could to keep the little man from going over the edge.

She finished the Bloody Mary, mixed a second one, and took it across the room to sit on the couch to look out at the ocean and the haystack-shaped rocks in the distance. A few boats bobbed on the gentle swells a mile offshore. Further north, large pleasure boats shaped like Clorox bottles headed toward the entrance to the marina.

A few days ago, Standard knew nothing about Raphael, his painting, or what it was worth. Now, he's got it stashed away and won't tell her where it is. He had become some sort of sun-soaked amateur gumshoe trying to solve murders of people he didn't know, including her husband's, all the while keeping the police in the dark and hoarding a priceless piece of art. Not exactly Charlie Chan, she thought, but just as inscrutable.

Money. Maybe that's what Standard was after and this talk about finding a killer was just that—talk. If that was the case, fine. There was plenty of money to go around. Before he died, Simon told her in an email that he promised Standard and his friend twenty thousand dollars each for bringing her and the Raphael from the airport to the hotel. She would happily pay that. He just had to return the painting.

She found her cell phone on the coffee table and called Standard. When he didn't answer, she left a message asking him to come and see her. Halfway through her second drink, he called back.

"I think we should meet and discuss how to resolve all of this in a manner that is satisfactory to everyone," she said. "Would you be willing to come to my hotel around, say, one p.m.? We could have lunch in my room and work this out."

When he agreed, she thanked him, hung up, and called the hotel manager. "I need to cash a forty-thousand-dollar check. I'll need the money in U.S. dollars. Can you handle that? Good. I'll be down in a couple of hours. Please have the money ready."

CHAPTER 40

Not even a half-bottle of eighteen-year-old The Macallan could wipe away the humiliation. The scene on the City Pier would stay with him forever. He knew it. He could feel it. Never in Carlos Strasser's life had he been treated that way. He was wealthy, educated, privileged. He deserved respect and deference. Being humiliated by some kicked-up beach bum that he could buy and sell a billion times over would not stand.

Reliving what happened kept him awake all night plotting ways to get revenge, to show John Standard that he was not someone to be taken lightly, and to get the Raphael. He kept coming back to the same answer: After ordering the deaths of five people, what's one more?

For a brief moment, he thought that if killing John Standard meant losing *Portrait of a Young Woman*, then goodbye Raphael. The moment passed quickly. It wouldn't work. Standard was the only one who knew the location of the painting. Killing him might mean losing it forever. There were other means of getting information out of Standard, but something told Strasser that finding him wouldn't be easy. Neither would be getting him to talk. Standard knew the territory; Strasser didn't. Heinz had been in Zihuatanejo long enough to get a lay of the land but never enough to match Standard.

Now, seeing Standard in action, gave Strasser a certain grudging respect for him. The report he'd gotten from his office in Johannesburg included warnings not to underestimate Standard. He had not taken them seriously. Why would he? He was one of the richest men in the world. Who was Standard? No one. A man laid low by his own mistakes, living a life of sun and beer in the middle of nowhere.

The humiliation on the pier had cost him a chance to get his hands on the painting. He would be smarter next time and more ruthless.

Strasser spun around in his office chair, admiring all the technology at his fingertips and how it kept him up to date on a conglomerate that circled the globe and the world events that affected his businesses. Satellites, servers, computers, televisions linked to every news organization in the world. A constant stream of information on world markets and international relations. Yet, here he was, stuck in a backwater Mexican bay, being held hostage by someone who probably didn't know a Raphael from a Grandma Moses.

The whole idea of it made him do more damage to The Macallan.

He thought about calling in reinforcements. Heinz was the pointy end of Strasser's arsenal, but he had other weapons. He could fill the town with more like Heinz, some worse, each with orders to find the painting. In the end, though, he decided against it. It would take days for them to get there and even longer to get the lay of the land and up to speed on what needed to be done. For now, he had to rely on Heinz.

It wasn't a bad choice. Heinz was brutal and remorseless.

The product of German military engineering. Aloof, stoic, and totally without a conscience. Strasser never knew if Heinz even thought that what he was doing was wrong or the consequences. If he did, Strasser had never seen it. Heinz just did whatever needed to be done. He had been that way ever since Strasser hired him away from the security company. Strasser purposely avoided knowing the details of how Heinz did away with those who tried to outbid him for the Raphael. What he did know, gave him newfound respect for his longtime enforcer. Heinz had gotten him this far. The best path forward was to turn Heinz loose once again. He picked up the phone and dialed.

"Last night was a travesty. We can't let it pass."

"I know," Heinz said.

"Learn all you can about Standard today, then we'll talk tonight."

Strasser hung up and called Blessing Sbuso in Johannesburg. "Thank you for your earlier report on John Standard and Dragovitch. It was extremely helpful. Have you learned anything more? I'm particularly interested in where Mr. Standard lives."

"I'm afraid not, sir," Sbuso said. "He's a bit of a mystery man. He doesn't have a computer that we can find. No email address or social media presence. All we learned from a search of his phone is that all his calls are from Zihuantanejo, Mexico. But I believe you already know that."

"What numbers has he called?"

"We've managed to track some of them, but we're not sure who they are."

"Names?"

Strasser waited while listening to Blessing tap her keyboard. "There are four frequent calls. One to a deep-sea fishing charter service, but not one with a website or any kind of advertising that we can find. When we called the number, a man answered, said he was busy, and to call back in a week. One is to a Richard Donlan in Zihuatanejo. Like Standard, he is off the grid. Just a phone and no address. One is to Benjamin Orlando in Portland, Oregon. I believe we mentioned him in our report as Standard's former landlord."

"And the fourth?"

"Emma Parrish in Zihuantanejo."

"Thank you, Blessing." Strasser hung up and called Heinz again. "I have another name for you."

CHAPTER 41

MAI NAZARETH SAT IN THE CORNER OF THE COUCH, HER arms crossed, a defiant look on her face. She wore a white pantsuit with gold trim and rhinestone-encrusted sandals. A large pair of sunglasses sat embedded in long black hair pulled back into a ponytail tight enough to show off her almond eyes and diamond earrings.

None of it was lost on John Standard. The attitude, the clothes, and the look were of somebody determined to get what she wanted. The meeting had been her idea but without mentioning what she wanted to talk about. Even before sitting down with her, he was sure what it was. He was right.

"I need that painting, Mr. Standard. This started out as a large but simple transaction. A painting and money. Now it's become a matter of life or death. If you had met Carlos Strasser face-to-face like I did, you would understand."

"I know Strasser," Standard said but stopped short of giving her a full description of what happened the previous night. "I think he wants the painting but doesn't want to pay for it."

"You really believe that? You can't be right."

"Even to a guy like Strasser, three hundred million or more is still a lot of money. Why would he pay hundreds of millions for it if he thought there was a way to get it for free."

"But he came here with his accountant and a laptop ready to transfer the money to our account."

"That was when he thought your husband was still alive, and that was not his accountant. That's his enforcer, his pit bull. Heinz is the gun. Strasser is the trigger. I figure them for at least five deaths. What happened last night just plain pissed me off."

She stood up and walked toward the bar. "Drink, Mr. Standard?"

"I'll pass."

He watched as she made what looked like a gin and tonic that was light on the tonic. "What do you propose?" she asked, tasting her drink then adding more gin.

"None of this is your fault, Mrs. Nazareth. Strasser knows that. His beef is with me. He's already threatened one of my friends. My guess is that he'll keep threatening or worse until he gets what he wants."

"The Raphael without paying?"

"Exactly."

"Let me make you an offer, Mr. Standard. I have the forty-thousand dollars my husband was going to pay you and your friend. I will give it to you right now if you'll return the painting and let me deal with Strasser. That gets you out of the middle and keeps your friends out of any further danger."

Standard intended to bring up the money he and Itchy were owed. That she brought it up instead surprised him. Taking the money, returning the painting, and walking away was tempting. Twenty thousand would go a long way in helping Emma with her desire to move to Troncones. Any risk-averse person with common sense would agree. He was neither of those things.

"Seems like everyone wants to get me out of this," Standard said. "That's my call, and I'm not ready to make it. Last night on the pier, he all but admitted that he ordered the deaths of those five men. I need to figure the rest out."

"What about your friends?"

"I'll take care of them."

"And the money?"

"I'll take twenty thousand and give it to Itchy," he said. "You can keep my share until I'm done with Strasser."

Mai Nazareth looked surprised. "Done?"

"Strasser is a killer who kidnapped and threatened one of my friends. I'm not going to let that go."

"Isn't that something for the police?"

"What have they told you about your husband's murder?" She looked chagrined, then shook her head. "Nothing."

"Enough said. I'll tell the police what I know when I know something, or I have no other choice. Until then, they can bumble around all they like trying to look busy when what they really want is to protect the tourism business."

"You're a complicated man, Mr. Standard."

"I've been called worse."

"I don't doubt it." She stood up and walked to the bedroom. She came back with a fat envelope. "Here's your friend's money. I'll keep the rest until you come to your senses and return the painting."

Standard put the envelope in his backpack and left. On the ride down the elevator, he called Itchy Donlan. "Where are you?"

"Ed's boat."

"Meet me at Mango's in an hour."

When Standard reached the lobby, he asked the woman at

the front desk to call Marie Mitchell's room. When she didn't answer, he walked out to one of the three swimming pools. He found her sitting under a large umbrella, a towel across her legs, and watching children frolic and yell "Marco Polo" over and over again in the pool a few feet away.

"Ms. Mitchell. John Standard. We need to talk."

She gave him a blank look, as if unsure who he was or why he wanted to talk to her. Gradually she came around. "Of course. Please sit down. What can I do for you?"

"I need a favor. Itchy's run into a little bit of trouble." Standard tried giving her a highly sanitized version of what happened the previous night, but even with what little he explained, the more horrified she looked. "The short of it is that he can't go home yet. I was hoping he could stay here with you. I don't think it will be more than a few days."

Marie Mitchell's reaction was less than enthusiastic, which made Standard think that she, like the long string of others before her, had grown tired of Itchy's freeloading and Irish blarney.

"He took some money from me," she said.

"I'll make sure he pays it back ... with interest. He's in danger, Ms. Mitchell. I really need your help."

When she finally relented, Standard thanked her and left. He got a taxi outside the hotel for the ride to Mango's.

CHAPTER 42

STANDARD WAS SITTING AT THE BAR AT MANGO'S DRINKING a beer and eating from a small bowl of salty nuts when Itchy Donlan suddenly popped up out of nowhere.

He grabbed Standard's shirt sleeve and pulled him to a small corner table away from the bar and restaurant. He was nervous and sweaty, his eyes, feral like, kept darting over Standard's shoulder. The bruises on his face an angry purple. His cut lip a bloody scab. He seemed to be having a hard time shaking the effects of what happened to him on Strasser's yacht. Standard couldn't blame him. Whatever happened to Itchy in the past was nothing compared to being kidnapped, beaten, and tied up with a gun to his head.

"Do you think Strasser and that guy are still after me?" he said, his voice higher than normal and stressed. "I've had this feeling all day that someone was following me. I must have looked over my shoulder a thousand times. Man, my neck."

"I doubt that, but we need to be sure." When Itchy gave him a confused look, Standard explained that going back to his house might not be the best idea.

"What about Yolanda? She's at the house."

"I'll square things with her. But don't worry. She'll be fine. She's not involved in this. Neither Strasser nor anyone else needs to bother her. You're safe now because he knows you don't have the painting or know where it is. Also, Yolanda never knows where you are anyway. You need to stay with Marie until this is over. You also need to repay any money you stole from her and help her with her hotel bill."

"How do I do that?"

Standard reached into his backpack, pulled out the envelope, and slid it across the table. "There's your fee for the airport trip."

Stunned, Itchy grabbed the envelope, then thumbed through the bills inside. "Twenty K? All of it? John, how did you ...?"

"Mai Nazareth. She knows when a deal is a deal. Now, get out of here. Take a taxi to Ixtapa and stay with Marie. I've already talked to her. She's good with it. Don't stop anywhere. Do as I say. You don't want another visit to Strasser's yacht. So, stay out of sight as much as you can until you hear from me. As for the money, you're an accountant. You can figure out tomorrow what to do with it."

Itchy didn't have to say thanks. The look on his face said it and more.

"One more thing, Itchy. Did you tell Strasser about Emma? Does he know I have a girlfriend?"

"No. No. No. He asked, but I lied. It was the only thing I lied about. I told him you played the field, made up stories about the two of us cruising the discos in Ixtapa picking up girls. He bought it all. I'm sure of it."

"Okay, thanks for that. I'm sorry what happened to you. I didn't see that coming. I should have."

"It's okay. Over and done." Itchy held up the envelope. "John, I don't know what to say."

"Nothing to say. You made the deal, and you earned the money. Now, get out of here." Standard thought Itchy left out a back door before he started crying.

Standard went back to the bar, sipped his beer, and stared across at the regulars with their Margaritas and Mojitos, oblivious to what was going on or that six people were dead. If only he could be so lucky. They didn't care. He did.

It was easy to figure out Strasser's next moves. Grabbing Itchy was just the start. He was low-hanging fruit: Easy to find and intimidate. He just didn't know anything. But who was next? Standard knew he was on the list, but there were others. No way Strasser knew about Special Ed, other than he was some guy dressed like a pirate and holding a shotgun. Same story with Emma, although thinking that he might be wrong sent shivers through him. He believed Itchy about not telling Strasser, but there may be other ways to learn about her and where they lived.

It was time to take precautions.

Standard left Mango's and walked the few blocks to the Artisan Market and Yolanda's stall. He told her a made-up story that he'd needed Itchy's help with a business matter out of town, that he'd be back in a few days, and not to worry. He gave her two hundred pesos and said it was from Itchy.

He walked across the street to a bar called Banditos, ordered a beer, and called Arturo. By the time he finished drinking, Arturo was outside waiting for him.

"Where to, Señor Juan?" Arturo was dressed in his usual pressed white shirt and pants, hair combed, dress shoes shiny. Inside, the taxi was clean and smelled of a cologne that Standard didn't recognize.

"Home, Arturo."

The taxi wound through town, took a right at Kyoto Circle, then along the road to *Playa la Ropa*. Standard made the same trip hundreds of times, but never got tired of it. The hustle and bustle of downtown Zihuatanejo gradually gave way to something calmer and more soothing. Knowing Emma was waiting for him gave him both a sense of comfort and concern.

He had put Emma through a lot in the last two years, so much that sometimes he wondered why she stayed with him. That she did only added to his feelings about her. He had promised himself to protect her if anything else were to happen. He sensed that this was one of those times.

"Stay loose tomorrow or the next day, Arturo," Standard said. "We may need you."

"Of course. I am always ready to take Señora Parrish anywhere she wants to go. Oh, and you too, Señor Juan."

CHAPTER 43

⤬

Mornings were the best time of day in Zihuatanejo. With the sun still behind the mountains to the east, the fragrance of bougainvillea and frangipani filled the cool air. Magpie jays skimmed the tops of the trees on their way to the cliffs overlooking the ocean. Red-butted squirrels scurried from tree to tree in their relentless and mysterious search for food. Something unseen continued to move through the dry leaves next to the fence surrounding the property. Then there was always the occasional boa constrictor hanging from the low branches of a madrone tree. Emma tolerated them because they kept the rat population under control.

Standard wasn't so sure.

The smell of fresh-brewed coffee filled the house along with the sound of Emma in the kitchen heating up pastries she'd bought the day before at the Central Mercado. She wore a thin silk robe and flip-flops, her hair still mussed from a night's sleep. Just watching her made Standard even more sure that he needed to do something to get her—and him—out of harm's way, at least for a while. He felt that Strasser could be unpredictable, especially after his humiliation at the City Pier.

Best to make things as difficult for him as possible.

"I have an idea," he said, going into the kitchen and leaning against the counter.

"If it's the same idea you had last night, you're going to have to wait. I haven't had my second cup of coffee." She said it with a suggestive smile.

"I think we should go back to Troncones, spend a few days, and see if we like it. You know, get a feel for what it would be like to live there. What do you think?"

She walked over and put her arms around his neck. "A few days, huh? Maybe you're starting to like this idea of moving."

"Change is good, most of the time."

"Then let's do it."

While Emma called her realtor friend for help finding a place to stay, Standard phoned Arturo, telling him to meet them at the turnaround at the bottom of the hill for a ride to Ixtapa to get *El Furioso*.

"Road trip, Señor Juan? Acapulco maybe? Tosco?"

"Just to Troncones for a few days."

Despite Arturo's insistence that they didn't need the Plymouth because he would happily drive them to Troncones, Emma said no. She loved driving *El Furioso*, and besides, it needed some more highway time, and she wanted the freedom to leave when they wanted. As usual, she won the argument.

By the time they packed, got the Plymouth, and headed north, it was midafternoon before they reached Troncones. This time there was no truckload of chickens or busloads of happy school kids. Just a couple of pickup trucks and a few taxis. Once clear of them, Emma boosted the speed to something over sixty, which was about max for Mexican roads. She slowed for a couple of makeshift speed bumps before turning west on the road into town.

The place Emma's realtor found was a spacious, decked-out two-story, beachfront condo on the north end of town. One room upstairs, one down. Both empty. The manager met them as soon as they drove up. Glad for some business, he eagerly gave them a choice of rooms. They took the one upstairs, thinking it would be quieter. It had a king-sized bed, a small kitchen, walk-in shower, and rustic couch and chairs. A wide terrace overlooked a large swimming pool surrounded by lounge chairs, tables, umbrellas, and Tiki torches. In the distance, waves crashing on the beach added some soothing background noise.

"Maybe we could buy this place," Emma said, looking around. "Live on both levels. What do you think?"

"Could be. Not sure it's for sale. We can ask, but let's look around some more tomorrow."

As the sun was setting, they walked four blocks down the street to a dark, cozy restaurant with a menu that was a cut above the usual grilled shrimp, rice, and salad. Standard ordered *chili rellenos*. Emma went with the grilled lobster. They washed it down with a wine from California rather than the usual from Chile.

"At least there's one good restaurant in town," Emma said. "That's a point in its favor."

Standard nodded in agreement. The more he came here, the more the place grew on him. Quieter. Calmer. Different vibe. But how would he feel living here permanently?

"Coming here for a few days was a great idea," Emma said, "but what about Strasser and the painting?"

The day before he'd given Emma a blow-by-blow description of what happened that night on the City Pier, she took it in stride. It wasn't the first late-night adventure Standard had taken and she knew it wouldn't be the last. That was life with John Standard. He was sure she would bring it up again, but fine if she decided not to.

"Strasser can wait. Let him cool off. He's probably still pissed about what happened. In time, he'll get over it. In the meantime, the painting is safe."

"We're not here just to look at property, are we?" Emma said.

No way of getting anything by her. Standard explained his fears that by not getting what he wanted from Itchy Donlan, Strasser might start working his way up the food chain.

"You mean me first, you next?"

"Something like that, but there's nothing to worry about. I just need time to figure out what to do. Staying here for a few days gives me ... us ... some breathing room."

"Maybe another Margarita will provide some inspiration."

On the walk home they stopped at a tienda a block from their condo for eggs, orange juice, and more pastries for a quick breakfast the next morning. Later, they sat on the terrace watching the waves in the distance. Lit tiki torches surrounding the pool flickered in a light breeze off the ocean. He ran through all the possibilities of what could happen next. There were more bad things than good.

The feeling that he'd overplayed his hand came creeping back. They were safe here, he thought, but they couldn't stay forever. At least not yet.

CHAPTER 44

Finding Itchy Donlan had been easy. A few bars, a bunch of waiters and waitresses, and a few jokes gave him most of what he needed to know. Heinz was finding Emma Parrish to be more of a challenge.

During his time in Zihuatanejo, Heinz Richter had done his best to learn about the area of town known as El Centro, the city center. A place where even the most circumspect tourist could feel safe, providing they could find their way around. He saw it as a confusing set of streets with narrow, crowded sidewalks that all looked alike, each lined with bars, restaurants, tiendas, and shops selling beachwear, sunglasses, and cell phones. There were small open-air meat, fruit, and vegetable markets mixed in with a scattering of auto repair garages, welding shops, and *lavados de autos*. There were no McDonald's, Starbucks, or Chevron stations.

The chain stores sold, well, chains: gold and silver with circular clasps and a crucifix. Over time, he'd come to use restaurants as landmarks to remind him which street he was on and where it was in relation to the Central Mercado, the hub of Zihuantanejo life.

In his search for Emma Parrish, he stopped at bars and restaurants for a drink at one, something to eat at another. Each time he asked about her, waiters and bartenders clammed up, shook their heads, or just walked away. Others asked questions that he didn't want to answer, such as "Why do you want to know?" Some said they'd heard her name but that was all. It was like she had some mysterious protected status, surrounded by a cone of silence when it came to who she was and where she lived. When he asked about John Standard, he got pretty much the same reaction, except with more shrugs and less reverence.

Not knowing what she looked like wasn't helping. He could pass her on the street and be none the wiser. All he knew was that she was American but, thanks to the tourist season, so were half the women in town. Having seen Standard, Heinz was pretty sure she wasn't some middle-aged, sunburned muffin top in Bermuda shorts and a straw hat. Whatever she was, after a full day of looking he was no closer to finding her than when he started. When he saw someone he thought might be her, he would follow only to see her go into a budget hotel in the middle of El Centro. He didn't know much about Emma Parrish, but he was pretty sure she was not the budget hotel type.

After getting the same reaction at the beachfront restaurants along *Playa la Madera*, he took a taxi to *Playa la Ropa*. He got out at a street that led into the hotel district. He walked down the hill and came out at the north end of the beach. The first restaurant was a hundred yards away. Good place as any to start. When he asked a waitress about her, she nodded and pointed south down the beach.

In broken English she said Emma Parrish lived where the

sand ends and turns into a rocky path along the south side of the bay. He was told the same thing by a beach vendor selling homemade cheese out of a bucket. At a place called The Tortuga, a sad-sack waiter shrugged and walked away when he asked where she lived. At a table where five people were playing backgammon he was greeted by four weak smiles and one "fuck off."

He walked to the end of the beach past the last restaurant and a small picnic area where a group of locals had set up a barbecue and plastic tables and chairs.

There were a couple of one-room cabins on a small bluff overlooking the beach. He followed the dirt road until he reached cliffs covered with a patchwork of houses, but none of them looked like they had beach access. Not that it mattered.

There was no way he could know which house belonged to Emma Parrish and Standard. It wasn't like anything around there had an address on it.

Since it was getting late and thinking that Parrish and Standard might be home soon, he went into a beachfront restaurant and took a seat at the bar. He had a view of the end of the road from town. He waited for an hour.

Nothing.

He left the bar and walked down the dusty path that led from the beach to the parking area where the bus line from the city ended. Rather than wait for the next crowded bus, he took a taxi back to town. He got out in the middle of El Centro, then walked around for another hour looking for anything that qualified as an upscale restaurant that Parrish might frequent. The only one that qualified was one he'd been to before—Mango's. That was where he got the lead that led him to Itchy Donlan. Maybe if the same sad collection of regulars was around, they might do the same in helping him find Emma Parrish.

He was wrong.

While the tequila-soaked crew was more than happy to give up Itchy Donlan, they wanted nothing to do with any questions about Emma Parrish, or Standard for that matter. The same old guy who told him where Itchy might live, turned and walked away when Heinz mentioned her name. After that, none of the other barflies would even look at him. Heinz left feeling more and more intrigued by her and why she deserved so much loyalty. His determination to find her only grew stronger.

He had dinner at a bustling taco place on a busy street, grabbing a table near the street on the off chance that she or someone like her would walk by. All he saw were businessmen in white shirts and pants, women with groceries, and teenagers with cell phones. By nine p.m., the streets were starting to empty. Deciding to call it a day and start again in the morning, he hailed a taxi and climbed in the back.

"¿Cuál es su nombre?" the driver said, looking over his shoulder.

"I'm sorry. I don't speak Spanish."

"That is okay. I speak good English. What is your name?"

"Heinz."

"My name is Arturo. I am the best taxi driver in all Zihuatanejo. Ask anybody." He reached back to hand Heinz a business card. "You need a taxi. You call Arturo. I know everyplace and everybody."

What the hell, Heinz thought, and leaned forward, his head between the two front seats. "Do you know Emma Parrish?"

"Of course. I am her personal driver. I take her anywhere she wants to go. I have done that for years. Shopping. Out to dinner. Running errands. Señora Emma always asks for Arturo. Do you know her?"

"We met a few months ago at a party in Mexico City,"

Heinz lied. "She said I should look her up if I'm ever in Zihuatanejo, but I don't know where she lives."

"I do. I could take you there, but she is not home. Her and her *novio*, Señor Juan, went to Troncones for a few days. A little romance, I think. They are very much in love. I know about such things. I have known Señora Emma for a long time, and I have never seen her so happy."

"Troncones?"

"It's a little town on the beach a half-hour north of here. More if there's traffic."

"Did you take them?" Heinz was having a hard time believing his luck. Of all the taxi drivers in the city, he found the one with everything he needed to know and wasn't shy talking about it.

"No. No. Señora Emma has her own car. You should see it. It is beautiful. A bright red Plymouth *El Furioso*. Very old. She is very proud of it. Many people have tried to buy it, but she will never sell. It is her ... *bebe*. Sometimes I offer to take her on trips to Potosi, Petetlan, even Troncones, but she always says no. She loves driving that car."

"She drove the car to Troncones?"

"*Si*. She is the only one to drive. I have never seen Señor Juan drive. I think maybe something happened."

After Arturo dropped him off at his hotel in the la Madera section of town, Heinz asked the woman at the reception desk what he had to do to rent another car. He had turned the earlier one back in after damaging the front fender when he rear-ended the Russians. She agreed to call a rental company at the airport and have a car ready for him in the morning.

In his room, he fired up his laptop to do a search for Emma Parrish. He didn't find much other than a few TikTok-obsessed teenagers with the same name. He finally gave up after thinking that maybe Mexico is where social media goes to die.

He thought about calling Strasser with an update but decided against it. He would let him know once he found her. He'd caught a break with Arturo the taxi driver. Let's see how things turn out.

He poured a shot of whiskey and sat on the balcony looking out at the bay.

Nothing had changed. The City Pier jutting out into the water. Sailboats bobbing on the gentle swells. *El Obra Maestro* lurking in the darkness, sucking in all the life around it.

He lay awake most of the night planning his next move before deciding that he needed to play it by ear. Since he didn't know where in Troncones Parrish and Standard were staying, there wasn't much he could do until he got there.

The car that showed up outside the hotel the next day was a battered Nissan Sentra with a manual transmission and a broken radio, something he didn't find out until after he signed the rental agreement and the representative had left. Heinz was gradually coming to the realization that Mexico is not the place to seek perfection.

He used the GPS on his cell phone to plot the route from his hotel to Troncones. It took him along a confusing set of surface streets through town then on to Ruta 200. He turned north, enduring the stop-and-go traffic until he reached the edge of town. After forty-five minutes of a maddeningly slow pace, he turned left off the highway at a sign reading "Troncones" and an arrow pointing west. The narrow road came to a dead end at a street that paralleled the beach. He stopped, looked both ways then decided to turn left. He was sure they would be staying at some place on the beach with parking for a bright red Plymouth. Shouldn't be that hard.

He slowly drove by beachfront restaurants, bungalows for rent, private villas, and thatch-roofed stalls selling serapes, hammocks, and beach toys. More stalls were stocked with fresh mangos, pineapples, bananas, and limes. An open-air market featured strange cuts of beef, whole chickens, and fish and shrimp on ice. Cheap motorcycles zoomed past in each direction. Signs pointing toward more restaurants and yoga studios covered light poles. Hotels ranged from modest to what some would consider upscale. None of them had a bright red Plymouth Fury parked nearby.

He was beginning to think that Arturo had fed him a line of bullshit, another local trying to protect Standard and his girlfriend.

When he reached the southern edge of town, he turned around and headed back, passing the same shops and side streets. The north end was less commercial, but with more dusty roads leading up into the hills above town. Beachfront homes with signs in Spanish that read *"En Venta"* or *"En Renta,"* which he took to mean for sale or for rent, dotted the side of the road. He spotted the Plymouth from two blocks away. It stood out like a flare at dusk, bright red against the dull yellow of a two-story house.

He slowly drove by, turned around, and headed back toward town. He called Strasser.

"Found both of them," he said.

Strasser didn't answer right away. Finally, he said, "You know what to do."

Now he had to wait, find a place to hole up for a few hours, get something to eat. What he had to do was best done at night.

CHAPTER 45

That morning, Standard and Emma slept in, then made love to the rhythm of the waves crashing on the beach that sounded like the distant roar of an approving audience.

"If every morning in Troncones is like this, then I'm all in," he said.

She put her head on his chest and looked out at the beach and the waves beyond the swimming pool. "It is nice, isn't it? Having the ocean right there changes everything."

They dozed for another hour before she got up to make breakfast, while he made a couple of calls.

First, he checked on Itchy Donlan to make sure he was still laying low with Marie at the VistaPacifica.

"I'm fine," Itchy said. "Marie is still acting a little weird, but I can stick it out for a few more days. Having the money you got for me gives me room to breathe. If Marie kicks me out, I'll be able to afford something else."

Next, Standard called Special Ed to see if anything had changed with Strasser's yacht.

"It's still there," Ed said. "No one has come or gone that I can tell. I've got a charter this afternoon, so if anything happens, I won't be around to see it."

He thought about calling Strasser but decided not to. What good would it do? They both knew what the other wanted.

After breakfast, they walked down the beach, stopping to watch a couple of surfers catch a few waves, then take a closer look at two of the vacant beachfront lots they saw on their last trip. At the south end of the beach, they walked inland to the road then headed north back toward the center of town.

Emma had a short list of available houses for sale she'd gotten from her realtor. The first two were nice but needed a lot of work to make anything even close to what they already had. The other two were lost causes, ramshackle dumps built of cement blocks, scraps of wood, and bamboo. The only keeper was the last one on the list. The two-story, thatch-roofed bungalow sat on a long, wide lot that ran from the road to the beach. The hand-carved sign on the wrought-iron gate read *Casa Tranquilidad*, Tranquil House. The gate was set in a five-foot cement wall painted yellow that surrounded the property. Inside the gate was a short driveway that led to a garage that Emma was sure would fit *El Furioso*. After peeking through the gate, they followed a dirt path that ran along the north side of the wall toward the beach. At the end of the property facing the ocean the wall was just two feet high, giving them a view of the entire length of the property.

The large swimming pool had a cement apron surrounded by grass. Bougainvillea lined the walls on each side while palm trees loomed over everything. The house at the far end of the pool was open air with a peaked roof of thatch and natural wood railings and posts. The best they could tell, the master bedroom was on the top floor. The living room and kitchen were on the main floor, and what looked like guest rooms flanking each side.

"It's beautiful," Emma said, looking at the flyer the realtor had given her, then sighing. "Too bad we can't afford it. No way could I sell my place for enough to buy this."

"Let's talk to the realtor again when we get back," Standard said. "Maybe we can figure something out."

Standard had pulled in a fair amount of money since coming to Mexico. It came from helping a wealthy contractor find his daughter's killer and working with the DEA to bring down a drug cartel's accountant. Emma knew about that money. She also knew it would fall short of making the place affordable. Squeezing a little more out of Fat Tony at Sticky Fingers was an option, but not a good one. Tony had his own bills to deal with. What she didn't know about was the quarter million Standard had sitting in a Vanguard account back in the States. He was willing to cash some of it in if it meant they could buy the house of Emma's dreams.

"Let's find out what the *Playa la Ropa* house is worth then go from there," he said.

From the way Emma stared at the house, it was clear that she'd be disappointed if it slipped through her fingers, and she had to settle for something less. After taking her hand, they walked back along the wall toward the road, Emma running her fingers along the stucco-covered cement.

Standard still wasn't totally sold on the idea of moving to Troncones, especially if it was just Emma's way of keeping him out of trouble. Coming here to take a breather for a few days and figure things out was one thing. Permanence was a whole lot different. Now, seeing the house he knew she wanted, he could easily see them living there, enjoying life and each other. Keeping the chaos at bay might make life a little less exciting, but in this case it might be worth it.

They lingered outside the house for a few more minutes, then headed into town, stopping for a late lunch of ceviche and Caesar salad at a beachfront restaurant. Lingering over a glass of wine, they talked about all the things they wanted in a new house, most of which already existed at *Casa Tranquilidad*. Although neither one said it, they were getting close to a decision. Standard felt like they were at the point of committing to a move without knowing what they would move into. He was beginning to feel the same way as Emma: Anything short of the house they just looked at would be a letdown.

After lunch they poked their heads into a few shops. Emma bought a hand-painted plate and two ceramic coffee mugs. Standard picked up a white linen shirt and a pair of sandals. It was late afternoon when they got back to the condo. They showered together then Emma, wearing only a pareo around her waist, made a pitcher of Margaritas. They spent two hours sitting on the terrace, drinking, not saying much, and watching the sun go down.

"There's a food cart next to the tienda up the street," Standard said. "How about tacos for dinner and a bottle of wine? The tienda probably has ice cream."

"My intrepid hunter and gatherer," she said, kissing him on the cheek. "I'll wait here with another pitcher of Margaritas."

"Are you going to get dressed?" he asked.

"No."

"Then I'll hurry." He kissed her, squeezed one of her breasts, and left.

Fifty yards away, the ocean sounded angry and unpredictable. The roar was constant, broken only by the crash of giant waves hitting the beach like they were mad at it; a brutish boxer pummeling the sand as if it were an outclassed opponent. Nothing like *Playa la Ropa* where anemic waves did little more than create scallop-like designs on the dry sand. The swimming pool's underwater lights gave off a soft, aqua glow. Tiki torches flickered in a light breeze, giving off an oily smoke that mixed with the heavy salt air.

It would take some getting used to, Emma Parrish thought.

She stayed on the terrace, finishing the last of her Margarita, and contemplating life in a place of constant noise, no matter how soothing some people found it. After a while, would it just become little more than background noise, like the sound of traffic to people who lived in cities? Maybe a less damaging form of tinnitus. Would it sound too much like gunfire, which would bring back memories of things John had gone through and what she had witnessed in its aftermath?

Ever since she talked to John about it, the idea of moving had taken on a life of its own. The biggest reason for doing it was to get John out of harm's way. She and trouble were attracted to him in equal measure. There had to be a way of winning, of throwing trouble off the scent and having him all to herself. If that was the eventual outcome, then she could put up with the constant crashing of waves. To say nothing of how the trouble that found him also meant it wasn't too far away from her. In fact, more than once it had been close, too close.

What surprised her was how open John was to the idea. He had his favorite hangouts in Zihuatanejo and, together, they enjoyed finding restaurants that had just opened and lamenting some favorites that had closed. The same things might happen in Troncones, but on a much smaller and laid-back scale. On the other hand, he was adaptable. He had eased into the Mexican way of life almost from the first day he arrived. If he missed Oregon or Portland, he didn't show it and certainly didn't talk about it. A refugee from the digital world, totally at ease with an analog lifestyle. She liked thinking that living with her had something to do with it. She had done her best to exorcise the demons he came with. Throwing trouble off the track would be just one more step to having him all to herself.

She picked up her glass, walked to the small kitchen, and got everything ready for another pitcher of Margaritas once John got back with more tequila and food. No matter where they lived, that would always be part of their lives. Neither of them had the kind of jobs that kept them busy—John even less than her—then things would pretty much go on as they were other than a change in scenery and places to eat. Life had been good for the last two years. Was there really a way to make it better? To enjoy what life had to offer even more than they already did? There was no Central Mercado or supermercado in Troncones, but the scattering of small tiendas around town carried the staples.

She pulled fruit out of the small refrigerator and had just started cutting it up when she heard a noise at the front door. John was back with supplies for the night.

She put down the knife and went to greet him.

The tienda two blocks down the street carried all the items that Standard had come to associate with Mexico: fresh fruit, five different kinds of chips, a few bottles of tequila and wine, and cookies and cupcakes made by Latin America's answer to Hostess. His favorite item was *Zucaritas*, with Tony the Tiger on the box. They're "*Gr-Riquisimas.*" The ten different kinds of ice cream were in a small freezer with a sliding glass top. The wine selection was limited to two kinds of white and three kinds of red. The tequila selection wasn't much better, but good enough for Margaritas.

Stocked up on food and liquor, Standard went next door to the food cart. He stood in line for a few minutes before ordering six *tacos carnitas* to go with *salsa verde*, rice, and a salad, then waited. The few cars that went by all looked like airport rentals. He watched kids on motorcycles and mopeds, some with girls on the back, race up and down the street. He had never been sure where kids got their money. He wasn't even sure when they went to school. It all seemed fluid to him and very ... Mexican.

With plastic bags hanging from his hands, Standard headed back to the condo. The more he walked around Troncones, the more it felt like he could live there, but it would take some getting used to. There was also no guarantee that the kind of trouble he attracted wouldn't find him. In his experience, trouble could thrive anywhere, even in dusty, bucolic, seaside towns.

He climbed the stairs to their room, thinking that with his hands full, he would have to kick at the door. Instead, it was open. He was only two steps inside when he saw Heinz Richter with a gun to Emma's head.

CHAPTER 46

It was one of those moments when life seemed to stand still, posing long enough for the mind's camera to take a picture and burn it into the brain.

Something indelible and unforgettable to be revisited on dark, sleepless nights when it was impossible to remember anything good about life and the things it offered. Glimpses of the past and those moments when things could go so wrong it would change things forever. A time that teetered on the dull edge of a rusty knife.

One wrong move and the world would come crashing down.

Emma was sitting in a chair, still naked from the waist up. Heinz stood behind her with a handful of her hair in one hand. The gun in his other hand was pressed against her temple. The fear etched on Emma's face looked real and felt permanent.

"Whoa. Whoa. Whoa." Standard pleaded, dropping the bags of food and liquor. Glass banged against glass. Salsa and rice spilled across the linoleum. "Don't do anything crazy. We can work this out. Just put down the gun."

"I'm here for the painting." Heinz pressed the gun harder against her head. "And maybe a little extra." He let go of her hair long enough to stroke one of her breasts. "Not really my thing, but tits are tits, and these are pretty nice." He laughed when Emma tried to squirm away. He grabbed her hair again. Standard held up his hands in a silent attempt to keep her calm. It wasn't working.

"I don't want to die." Tears filled her eyes. The normally lusty voice was little more than a squeak.

"You're not going to die. No one is going to die." Standard looked at Heinz. "How did you ...?

"Did I find you? One of the great truths in the world is that taxi drivers in every city in the world have all the best information. Where to stay. Where to eat. Where to find a woman. Where to find an art thief."

"Arturo," Standard said to himself, but loud enough for Heinz to hear.

"I believe that was his name." Heinz had the smirk of someone with the upper hand and knew it. "Nice man. Chatty. Very helpful. He even gave me his card. I have it here somewhere, but you already know him. Says he's the woman's personal driver. Personal idiot would be more like it. Anyway, I'm here for the painting. Tell me where it is, and no one gets hurt."

When Emma tried to pull away again, Heinz took a firmer grip on her hair.

She looked too scared to scream.

This had been Standard's worst fear. He'd put those closest to him in jeopardy. First Itchy. Now Emma. Why didn't Strasser come directly at him? Why involve others? This had always been between the two of them. Why not leave it that way? No time for that now.

"Emma, stay calm. We can work this out," Standard said.

She didn't look convinced. All she could do was squeeze her eyes shut and sob.

"Listen, Heinz. You kill her, then you're going to have to kill me. If that happens there's no painting. I'm the only one who knows where it is. Strasser will blame you. I don't think you want that."

"Who said anything about killing you?"

"I did, because if you harm her, you'll need to kill me before I rip your heart out with my bare hands."

"Talk is cheap. The painting, Mr. Standard. Tell me."

When he said "no," Emma's eyes got big, her face said, "What are you doing?"

"You know my price." Standard didn't like the idea of negotiating with a gun to Emma's head. Nothing he could do about it. "It hasn't changed since that night on the pier. I think you killed the five foreigners, six if you count Simon Nazareth. Strasser's orders to eliminate the competition. So, turn yourself in. Confess. I give the painting to your boss. The way I see it, you're the only thing standing between Strasser and his painting. Give yourself up and this all goes away."

"What makes you think I killed anybody?"

"Come on, Heinz. Look at yourself? You have a gun to the head of a half-naked, helpless woman, and you want me to think that you wouldn't kill for your boss? Let's not forget what you are—Strasser's enforcer, his attack dog. If I die all bets are off. If he really wants the painting, then he needs to throw you under the bus. Goodbye, Heinz. Hello, Raphael."

Standard gave Emma a pleading look, trying to make her understand that he was doing everything he could. All he got back was frozen fear.

"He would never do that," Heinz said. "I have been loyal to him."

"Just following orders, huh. I've heard that before. It's sort of a German thing."

"It's not the same."

Standard felt an opening. "Tell you what. Let's call Strasser. Have him decide. The two of us die or you turn yourself in." He carefully used two fingers to pull his cell phone out of his pants pocket. "No offense, but my money is on Strasser choosing the painting over you."

"I am more important to him than the painting," Heinz said. "Dial his number and give me the phone."

Standard really didn't have a plan. It was something closer to recklessness, an impulse rather than a carefully detailed and well-thought-out blueprint. All of it fueled by equal parts adrenaline and fear. For sure it was anger. A lot of anger

He looked at his phone then poked at the numbers. "It's ringing," he said, then tossed the phone far enough to Heinz's left that he had to step away from the chair ... and Emma ... to catch it. That's when the reckless impulse thing kicked in. It was his one and only chance.

As soon as Heinz looked to catch the phone, Standard leaped forward as fast as he could. He brushed by Emma before lowering his shoulder into Heinz's chest, driving him backward onto the terrace. As Heinz beat on Standard's back with the butt of the gun, they flew through the terrace's wooden railing, and over the edge.

Later, Standard would barely remember what happened during the next seconds, except that everything seemed in slow motion. He wondered how far it was to the ground or what would happen when he reached it. He hadn't thought that far ahead. They were airborne and then they weren't. He just wanted to get Heinz and the gun away from Emma. What he did made sense at the time. Less so as they hit the railing. He had a vague memory of Heinz's face beneath him, then pushing him away.

Standard braced himself to hit the ground. The swimming pool never crossed his mind, until he landed in it. The next thing he knew, he was at the bottom of the pool. He surfaced at the same time he realized where he was and what had happened. The pool had saved his life.

Heinz wasn't so lucky.

The German was impaled face up, on a smoldering tiki torch. The torch's shaft running through his back and out his chest. The pistol still clutched in his left hand. His arms and legs twitched a couple of times then went limp. Slowly, the skewered Heinz fell sideways, coughing up what little was left of his life onto the cushion of a lawn chair. All Standard could smell was burning flesh.

He looked up at the terrace. Emma was kneeling in the gap in the railing, her hand over her mouth. The fear on her face had been replaced by something just short of hysterical. He knew she was strong. He just wasn't sure how strong.

When the manager appeared, he stared at Heinz's body, then at Standard starting to climb out of the pool, then up at Emma looking down on all of it. He fumbled for his cell phone, dialed, then started talking in panic-stricken Spanish.

CHAPTER 47

THE FIRST POLICE CAR SHOWED UP BEFORE STANDARD HAD a chance to change into dry clothes and get the still-stunned Emma into a robe. She was shivering from fear, her mouth forming words but nothing coming out. He put her on the bed and pulled a blanket over her.

Two more cops arrived five minutes later, turning the street into a carnival of flashing lights, curious locals, and confused visitors. A circus with pistols and cherry tops instead of elephants and clowns. No cheering spectators, just rubber-necking gawkers with cameras and cell phones. From the terrace, he could see four cops gathered around Heinz's body looking like they weren't sure what to do next. In unison, they all looked up at Standard and the broken railing. They were all young and fresh-faced. He got that feeling that this may be their first dead body. If it wasn't, then it's not one they'll soon forget. Standard knew he wouldn't.

The cop that came up to their room was a little older than the others and spoke a less-than-passable English, leaving Standard to answer what he thought were questions with a shrug or a *"no sé."* or a *"lo siento."* When he finally figured out that *ladrón* meant burglar, he nodded his head then made a motion like he was wrestling someone. The cop wrote in his notebook, then in rapid Spanish, said something into the radio microphone attached to the lapel of his shirt and left.

Emma sat on the bed, her blanketed legs pulled up tight against her chest. Standard thought she was in either shock or major-league pissed. A little bit of both, he finally decided. When he sat down beside her, she looked at him, tears in her eyes. She slapped him across the face, then started beating on his chest.

"What were you thinking? Did you know the pool was there or that you would land in it?"

"As John Burroughs said, 'Leap, and the net will appear.'"

"I don't think Burroughs meant flying off a balcony. You could have been killed. That could be you down there pierced like some ... Swedish meatball."

"I was going for schnitzel on a stick." Standard gave her a weak smile.

"Damn it, John. That's not funny. First, I thought I was going to die, then I thought you had. That bastard! God, I can still feel his hands on me. I can still see the two of you going through the railing." She shivered and pulled the blanket a little tighter around her chest. "So much for a quiet few days of house hunting."

He was searching for some way to tell Emma that luck was on his side, not that it needed any explaining. He was still looking for words that would help Emma cope, when Vega showed up.

The comandante knocked on the door then came in before Standard could answer. He apologized to Emma for barging in, then told Standard to sit down.

"My man told me you believe that guy down there was a

burglar," Vega said, looming over Standard, his face grim and dark. He was in full-cop mode, something Standard had rarely seen. This was not going to be a friendly chat. "You want to tell me the truth?"

Standard knew he didn't have much choice. A day of reckoning with Vega had never been far away. Now it was here.

"His name is Heinz Richter. He works for Carlos Strasser, the guy who owns the yacht anchored in the bay. I believe Richter killed those five foreign nationals and maybe Simon Nazareth as well."

"Why would he do that?"

"Because Strasser told him to."

"Proof."

Standard explained what happened at the pier and the gun Special Ed took from Richter that night. "If that doesn't match the weapon used to commit the murders, then the one he had tonight probably will. The last time I saw it, it was still in his hand."

Vega looked around at the shattered railing and Emma curled up in the bed. "What's this all about? And don't give me the usual *tonterías*."

Standard filled in the gaps, beginning with picking up the painting and ending with Heinz Richter and the tiki torch.

"So, this is all about a painting? Is that it?"

"Well, not just any painting, but it is the one thing that connects all the dots."

"Let me guess. You have it and this Richter fellow wanted it."

Standard shrugged. "Sort of. It's Strasser that wants it. He sent Richter to get it."

"Why not just give it to him?" Vega asked.

Emma muttered a faint, "Amen to that."

"It's complicated," Standard said.

"Must be some painting," Vega said.

"You have no idea."

"Tell me about Strasser."

"Rich. Art collector. Seems a little obsessive when it comes to this particular painting."

Standard and Vega walked out onto the terrace to look down through the broken railing at Richter's speared body still lying on the ground. Vega's men stopped taking pictures with their smartphones and moved to one side to let a trio of men in hazmat onesies get closer. They had *Laboratorio Criminal* stenciled on their backs and on their boxes of equipment. One of them began moving around the body taking pictures from several different angles. When they started talking to each other, Standard guessed that there was a question about whether to take the six-foot tiki torch out of his chest, and if they didn't, how to get him on a gurney and into an ambulance. From what Standard could see, no one seemed to have an answer.

"Did you push him?" Vega asked.

"Sort of," Standard said, then gave a short description of what happened.

"You're a lucky man, John." Vega gestured to Emma still on the bed staring into space. "She saw it all, I take it."

"He held a gun to her head. She's tough. It will be a while. Things like that leave a mark."

Vega nodded. "I'll need you to come to the station tomorrow to make a statement. Bring the gun you say you have. I'll need a statement from Señora Parrish as well." He glanced over at her again. "But that can wait."

"And you?"

"I need to talk to Señor Strasser." Vega took it all in one more time, then shook his head. "When I retire, I'm not going to miss you."

CHAPTER 48

Standard and Emma spent a sleepless night in their room. She had nothing to say. He couldn't blame her, so he left her alone. No words were going to change what had happened to her and what she had seen. Early the next morning, they got dressed, packed, and left. When they reached the Plymouth, she threw him the keys, then sat silently in the passenger seat while he drove.

"No place is ever going to be safe, is it?" she said when they were a few miles north of Ixtapa. Her voice sounded weak, tired, and defeated. "Not even a quiet, bucolic, harmless, tranquil little place like Troncones. Now, what's the point of moving? It's going to be the same wherever we go. Wherever you go."

Standard wanted to believe she was wrong, but history said otherwise. She was caught in the recurring maelstrom of violence that swirled around him. If they were together, would she ever be safe? Would he? Love and passion kept them together. Would violence and mayhem pull them apart? He badly wanted to believe that the danger that followed him around would eventually lose interest, fade away, find some other poor bastard to torment. There was just no way to guarantee it.

As they drove through Ixtapa toward the condo where Emma kept *El Furioso,* Standard thought about calling Arturo for a taxi ride home and, on the way, giving him a lecture about keeping his mouth shut. He decided against it.

Maybe in a few days after he'd calmed down and memories of what had just happened had faded a bit. He knew that when Arturo learned the truth, he would be upset and beg for forgiveness. Just the thought of a groveling Arturo made Standard think that he might not tell him at all. He called another taxi. They stood silently outside the condo until it arrived.

After helping Emma take the luggage up the stairs to their house, Standard gathered up a few things, stuffed them in his backpack, and left to catch another taxi. She needed time to sort things out. Even though it was still fresh in their minds, having him around would only remind her of what had happened and the fear and disappointment that went with it. A few hours apart couldn't make things any worse. If events were taking away her love of Mexico, only time would bring it back.

Police headquarters on the south edge of town just off Ruta 200 was a two-story, cinderblock building with a dirt parking lot encased in razor wire, glass bricks for windows, and a revolving front door. Three police cars were parked in the lot. A half dozen officers in brown and black uniforms stood out front smoking cigarettes.

Inside was a collection of battleship-gray desks, ten-year-old computers, and squawking police radios. Flies and other insects that looked big enough to have their own badges bounced against the windows. The once-white walls had turned a pale yellow from years of tobacco smoke. The floor was a dingy chessboard of scuffed black-and-white tiles. Standard told a female officer at the front desk he was there to see Comandante Vega. She picked up the phone, talked in Spanish, then got up to escort him in.

"I know the way," Standard said, then walked around her desk and up a spiral staircase to the second floor. The first time Standard visited Vega's office it was little more than a card table, a well-worn leather couch about to lose its stuffing, and bullfighting posters thumb-tacked to the wall. That was two years ago. Since then, Vega had upgraded to a large wooden desk, new leather couch with matching chairs, and framed art on the wall. Standard recognized one of the works as an original Serrano. Worth six figures in the States but was probably Vega's for the price of turning the artist's electricity back on. Vega was sitting behind his desk still in cop mode and appearing determined to stay that way.

Standard sat down in a chair across from him.

"Here's the statement you gave me and the other officers last night." Vega slid a single sheet of paper across his desk. "If it is an accurate description of what transpired, then please sign and date it."

Standard picked it up. "This is in Spanish."

Vega looked offended. "What? You don't trust me?"

Standard shook his head, signed it, then pulled Heinz's revolver out of his backpack and set it on the desk.

"You're positive this belonged to the dead man?"

"Special Ed can back me up."

"Anyone else?"

"Itchy Donlan was there, but he had a bag over his head."

Vega pulled an evidence bag out of the bottom drawer of his desk, carefully slid the gun inside, and put it back in the drawer. "I'll have ballistics compare it to the bullets taken from the scene. We can still check it for fingerprints. Same with the one we recovered last night."

"When are you going to question Strasser?"

Vega sighed. "Señor Strasser is a very well-connected man, both in Mexico and elsewhere. Bringing him in for questioning is going to cause a certain amount of *excitation*."

"But you are going to bring him in?"

Vega looked at his watch. "I have arranged for one of the naval vessels to take me and some of my men out to his yacht later today." Vega smiled. "The boat has a machine gun mounted on the bow. Hopefully, that will be enough to convince Señor Strasser that we are serious about talking to him. We'll bring him back here for questioning. Two of my men will stay on the yacht until he gets back. It might be a couple of days."

Standard knew the wily old cop was playing the odds, which favored Richter as the killer. Richter worked for Strasser. Questioning him about a dead employee was just good police work, or at least that's what he hoped his superiors would think.

"Aggressive, and risky."

"*¿Por qué?*"

"If you agree with me and believe that Strasser ordered those murders, then you know what he's going to do." Standard said. "He'll deny it. It will be hard to prove otherwise. Just because Richter worked for Strasser doesn't necessarily mean Strasser is responsible for the murders."

"I know all that," Vega said, "but I have all the probable cause I need."

"Everything I believe about Strasser is circumstantial," Standard said. "That's good enough for me, but not for you or your superiors. I get that. You'll question him for a couple of days, then release him. You'll probably also get a call from your government asking what the hell you're doing detaining one of the richest men in the world. After that, you'll let him go."

Vega gave a resigned nod.

"Here's the good news. By then, you'll know that one or both of Richter's guns was used in the five murders. You'll be a hero. Two foreign governments and The Vatican will thank Mexico for finding the killer. Mexico will thank you, and you can retire a hero. You might even get a letter from the Pope. Now, that's a career topper. So, what if Strasser walks, which he probably will. No one will care. Murders solved. Killer dead. Case closed. Pretty good deal, yeah?"

Vega leaned back in his chair, a smug look on his face. He reached into his desk and pulled out a bottle of tequila, two glasses, and a pair of cigars. "I was just thinking the same thing. We are both very clever men."

CHAPTER 49

❧

Standard talked one of Vega's men into giving him a ride back to *Playa la Ropa*. After being dropped off, he thought about going up to their house to see how Emma was doing but decided instead to give her some more space. He walked up the beach to The Tortuga, sat at a table away from the kitchen, and waved at the usual customers playing backgammon. After a few minutes, Ranger Bob came over to say that some guy had come around asking about Emma. "I told him to fuck off. Hope I did the right thing."

"Blond? T-Shirt? Jeans? German accent?" Standard asked.

"That's him. Everything okay?"

"Yeah. He found her. We're good."

Standard ordered a plate of tacos and a beer from Pablo the waiter, then pulled a lounge out into the sun. He put his hands behind his head and looked out at the *El Obra Maestro* still anchored in the bay like some black hole sucking in air, light, and bodies. He wondered if Strasser knew that his pit bull was dead and what the billionaire's reaction would be when Vega pulls up in a cutter from the Mexican navy and hauls him off for questioning and a couple of nights in jail.

What he'd told Strasser that night on the City Pier was all coming true. Sweet.

Whatever was going to happen, there was a strong chance Standard might at least get a couple of days of peace and quiet before Vega turned Strasser loose. In the meantime, he needed to decide what to do about the painting. With Richter dead and getting the blame for the murders, his reason for keeping it was gone.

Even so, did he really want Strasser to have it? Maybe there were other options.

He was still mulling over what to do next when the navy cutter entered the bay. The ship wasn't exactly what Vega had promised. It was more of a tricked-out PT boat loaded down with satellite dishes and antennae instead of torpedo tubes. Its motors putting out exhaust fumes and a deep-throated rumble. As Vega promised, it did have a machine gun mounted on the stern. Once inside the bay, the boat seemed to purposely cross the bow of the *El Obra Maestro* before veering north toward the City Pier. Standard didn't want to miss this. He threw some money on the table, walked back down the beach, and got a taxi into town.

By the time he got to the pier, the navy cutter was cruising slowly toward *El Obra Maestro*. One of the sailors dressed all in white stood behind the machine gun. Vega and three of his men stood on the back deck, clinging to the railing.

Standard joined the crowd of onlookers watching the cutter circle the yacht a few times then stop on its starboard side. The clumsy, overweight Vega struggled to climb over the railing and onto the yacht. Two of his nimbler men followed.

Watching Vega go inside the yacht, it was all Standard could do not to laugh. He tried to imagine the self-absorbed and mildly corrupt police chief from a backwater beach town confronting the equally self-absorbed billionaire head of a worldwide conglomerate. If the stakes weren't so high, he could easily imagine Vega negotiating a discreet bribe in exchange for a few softball questions about some dead guys. Strasser would jump at the chance to add to Vega's retirement account if it meant the whole thing would be written off as a misunderstanding.

But the stakes were high. Vega knew that gushing praise from higher-ups and foreign governments for solving the murders of six foreign nationals without causing a major scandal trumped a substantial bribe. Based on Standard's experience with Vega, that doesn't happen every day. More like genetic realignment.

Vega would do the right thing, and Strasser would spend a couple of days in a feces-and-urine-stained cell. For Standard, it would make the moment that much richer.

After fifteen minutes, Vega came out on the back deck of the yacht with Strasser, the multi-billionaire's hands behind his back. With him was a man in a white uniform with a peaked hat that Standard assumed was the yacht's captain. Vega said something to his men, after which they went back inside the yacht. With Vega and Strasser on board, the cutter pulled away and headed for the pier.

Standard moved to where he could get a good look.

Vega was the first one up the stairs from the dock, Strasser a few feet behind being gently pushed by another cop. He was handcuffed and bent over at the waist for the perp walk up the pier to a waiting police car. When he looked around at the crowd, he spotted Standard. They locked eyes for a second, then Standard nodded his head. If Strasser was confused about what was happening and why, he wasn't anymore.

CHAPTER 50

STANDARD AND ADAM BOVARY JONES MET FOR LUNCH AT Fonda Irma in the Central Mercado. They ordered chili rellenos with rice, beans, and Corona, then sat in an eating area across the aisle and as far away from the lunch crowd as they could get.

"Are you here to tell me more about Dragovitch?" Jones asked.

"No, but his name keeps popping up. I don't know where he fits into all of this except that he sent two men to apparently steal the painting I told you about and he's *numero uno* on Mai Nazareth's list of who killed her husband."

"So, why am I here?"

"I need another favor."

"Of course you do."

Standard described what happened in Troncones and the effect it had on Emma.

"A tiki torch, huh? Sorry I missed that. You get any pictures?"

Standard said no. "You're used to guns. I'm less so. Emma

not at all. I'd like to get her away for a while so we can work things out."

"I take it you want to use the safe house in Potosi."

When Standard nodded, Jones said he would take care of it and that he and Emma should let him know when they're ready to go.

"I think right away would be best."

Barre de Potosi is a small, dusty, village fifteen miles south of Zihuatanejo. It sits at the mouth of a caiman-filled estuary that empties into the ocean. To the north are miles of beaches lined with everything from tents to three-story hotels. Cattle mesmerized by the heat and humidity wandered up and down the paved road leading into town. The only store was the *Cristo Jesus Tienda*. Each of the beachfront restaurants were called *Enramada* something.

Standard and Emma had been there a dozen times, including a few nights at the DEA safe house the previous spring. He called Arturo to drive them down, but only after Emma made him agree not to bring up what happened in Troncones and why. She was right. Standard would find a better time to fill Arturo in on the finer points of discretion.

The safe house was on the north edge of town, conveniently located near a liquor store. One of Jones' men was there to greet them, unlock the front gate, and give them his phone number when they were ready to leave. The roomy, two-story house had a fully equipped kitchen, a well-stocked wine rack, and an ample pantry. It included a pool, 85-inch television, and soft leather furniture. The house was surrounded by a cement wall. The gate had a lock with a four-digit code they got from Jones's man. If there was anything that set it apart from the modest homes nearby, it was the array of antennae and satellite dishes on the terra cotta roof.

For two days, they sat in the sun, walked the beach, and

dined at the string of modest palapa restaurants that lined the entrance to the estuary. They read cheap novels left behind by those in the DEA's witness protection program, drank Margaritas poolside, and binge-watched *Game of Thrones*. The hardest part for Standard was sleeping in separate rooms.

On the second day, they walked north along the beach, marveling at the shacks with million-dollar views, short-and-long-term rentals with pools, and modest homes with armed guards. Never once did what happened in Troncones come up. Neither did how much more of Standard's curse of chaos she was willing to endure. She would eventually decide whether having him around was better than not. He had two choices: Wait for her to figure it out or take himself out of the picture.

He could leave, go back to Portland, restart his life as a freelancer. But why go back to what made him come to Mexico in the first place? He would leave if that's what she wanted. He could not do it on his own.

Arturo returned on the third day to pick them up for the ride back to *Playa la Ropa*. On the way, he talked about his five children and how well they were doing in school while Standard and Emma sat in the back barely listening. After a while, Arturo seemed to sense that all was not right and stayed quiet for the rest of the trip. When they reached *Playa la Ropa*, Standard thanked Arturo, paid him, and schlepped their luggage up the cement stairs to their house. Sweaty and tired, he plopped down in a chair. Emma disappeared into the bedroom.

Standard was in the shower when Emma stepped in beside him. She put her arms around his neck and pulled him close.

"Before you I had a good but boring life here. It's still good, but I miss boring. The problem is I would miss you more. I don't want to lose you, but I need you to do two things."

"Anything."

"First, give that damn painting back to whoever owns it.

Second, all bets are off if I ever see anything even remotely resembling that German asshole impaled on a tiki torch. Deal?"

"Deal."

"I hope you realize that I'm giving up my childhood dream of a Hallmark movie kind of life."

"I would hope so."

"One more thing. You don't get laid for a week." The disappointment on Standard's face made her laugh. "Just kidding."

Emma had recovered on the outside. He wasn't sure about what kind of scars were left festering on the inside. Time would tell. He just needed to make sure that she got that time.

That night they had dinner at a rooftop restaurant overlooking *Playa la Ropa* and the bay. A below-average marimba band made the place sound more like Trinidad than Mexico, but they sat far enough away that it didn't make conversation impossible. While lights on the anchored sailboats rocked back and forth in the gentle swells, the *El Obra Maestro* lay quiet and dark except for a few dim running lights. He thought about the two men Vega left on board when he took Strasser in for questioning and hoped they had taken full advantage of their assignment. They would have at least gotten away with a few bottles of wine and a laptop or two. If they took any of the paintings, they were a lot smarter than Standard gave them credit for.

"So," Emma said, leaning across the table, "you can tell me now. Where's the painting?"

Standard put up his arms, the international sign of surrender. "It's with your friend Don Pedro Serrano. Thanks for telling me about him, by the way. That really worked out. He kept the Raphael safe and verified that it's real ... or as real as he can determine without looking at the provenance."

"So, what's keeping you from returning it to Simon Nazareth's widow?"

"Nothing, other than the thought of Strasser owning it. The man is a killer once removed who may very well get away with it. He kidnapped Itchy and scared the hell out of him. He probably okayed Heinz's little visit to us in Troncones. After all that, the idea of him owning a priceless masterpiece just doesn't sit well. I'm not one to reward bad behavior."

"John, at what point do you say, 'I don't have a dog in this fight' and walk away?"

Having asked himself the same question, Standard didn't have to think long. "Probably right now, but I have one more card to play. There's no risk. If it works out, fine. If not, that's fine too."

"Then you're done with it, right?"

"Promise."

They topped off dinner and a bottle of cabernet from Chile with glasses of Amaretto. The tension between them had faded. He had agreed to get rid of the painting. A repeat of anything that resembled a man on a tiki torch was next to impossible. What he wasn't sure of was Strasser's next move. Without Heinz Richter, Strasser had lost the pointy end of his spear. That didn't mean he was totally without resources. Heinz may have been his best man, but Standard doubted he was his only man.

CHAPTER 51

THE NEXT MORNING, STANDARD CALLED VEGA TO MAKE sure Strasser was out of jail and back on his yacht.

"We cut him loose last night," Vega said. "We had nothing to hold him on and I was getting strange phone calls from the National Police as well as the secretary of foreign affairs and the ambassadors of Argentina and Uruguay."

"What did he tell you?"

"Just what you'd expect. He admitted that Richter worked for him but claimed to know nothing about any murders. He made Richter sound like little more than a deck hand. He didn't know the names of the first three victims but recognized who they worked for. That was no surprise. He did admit that there were competitors who wanted to obtain the painting, but that he and Simon Nazareth had an agreement. They set a price. The painting was his. Anyone else who wanted it showed up too late with too little. He claimed to know nothing about the dead Russians or why they would be in Mexico."

"And Simon Nazareth?"

"He probably told me the same thing he told you: Simon

Nazareth's death was not to his advantage. He made it clear that all he wants is to get the painting and leave here. He is not a fan of our little city."

"If he gets the painting and leaves town, he will get away with murder."

"Perhaps."

The tone in Vega's voice was begging Standard to stop, that there was more going on than just a painting, no matter who painted it or how old it was. Vega was a small-time cop with a big-time problem. The pressure was getting to him. He was not in the business of fielding calls from other countries, and certainly not from The Vatican. In his world, the sooner Strasser left town, the better.

"The only way that can happen, John, is for you to give him the painting and be done with it. I don't care who he pays or how much. I just want him gone. Am I clear?"

"I'll take care of it," Standard said, then hung up.

When Emma left to go shopping and run some errands, Standard grabbed his backpack and hit The Tortuga. He was well into a plate of *huevos rancheros* and a Bloody Mary when Special Ed showed up, doing what he liked to call retail marketing. That meant roaming the beaches offering deep-sea fishing trips to sunbathing tourists. In reality, it was an excuse to stop at restaurants and bars, drink a few beers, and chat up the locals. If someone wanted to buy an over-priced trip on the *Tuna Warrior* to catch a Dorado or a sailfish, so much the better. It wasn't like he needed the money, just the enjoyment of going fishing.

"Lots of activity lately around that yacht in the bay," Ed said, grabbing a piece of Standard's toast and using it to point toward *El Obra Maestro*. "Care to tell me what's going on?"

After Standard filled him in on everything that happened since that night on the pier. He got the predictable reaction after describing what happened in Troncones. Ed had one suggestion. "I think it's time we went fishing."

The *Tuna Warrior* was tied up at the fuel dock on the west side of the bay near the marina. Gassed and ready to go, Ed let Standard take the wheel. He carefully weaved through a handful of moored yachts and pangas, then picked up speed as they went out the mouth of the bay into the ocean. Ed stayed on the rear deck rigging two poles, baiting hooks, and drinking *Tecate* from a can. Finished with that, he disappeared into the cabin. A few minutes later music from the album *Desperado* by the Eagles blasted out over the gentle swells.

Ed came back on deck, raised his beer in Standard's direction, and started singing. "Saddle up boys we're going to ride into town and get a little out of control."

The mixture of wind and sea air produced a welcome, but long-overdue sense of freedom. The further from shore, the more Standard realized the importance of getting rid of the Raphael and simplifying his life again. He owed himself and Vega that much. He owed Emma even more. He knew how he wanted everything to end. He was just going to need some luck to get there.

"Let's try for a sailfish," Ed shouted once they were about two miles offshore. "Head northwest. Slow her down a bit."

Ed picked up one of the poles and started stripping out line. On the end was an exotic-looking lure shaped like a fish. He let it skip across the light swells as he pulled out more line until the lure was fifty yards off the stern. Standard kept one eye ahead and the other on Ed sitting in one of the chairs on the back deck. He had a fresh beer in one hand and a joint in the other. Twenty minutes later, he dropped the beer, threw the joint over the side, and stood up.

"There. There." He pointed at the fan-like fin of a sailfish swimming through the boat's wake. He grabbed the pole, reeled in the lure, then grabbed the other pole with the bait and hook.

"That lure went right across his nose," Ed yelled. "Now he's headed for the bait. Get down here. He's going to hit it any second now."

Standard put the engines in idle and climbed down from the flying bridge. When he sat down in the chair facing the stern, Ed buckled him in and handed over the pole. "When he takes the bait, let him run. I'll tell you when to set the hook."

Suddenly there was a splash off the stern. Line flying off the reel made a high-pitched whir. As more and more line went out, the more Standard wanted to jerk the pole back to set the hook. Ed sensed it.

"Not yet," he said. "Just a few more seconds." The line finally slowed, Ed shouted "Now," and Standard pulled hard on the pole. Seventy-five yards out the sailfish broke the surface, tail danced across the water shaking its head, then disappeared. The pull on the line told Standard the fish was still there. It wasn't his first sailfish, but the feeling never grew old. The energy of a hundred-and-fifty-pound fish came up the line, down the pole, and into his arms. The fish came out of the water again and again, violently shaking its entire body. Each time, Standard pulled on the pole, reeling in the slack, then pulling again. When the fish started to run, he let the line run out then started all over again when the fish slowed.

It took the better part of an hour to get the fish alongside the boat. Standard was drenched in sweat, his arms and back screaming in pain. But a pain that disappeared once he got a look at the fish. It was eight feet long and iridescent. Its sail-like fin stretched from the back of its head to its tail. Tired after the long fight, the fish hung by the side of the boat as if waiting for its fate. One eye looked right at Standard.

"Cut it loose," Standard said.

"You sure? Pretty good eating here and not just for us. There are those locals who might not have been as lucky today."

"I know but cut it loose anyway. I've seen enough blood."

"Gotcha," Ed said.

He pulled a large pair of pliers out of his cargo shorts, leaned over the side, and yanked the hook out. The fish slowly drifted away, as if not sure what had just happened, then, with a flick of its tail, was gone.

Ed left the boat in idle to drift with the current. He pulled two cans of beer from a cooler under one of the bench seats on the back deck. Standard rubbed his arms, stretched his back, and took off his shirt. He felt as good about letting the fish go as he did landing it. They toasted each other and drank.

"This is the first time we've come out here together that you didn't whine about getting seasick," Ed said. "I guess those pills I gave you did the trick."

"Pills? Oh yeah. I forgot them. I didn't think about getting sick until you just brought it up."

"Told you they'd work."

The current was taking them north and closer to shore. They could see Ixtapa in the distance, its high-rise hotels and condos lining the beach like so many tombstones. A few pangas hung close to the rocky shore, probably divers looking for lobsters or octopus.

"That little trick you pulled with the two poles," Standard said. "What was that all about?"

"A technique I learned from one of the locals. It didn't make sense at first until I realized he was catching more fish than the other boats. The first pole has a barbless lure on it meant to imitate a food fish and get the sailfish's attention. It's a lure the fisherman designed and carved himself. It seems to imitate a real fish better than anything else I can find. Once the fish sees it, you replace the barbless lure with bait full of hooks. Doesn't always work, but it did this time. I can't remember what the Mexican skipper called it. I like to think of it as a kind of bait and switch. Clever, yeah?"

"Bait and switch? You mean the old marketing term for luring customers in with one product then selling them something more expensive?"

"That's it. I learned about it at Harvard."

"Yeah," Standard said. "Bait and switch. It did work."

They sat in silence enjoying the cool breeze while Standard's arms slowly returned to normal. He thought about what Ed said and the technique he used to catch the sailfish.

"How about we head back in," Standard said. "There's something I need to take care of."

"Anything I can help with?"

"As a matter of fact, there is but I need to talk to Serrano first. I'll explain on the way."

CHAPTER 52

Standard had Ed drop him off at *Playa las Gatas*. He eased the big boat between the smaller pangas bringing passengers from across the bay or taking them back. He thanked Ed, said he would be in touch soon, and jumped off onto the rickety dock. He once again waved off waiters from the palapa restaurants as he trudged up the beach to Don Pedro Serrano's home and studio. He found Serrano standing at an easel, a palette in his left hand, a brush in the right. Paint spatters on the floor looked like crushed M&Ms. The ones on his white pants resembled blood spots. In between glances out at the palm trees in front of his studio, he dabbed at a painting. He ignored Standard for a few minutes, stepped back to look at his work, then came out.

"I saw the navy pull up alongside *El Obra Maestro*. The machine gun was a nice touch." Serrano smiled, yelled to his house boy, and held up two fingers. The cold Coronas arrived before they could sit down in the Adirondack chairs overlooking the bay. "I'm going to assume that you had something to do with that."

Standard brought Serrano up to speed on everything that had happened in Troncones and Vega's decision to question Strasser.

Serrano sipped his beer and looked concerned. "Señora Emma? She is doing okay?"

"Better, but I've given her some room. In the past, she'd work it out on her own. This time it could be a little harder."

"She is a *mujer fuerte*. I believe she will be fine. And this Heinz person? A tiki torch? Seriously?" When Standard nodded Serrano shook his head. "If I were younger, I think you and I would have many wonderful adventures together. I would enjoy that."

"Be careful what you wish for."

"So, what now?"

"That's what I came here to talk about. The Raphael. I think it needs to go back to its owners or at least to Mai Nazareth. They can do what they want with it. Selling to anybody, even Strasser. I've got what I wanted."

"Heinz killed the three men from the museums and two Russians. Did he also kill Simon Nazareth?"

"Could be. That's what Vega wants to believe. Nobody else was running around town killing people. But Nazareth? Strasser told me Nazareth's death only made this harder for him. Had he lived, Strasser believed he would have the painting and be out of town by now. That makes a lot of sense."

"Unless Strasser never intended to pay for the painting. With Simon Nazareth out of the way, maybe he felt he had a chance of duping his widow."

Standard had told Mai Nazareth the same thing, but the more he mulled it over the more it sounded a little too clever by half. To Strasser, punching the ticket of five rivals for the Raphael was probably the price of doing business, the kind of thing someone who believes they are above the law would do.

That didn't necessarily make him an art thief or a swindler. Everything Standard knew about Strasser was that he was a serious art collector willing to part with several hundred million dollars to indulge his love of lost masterpieces. Killing someone to get what he already agreed to buy didn't seem out of the question. It just sounded unlikely.

"What about the Russian, Dragovitch?"

Standard shrugged. "Who knows? He's on Mai Nazareth's most wanted list. I'm not sure how that works since his two men were killed at about the same time as he was. What do you know about Russian oligarchs and art?"

"Not much, other than they're like a lot of rich people who use art to hide assets from taxes. There are things called freeports, which are little more than high-end storage facilities free from any serious taxation. If Dragovitch owns any art worth having, then that's where he would keep it."

"Why do you think he wants the painting so badly?"

"These are tough times for oligarchs aligned with Putin. Sanctions are having an effect. He may just want to sell it because he needs the money." Serrano finished his beer and set the bottle on the ground. "So?"

"I think Strasser and I need to talk," Standard said. "I'm not comfortable with just telling him 'Here's the painting' and letting him and Mai Nazareth work out the details. Certainly not after he sent Heinz to kill us."

"You need to figure it out."

"You're right, but I need to know one thing first."

Serrano looked suspicious until Standard explained what he had in mind.

Then he smiled. "I'm way ahead of you, amigo."

CHAPTER 53

STANDARD CAUGHT A PANGA BACK ACROSS THE BAY BUT rather than go home, he headed to Mango's for a drink and time to think. The place was nearly empty. The lunch crowd gone. The usuals yet to arrive. He got a Corona, found a table in a quiet corner, and called Itchy Donlan.

"Heinz Richter is dead," Standard said. "You're safe. You can stay there with Marie, go home, or do whatever you like. As far as you're concerned this is all over."

"Dead? Really? How?"

"It's a long story. I'll tell you some other time."

"What about Strasser?"

"Unless he has another apex predator like Heinz Richter onboard that yacht,

I wouldn't worry about him." Standard could hear Itchy's sigh of relief over the phone.

"And the painting?"

"I think I've figured it out. I'll let you know what happens." Standard knew what he needed to do. He just wasn't going to share any of it with Itchy. "I just want to get it off my hands."

"You could keep it. It's worth a buck or two."

"It's not mine," Standard said, then quickly changed the subject. "So, how's Marie? She tired of you yet?"

"Not as much as I'm tired of her. She barely says ten words a day. Spends all her time by the pool drinking or in our room doing the same thing. She keeps mumbling things that I can't understand, but probably has something to do with who or what died back in New York. Not that I care. I'm out of here now that it's safe. The twenty K makes this a lot easier decision. I have you to thank for that. I was ready to kiss the cash goodbye."

"You earned it. Make it last."

Standard hung up and called Mai Nazareth. "You still want to sell the painting to him?" he said, not sure how she would answer.

"Personally? No. Not if it's true that he had all those people killed, but I have my clients' interest to consider. If Strasser pays the price, then I'm obligated to sell it to him."

"Okay. If that's what you feel you need to do, then let me take care of it."

"How are you going to do that?"

Mai Nazareth listened while Standard laid out what he was going to do over the next twenty-four hours. When he was done, all she said was, "If that gets this over with, then it's fine with me."

The next call was going to be more difficult. He fortified himself with a second beer, chased it with a shot of Don Julio, and picked up the phone again.

"Mr. Standard," Carlos Strasser said. "I've been expecting your call."

"We need to talk."

"So, talk."

"No. Face to face. Meet me at nine tonight at the basketball court on the bay front. If you want your painting, come alone."

"You've said that before."

"Just be there."

Standard hung up, ordered another shot of tequila, then took a taxi home.

When he got there, Emma was putting away groceries. When she was done, they sat in the living room where he told her about the fishing trip, the sailfish, the calls he'd made, and his meeting that night with Strasser. He didn't tell her about his talk with Serrano. That would have to come later.

Meeting Strasser didn't go over well. "John! He's a killer. Why would you go near him?"

"He's a killer once removed. Heinz Richter did the dirty work and he's dead. He wants the painting and then to get out of town. I said all along that I'm the only one who can make that happen. That's what I intend to do. Get this whole thing over with."

Emma shrugged her shoulders, resigned to whatever Standard felt he needed to do. "As long as there are no tiki torches involved, I'm good with whatever you want to do to end this. Now, I'm going to start dinner."

Dinner was shrimp pasta and a tomato salad. Standard went easy on the wine. He wanted all his wits about him when he met with Strasser. Emma said so little that she made him feel like this was the last supper. He doubted it, but nothing he could say to her would change anything.

CHAPTER 54

AT HALF PAST EIGHT, STANDARD WALKED DOWN THE HILL to where Arturo was waiting. On the ride into town, he tuned out Arturo's gossip about who came to town and who left. The night was warm, the humidity low, the road empty except for the usual parade of taxis and buses headed in both directions.

Twenty minutes later, he got out a block from the basketball court. The bayfront was busy with locals and tourists headed home or out to dinner. He bought a bag of popcorn from a street vendor then stood in the shadows of a palm tree at the far end of the court, waiting.

At a little after nine, Standard spotted Strasser walking past the bay side restaurants. He waved off waiters with menus and ignored diners eating at outdoor tables. When he reached the basketball court, he stopped, looked around, then sat in the top row of the bleachers. Two basketball teams raced up and down in what was part basketball, part *West Side Story*. Best he could tell, Strasser had come alone.

He just needed to be sure.

He dialed. Special Ed answered on the first ring.

"He came alone," Ed said. "No one followed him up the pier from the dock. If someone else was in the Zodiac, I haven't seen him. Probably still waiting to take him back. I'll check it out. If it's something different than that, I'll let you know."

"Thanks. Texts are best."

Standard waited, watching Strasser for another few minutes before moving out of the shadows.

"My friend Itchy Donlan—you remember him?—likes to call Mexican basketball Juan on Juan," Standard said as he walked up behind Strasser, sat next to him, and held out the greasy paper bag. "Popcorn?"

Strasser shook his head. His face was a doughy white with a look that said he didn't want to be there but had no choice.

"Why am I here, Mr. Standard?"

"You're here so I can tell you exactly what you are going to do in the next twenty-four hours if you want to leave with what you came for."

Strasser bristled, then took a deep breath. "Go on."

"You are going to transfer the money you agreed to pay for the Raphael to Mai Nazareth. I believe you have all the necessary account numbers. When the money is in her account, she will call me. I will contact you and arrange to deliver the painting. If the money is not in her account in twenty-four hours or it's the wrong amount, I will contact the painting's owners and tell them that I will return it to them under one condition: They never sell it to you. One more thing, this offer is non-negotiable."

Strasser didn't move for several minutes. His eyes followed the two teams up and down the court, but Standard doubted he really saw them. Strasser was a businessman and he'd just been given a business deal. It was essentially the same deal he'd made before coming to Zihuatanejo.

"Can I trust you, Mr. Standard?"

"Do you trust anyone?"

Strasser thought for a few moments. "Sadly. No."

"In this case, you have no choice."

"Let me tell you something, Mr. Standard. By the way, may I call you John?"

"No."

"Very well then. My father was a Nazi who stole millions from the Third Reich. Mostly it was money and assets taken from Jews, Gypsies, and others who were not part of the master race. It is a legacy that is hard to face. I wish it wasn't true, but it is and there is nothing I can do about it. At the end of the war, he abandoned his family, a wife and two sons, left Berlin, and took his fortune to South America. He married the daughter of another refugee from the Reich and started a cattle ranch that grew into the global conglomerate I now own and run. I can honestly say that he was the worst person I have ever met. A terrible man. Brutal. Racist. Abusive. Chauvinist to the ultimate degree. Dismissive of everything and everyone that was not Aryan. He even believed Hitler survived the war and was living in Switzerland. When he died, my mother left the funeral and never mentioned his name again for the rest of her life. She even refused to be buried anywhere near him."

"Are you going anywhere with this?" Standard was trying to be patient. "Some kind of self-help thing."

Strasser watched the two teams race up and down the court, having to peek around a cheering woman standing in front of him when someone finally scored.

Standard offered the popcorn again. Strasser waved him away.

"To his credit, near the end of his life, he gave me a piece of advice that I never forgot, but, in this case, failed to follow. 'Carlos,' he said to me, 'never play the other man's game and if you do, don't play it on his ground.'" After everyone sat down,

Strasser leaned back against the bench seat behind him. "I give you credit, Mr. Standard. You have outsmarted me at every turn. I commend you. I played your game on your turf, and I lost. It's not like I wasn't warned. I should have known. I ignored my instincts and my grandfather's advice to my own detriment. Your offer is a fair one. I will consider it. All I want is to leave with the Raphael. It would be a victory that came with a hard lesson."

"Your mistake was threatening me and my friends. You're supposed to be smarter than that. One of the masters of the universe. Yet all you did was make me dig in deeper."

"Perhaps you're right." Strasser stood up and turned to face Standard. "Let's take a walk and talk some more. This humbling experience is new for me. It has made me philosophical. Indulge me." When Standard hesitated, Strasser smiled. "It is okay. I am alone. You're safe."

They walked east, past the archaeological museum, and over the bridge where the canal that splits the city empties into the bay. They passed restaurants and street musicians and waved off waiters, then into the la Madera section of town on Adelita Street.

"While my family is from Germany, I find that I have very little in common with the German people." Strasser's head was down, his hands behind his back. "I spent most of my life in South America and western Europe. Argentina where our cattle ranches are. Paris and London, although I felt most at home in Madrid and Barcelona."

"No time in the homeland?"

"I find that Germans lack a certain ... gentility. Granted, my bias is a product of my malevolent father, but I have seen very little to prove otherwise. He was slow to admit when he was wrong and even slower to apologize for it. In fact, in hindsight, he didn't have the character to do either. Instead, he held grudges, had a loose relationship with the truth, and reveled in a feeling of superiority he never earned. The horrors of World War II clung to him like the odor of spoiled milk"

"Pretty harsh."

"Yes, but true. I'd like to think that I am better than that. I want to believe that time has washed my father's prejudices out of my system. Unfortunately, my time in your little city makes me think that I still hold some of those same grudges. Maybe they're ingrained in me. I chose this place to get the painting because it looked quiet and out of the way, a harmless place with harmless people that no one in the world of art and lost masterpieces cared about or even knew about. Backward. Unsophisticated. Uneducated. Non-threatening. Nothing here could ever get in my way."

Strasser seemed to slump a little, like air was leaking out of him. If he wanted to turn into a puddle on the cobblestones, Standard was good with it.

"I have learned a very important lesson," Strasser said. "It was a mistake to take anyone or anyplace for granted."

"Pretty generous for someone who ordered the murders of at least five people and probably okayed Heinz Richter's attack on me and my girlfriend. Sounds to me like you have more in common with your Nazi roots than you care to admit."

"Speaking of harsh, Mr. Standard."

"Really? Murder to get a priceless painting for nothing. It's happened before. Steal billions in great art thinking your Third Reich would last forever, then burning it all when things don't go your way."

When Strasser looked surprised, Standard laughed.

"Come on, Strasser. You had no intention of paying for that painting unless you had to. It looked that way for a while, but with Simon Nazareth dead, you saw a chance to get the painting for nothing. When you learned I had it, you tried to get it by threatening me and my friends. You offered me money that was a fraction of what you offered the Nazareths. It didn't work out. Back to Plan A."

Standard stopped to look Strasser in the face. "If you want it as badly as you say, then now you know how to get it. Let's end this. Right here. Right now."

Standard was starting to enjoy himself. He didn't know a lot about multibillionaires, but he was pretty sure they weren't used to hearing what he'd been saying.

"The problem with you Strasser is that you're everything that's wrong with the world. Wealth without humility. Excess without empathy. Your only saving grace is that you use your money to buy art rather than joyrides into the stratosphere."

"I don't need to be lectured by someone who hides from life in a Mexican beach town."

"I like it here because there are no people like you."

At the end of Adelita Street, they turned right and looped around to an alley that ran down to *Playa la Madera*. They walked the two hundred yards to the end of the beach then followed a paved, winding pathway back into town. Neither one of them had anything left to say. Strasser started a few times but stopped. By the time they reached the basketball court again, Strasser seemed to have aged ten years. He looked defeated, tired, and ready for a nap.

"The police chief told me Heinz was dead, but not how he died," Strasser said. "Care to tell me."

"He was impaled on a tiki torch after falling off a balcony. I'll never forget the smell of burning flesh."

Strasser looked startled for a few seconds. "I'll add candor to your list of attributes." He held his hand out. Standard ignored it. "As I said, I will consider your offer. If I decide to accept, I will transfer the money to Ms. Nazareth and arrange for the painting. Either way, the sooner I am rid of this place, the happier I'll be."

"It's not all that bad if you give it a chance."

"You're a very clever and resourceful man, Mr. Standard. Certainly not someone I expected to deal with in a place like this. I'd like to say it's been a pleasure, but I just can't do it. I'm sorry. I hope you understand."

"Don't overthink this. You could have your painting and at the same time get away with murder, all for the same price. Justice is blind, but in your case, it doesn't give a shit. That goes against my nature. So does giving you a pass on sending Heinz to Troncones. Left to me, you'd be back in one of Vega's cells with the rats and roaches."

Strasser started to walk away then turned around and came back. "Let's sit down again." He motioned toward empty seats in the bleachers overlooking another game. "Are you a religious man, Mr. Standard?"

"I'm not much on going to church."

Strasser gave him a wry smile. "Going to church has nothing to do with being religious. It's just showing off. I was a teenager when my grandmother died. She was the most religious person I've ever known, but she seldom went to church. Christmas and Easter maybe. Instead, she had a chapel built in her home. She prayed there twice a day. Before she passed away, she asked to see me. When I sat on the side of her bed, she took my hand and told me that she believed that there were as many souls in hell as in heaven. 'Lead a good life, Carlos.' Those were her last words."

Standard felt like he was supposed to say something. Instead, he waited while Strasser wiped his eyes and tried not to look embarrassed.

"When you're a young man you look ahead and think in terms of decades with plenty of time to achieve your goals. The decades become years, followed by months, weeks, and days. In the end you're down to hours, minutes, seconds, and asking yourself if you've accomplished what you set out to do. In my case, Mr. Standard, I will be seventy years old this year and I have achieved those goals ... with one exception."

Strasser looked at Standard, then put a hand on his shoulder.

"I'm afraid that in my obsession to possess something I have wanted all my life I have forgotten the words of my grandmother. Good night, Mr. Standard."

CHAPTER 55

THE WAY STRASSER WALKED AWAY MADE STANDARD THINK
that the multibillionaire was a beaten man forced to swallow
hard to get what he coveted the most. That was something he
wasn't used to and was having a hard time accepting. Maybe he
was someone past his prime and unable to cope with a harsher,
more cynical world. One thing was certain: He had underesti-
mated Mexico... and Standard.

Then again, Standard might have been played and Strasser
wasn't as down and out as he thought. If he wanted to find out,
he would need to be patient.

He hit Mango's for a drink, called Arturo to pick him up,
then had another drink while he waited.

"How was your time in Troncones, Señor Juan?" Arturo
said, steering the taxi through the late-night traffic.

If ever there was a time to tell Arturo what happened and
why, this was it.

Standard just wasn't up to it. The stress of dealing with
Strasser and wondering if the mysterious and so-far absent
Drago Dragovich was more than an idle threat had taken its

toll. Confronting Arturo then watching him beg and grovel for forgiveness would be more than he could handle.

Maybe there was a middle ground, a way to make a point without humiliating him.

"Do you know why Emma likes to have you drive her around?" Standard said. They were a half mile from the end of *Playa la Ropa*. The windows were down, warm air easily filling the small car. "It's because she trusts you. She knows that you will always protect her and never betray a confidence. This town looks out for Emma, no one more than you. If she trusts you, then so do I."

Arturo looked confused for a few seconds, then the look on his face told Standard that he'd made his point. Arturo mumbled a weak "*gracias.*" He didn't say anything for the rest of the trip.

"That part about never betraying a confidence is very important to Emma," Standard said before climbing out. "I'm sure you understand that."

"Of course, Señor Juan. You and Señora Emma are *muy importante.*"

"Good. I hope we never have to talk about this again."

"*Nunca*, Señor Juan."

When Standard got to the house, Emma was sitting in the front room, feet on the railing, a bottle of Patrón *Anejo* on the table next to her, a joint smoldering in her left hand. The shot glass in her other hand was empty but hadn't been for long. She looked at him with a face that said she was still pissed that he left but thrilled that he came back.

"So?" she asked.

"The ball is in Strasser's court. Either he is going to pay for the painting, or he isn't. He has until this time tomorrow."

Standard took a glass off the kitchen counter and poured himself a shot of tequila. It tasted good and felt better. The one thing he and Emma agreed on was that life was too short for cheap tequila. He half fell, half sat in a chair next to her. The beachfront restaurants were closed, so the only sound was the muted rumble of waves on the beach, something running across the roof, and the nightly gecko races inside the lampshade.

"You talked to Arturo, didn't you?" she said.

Standard nodded. "It was a soft touch. He got the message."

"Any more thoughts about Troncones?"

"Plenty," he said. "I think we should give it a second chance. Not let what happened make a difference. That was a one-off. No way anything like that could happen again. It's just that moving there doesn't feel like my call. It's yours. I'm happy where you're happy."

Emma leaned over to kiss him on the cheek. "I learned today that the man who owns the property next door would pay cash for this place. He's wanted it for years and he's a nice old guy. He wants his daughter, son-in-law, and his grandchildren to live here so he can be close to them. That means no realty fees. Together he and I can navigate the sale. Mexican law can be a little complicated, especially since I'm not a citizen."

"Price?"

"We're not that far yet, but I don't think it would be enough for that place we looked at."

Standard thought once again about the quarter million he had in the Vanguard account. It was an ace in the hole until Emma had run all the numbers. He still felt that if, in the end, what he had would get her what she wanted, he would be all in.

After Emma went to bed, Standard called Mai Nazareth to tell her to look for Strasser's money in her account sometime in the next twenty-four hours and what he would do if it showed up.

"And if it doesn't?" she said. Standard heard ice rattle in a glass.

"Then you're back in the business of finding another buyer or looking at other options. The Louvre, Prado, and The Vatican were interested enough to send representatives here. Maybe they still are."

CHAPTER 56

THE FIRST THING STANDARD DID THE NEXT MORNING WAS look out at the bay to see if *El Obra Maestro* was still there. Not surprisingly it was, further evidence that Strasser hadn't given up his quest and slinked off into the night. He had another twelve hours to pay up.

Standard and Emma had breakfast at The Tortuga before she went into town.

She didn't tell him where she was going, but he guessed that it had something to do with selling the house and financing a new one. Standard stayed to catch some sun, have a beer, and read a two-day-old *USA Today* he bought from a beach vendor. An old man with a still in the jungle behind *Playa las Gatas* came by offering mescal in plastic water bottles. Standard bought a bottle with no intention of drinking it. He'd made that mistake before. It would go under the sink with the other five bottles he bought in the past just to help the old guy out. Emma had used it to clean the oven.

Itchy Donlan called to say he and Yolanda had found an

apartment in El Centro they could afford thanks to the twenty thousand from Mai Nazareth. "It's on the top floor just two blocks from the bayfront. Big improvement from that shack we were living in. No more dirt floors and outdoor plumbing."

Standard couldn't remember a time when Itchy sounded happier. He just hoped he didn't blow through the money too fast and end up back in the hillside hovel. When he asked about Marie Mitchell, Itchy was generous but relieved to be away from her.

"Thanks to you, John, I'm off the Ixtapa circuit for a while. Maybe forever when the money from my divorce and sale of my business comes through. Things are looking up."

When Itchy asked where things stood with Strasser and the Raphael, Standard stayed vague. He had no idea which way things were going to go. Once it was over, he would tell the little guy everything. There was no hurry. Itchy was out of harm's way. He could deal with him after everything was over.

By mid-afternoon and Emma still not back, Standard packed up and walked back to the house. He showered, dressed, pulled a beer from the refrigerator under the kitchen counter, and sat down to wait.

"Tik tok, tik tok, Mr. Strasser," he said, looking out at the billionaire's yacht.

It was a little after three o'clock when Mai Nazareth called to say the full amount had been deposited in her account. "It just popped up. No warning. No phone call. Nothing. Three-hundred-and-fifty-million dollars. Just like that. I don't know what you did, Mr. Standard, but I can't thank you enough."

"Don't thank me. I made things harder for everyone. Anyway, I'll take care of everything else. The only thing I need is the provenance to give to Strasser along with the painting. I'll be there in half an hour."

Mai Nazareth was waiting in the lobby of the VistaPacifica

when he showed up. She handed him a manila envelope and thanked him again.

"Will you be staying here, or have you had enough of paradise?" Standard asked her. He wouldn't be surprised if she was eager to leave or at least get out of the hotel where her husband was killed.

"You know, I think I'll stay a while. It's cold in New York this time of year and I've come to enjoy the sun and warmth. I also think there might be more to this story, and I wouldn't want to miss it."

"Such as?"

"Who killed Simon. I told you and Strasser that I thought Drago Dragovitch was responsible. I still believe that, but I don't know for sure. Maybe if I stay a little longer, I'll find out."

Standard had been too busy to think about how Simon Nazareth died. He had a hard time believing that Strasser wasn't involved somehow, but his excuse always made sense. Besides, Heinz was more of a gun guy. He'd shot five people and held a gun to the heads of Itchy and Emma. He even died with a gun in his hand. For him to pick up a steak knife off a room service tray and stab someone in the chest seemed out of character. Too rash and opportunistic instead of cold and calculated. Whoever it was, it would have to wait. There was still a lot to do.

After Mai Nazareth went back to her room, Standard found a seat at the lobby bar, ordered a beer, and called Strasser. "I'm bringing the painting to you. Two hours. After that, make sure I never see you again."

He hung up and called Don Pedro Serrano. They talked for just a few seconds then Standard called Special Ed. After that he caught a taxi to the marina where Ed was waiting with the *Tuna Warrior*.

"The shotgun is loaded and ready," Ed said as he fired up the boat's powerful engines. "Am I going to need it?"

"Let's hope not. I want to make this as quick and simple as possible."

CHAPTER 57

They crossed the bay to *Playa las Gatas* where Serrano stood on the dock with the metal case containing *Portrait of a Young Woman.* Serrano carefully handed it to Standard, then climbed aboard. Ed pulled the boat away from the dock and made a wide turn around the bay until they were idling thirty yards off the stern of the *El Obra Maestro.*

Standard called Strasser. "You held up your end of the deal. I'm here to hold up mine."

Standard hung up. The three of them stood on the back deck of the *Tuna Warrior* and waited. There was little chance that Strasser and some of his crew would come out guns blazing, but there was no way to be sure. That gave Special Ed all the reason he needed to grab his shotgun and climb up to the flying bridge and stand at the wheel, the gun under his arm. No way anyone on the yacht could miss that.

When the billionaire appeared alone on the back deck of the yacht, Ed set the gun down, took the wheel, and eased the *Tuna Warrior* along the port side.

Strasser opened a gate in the railing and lowered a short

ladder. Standard climbed up. Once on deck, he leaned over the side. Serrano handed him the case with the painting and the manila envelope containing the provenance.

"Is the man with the shotgun necessary?" Strasser asked, looking up at Special Ed.

"No more than Heinz Richter was."

Strasser answered with a weak smile then nodded toward the case containing the painting. Standard handed it to him.

"You won't mind if I verify that this is the painting I purchased," Strasser said.

"Of course not." Standard glanced at Serrano then followed Strasser across the deck into a large parlor. "Nice boat."

"Thank you. Forgive me if I don't show you around."

Banquettes with blue velvet cushions circled the outside of the room. At one end was a fully stocked bar. At the other, a large flat-screen television. In the middle, a massive mahogany table surrounded by twelve chairs. Strasser pulled three of them away, then carefully laid the metal case on the table. He stepped back as if savoring the moment. Then, slowly opened it.

Inside, the painting was encased in thin wooden laths. He carefully began removing the screws, gently lifting off each piece of wood and setting it on the table. Underneath was a layer of heavy paper. With the same patience he showed with the wooden laths, he removed the paper, peeling from top to bottom and revealing the painting. Slowly, Strasser picked up *Portrait of a Young Woman* and held it at arm's length.

"This painting is more than seven hundred years old," Strasser said, tears in his eyes. "It's incredible, isn't it? More beautiful than I ever imagined. The word masterpiece seems inadequate somehow."

As much time as Standard had spent dealing with the painting, this was seeing it for the first time. Its small size surprised him. The heavy frame seemed to dwarf the painting, making it appear smaller than it really was. The colors were muted, the look on the young woman's face enigmatic with neither a smile nor a frown. Da Vinci's influence, Standard thought. He was underwhelmed at first, then gradually came to see that the brush strokes and paint gave off a subtle, mesmerizing elegance.

Standard's reaction was nothing compared to Strasser's. More tears welled up in the billionaire's eyes and his hands started shaking so bad Standard thought he was going to drop the painting.

"What we are looking at, Mr. Standard, is what could very well be the last masterpiece. More works of art by the great masters—Botticelli, da Vinci, Michelangelo, Titian—may be lost forever, never to be found or admired. The last da Vinci was found more than a hundred years ago. There will be no more. I'm sure of it."

He gently put the painting back on the table. "I have spent forty years believing this painting endured while others said it would never be found or never existed. They were wrong and now it is mine. Mine! Finally. You have no idea how satisfying that is."

Strasser turned to Standard, the emotion of the moment still etched on his face. "You didn't make it easy, Mr. Standard, but I suppose anything worth having should be hard to get." He held out his hand. Standard hesitated then shook it. No reason to be a sore winner. "I'd like to say it's been a pleasure doing business with you but I'm sure you'll understand if I don't."

"You know you're getting away with a priceless masterpiece and with murder, five to be exact, maybe six. If I were you, I'd call that a good day."

"Wealth does have its privileges, Mr. Standard. Now, forgive me. I need to get ready to leave."

"Sailing away tonight?"

"No. My plane will be arriving soon. I will take the helicopter to the airport. By this time tomorrow, the Raphael will be in a place of honor in my home."

"For no one to admire it but you."

"Precisely. The only thing the world needs to know is that I have it, that I was right and all of them were wrong. Why should they be allowed to see something they never thought existed in the first place?"

"There are those who knew nothing about the painting. You know, the unwashed masses. They might like to see it."

Strasser gave Standard a tolerant look. "I'll keep that in mind. Now, it's time to go."

After Standard climbed back aboard the *Tuna Warrior,* Ed pulled the boat away from the yacht and slowly headed across the bay to the City Pier. After tying up at the dock, Ed broke out three ice-cold bottles of beer and a bottle of Don Julio Especial. They toasted, drank, then toasted again.

"How did it go?" Serrano asked.

"Perfect." Standard said, smiling. "Perfect."

CHAPTER 58

After one more beer and two shots of tequila, Standard said goodbye to Serrano and Special Ed then caught a taxi back to the VistaPacifica. He needed to tell Mai Nazareth that Strasser had his painting and to collect the twenty thousand she still owed him.

The ride to Ixtapa gave him time to think about all that had happened since first meeting Simon Nazareth. Had he known what lay ahead, he would have eagerly told Nazareth thanks, but no thanks and walked away. He'd be out twenty K, but at least Itchy and Emma would have been spared having their lives threatened by Strasser's pit bull and the image of Heinz Richter impaled on a tiki torch wouldn't be etched forever in his mind. Maybe Simon would still be dead, but at least it wouldn't be any of his concern. In fact, he probably wouldn't know about it.

He got out of the taxi, walked through the hotel lobby filled with tourists and luggage, and into the elevator with a feeling of relief and accomplishment. He played most of the last few days by ear, freelancing in a way that was much different from what

307

he once did. It had all worked out. There were still a few things left to do, but nothing he couldn't handle. In fact, he looked forward to it.

Remembering the look on Strasser's face when he held up the Raphael was worth the price of admission.

He was still smiling when he got off the elevator and knocked on Mai Nazareth's door. He stopped smiling when it flew open, and a hand grabbed the front of his shirt. A man with a brutish face and tattooed forearms the size of pork roasts pulled him into the room and flung him into an end table, knocking a lamp on the floor. He looked up to see a second man holding an ice pick in Mai Nazareth's ear.

"Let me introduce you to my associate. His name is Igor."

"Of course it is," Standard said, rubbing the back of his head where it hit the table. "That would make you Drago Dragovitch."

"At your service," he said with a smile.

Dragovitch wore a dark three-piece suit with a bright pink shirt, no tie, and open at the collar. He had a square head, broad Slavic face, and a full head of red hair combed back and tucked behind his ears. Diamond pinky rings on both hands made him even more unlikeable, if that was possible.

"Ms. Nazareth tells me you have the painting. Where is it?" Dragovitch had a heavy accent, but that didn't make it hard to figure out what he wanted.

Standard started to get up but decided it might be better to stay on the floor. "Do you know how many times I've been asked that in the last five days?"

'I don't care. She says you have it. I want it."

When Standard looked at Mai, he could see the fear on her face, but still alert enough to give him an almost imperceptible shake of her head. "This woman has told me everything that has happened over the last few days, including your role in it.

That makes you being here at this moment very convenient. Now, the painting." Drago slipped the ice pick a little further into her ear. "Where is it?"

"You know, Drago. There are people who think you're responsible for killing her husband. Can we clear that up before getting to the painting?"

"I haven't killed anybody. At least not recently." He smiled and jiggled the ice pick. "That doesn't mean I won't."

"That's reassuring. I'll take your word for it. As for the painting, I gave it to Strasser."

Drago looked confused at first, then surprised. "Gave it?"

"He threatened me and my friends and he's responsible for the deaths of at least five people, including your two men."

"Did he pay for it? Where's the money?"

"I didn't get any money. I just wanted him gone. The man is a menace, but you probably already know that."

"You just gave him a priceless painting? Are you an idiot?"

"It made sense at the time."

"Where is Strasser now?"

"Last time I saw him, he was on his yacht in the bay. He told me his plane would be here soon to take him and the painting to wherever he lives, Montevideo, I think. His yacht has a helicopter."

Dragovitch looked at Standard like a rube in town to buy barn boots. "All yachts have helicopters."

"Well, I guess you would know."

Dragovitch pushed Mai down on the couch, then said something in Russian to Igor, who pulled a revolver from the small of his back, flipped open the cylinder, spun it around, and snapped it shut.

"Do you know the origins of Russian Roulette," Drago said. "It is from the revolution in 1917. They used to play it with only one empty cylinder. Stupid Bolsheviks. Now, there is only one bullet. That seems more sporting, don't you think?"

Dragovitch nodded to Igor, who put the revolver to Standard's head and pulled the trigger.

Click.

It happened so fast Standard didn't know what to do, then yelled "Whoa. Whoa. Hold on a second."

Igor spun the cylinder again, closed it, put it to Standard's head a second time, and pulled the trigger.

Click.

"God damn it," Standard yelled. He tried pulling away but there was nowhere to go.

"The painting, Mr. Standard."

"I already told you. Strasser has it and he's on his way to the airport."

Dragovitch said something in Russian to Igor, who put away the gun, smirked at Standard, and left. Dragovitch went to the bar. He poked around at the bottles until he found the vodka. He poured a tumbler full and drank it down in two gulps.

"Not bad," he said, pouring another and knocking it back. "Do you suppose room service has caviar? Probably not, and if it did, it wouldn't be any good. They'd probably serve it on a tortilla. Philistines." He poured a third shot and drank it, slower this time.

"You gave away a priceless painting for nothing." He looked at Standard with disgust. "I still can't believe it."

"It's hard to explain. You got here a little late. The good news is that if you leave now and head to the airport, you might have one last chance to steal it. I know the first time didn't work out. Maybe this time you'll have more luck."

"I know. My plane and my men are at the airport. Igor is

calling them now. The question I have is what to do with the two of you. Any suggestions?"

"You could start by thanking us for telling you where the painting is and who has it."

"I could also cut your throats and leave." He smiled at them with a mouthful of yellow, uneven teeth. "That, however, seems unfair since neither of you have done anything to deserve that." He pointed at Standard. "But you did give a priceless painting away for free. That kind of stupidity deserves some sort of punishment."

"Only because I didn't know you were here. Had I known what you were going to do to us, I would have given it to you for the same price."

"The two Russians killed trying to steal the painting were my brother and a nephew. Igor thinks you are responsible. That is reason enough to kill you."

"Igor's wrong. A man named Heinz Richter killed them. He worked for Strasser."

"And where is this Richter now?"

"He's dead. I killed him. The local cops have the evidence. You can check with them, although that might not be a good idea given your ... reputation."

"You killed the man who killed my family members?" He thought about that for a few seconds. "Maybe I will not kill you."

Dragovitch was still thinking when his phone rang. He listened, said something in Russian, then hung up. "I need to go. It would be best if both of you stayed here for a few hours until this business at the airport is finished. After that, you are free to count your blessings and thank me for not killing you."

He walked across the room to where Mai was sitting on the couch. He held her chin in his hand then gave her a long, wet kiss. "Now that you are a widow, perhaps we could have dinner sometime. I am very fond of Asian cuisine."

Mai held herself together until Dragovitch was gone, then broke down sobbing. All Standard could do was stare at her. It would take a while to get Igor and his revolver out of his head. Two clicks. Two chances to die. The term dodging a bullet had taken on a new, more personal meaning. If Mai had lingering issues, she could deal with them in her own way.

He got up and went to the bar to get a glass of whatever he could put his hands on as long as it was alcoholic. He found tequila for himself and water for her. They both drank while he fished his cell phone out of his backpack and dialed.

Adam Bovary Jones answered on the third ring. "You still interested in Drago Dragovitch?"

"Of course."

"He just left Ixtapa headed for the airport. He's going to try to steal that painting from Carlos Strasser. The one I told you about. Looks like a clash of billionaires. He has men with him. Watch out for a guy named Igor. I'd appreciate it if you could find a reason to shoot both of them. Sorry for the short notice. I'll explain later."

"Who was that?" Mai asked after he hung up.

"DEA. Can't wait to hear how that turns out."

Standard went back to the bar. He found a cold beer in the mini fridge. "I hate to bring this up after what just happened, but I need a couple of things."

The fear drained from her face a bit, replaced by a dose of reality. "Yes. Yes. Of course. Your money. I have it right here." She went into the bedroom and came back with a fat envelope. "I can't thank you enough, and maybe one day I'll understand why you did it."

"One more thing," Standard said, taking the envelope. "I'd

like the email address for the people who found the Raphael. I think you said their name was Bergen."

CHAPTER 59

IT DIDN'T TAKE LONG FOR STANDARD TO START BURNING through the money from Mai Nazareth. Even though he was more interested in drinking than eating, he took Emma to an intimate cliff-top restaurant overlooking the bay. Over a bottle of Veuve Clicquot he told her about what happened that day, leaving out any mention of Drago Dragovitch, Igor, and the little game of Russian Roulette. Sharing it with her or anyone else would only make him live it all over again. Not even French champagne or a temporarily fat bank account could make him forget that.

"Strasser is gone. Mai Nazareth has her money and so have the owners."

Emma saluted him with her glass. "That was all pretty ugly, but a win is a win."

Still drinking champagne, they ordered food. She devoured a large piece of lasagna. He pushed around a plate full of pasta primavera and thought about ordering more champagne. They decided on glasses of wine instead. When she asked what they were celebrating, he told her about getting the twenty thousand from Mai Nazareth.

"Finally," she said, "but twenty thousand for delivering a three-hundred-and-fifty-million-dollar painting. Sounds like you sold yourself too cheap."

"It is, but that was the deal Itchy and I cut with Simon Nazareth. His original offer was two thousand, so twenty was a big jump."

"So," she said. "A successful end to another of your adventures. Order more wine and we'll toast to the hope that you never have another one."

"My twenty thousand and what you could sell your house for isn't going to be enough to buy that place in Troncones, is it? The one with the wall around it and the swimming pool."

"Probably not." She gave him a disappointed look that said all anyone needed to know about how much she wanted that house. "Too bad."

Instead of more wine, he ordered two snifters of Grand Marnier. "There's something I need to tell you." She gave him the concerned look he expected. She knew him too well. "All of this isn't ... quite ... over."

"This better be good," she said, leaning back in her chair, drink in hand.

Even though she had heard some of it before, Standard explained everything again along with a few things she didn't know. When he was done, he wasn't sure if she was going to laugh or cry. It turned out to be a little of both. At least she wasn't throwing food or utensils at him.

"I can't believe you did that." She put her face in her hands and elbows on the table. "Did you and Serrano dream this up, or was it all your idea?"

"A little of both. It seemed like a good idea at the time," he said. "Still does, depending on how things work out over the next few days."

"So, what now?"

"I have two options." He explained both then waited for her answer.

"I like the second option."

"Yeah. Me too."

"This better be the end. I mean the real end."

They finished dinner, paid, and took a taxi back to *Playa la Ropa*. Emma clung to his arm, her head against his shoulder. "You really are a piece of work, no pun intended."

After Emma went to bed, Standard got out her laptop and wrote a long email to the Bergens. He explained who he was, how he got involved with *Portrait of a Young Woman,* and everything that happened between when Simon Nazareth was killed, and Carlos Strasser left. It was cathartic, a way to look back on what happened and see it in a larger context. At the end of the email, he asked what they would like to do.

He read the email again, made a few changes, then decided to wait until morning to send it, if at all. He still wasn't sure of the right thing to do.

The next morning, he read it a third and fourth time, made two small changes, then left for the beach. Over a plate of *huevos rancheros,* he decided he had no choice. He was out of options. He packed up his things, threw some money on the table, and walked home. He sat down at the laptop, paused for a few minutes, then hit "Send."

The answer came two hours later in an email. "We will be there in 48 hrs. I'll contact you when we land."

CHAPTER 60

LATER THAT DAY, STANDARD SAT IN THE LIVING ROOM watching as *El Obra Maestro* sailed away, leaving the bay looking lost, empty, and a little smaller. The yacht headed due west, then, just as it was about to disappear over the horizon, turned south. The only thing he noticed about it was that the helicopter was back on the foredeck and lashed down.

He walked back down to The Tortuga, pulled a lounge chair out into the sun, and called Adam Bovary Jones.

"What did I miss?" he asked.

"Not much, considering who we were dealing with. When we got to the airport, Dragovitch was standing next to his jet watching another plane take off and head southeast. I had five men with me, all in full gear. He took one look at us and nodded to his men. They all stood down except one. He decided to shoot it out. He got off one round before we hit him with five in the chest."

"That must have been Igor I told you about. Can't say I'm sorry to see him go. What about the rest?"

"We turned them over to the federales. They can do what-

317

ever they want. Knowing them, probably nothing. I only wanted Dragovitch. We'll hold him here until we get a plane to take him to the States. Your government owes you one, John."

"What will happen to him?"

"We'll charge him with drug trafficking, stick him in a federal prison somewhere, slow walk the whole thing, and hang on to him until he becomes fodder for some prisoner exchange. He's tight with Putin. I doubt we'll have him for long. He'll probably get swapped out for some reporter or a dissident who's been rotting away in some Russian prison." Jones paused for a few seconds."There's one thing you need to know. As we were cuffing Dragovitch and putting him in my SUV, he looked at me and said 'Fuck that Standard guy.'"

"Was he serious?"

"I doubt it. He has a lot more to worry about than you. I wouldn't sweat it. I just thought you should know."

"The plane that took off. Strasser?"

"Yeah," Jones said. "We got the plane's numbers and its flight plan. Registered to him and headed for Montevideo."

"For what it's worth, I don't believe Dragovitch killed Simon Nazareth."

"So what? We got plenty of other things to charge him with. By the way, arresting Dragovitch may come with a reward. Want me to check it out?

"Why not?"

Standard spent the rest of the day at the beach. Breakfast led to lunch, lunch led to a Margarita, Margarita led to a second one. At late afternoon, he walked home. Emma was gone but left a note to meet her at Mango's for dinner. He took a nap, showered, dressed, and got a taxi into town.

He got to Mango's a little after six. Emma could show up in five minutes or an hour, whichever it was it gave him time to spend more of Mai Nazareth's money on high-end tequila. As if sensing that Standard was about to buy a drink, Itchy Donlan showed up and sat next to him. He stared across at the other side of the circular bar where the regulars were gathering for their nightly round of gossip, Margaritas, air kisses, and man hugs.

Standard ordered two shots of Gran Patrón Burdeos, one for each of them.

"That stuff is four hundred dollars a bottle," Itchy said, running the glass under his nose, taking a sip, and savoring it. "I take it that asshole Strasser has his painting and you settled up with the Nazareth woman." They clinked glasses as a toast to their mutual payday. "Now, tell me what happened to that Heinz guy." Standard described the night in Troncones, including Heinz holding a gun to Emma's head and the fall off the terrace.

"A tiki torch," Itchy said. "Sorry I missed that. Anyway, another successful case, eh John. I think this partnership of ours is really working out."

Standard didn't bother to tell Itchy for the hundredth time that there was no partnership. Instead, he ordered two more shots of tequila then asked whether Marie Mitchell was really out of the picture.

"I'm done with her, John. The last time I saw her all she was doing was drinking and mumbling to herself. Instead of rambling on about some dead cat back in New York it was about some business deal that went bad. Best I could tell, she and her husband lost a lot of money. They tried to get it back then couldn't. Then he committed suicide. Best I could tell it was just a few years ago."

"Sounds terrible. What was this business deal?"

"Not sure. Something they bought thinking it would turn a quick profit. That's all I know and all I want to know. The good news is that Yolanda and I have moved into our new apartment. It will feel like having a real place to live again."

Itchy made a strategic retreat when Emma showed up. Standard ordered her a shot of the same expensive tequila then asked the maître d' to get them a table in the dining room.

"Are we still celebrating?" she asked when they sat down. When he said yes, she ordered a steak and a bottle of Veuve Clicquot. "I'm beginning to enjoy your newfound wealth. How long will it last and what are you going to do when it's gone?"

"Let's enjoy. I'll figure it out when the time comes."

"John, I don't think you realize that the only way you earn money is on adventures that endanger both of our lives. That is not a sustainable business model."

"You're right. Now, can we talk about something else?"

Over dinner and on the taxi ride home, Emma told him about her visit with her realtor and a banker. By her estimate, she was about a hundred-thousand dollars short of what she needed to buy the house in Troncones.

"I could take out a loan," she said, "but I'm worried about paying it back. My income here is steady, but this is a place where the future is always uncertain. I need to think about it."

Standard made up his mind that he would cash in enough of his Vanguard account to get her over the top. He just wouldn't tell her about it until he had time to open an account at a local bank and the money showed up.

That night, Standard couldn't sleep. He kept thinking about what Itchy had said about Marie Mitchell. He tossed and turned until Emma finally asked him what was wrong.

"Something Itchy said. Probably no big deal."

"This better not be the start of another adventure, and if it is make sure it doesn't involve guns, homicidal Germans, and tiki torches."

Standard stayed in bed for a couple of more hours, then,

just before dawn, he dressed, made coffee, and fired up the laptop. It took him two hours of searching various websites before finding what he was looking for. To make sure he was right, he sent an email to Benny Orlando and gave him one name and a brief explanation.

"Just check my work," he wrote. "I need to be sure I'm on the right track."

It didn't take Benny long to answer. He confirmed what Standard had learned on his own, plus a law review article from a small university in New York state. He read the article once, then a second time. He closed the computer, poured more coffee, and went into the living room to stare into the jungle and listen to the birds and squirrels run through the treetops.

At ten a.m., he finished the breakfast that Emma had made, then walked down the hill to catch a taxi. No surprise Arturo was there. It was Tuesday and he always took Emma shopping on Tuesdays. Standard climbed in the back.

"Is Señora Emma coming? Should I wait?"

"No. Take me to the state police station. You can come back after that."

They drove by hotel maids dressed in black with white aprons getting on and off buses in the hotel district. A utility crew blocked the road for ten minutes. They spent the time staring at the back of a school bus, the happy children making faces at them out the back window.

Vega was in his office, coffee in one hand, a half-eaten pastry in the other. On his lap was an open file covered in crumbs and coffee stains. He was surprised to see Standard. More surprised with what Standard told him.

"I don't agree. The man who died in Troncones, Heinz Richter, killed Simon Nazareth along with the other five," Vega said when Standard finished. "That's what my official report says."

"Come on, Alejandro, you're using a dead man to clear all your unsolved cases."

Vega looked embarrassed but didn't say anything. Instead, he took Standard's cell phone and read the information from Benny Orlando, including the law review article.

Standard waited while Vega read, sipped coffee, and downed two more flaky pastries.

"You're sure about all this," Vega said.

"Ninety percent."

"Then I guess we better start asking some questions."

CHAPTER 61

AT NOON, THE LOBBY OF THE VISTAPACIFICA WAS FILLED with guests checking out and arranging rides to the airport for the afternoon flights out of town. Children sat on over-stuffed luggage looking tired, sunburned, and ready for home. Taxis and shuttle buses arrived empty and left full. They would return in a few hours with pale and excited replacements.

As a courtesy, Vega let the hotel's director of security know he was there but stayed vague about the reason why. Seeming only mildly interested, the security director nodded then thanked Vega for letting him know.

Vega waited while Standard found a house phone, called, then hung up when no one answered. They walked through the restaurant, past the lunch buffet, and out to one of the three swimming pools. It was the heat of the day. Screaming children filled the pool. Adults sat in the shade of a swim-up bar drinking Margaritas and Mai Tais. A half dozen fat iguanas dozed on the island in the middle of the pool.

Marie Mitchell was sitting in a pool-side lounge chair asleep, a towel over her legs, the ice in her Margarita half melted. Standard guessed that it wasn't her first. He pulled over a chair and sat beside her. Vega did the same on the other side.

"Marie?" Standard said. "Wake up. We need to talk."

When Marie Mitchell slowly opened her eyes, she looked scared and confused for a moment as if not knowing where she was. After a few seconds she focused on Standard's face and smiled. "Mr. Standard, how nice to see you again. It's been forever."

It had only been a few days but there was no reason to debate the point.

"Marie, this is Alejandro Vega. He's with the local police. We need to ask you a few things."

"Police, oh my," she said, slowly shifting her gaze toward Vega. "Did something bad happen? Did someone die? Is Itchy okay?"

"Itchy's fine, but he's not why we're here." Standard waited for her gaze to shift back to him, then started explaining. "Several years ago, you and your husband purchased an expensive piece of art, a painting, as an investment. You thought it was an original Monet, but it turned out to be a fake. You sued to get your money back. It didn't work. You lost almost two million dollars. Several months later, your husband committed suicide."

Marie Mitchell continued looking at Standard, her mouth open. "How do you know about that?"

"There are no secrets anymore, Marie. I found articles about your lawsuit, what happened with it, and your husband's death. The man who sold you the fake painting was Simon Nazareth, wasn't it?" She didn't have to answer, so Standard kept going. "You've hated him ever since, and with good reason. He cheated you. Cost you a more comfortable retirement. You blamed him for your husband's suicide. Then you come down here on vacation and who do you see? Simon Nazareth, staying in the same hotel."

"Do you want to tell us the rest, Señora Mitchell?" Vega said. "However, I need to warn you about self-incrimination and how what you say can be used against you in our courts of law."

Marie Mitchell gave Vega a vacant smile. "That's very sweet, but I don't believe that will be necessary."

She pulled herself up, straightened the towel around her feet, and motioned to a passing waiter for a bottle of water. Standard and Vega waited for her to get situated and for the water to show up.

"I killed the bastard," she said, finally. "I don't regret it and I'd do it again. He was a crook who ruined our lives. He deserved to die."

Surprised, Vega took it in stride. "That's what we thought, Señora Mitchell, but we weren't sure. Thank you for clearing that up and doing it so ... quickly."

"Tell us about it, Marie," Standard said. "What happened?"

"I was in the restaurant with Itchy. It was the day he introduced you to me. The two of you left, saying you had business to do. I watched both of you walk away to a table in the corner, and there he was. At first, I thought I was mistaken until I saw him again talking to you out here by the pool. I couldn't believe it. What were the chances?"

Standard remembered both meetings with Nazareth and seeing her at the same time. It was on the second visit that he noticed her standing in the lobby looking outside at the pool, and, apparently, at Nazareth.

"When I was sure it was him, I didn't know what to do. I tried to let it go, to not let it bother me. But I just couldn't get him out of my mind. What he did to us. What happened to my husband. It all came back to me like a recurring nightmare.

Finally, I decided to meet him face to face, ask him if he remembered my husband, tell him that Edwin was dead because of him. I found out what room he was staying in and went to see him. When I got there the door was unlocked. I said hello. I think I might have knocked."

That made sense. Nazareth was killed while waiting for Standard, his wife, and the painting to arrive from the airport. He left the door unlocked so he wouldn't have to get out of the hot tub when they showed up.

"There he was in all his glory," Marie continued. "Staying in a beautiful penthouse, sitting in a hot tub, gazing out at the ocean. All of it probably paid for with money he stole from us. The knife was on a room service tray. I don't remember picking it up. What I do remember is standing behind him thinking about everything he had done. Thinking about my husband. The money we had spent a lifetime earning—money that would have allowed us to retire and travel together like we had always dreamed about. He didn't know I was there at first. I only remember him turning his head when I reached over his shoulder. He didn't look surprised at first. I think he was expecting someone else. When I stuck the knife in his chest he looked down. Blood was running into the water, turning it a lovely shade of pink. More blood came out of his mouth when he coughed. I left after that."

Vega and Standard glanced at each other. Standard had been right, and Vega had been right to believe him.

"I didn't realize what I'd done or what it meant until I got back to my room," Marie said. "I felt remorse and at the same time satisfied. The man responsible for so much misery was now dead himself. It was later that the guilt set in. I thought drinking would help. It did, a little."

Vega got out his cell phone. Even with Standard's severely

limited Spanish, he knew the *comandante* was calling a patrol car to come and arrest her.

"I feel better having told you all of this," Marie said. "Please tell Itchy goodbye and that I'm sorry." Then, she seemed to slide back into whatever happy place she'd been in before they got there.

Vega and Standard moved to another table—far enough away that she couldn't hear them, close enough to keep an eye on her.

"What's going to happen now?" Standard asked.

"We'll get her confession. She might get a lawyer. Eventually, she will go before a judge and be sentenced. Likely she will go to prison, but there are facilities in Mexico for people like her, ones that are more... civilized. I'll have to amend my earlier report. Probably say something like 'based on new evidence.'"

Standard looked over at her. She seemed to be asleep or at least at peace with what she'd done now that it was no longer a secret that gnawed at her.

When Vega's men arrived, he talked to them privately for a few minutes then watched as they gently helped the compliant Marie out of her lounge chair and along the pool into the lobby. Standard thought it was a nice touch that they didn't handcuff her in front of the other, gawking guests. He knew that had been Vega's idea and he thanked him for it.

"Feel better now?" Standard said. "Justice is done."

"Not really. She's a nice woman who was wronged. I would have been more than happy to continue blaming Richter for everything." He watched Marie leave with his men. "Let's see what happens."

CHAPTER 62

THE NEXT MORNING, STANDARD GOT A TEXT FROM FRED Bergen asking to meet in Mai Nazareth's room at the VistaPacifica. Standard answered that he would be there by three in the afternoon, then called Don Pedro Serrano.

"It's time to close the book on all of this," Standard said.

"I'll get everything ready."

Standard took his time having breakfast with Emma and telling her what was about to happen.

"That means it's time to settle up," Emma said, putting her arms around him. "Finally. It's long overdue. I'd wish you luck, but you don't need it. You played this one right even though there were times it didn't look that way. Now, say hello to Don Pedro for me and invite him to dinner."

Standard took a taxi into town, then a *panga* across the bay to *Playa las Gatas*. Serrano was waiting for him at his compound. He was standing next to a table with two shot glasses, the bottle of boutique tequila in one hand, and a metal case in the other.

"First, a toast," he said, pouring two shots. "To you, John.

Thank you for giving me the opportunity to possess, even for a short time, a priceless painting by one of the great masters. It was the privilege of a lifetime. *Gracias.*"

They clinked glasses. Serrano poured two more.

"When did you start on the forgery?" Standard asked. "It must have taken a while given how convincing it was. Strasser never doubted for a moment that it was the real thing."

"Right after we brought it here. I knew enough about the players involved in wanting it that a copy might come in handy. If it didn't, then so what? Fortunately, it did. I have to admit, it was a pretty good replica for someone out of practice, but it wasn't easy. I found an ancient door panel at an old mission in Petatlán that was nearly the exact size of the Raphael painting. There was also a large, sixteenth-century portrait of an early priest. I took some scrapings and reconstituted the paint with various colors mixed with linseed oil and varnish."

Serrano poured two more shots, and they toasted his success. "How long do you think it will take Strasser to figure out that he paid three-hundred-fifty million for a forgery?" Standard asked.

"Depends. He is more of a collector than an expert, so it could be a while. I think once he gets it home and takes a closer look, he will realize what happened."

Serrano smiled and sipped his drink. "Not that it matters. There's not much he can do now."

"What you learned paying for art school didn't go to waste. Now it's time to return the real thing to its owners."

"*Sí*, but not the rightful owners. Works of art like *Portrait of a Young Woman* belong to the world. Not one man or woman, and certainly not one like Carlos Strasser. By denying it to him, you have struck a blow for beauty over avarice. Let's hope the owners feel the same way. Given that they agreed to sell the painting to Strasser in the first place, I don't hold out much hope. I would gladly be wrong."

After drinking two more toasts, Standard thanked Serrano again, then took the original Raphael back across the bay. Arturo was waiting at the base of the City Pier. "Where to, Señor Juan?"

"Ixtapa. VistaPacifica."

CHAPTER 63

MAI NAZARETH WAS WAITING FOR HIM WHEN HE KNOCKED on the door of her penthouse suite. She gave him a hug, then led him inside to where two people were sitting at the dining room table, sliding glass doors behind them open to let in a warm breeze and the sound of waves.

"John Standard," Mai said. "This is Fred and Tiffany Bergen. The owners of *Portrait of a Young Woman.*"

Fred Bergen looked to be in his fifties, small, owlish, and with thinning hair and dark-framed glasses. He was wearing a light-green golf shirt with a St. Andrews logo, white pants, and penny loafers. Tiffany Bergen looked half his age. She had a mane of blonde hair combed back over the top of her head, a toothy smile, and maybe a touch of Botox. She wore Bermuda shorts, a crop top, and sandals.

After shaking hands, Standard sat down across from them. Mai took a chair at the far end of the table. Whatever was going to happen next was between Standard and the Bergens.

"Thank you for coming, Mr. Standard," Fred Bergen said. He stood up, shook Standard's hand, then looked at his wife.

"We came to get the Raphael, but we also wanted to personally thank you for everything you've done. Mai has told us all of it, including the gory details. To be honest, what has happened down here and your role in it has been something of an epiphany for us. Isn't that right, Tiff?"

Tiffany Bergen dutifully nodded in agreement then flashed Standard a practiced smile.

Standard handed the metal case containing the original Raphael to Fred Bergen. He took it and set it gently in the middle of the table.

"Don't you want to make sure it's the original?" Standard asked.

Bergen smiled. "I'm not going to insult you, Mr. Standard. Your email made it clear that your motives in all of this are honorable. Besides, I believe that the bad guys in this story are either dead or have left town."

When there was a knock on the door, Tiffany Bergen got up and came back with a tray filled with glasses and a pitcher of Margaritas. Fred Bergen poured for each of them.

"So, what happens now?" Standard asked.

"We've decided to keep the painting for the time being," Fred Bergen said. "We've been rethinking everything, so rather than sell it I believe we will eventually donate it to a museum. There are certain tax advantages to doing that, but we still need to explore it further."

The four of them toasted Bergen's decision.

"In hindsight, we regret attempting to sell it in the first place and, after what we've learned from you and Mai about what has happened over the last few days, certainly not to Carlos Strasser. We don't blame Simon Nazareth." He nodded toward Mai Nazareth. "That was not his fault. He only did what we asked him to do. It was the wrong thing. We'll take the blame for that."

"For what it's worth, Simon's death had nothing to do with the painting," Standard said, then explained about Marie Mitchell. "Wrong place, wrong time, I guess."

Mai Nazareth looked surprised at first, then gave Standard a weak nod of acknowledgment. If she played a role in bilking the Mitchells, this was not the time or place to talk about it.

"There is one thing you could clear up for us," Fred Bergen said. "Why did you get so deeply involved in this? I understand taking the job of picking up and delivering the Raphael and Mai to her husband. What you did after that is something of a mystery to us."

"I've asked myself the same question. I keep coming up with the same answer: Character flaw. I don't like people who kill other people and threaten my friends."

The Bergens smiled at each other. "Then you'll get a little more satisfaction from what we are about to tell you."

"Strasser?"

"Indeed. Two hours after I got your email, I got one from Strasser. When he got the painting back to Montevideo, he discovered that you had given him a forgery. He wanted his money back. All of it. I have to say it was a very... heated conversation, to say the least."

"If it's the Strasser I know, he probably threatened to kill you or have someone else do it for him."

Fred Bergen laughed. "Not quite, but close. So, tell me. Where did you get a forgery capable of fooling one of the world's foremost art collectors?"

Expecting the question, Standard was ready. "There are two answers to that. The first is no, I won't tell you except to say that Zihuatanejo is a city of surprises. All you need to do is poke around and get to know the right people."

"And the second?"

"Maybe Strasser is not what you all think he is. As someone just told me, the fake only needed to fool one person."

Fred Bergen laughed. "You may be right. Anyway, after Strasser calmed down, we were able to reach an agreement. I will repay him, minus Mai's fee, plus several million more in compensation to the organizations of the people he had killed. In exchange, we agreed not to tell the art world that he had been duped into buying a fake Raphael. Apparently, saving one's reputation comes with a price. In this case, we returned roughly half of what he paid for the forgery."

Standard looked down the table at Mai Nazareth. She smiled, raised her glass, and said, "Freedom, Mr. Standard. Freedom."

Standard knew immediately what she meant. She just earned roughly seventy-million-dollars, all of it coming out of Carlos Strasser's pocket.

"Thanks to your efforts, Mr. Standard, we learned what kind of person Strasser really is and what a travesty it would have been had the Raphael ended up in his hands. As I said, we have you to thank for that."

"You know what Strasser and Heinz Richter did while they were here. I couldn't let any of it pass. By simply giving him the painting, even though he'd paid for it, I was rewarding bad behavior. I don't do that. Sounds like you don't either."

"No, Mr. Standard, we don't. Now that we fully understand everything that happened since the painting arrived in Zihuatanejo, we need to do a little business."

Tiffany Bergen poured another round of drinks while her husband produced a small leather portfolio, set it on the table, and unzipped it. Inside were several forms and a white envelope.

"As a way of showing our appreciation, I have taken the liberty of establishing an account in your name at the CIBC

First Caribbean International Bank in the Cayman Islands. The account contains five million dollars."

Fred Bergen slid two forms across the table and handed the confused Standard a pen. "If you'll sign these documents, I will have my people take care of the rest." He slid the envelope across the table. "This contains all the account information, contacts at the bank, and instructions on how to access the money. I hope this meets with your satisfaction."

Stunned, Standard looked at Fred Bergen and his wife. They were all smiles. Same with Mai Nazareth, who raised her glass and said, "Freedom," a second time.

"Five million! Seems like a lot for all the trouble I put everyone through."

"Trouble, yes?" Fred Bergen said. "But good trouble as someone once said."

Standard stared at the forms for a few seconds, then gave Fred Bergen a questioning look. "On the level?"

"Completely. We are playing with house money. Remember, thanks to you, we have a hundred-million dollars of Carlos Strasser's money to do with whatever we wish, and we still have the Raphael. I'm hard pressed to imagine a better outcome as far as we are concerned. I hope that having a substantial chunk of Strasser's money will mitigate your frustration that he got away with murder."

"No argument from me," Standard said as he looked through the documents. It was all straightforward.

"Forgive me for asking," Fred Bergen said, "but while this is a lovely place and you appear to be at home here, it makes me think that perhaps your talents are wasted in this place. What you've accomplished is something worthy of Wall Street. Why stay?"

"If you'd asked me that ten minutes ago, I might not have had an answer. Now I have five million of them."

Fred and Tiffany Bergen nodded in unison.

Standard signed the forms then slipped the envelope into his backpack. "Saying thank you doesn't seem adequate, but I can't think of anything better."

"No need, but there are two other items of business," Fred Bergen handed Standard a second envelope. "I understand you have a partner of sorts. A Mr. Donlan, I believe. Mai has told us all about him and the deal he made with Simon. Please give him this with our sincere thanks for his role in what has happened. I hope he feels that a hundred thousand dollars is just compensation for his efforts. Courtesy of Mr. Strasser, of course." Bergen smiled. "We have come to think of him as the gift that keeps on giving."

Standard took the envelope and laughed. "I'm sure Itchy will be more than happy."

"One last thing. Tiffany and I have opened a five-star hotel and restaurant in a refurbished nunnery in the south of France. I believe Simon told you about it. It was where we found the painting. We have named it The Raphael. You'll be pleased to know that as part of our agreement with Strasser, he is sending us the forgery. We plan on displaying it at the hotel with all the proper disclaimers, of course. You are welcome to come and stay with us for as long as you like. On the house, of course."

"This is all very generous," Standard said, feeling a little embarrassed.

Tiffany Bergen took away the Margarita pitcher and glasses then came back with a bottle of champagne. After they toasted and drank, Standard said his goodbyes.

Mai Nazareth followed him out the door and down the elevator to the lobby.

"I want to thank you, John. This all turned out better than I ever dreamed. After what happened to Simon, then Strasser, and finally that awful Russian. I had lost all hope."

"No need. I made things more complicated for everybody. That's just me. It's happened before. I just hope it never happens again. What will you do now?"

"Simon and I talked about buying a villa in Mallorca once this deal was done. I suppose I'll go there now, alone. It's what he would have wanted."

"Sounds nice."

"If you ever take up the Bergen's offer to stay at their hotel, Mallorca is not that far away. You're welcome to visit."

Standard smiled to himself. A half hour earlier he was just some guy hanging out in bars and beachfront restaurants trying to figure out how to scrape together enough money to help Emma buy her dream house. Now he was getting invitations to a five-star hotel in the south of France and a villa in the Mediterranean.

"I'll keep that in mind. Thank you."

"And you?"

"I'll stick around here."

Standard went into the hotel bar, ordered a beer, and took out the papers Fred Bergen had given him. Five million dollars. Maybe there is a pot of gold at the end of the rainbow, but for Standard it wasn't a beautiful arc through a misty sky, but a twisting path of good and bad decisions and paths not taken; of equal parts luck and calculation; of believing that the best justice in the world was a bad thing happening to bad people. He looked again at the five-million-dollar bottom line and decided that whatever he'd done had all been worth it.

CHAPTER 64

WITH THE LAST PIECE OF THE PUZZLE IN PLACE, STANDARD went back to doing what he did best: Nothing.

For the next two weeks, he did little but spend his days on the beach at The Tortuga and his nights taking Emma to dinner. *Playa la Ropa* was once again in full bloom, a kaleidoscope of colorful swimsuits, shorts, and T-shirts parading back and forth in front of him. Only the faces and shapes changed. Young replaced old. Fat replaced slim. Tall replaced short. And then all of it vice versa. A parade of newlyweds and nearly deads. The sailboats in the bay had their own dance. Some came. Some left. Some never moved. Banana boats with screaming children sped by. Further out, jet skis raced across the bay, rooster tails shooting out the back. Parasails towed by speedboats floated around the bay before depositing their passengers back on the beach, usually without injuries. Pangas came and went from the marina. Others ferried tourists back and forth across the bay between *Playa las Gatas* and the City Pier. He started jogging along the beach each morning. He killed time by reading *Lord of the Rings* for the first time since college.

It took a stunned Emma a while to understand everything that had happened and what it meant for all the things they had talked about. When he told her that now anything was possible, it brought her to tears. She hugged him, gave him a kiss, then made plans to meet with her realtor and a lawyer. The first thing she learned was that the house in Troncones was still on the market and theirs if they wanted it. Emma couldn't say yes fast enough.

While the details were being worked out, he and Emma flew to Mexico City for a week of shopping, sightseeing, and dining out. Emma picked out rugs and art, leaving Standard to do little more than nod in agreement. Seeing her that happy was all he needed.

Evenings were spent drinking wine and talking about what their new life would look like. Left unsaid was whether a change of scenery would also mean a change in his luck. They both wanted to put the chaos behind them so badly they didn't even talk about it. If it went unsaid, maybe it would happen.

CHAPTER 65

EMMA'S REALTOR WAS WAITING AT THE GATE TO THE house in Troncones. After handing over the keys along with a congratulatory bottle of high-end tequila, they unlocked the gate, drove in, parked *El Furioso* in the spacious two-car garage, and got out. Before going inside, Emma gave Standard another in a long series of hugs, kisses, and more.

"This place belongs to both of us," he said. "We made this happen together."

It only took a few days for Standard to get money out of the account in The Caymans and into one at the local Scotia Bank. What followed were two months of negotiating Mexico's byzantine laws regarding the sale of property to non-citizens. It took an intervention from Vega and Serrano to get it done. While they waited it out, Emma put her house up for rent. Selling it was no longer necessary. She could keep it and earn income even though they didn't need it anymore. The old man who wanted to buy it for his family was disappointed, but agreed to rent it for his daughter, son-in-law, and their children. Emma gave them a bargain-basement rate.

That didn't make leaving any easier.

Emma got tears in her eyes as movers loaded their belongings into a van for the trip north. She left enough behind to make sure the old man's family would have everything they needed. Even then, she had no trouble filling the van with things she couldn't part with. Still, leaving was hard. She had designed, built, and paid for the house herself with no help. It had been her life for fifteen years. Deciding to rent it gave her a softer landing, but not that soft.

Then, in true Emma fashion, she quickly put it behind her and looked to what was ahead.

No sooner had they parked the Plymouth in its new home, then the van with their belongings showed up. Emma barked orders to the movers, while Standard walked through the house for the tenth time. The spacious living room. Gourmet kitchen. Guest rooms on the first floor. The spacious master bedroom on the second floor looking out over the pool with the ocean beyond a line of stately palm trees. The large bathroom with the tiled, walk-in shower.

He stayed out of the way until the movers were done and their belongings sitting in boxes in the middle of the living room. After that, the delivery trucks arrived with new furniture, including a king-sized bed with headboard, dressers, couches, chairs, end tables, and lamps. There were new dishes, pots, pans, and silverware. Emma ordered the delivery men around until by late afternoon everything was exactly where and how she wanted it. She started opening one of the packing boxes, then decided it could wait. There was no hurry. The hardest parts were over.

"I'm hungry and sweaty," she said. "Why don't you go find some food and I'll take a shower."

Standard walked up the street to a tienda for food, beer,

and tequila. When he got back, Special Ed's Pontiac Bonneville was parked in the street outside the gate.

Inside, Emma was proudly showing Ed, Itchy Donlan, and Don Pedro Serrano around the house. She wore a silk robe, her hair still wet from the shower.

"Nice digs," Ed said, giving Standard a congratulatory handshake and two bottles of champagne as a housewarming gift. "Sorry to show up unannounced. We thought we'd surprise you. Maybe help out a little bit." He looked around the house and then at Emma. "But it looks like she has everything under control."

Itchy could only stand and stare at the front room, kitchen, and the pool turned a soft blue from the underwater lights.

"Incredible," Itchy said when Standard handed him a beer and a shot. "Kind of quiet though, isn't it? And a long way from Mango's. I'm going to miss meeting you there and going on cases together."

"I'm all in with quiet," Standard said.

Serrano stood to one side looking at the walls, then went back to the car and returned with one of his paintings. It was a large, colorful depiction of a house with walls covered in bougainvillea. "I think it will look nice right over there," he said to Emma, pointing to a vacant wall behind one of the new couches.

"I think that's perfect." She gave him a long hug and a heartfelt thank you.

They sat around the new dining room table drinking and munching on the snacks Standard had picked up at the store. When Ed asked what he had missed, Standard filled them in, including the windfall from Strasser via the Bergens. Just not how much it was.

Standard had given Itchy his hundred K the same day he got the check from the Bergens. The little man was speechless.

In less than two weeks he had gone from dead broke to a bank account filled with money from the Nazareths, the sale of his business, his divorce, and Carlos Strasser.

Now, he eagerly told all of them that he and Yolanda were going to open a small restaurant on Adelita Street in La Madera, otherwise known as Gringo Gulch. "Turns out Yolanda is better at cooking than at making baby clothes. The place even has an apartment upstairs."

That called for a round of toasts then a short walk into town for dinner. It was late when they got back. They said their goodbyes in the street outside the house. Emma and Standard watched the Bonneville head up the street.

"The hardest part about living here is that I'll see less of those guys," Standard said.

"We're not that far away. You can see them whenever we go to town."

"Even Itchy?"

She smiled. "Even Itchy."

CHAPTER 66

Alejandro Vega showed up the next morning just as Emma and Standard were finishing breakfast. He greeted Standard with a handshake and Emma with a polite hug, handing her a ceramic vase as a housewarming present.

"How's retirement?" Standard asked after pouring him a cup of coffee.

"It is hard to find the words. It's been a month and I still wake up every morning feeling like someone just pulled a knife out of my back. The best part is that I went out on top."

"Must feel good not to deal with drug lords anymore, although you did a good job holding them at bay for the good of the city."

"Thank you. It was not easy."

"Travel plans?"

"France in the fall. My wife is making the arrangements now."

Standard made more coffee while Emma warmed up some pastries for Vega. They sat by the pool. Wind off the ocean rattling the palm trees along the beach.

"And Marie Mitchell?" Standard asked.

"She went before a judge two weeks ago. I appeared on her behalf. I told the judge that I stand by my initial report that said Heinz Richter killed Simon Nazareth. Ms. Mitchell may have confessed, but I didn't believe her. I said she may have emotional issues that were better dealt with at her home in New York City." Vega shrugged. "The judge let her go. She flew home two days ago. I consider it my last official act."

Standard smiled and raised his glass in a toast to Vega. Emma knew enough about Marie Mitchell and the part she played to do the same.

"Thank you for that," Standard said. "Add one more name to the list of those getting away with murder."

While Emma cleared the dishes and looked for where to put her new vase, Vega handed Standard an envelope. "This is from our friend at the DEA, Agent Jones. He says it's a reward for helping with that Russian, Dragovitch." Vega looked around the house. "I guess the rich get richer."

Before he left, Emma showed Vega around the house. She put her arm through his and invited him and his family to come and visit them anytime.

After he left, Standard opened the envelope. It contained twenty-five thousand US dollars and a note that read: "There wasn't a reward, but I managed to scrape together something as a way of saying thanks. Drago is out of circulation. Rest easy. I'll drop by when I can."

Vega left after congratulating them on their new house and promising not to be a stranger.

They slept in the next morning, then spent the rest of the day unpacking the last of the boxes and filling the closets and bureaus with their clothes. Late in the afternoon, Emma gave Standard a list and sent him to the store. That night, she made chili rellenos with rice and fried plantains. Standard watched her from the living room as she happily moved around the kitchen, cooking, and learning where everything went. When dinner was ready, she set the table with their new plates.

After dinner, they washed the dishes and cleaned up the kitchen before taking a bottle of wine outside to sit by the pool. Palm trees waving back and forth in a gentle wind looked like old ladies with bad hair passing rumors from one to the other. Waves pounding the beach, people rode by on horseback, and small birds hopped along the bougainvillea that covered the walls.

Saying she was tired, Emma took her wine and headed off to bed. Standard stayed behind, finishing his glass, then deciding to take a swim. He slipped into some shorts, dived in, swam a couple of laps before finishing at the far end of the pool.

He had just draped his arms over the edge to look out at the ocean when he saw the shadow move between two of the palm trees fronting the beach.

He slowly climbed out of the pool and walked back toward the house. The laundry room was behind the kitchen near the garage door. The Glock was on the top shelf above the dryer. A pair of Topsiders were on the floor near the washer.

Two steps outside into the street, he turned left, and followed the wall along the north side of the property. He made as little noise as possible as he moved down the sandy path toward the beach. At the end of the wall, he stopped, held the pistol in front of his face, and peeked around the corner.

The man crouched in the sand was dressed in camo with face paint and a safari hat. The sniper rifle perched on top of the wall was pointed toward the house—pointed toward Emma.

Emma.

Without a thought, Standard stepped around the corner. The butt of the Glock hit the side of the sniper's head. He went down with a groan, face in the sand, blood leaking from a large gash above his right ear. Standard sat on the sniper's back and waited. Gradually, he came to, groaned again, then tried to move. Standard's weight kept him pressed into the soft sand.

"Who sent you?" Standard asked.

"Fuck you." The sniper said it with a heavy Slavic accent.

Standard reached around behind him, put the gun to the fat part of the sniper's thigh, and pulled the trigger. The muffled pop blew flesh, meat, and blood out through the sniper's pants. When he started to scream, Standard put a hand around his throat.

"I tried my best not to hit any vital arteries, but I can't be certain. So, you better tell me who sent you if you want to live."

"Drago." He said it through teeth clenched in pain. It was more a plea than an answer.

"Drago's in prison."

"He has ways."

"Why?"

"You lied to him about the painting and the money. He thinks you ratted him out to the DEA."

Standard shook his head. All that was true, but he thought a drug-running oligarch sitting in a federal prison in the United States would have other things to worry about.

"Jesus, what's wrong with you people?"

Standard stood up, grabbed the sniper by the back of his shirt, and pulled him to his feet. "Give me your cell phone." When the sniper only groaned, he pushed him back to the ground and patted him down. The cell phone was in a pocket of his cargo pants. He pulled him back up. "You know how this ends, right?"

"Fuck you."

"Yeah, I know."

Standard pushed the sniper toward the beach, then reached back to pick up the rifle. The sniper fell twice as they moved between the palm trees, onto the beach, and toward the ocean. Each time he came up spitting sand. Standard kept the Glock pressed to the sniper's back.

When they reached the waterline, Standard wrapped the rifle strap around the sniper's neck then pushed him out into the surf. When they were waist deep in water, Standard shot him in the back of the head and shoved his body under the crest of an incoming wave. He took the Glock apart and tossed the pieces as far into the ocean as he could.

Back on the beach, he watched the waves, expecting to see the body surface and being pushed around by the pounding surf. Seeing nothing, he used the sniper's cell phone to call Adam Bovary Jones.

"Drago sent a man to kill me. I killed him instead. Now I need one more favor. Get a message to Drago. Tell him I'm dead, but so is the man he sent."

"We can do that."

"Good. You can also tell the same thing to anyone who asks about me."

"Anything else?"

"What are the chances of putting Drago in general population and tell the Hispanic gangs he's a chicken hawk."

"That might be more of a problem."

"Too bad."

Standard hung up, took one more look at the ocean, muttered "Stupid Russians," then threw the phone into the waves. He walked back to the house, jumped the wall, and dived into the pool to get the sand off his feet. Reaching the end, he climbed out, dried off with a towel left on a lounge chair, and went upstairs.

Emma was in bed, *Jane Eyre* on her knees, and a glass of wine in one hand. The bottle sat on the bedside table. "How was your swim?"

"It was good exercise."

She put down her glass and watched him while he pulled on a pair of pajama bottoms.

"It's really quiet here," she said. "I hadn't noticed until everything had been put away. Do you think you can get used to it?"

"Yeah."

"You sure?"

"Everything is going to be fine from now on." He picked up the bottle and held it out. "Now, more wine?"

THE END

ABOUT THE AUTHOR

Tom Towslee is a former newspaper and wire service reporter. After leaving journalism he worked in corporate public relations and was communications director for a governor and a United States senator. Tom and Dinah Adkins live in Portland, Oregon, with their dog, Tessa, and cats Sancho and Vincent.

∽

To learn more about Tom Towslee and discover more Next Chapter authors, visit our website at www.nextchapter.pub.

The Last Masterpiece
ISBN: 978-4-82419-502-9

Published by
Next Chapter
2-5-6 SANNO
SANNO BRIDGE
143-0023 Ota-Ku, Tokyo
+818035793528

27th June 2024

9 784824 195029